Clearing

OF THE

mist

CLEARING OF
THE MIST

Book Three

Owen Clough

weka
ficton

Cover design: Tania Hassounia of Drawer Full of Giants

National Library of New Zealand
Cataloging-in-Publication Data Weka Fiction 2020
ISBN 978-0-473-51066-4 Paperback
ISBN 978-0-473-51068-8 eBook
ISBN 978-0-473-51067-1 epub

Published in New Zealand

A catalogue record for this book is available from
the National Library of New Zealand.

Kei te pâtengi raraunga o Te Puna Mâtauranga o
Aotearoa te whakarâfangi o tênei pukapuka

This book is dedicated to my wife, Kaye,
for the support she has given me over the years
of my writing, for without her help this and
future books would never had come to fruition.

CONTENTS

ACKNOWLEDGEMENTS

To my wife Kaye, but for you I would have continued to be lost soul in the woods, never reaching this stage as an author. The hours you put into the editing this book is more than appreciated I cannot thank you enough, you in my opinion put the icing on the cake. I love you to bits.

To my daughter Tania, thank you for all of your assistance to get this book up and running. For using your illustrator skills, to design the book cover and keeping it in the same vein as the first two novels. Also, for creating my business cards and banner. And, finally, for being there for me whenever I had computer problems.

To my granddaughter Sofia for her continuing help updating my web page with new reviews and in general keeping it fresh. I'm so lucky to have talented women in my family.

To my son Brent who gave me his thoughts on the fight scenes in the book. In the past he was a 3rd Dan Black Belt in karate and was definitely the go-to person.

Also my sincere and grateful thanks goes out to the too numerous to mention people, who helped me with my research.

AUTHOR'S NOTE

"We know what we are but know
not what we may be."

—

William Shakespeare

FOREWORD

2024

Kia ora, Bob Kydd here. I felt it was time I continued with my tale about what happened after my friends disappeared. It all started such a long time ago. Hell, it must be ten years since it began. Where did that time go? That was when my friends Shane, Sam, and I inadvertently travelled back through the mists of time into the past, the year 1863, a time just before the beginning of the New Zealand Wars.

I've told you previously about how I found Shane, and as he was happily married in the nineteenth century, I was content to leave it there. However, my biggest concern has been with Sam—that's Samuel McInnes. I have spent these past years searching for the most likely scenario of what could have happened to my missing mate, and I think I've come to some sort of conclusion. Nevertheless, it's still not enough. I feel there's more to know, and the suspense is getting to me. Here's a recap of how it all began so as to jog your memory.

In 2014, we were on a wild-pig-culling exercise for the Department of Conservation in New

Zealand's Tongariro National Park. After walking into a cloud of mist, we were transported back in time to early New Zealand. While there, Shane met and fell in love with Tui, an attractive Maori woman, and before long married her.

In spite of that, our troubles really began later in Auckland when Sam was wounded with a head shot in the unforeseen Maori attack and lost his memory. We had put him into the care of the hospital ship in the harbour, but there was a mix-up, and the boat sailed unexpectedly. We were told they had left for Dunedin and presumed they meant Dunedin in New Zealand's South Island, but instead, he was shipped to Scotland. The army had assumed he was a Scotsman as his papers recorded his name as Samuel Mack, and Shane and Tui had already left for Dunedin to look for him. By that time, it eventually dawned on me that Dunedin means Edinburgh in Gaelic. So that's where Sam went, to Scotland in the UK, not Dunedin, New Zealand. I never saw either of my mates or Tui again. What a mess.

I hid for months waiting for Shane's expected message, but it never came about. Eventually, I gave up and decided to have a crack at returning home alone. Luckily, with the assistance from an incredible Maori friend, and a great deal of luck, I made it back. On the other hand, Sam and Shane never did make it home and were trapped in the middle of nineteenth-century New Zealand. Of course, it wasn't all smooth sailing for me. I was attacked while escaping, and I left that time zone pretty shot up and suffering from post-traumatic stress. I was quite a mess. At least I got home, but I had lost over a year of my life in the process.

Once back in my own century after recuperating, I made a commitment to myself, and to Sam's parents, to investigate the sequence of events of what could have happened to Sam. As my exploits gave me an unexpected windfall, I took a sabbatical from my work as a high school teacher and was prepared to spend a whole year doing research on what happened to my friend. I delved into it full on, following leads for nearly twelve months, but after I returned to work, my enterprise slowed right down. After all, I still had a life to get on with, although I did continue researching in dribs and drabs.

Looking back now, I was amazed at the amount of data I had accumulated during this time. it was really mind boggling. When you think about it, information wasn't as easy to come by when I started, not like it is now. I had compiled a list of all of Sam's family in Shrewsbury, England; it included his children's names along with their eventual families, and all of their life's achievements. I included all of Sam's schemes I had come across, as he was forward-thinking for the times and had introduced a lot of modern innovations. I suspect they must have come from his subconscious mind, as up until this moment, I don't think his memory returned because he's made no contact or left any clue of what has become of him.

I did, a while back, stop researching as I'd thought Sam's folks were happy with the knowledge I'd accumulated about their son's life in the nineteenth century. Be that as it may, after they thought about it, they asked me to continue to find his direct descendants as well as family who may be alive right now, and this is what I have been doing up to date.

CHAPTER ONE

Invercargill, New Zealand 2024

I discovered Sam's wife, Bella, a titled lady—unbeknownst to all the other nurses and the crew aboard the ship—had been his nurse on the HMS Esk on his trip to the UK. Sam and Bella married in Scotland not long after arriving and later moved to Shropshire, Shrewsbury where they eventually had their children. From the information I've gathered, he had a happy and fulfilling life, and I feel he mustn't have had any inkling of his past. Most likely, snippets of memory could have come through from his subconscious, and he used these ideas to his benefit, making a lot of money from them. I managed to collect photos of Sam, Bella, and his family, and have copies of the paintings that are still hanging in their family home, the manor house of Shadymore. All of my research regarding his life, I've passed on to Wayne and Mary McInnes, Sam's parents here in New Zealand, and to his sister Mary in Dunedin.

As Sam had lost both his memory and name, he settled on a moniker that made him feel comfortable and he could identify with. When we were together in the 1860s, we had changed our last names to prevent them from confusing future circumstances, and Sam, at that time, was known as Samuel Mack, a shorter version of his real name, McInnes. I was aware he really disliked being called Mack, so when he came across the name Selkirk, he used it. This must of felt familiar to him, as it was, after all, his grandmother's maiden name.

Then in one particular article I found important information I wished I had found ages ago. We were only just getting our heads around discovering that after he saved Queen Victoria from an assassination attempt in 1863, Sam received a knighthood. Then much later I came across the fact that he was given the title of earl as well. Well, it blew me away—all of us, in fact. We just couldn't believe it. His wife, Bella, had held the title of lady before they were married, as her parents were the Earl and Countess of Shadymore. The queen must have thought him an extraordinary man to go against custom and hand him the earl's title after his father-in-law passed away in 1889. Usually, that title becomes null and void when there are no sons to carry on the earldom. The earl's wife, Margaret, died in 1893. So, Sam and Bella became the Count and Countess of Shadymore. The papers were full of it and gave us most of his life story.

At this present time, we haven't tried to

contact any of Sam's descendants. I'm not sure whether Wayne and Mary will want to meet with this family yet, if at all, as they might just find it all too emotional. Of course, we would want to have all our facts confirmed first. But then if we proceeded, how would you explain the circumstances of Wayne and Mary's son being their great-great-grandfather? Who would believe it anyway? No one travels into the past, do they? Bugger it, I wasn't keen to broach that subject just yet, and if we did, there was the matter of creating complications with the New Zealand Security Intelligence Service. In all of this time I've been researching, I had to be very careful not to make waves and continually looked over my shoulder. Because when I had come home through the mist, they had forcibly warned me not to mess about with this time-travel stuff. What that was about, I had no idea.

The other thing that had me pulling my hair out was concerning Sam and Bella's second daughter, Margaret, who was born in 1866 in Shrewsbury. For goodness' sake, she actually came out to Dunedin, New Zealand to study medicine at Otago University from 1889 until 1893. While she was there, she met Adam Fenton, a young Kiwi bloke. I'm still trying to get my head around the chance of this happening. Adam Fenton—you could have knocked me over with a feather. She then went back to the UK with him, got married at St Chad's

Church, Shrewsbury, subsequently returning to New Zealand for a second ceremony at the Knox Church in Dunedin. From what I could gather, the reason for the additional ceremony was for the benefit of a few of the older Fenton family members. Travelling to and from New Zealand then was onerous, especially for the elderly. So they did the next best thing and formalised their nuptials twice.

Even so, her marrying Adam Fenton, of all people; the coincidence was so unbelievable. You see, Sam actually met his future son-in-law as a five-year-old back in New Zealand. For heaven's sake, the hairs stood up on the back of my neck. The astonishing fact was that we all had met both Fenton boys not long after their dad was killed in the attack of our wagon in Otahuhu. Our friend Stewart took the orphans under his wing and undertook putting them into the care of his sister down in Dunedin. To make this even more unbelievable, Stewart was Sam's third great-uncle. Boy, when you time travel, things can get complicated. This all happened the day before the Maori attacked Auckland, and that was when Sam was headshot. Who would have thought, in a million years, that Sam's daughter would come out to New Zealand and marry a bloke whom we'd met by pure accident back in 1863? This, in turn, means that presently, Sam's parents from Dunedin would have at least one of their grandchildren: Sam's daughter Margaret, living in Dunedin about a century and a half ago as well as her children with their descendants. Boy, working on this stuff muddles your brain.

Stewart, who we were with on that eventful day of the ambush, never saw my mate, Sam, again. If he had travelled to the UK to the wedding, he might have recognised Sam at the ceremony. Unfortunately, he didn't, so the connection between the two men never eventuated. It might have been just the thing to jog Sam's memory, but it was not to be. Then there was that other chance for recognition if only Sam and Bella had come out to New Zealand for their daughter's second ceremony. They would have met then, or he could have had the opportunity to run into Shane and Tui, who were living in Dunedin at that time. Now that would have been something.

The Fenton family are still living in New Zealand today. They are descendants of those two little boys Adam and Noah. Adam and Margaret's descendants are the direct lineage of Sam's parents here in New Zealand. I didn't feel we could just turn up at their place and say, 'Hi, I would like to introduce you to your third great-grandparents.' They would think both of Sam's parents and I were nuts. What to do, what to do? All this makes my bloody head hurt. So, I put it aside for later when I could figure out how to approach it. Anyway, that's only if Sam's parents want to make contact with them.

Would you believe it, I discovered later that these two little Fenton boys ended up becoming millionaires by the early twentieth century. They were one of the first to export meat using refrigeration from Dunedin to England and made a packet from it. The whole family were well educated, and Margaret was one of the first female doctors in New Zealand. She practised medicine for years. They also travelled a fair bit throughout Europe and the United States of America.

Her husband, after making his millions, retired very early and then sponsored young students from poorer homes, with grants for higher education. The Fenton Fund for Medical Studies is still going today. Their criteria is if you have low-income parents and have consistently high marks in high school, you have a good chance of qualifying for the fund. Not only are your university fees paid in full, they include the accommodation. They accept half-a-dozen young people a year to qualify for the trust money, and so far, it has never run out. They do have one stipulation though. Once you become a doctor, you must spend at least three years in New Zealand where they are short of doctors. After that, you can please yourself with where you go and what you do. This was Sam's New Zealand family.

I also found old newspapers on the net and located a collection of reports that mentioned a Mr Samuel Selkirk, Sam's second son who, along with his friend John Cotton, showed considerable interest in New Zealand's First National Park back in 1893 when they came to visit. There was a great deal about them in the papers. They spent many months tramping around Ruapehu and observing how the New Zealand government of the day ran it. It was like reading about my old mate, Sam, as he also would have done just that. It brought tears to my eyes when I recognised that he was so much like his dad, who was a big man as well, and both had identical red hair. Nearing the time of his sister Margaret's graduation, they left the bush to head south to Dunedin. They later took the opportunity, while still in the South Island, to check out Fiordland, eventually leaving New Zealand with his sister and her fiancé for the United Kingdom.

There was no reference to Sam and Bella ever coming out to New Zealand. However, I did come across a story in the New York Times citing their daughter, Mary. She and her twin brother, Bernard, were Sam and Bella's eldest. In the article, she spoke of her parents visiting her in Rhodesia, when she was a nurse out there. They must have gone incognito and not used their titles, as I couldn't find any reference to them. Thinking about it, there's a chance that Sam and Bella might have travelled anonymously often, as he wasn't one to draw attention to himself. Maybe even visiting their family in New Zealand after 1895, as his daughter Margaret had returned to New Zealand with her husband, Adam, and settled here.

Mary eventually married and ended up in the USA. I could understand Sam travelling incognito. Being an earl, he would have continually been in the limelight, so if he travelled under his chosen name of Selkirk or Mack or any other name he conjured up, he would have blended in. I added to my list of searches an investigation of whether a Mr and Mrs Selkirk came to New Zealand. Mind you, up until this time, he had never tried to leave a message for either his parents or me. So, it must be a given that his memory didn't return. My mate Shane never mentioned him, either, in his diary that was passed down through the generations until it reached my wife, Tui. She is the direct descendant of my friends Shane and Tui Lang. Funny how things work out, as I ended up married to my mate Shane's third great-granddaughter. This is pretty involved, so I hope you're getting the drift.

Then the day came when I had tracked down Sam and Bella up until 1894, and suddenly I lost them completely. In the census of 1891, they were at Bella's bridesmaid's place under the names E of Shadymore and C of Shadymore. I had noticed those names years before but didn't take a blind bit of notice, as at the time I didn't know he was an earl. That knowledge could have saved months of research if I had been more astute.

By the time I got to the 1901 census they had disappeared, and I never found them again. I did find an earl and countess in Shadymore, but it was his eldest son with his wife, so all I could think of was that my mate must have passed on. Even so, the most surprising thing that really got to me was that I couldn't find a death certificate for either of them. Yet they must have died, as his son had inherited the title. It was definitely a mystery—no sign of a death certificate or a burial in the whole United Kingdom.

I checked the records in South Africa also, as their daughter Mary was stationed there by then. She was a nurse with the British Army, fighting the Boers. I had thought they might have gone out to visit, but there was nothing. I looked at all the names I could think of, Selkirk, Mack, and even his real name of McInnes—nothing. By this time, he would have been close to sixty-one years old, and Bella in her late fifties. Where the hell did they go, and where did they die? So then I tried New Zealand; no luck there either. They had just vanished off the face of the earth. I think I'll have to go and revisit the online newspapers as I must have missed something. Let's face it, they were titled, and titled people just don't disappear; there's always some information about their activities. It will take some time to troll through them again, but it has to be done for my own piece of mind. I just can't let it rest there.

While searching, I came across the mention of a Maori delegation who petitioned the queen in regard to the New Zealand land confiscations in December 1894. They had arranged to talk to Queen Victoria at Buckingham Palace, but she had been unwell the week before, so they had to bide their time until the meeting could take place three weeks later. Of most of the dozen Maori who attended, I didn't recognise any of their names except the leader, Te Ruru Maniapoto, with his mother, Rita, who was, at that time, in her late eighties. Boy, their names brought back memories of 1863. That was the time we first realised we were not in the twenty-first century anymore but had been propelled back in time to just before the start of the New Zealand Wars. My mates and I had charged into the little Maori village of Pukekawa to assist Rita when a group of unauthorised English soldiers were ransacking the settlement. I can still see the picture of that day in my mind's eye. Then I noticed, included in that delegation, a group of service personnel involved in the New Zealand Wars: it involved both active and ex-servicemen. I ran down the list of names, and there he was, the Earl of Shadymore.

My God. Sam—he finally caught up with them again. I wondered… did he recognise any of them? I needed to find out more about this meeting and what it implied. I thought back and remembered Rita, the village spiritual leader—their tohunga. She had told me that I would eventually get home and be tied to both the Tainui and Ngaphui tribes in my lifetime. That confused me at the time, but it came to pass because when I married my wife, Tui; she was connected to them both. So now I wondered if when she saw Sam, did she manage to jog his memory? There must've been something significant about this meeting; there had to be. I had found it strange that Bella had not been mentioned after 1895 either. Could this meeting with Rita be the reason Sam and Bella disappeared? Bloody hell, it's so darn frustrating. It has been years since we were lost in the past, and it still hasn't finished. Until I find where Sam and Bella died, I can't let it rest. I need to find them, so I can finally move on with my life.

CHAPTER TWO

Invercargill, New Zealand 2026

I sat looking at the photos of my mates Shane and Sam on the mantelpiece.

I was disappointed with myself. A few years had slipped by since I last worked earnestly on my research, and I realised I was procrastinating again. I had all the best intentions, but I still hadn't finished what I had started, and not knowing where Sam had died plagued my mind. Oh, I performed short bursts of sleuthing on occasions, but I was mucking around. I suppose it was because I came across more dead ends now than before. I longed to know more about them, but it was hard going as this last chunk of their lives was tough to trace.

I had scrutinised all the UK records and found no death notice for either of them. Usually, a registered death would show up if they had passed away in that country, and I found no luck in the Scottish death records either. As they were an earl and countess, you would think it would be difficult for the records to disappear so easily. Surely their names should show up somewhere. I soon came to the realisation

that it was a safe bet they died outside the UK.
I scratched my head wondering where to start.
The known world wasn't so big in those days,
but it still was a huge area to cover. I also speculated that if you were titled, there would be
something in one   of the newspapers surely. At
the back of my mind, I reasoned that since I had
found their descendants, why not go straight to
the source and ask them. They might have heard
stories of their ancestors, especially if there
were unusual circumstances that might have
been remembered and eventually passed down
through the generations. However, I didn't
want to open that can of worms just yet.

I gazed up at his photo on the mantelpiece
again. 'Where the hell did you go, my friend?' I
shook my head. I really should be at peace knowing I had found him and his family. Oh no, not me
though. I'm the type of bloke who needs to have
closure, and it was taking me much longer than
I had anticipated. Heck, I'd started this when I
came through the mist all those years ago back
in 2015, and now, eleven years later, I was still
working through it. I could feel the despair start
to creep in.

Then I felt this shimmer of excitement run
through my body. I hadn't experienced this
awareness for ages. I felt certain that something
was going to happen. A sense of urgency hit me;
it felt so close. I grinned from ear to ear as I'd

had similar premonitions before, with startling results. Finally, the enthusiasm rose up inside of me, and I felt the commitment at last to push forward and find Sam and Bella.

I'll renew my endeavors and delve back into the period after Sam had received the earldom in 1889. In the past I'd found by using the English census online, it had been easy enough to search his immediate family, so my future sleuthing was assured. I was motivated again, at last. Thinking about it, I felt quite confident that all the children would have had to be grown up before they would have wanted to leave the UK. I rubbed my hands together. This was going to be my passion from now on, and I was determined not to stop until I found them.

I shut down my computer, went out to the car and sat in the driver's seat. Sam's smiling face came to mind. Never fear, mate. I'm back on your case. You won't get away from me that easily, my old cohort, even if it takes me another ten years. The enthusiasm coursed through my veins. I've traced all of your family right up to the present day. You can be assured, my friend, that I'll do my damnedest to find you and reveal your life story. I turned out of the drive and headed into Riverton to pick up my family.

In hindsight, knowing what I knew, I should have stopped my research right then and been content with what I'd already uncovered. I had no idea that governments would soon become involved, both from the United Kingdom and New Zealand, and this would affect all of Sam's and my own families. Unfortunately, I am like a dog with a bone, blinkers on and not seeing the consequences. I just kept going. When I returned from 1863 and came back through the mist to my time, our government stepped in and demanded that I was to let things be, not to communicate what I'd experienced. In other words, to forget that it ever happened. It never crossed my mind that while I was researching, some government agency would have been monitoring me and my searches closely. In my mind, I wasn't doing anything wrong, but in the eyes of the government, it was a different story.

You don't just disappear into the past and come back again without creating consequences. It's quite possible they were concerned about what information I might discover and perhaps alter what was going to happen down the line. Furthermore, I had noticed they were somewhat anxious about Sam still mucking about in the nineteenth century and how this might affect the world to come and possibly change our whole concept of time.

What worried me was if this idea of changing our future was right, it could even prevent Sam from getting home. After all, it's in the cards that if his memory did return in his later life, he might try to return to his own neck of the woods. However, in reality, I was sure that wasn't so. Still, how would I know? Anyway, he hadn't been in contact with me or his family up until now. Hey, there's a thought. If he did return, would he end up in the here and now, or end up further back in the past, or maybe even in future New Zealand? Maybe even in Britain, for that matter. I scratched my head. It was beginning to totally confuse me. I thought I'd put that away till later.

After picking the kids up from school and starting to fix them a snack, out of the blue, the doorbell rang. No rest for the wicked, I thought, as I wiped my hands on a towel and opened the door. Outside was a courier van, and the driver inquired, 'Mr Kydd?'

'Yep, mate, that's me.'

He handed me an iPad and asked, 'Will you sign here please?' I signed, and he handed me a large courier bag, turned, and shouted, 'Thanks' over his shoulder as he rushed away.

I returned to the kitchen, placed the parcel on the kitchen table, and finished the kids' snacks with my eyes flicking towards the parcel every few seconds. I wasn't expecting anything. I wonder what this is all about, I thought. 'Here you go, kids. It's ready,' I yelled, 'and don't forget your homework,' then added with emphasis, 'and remember your reading assignments.'

They grabbed their snacks, shouted, 'Thanks, Dad,' and were off out the door.

I looked down at the parcel wondering who could have sent it. I hadn't bought anything online lately, and Tui would have told me to be on the lookout for a package if she had. I took the scissors out of the kitchen drawer and cut the top off the package. As I pulled at the outer bag, what looked like a hefty manuscript, wrapped in old brown paper, came into view. My name and address were handwritten on it, with an added note. 'Please post to Robert Kydd no later than 2020.' What! It was now 2026. The postal service is impossible these days.

Of course, I knew what it was; I was just suppressing my emotions in case it wasn't what I had wished for. After all, I'd been waiting for it for years, and I couldn't really believe it had finally come. This had to be Sam reaching out from all those years ago. Suddenly I was overwhelmed and started to shake. I couldn't open it. I put it back on the table and stared at it, and my eyes filled with water. Hell, Sam, it's been so long. It's been too long, mate. My eyes were glued to the parcel, and all my old anxieties came back. My mind screamed at me, 'Get over it, you sook. You've waited for this for eleven years; get a grip on yourself.' Regardless, there was that little voice that told me to leave it until later when Tui comes home. After all, you'll need plenty of time to digest it all. Subsequently, my practical side shouted, 'Bullshit, just open the bloody parcel.' Well, that was pretty forceful, and it took over my actions. Slowly, I gingerly peeled back the very old paper. Inside was a blue book with a hard cover. I turned to the first page, yellowing with age.

Auckland 1895

Dear Bob,

I wrote this manuscript on the boat coming out to New Zealand. It is the story of my life to date. I'm sending it to you mate, I'm hoping that you are still in the same spot, as I know how much you love your place at Kawakaputa Bay, south of Riverton. I'm assuming my family members may have moved around as folks often do. I'm praying you are still there to receive it.

I'm sixty-four years old now, and my memory has returned at last. It has taken me practically my whole life to finally come to the realisation of who I am. So, I'm going to try to get home to see you and my family. At this time of writing, my son Sam is with me. He believes I'm away with the fairies, but he humours me though still sceptical. At any rate, he has agreed to come with me as does Abe. Do you remember Abe? He was the captain of the Auckland Rough

Riders Calvary Troop in the Auckland attack? He's coming, and there's a woman with us as well. They are both under our protection from government agents who are hunting us all and giving us no respite.

You remember that mist? I'll try to get back through it. Look out for me, won't you? Give me a couple of years, my friend. If I don't make it, well, at least you will know I have tried. Please don't tell my parents just yet, I would not like them to get their hopes up, and besides, it has been thirty-odd years. They will be into their late eighties and nineties or might not even be around. If I don't get home, and they are still alive, please pass this letter on to them or to Mary. In addition, could you hand it on to Shane?

I send my love to you and your family, if you were lucky enough to have found someone special, and also to your parents, and sister, Shane, and Tui, his parents, and of course, his two sisters. I also send my love to my cherished parents and my wee sister, Mary. I cannot wait until I see them again. It's hard to believe in all these years, everyone of you has been a closed book to me. I'm so overjoyed I'm finally whole again, and I cannot wait for the moment when we meet once again.

Your mate, Sam.

THE MANUSCRIPT

1863
HMS Esk, Tasman Sea

I was born on the 18 May 1863, at the age of thirty years or thereabouts. Nobody has a clue, but they reckoned that was how old I was when I regained consciousness.

I had only read a few lines when I stopped. Something wasn't right. He had said that thirty-odd years had passed, yet it has been only eleven years since we slipped back to 1863. Does that mean I have to wait another bloody twenty years before he tries to get home? The timing is all out of sync. Hell, this is confusing. Thinking about the complexity of time travel reminded me about that mob in Wellington keeping tabs on me. I had better make sure they don't know I have this manuscript, or the bastards will be around here like a shot making a nuisance of themselves. Now back to this letter. What did he mean when he mentioned 'a woman' returning with him? Isn't it Bella? If so, why refer to her as just 'a woman'? Anyway, if it's not his wife, and if his son does come through, how will they both cope? And what about Abe? Why is he coming? He would be about Sam's age by now. What the hell are you thinking of, Sam? These people are from the nineteenth century. It's a big ask. I guess after proper rehabilitation, I'm guessing they would eventually fit in, but hell, mate. Why couldn't you just leave them back there? You must realize that this century is so different compared to the time they are used to.

I glanced out the window to see a new EV black Mercedes slowly pass the front gate. I didn't take much notice as I turned back to gaze at the manuscript that had come to me out of the blue.

What am I going to do about meeting Sam, as he could turn up at any time? I could go up to the Tongariro National Park and hover around waiting for him to materialise, or I could monitor the airways, police, search and rescue, and government signals since the stuff you would need for that is easily available compared to ten years ago. I'll have to talk it over with Tui and ask her advice when she gets home from work.

It wasn't until eight in the evening that Tui and I sat down on the couch with Sam's manuscript. It had been a long day, but once the kids had done the dishes and watched a programme on TV, I finally placed it between us and we started to read. You could hear a pin drop and the slight moan of the wind as it whistled around the house while we read.

All the knowledge I'd gained in my research now lay before me verified as fact through the yellowing pages of Sam's life. It all came together to give the us the complete story of his life. What surprised us is that it took him thirty years to recover from his amnesia, to at last clear the mist from his mind to become Sam again. The progress of his journey was quite unbelievable, and by four in the morning, after a marathon read, we finally reached the last page.

All my questions I'd researched had been answered, and now our thoughts centred on when and where he will get home. That concerned me, and I was sure worried about him. How was he going to manage it? Have the conditions changed much since when we all went through the golden mist on Ruapehu back in 2015? Was that mist, that hole in time still there? I did know that parts of the National Park were completely out of bounds, and the government had justified the closure by stating it was for the safety of everyone. They had informed the public that there was a lot of seismic activity in the area. I know that area well, and that was a load of rubbish. They absolutely don't want people wandering around and slipping back through a time warp to goodness knows where. Mind you, I can understand that.

If Sam comes home through the mist from the past, will he arrive back at Ruapehu or somewhere else? It will be a brave thing to do and quite dangerous. I managed to return okay, but to bring his son and two others with him would be crazy. Though knowing my mate, his decision wouldn't have come lightly. The manuscript had not mentioned any of this. He had arrived in Auckland and was in the process of trying to come through the original cave we had found south of Pukekawa. For now, Tui and I will just have to wait and see as there's nothing else we can do. The timeline is too complex.

I left the manuscript on the table, with the idea of going over it again later in the day, and headed off to bed exhausted with all the bewildering information about Sam's life going through my head. I had mostly discovered all I could about the first part of his life with my research over the years. It was the second part from the time he was awarded the earldom that had left me amazed and emotional. I fell asleep with his words tumbling around in my head.

CHAPTER THREE

1893 Shadymore, Shropshire England

I was shot in the head in Auckland, New Zealand in 1863, during the Maori Wars, and since then my memory has been lost to me. So much has happened on my journey, but still, after thirty years I am none the wiser about my origins. Looking back on my life, I wonder where the hell all the years went. Funny, though, even now I still come out with words and statements that are bizarre, leaving people around me looking astounded. I think of my ideas as commonplace; however, they appear completely foreign to the others. Most days I take the time to gaze at the mounted silver kiwi given to me by Mary, who apparently is my sister. It torments me to not remember her or where she lives, or if she has other kin still alive. It concerns me that I have no recollection about this lost family. The head wound that I received back then has a lot to answer for.

From the manor house, I glanced over at Shadymore Forest Park, as I allowed my mind to slide back to my arrival and realise we have accomplished a lot over the years. One of our clan's best endeavors, that we are most proud of, is that we have turned our country estate into a conservation park, the first of its kind in the United Kingdom. I smile every time I look over the forest from where I am standing now, and see the hills rising up to the bushline on the horizon. Up there is the lake we named Victoria, and on its shore stands our hotel designed to look like a log cabin with rooms for thirty guests. Inside we have all the amenities of a modern-day lodge, including a large dining hall. The Victorian Spa as we call it, put us on the map, because it exhibits something quite different from any other hotel in the UK. It has its very own thermal hot springs, a gift from Mother Nature.

In 1871, Shropshire had an earthquake, the first in living memory. At the manor it upset almost everyone when the chandeliers started swaying and rattling. The servants couldn't stop chatting about it for weeks after. Luckily, it wasn't a large one but sufficient to crack the bedrock below Lake Victoria, creating a large hot-water spring that is still flowing freely today. The funny thing is, even though we were all excited about the quake and the discovery of the hot pools, I was certain I had seen it before.

As I stood there reminiscing, I recalled how at home I was with those hot pools when I first discovered them. Why I wondered. Suddenly I remembered the map that I had tucked away in my backpack. Blast I hadn't thought about it in years and I've no clue how it came to be in my possession. I rummaged around in our bedroom till I found it. It covered an area of the Tongariro National Park in New Zealand. The details it depicted were extraordinary and I could see, as plain as the nose on my face, there were many hot pools and mud pools clearly marked.

These pools felt so familiar to me. In fact, I felt really acquainted with this whole area. Strange, as I had read in the newspaper that the Maori of this region had recently gifted this whole area to the New Zealand government as New Zealand's only national park. What I'm getting at is this place has hardly been explored and certainly not mapped in such detail, and get this, I've had this map for thirty years. To add to the puzzle, it has the year 2014 printed along the edge. The answer to this mystery, along with the source of the map, is still an enigma to me to this day. I folded the map neatly and concealed it back in my pack where it had been hidden for the last thirty years.

I settled back and recalled that all this didn't stop me from recognising an opportunity when I saw one. I knew we could utilise the hot-water source somehow, and we did. We converted the hotel into a spa with heated pools for our guests. We went even further as each room had its own individual shower that had been invented back in 1811 and included a private soak bath, which proved to be very favoured. Before long, the hot spring water was piped down to the manor house, which gave us the honour of being one of the first houses in the UK to have fresh inside running hot and cold water.

Next, we progressed into the villages of Sledgemore and Brittermore and included all the farm tenants' cottages. Because of these innovations, the villages became so popular that we were pushed to extend the available accommodation just to cope with the influx of folk. They were keen to experience this novelty and wanted to travel up to the lodge to see the steam rising off the lake from the tearoom's window.

The public were aware of the hot-water springs in Bath, but our springs were set among pristine wilderness, which made it quite exceptional in the British Isles. Once Queen Victoria visited to take in the waters and to stay on at the lodge, it came to be 'by royal appointment.' So, it rapidly evolved into the place to visit. We were soon the envy of Britain, and it certainly made us a lot of money. We continued to develop the village with more homes for the necessary extra staff, built an additional hotel, then increased the diversity of shops, tearooms, and businesses. Eventually our village became a town.

I believe it was the cable car to the lodge that

led us to the head of the queue. It was quite an engineering feat. As a family, we sat down and thought hard on ways to develop the thermal area and the challenge of transporting our customers up to the lodge. I was against pushing a road up there as I did not want to ruin the untouched habitat and pristine nature of the forest. However, in spite of that, when I read about an aerial cableway for freight that had been built in the United States, I immediately wrote to the inventor, Andrew Hallidie, a Scot now living in California.

He later visited us, and after taking a good look at our problem, designed us a cable car to carry people. It covered fifteen miles as the crow flies, from the village up and down hills, skirting the treetops, then on up to the lake. Once the cableway was erected, we replanted the pathway that was built for the construction towers. It was a massive achievement and an astounding success for both Andrew and our family— and for the United Kingdom. It satisfied me that I achieved what I had hoped for, as it had left the bush in an untouched state, and people came from far and wide just to ride the cableway.

We had used the latest steam engine available to power the gondola, and all goods were sent up to the lake by this method. We built a small road on the Welsh side of the park just in case of emergencies. All this created even more jobs, and our little town kept on growing. As a side-line, to encourage visitors to explore the park, we included 'rambling' as part of our advertising in the newspapers. Somehow, the word rambling still did not sit right with me, and I continued to think of it as tramping.

Tracks crisscrossed the park for all types of walks, and huts were built throughout the forest to accommodate them. Our business grew rapidly, and a booking system had to be established to prevent the huts from becoming overcrowded. All of this soon became too much for just a few family members to cope with, and before we knew it, we were forced to train staff to lighten our load.

Thinking it would lessen our load, I now have other worries to contend with. I recently heard the notion that parliament could introduce a new law concerning death taxes by 1894. So, my biggest concern had become the need to put money aside for this future expense, otherwise we might lose everything we had built up. Then, the solution came to me. After inquiring if the idea was feasible, I gathered the family around and gave them my proposal. Why not put all monies into a conservation trust and change the name of the estate? That would mean the property would be run by a trust, with our family and friends on the board.

I suggested we could decide which family

members to include, but I wanted to invite my good friend Moshe from Selkirks to join us. It would be a reciprocal favor to his family, as I am on their firm's board. Furthermore, I recommended our forest warden Toby Cotton as he would be an excellent choice, and what about one of our tenant farmers. The farmers could elect who they would want to fill the position. We had recently come to the decision to include all the farm tenants to collect a share of the profits as part of the conservation park, giving them the confidence to improve their farms. This way, they would not only work for themselves, but also secure an income through the trust. The outcome of my scheme was that when the earl died, the only death duties we would have to pay would at the very most be solely on the manor house and the three acres it was sitting on. After deciding this was our best course, we put out feelers to the ministers of the crown to see if this was viable, and with the backing of Queen Victoria, we became the first conservation park. Right thinking was the order of the day, nevertheless, we were lucky as a lot of other family estates throughout the Kingdom had to sell their land just to pay for death duty taxes. Whereas, because we were getting paid from the trust to run our park with government backing, we were sitting pretty.

Thinking back, I believe that was our family's greatest achievement, and I say family, as each of us always had a say in the decision-making. The park was run with all the trustees involved each having an input, starting from the earl and going down to Toby our warden. We also encouraged anyone who had a suggestion to come forward. This type of arrangement had been unheard of until now, so it was a pat on the back for our UK, and I believe a lasting legacy for generations to come. The forest has been kept as pristine as it was for over four hundred years. We manage the wildlife, capturing where necessary and selling the excess deer and boar to other estates, or culling if needed. Moreover, our tenant farmers bred deer and boar for the park and were paid per head of adult animals they released into the wild. This was another revenue for the trust and farmers alike. We even had folk queuing for the right to cull our animals when we were over-stocked, creating an extra income earner for the trust every second year or so.

We were still taking gold from our small mine on the Welsh side of the property, and at this stage, it was looking good, as our minimum forecast was to continue doing so for at least another twenty years. Those profits also went back into the trust which paid all the directors and trustees remuneration; we were extremely fortunate. However, I always reiterated that it was wise to continue to use our expertise and business know-how with the skill we had learnt along the way, as it was most important that what we had built was to continue for generations to come.

Thinking of the families of our workers, we set up an education trust programme for when the children went off to school and university. It not only took their educational concerns off our employees and leaseholders' minds, but when they returned as adults, they brought their new perceptions with them and some even stayed on. On the other hand, most left but spread our new ideas out into the world, so the investment eventually came back to us twofold. They still keep in touch, and our estate and town has prospered.

A smile crossed my lips when I let my mind slip back to what happened in 1863 after I first woke on board the HMS Esk following being shot in Auckland New Zealand. Of course, I'm aware the beginning of my life as I know it, was a significant occasion, but even more far reaching was the moment I looked up into the most amazing green eyes I had ever seen. My heart leapt in my chest, and I could have sworn I heard bells ringing to signify the occasion. I was in love from that point on. I soon discovered I had given my heart to my nurse, Bella. As we sailed our way to the UK, we became very close and spent as much time together as we could; that was when I discovered she was a titled lady. After arriving in Scotland, unbeknownst to her parents, we married promptly to avoid her father's interference. However, it played on my mind that I couldn't avoid him forever and eventually would have to face her father's wrath. After all, I did steal away his first born. Nevertheless, the day arrived and fortunately it wasn't as arduous as I had thought, and by the end of the first weekend, we were family. Some things are just meant to be.

Bernard—that's Bella's dad the earl—and I quickly became best friends. Shortly after that I dragged out my sports rifle. I had kept it hidden until then, but felt convinced that he was the person to show it to. He stared at it in awe, and I could see he desperately wanted to touch it, so I offered it to him, and he inspected it with the respect he felt it deserved. Apparently, there was nothing quite like it here in the UK. With me in agreement, Bernard promptly contacted Lord Winter, a prestigious rifle manufacturer he knew in Briton, and before long they both salivated over it. To cut a long story short, we were offered fifteen hundred pounds up front, plus two shillings a gun, and on top of that an additional 2 percent profit paid quarterly. Thinking back, Bella and I made an excellent deal. To date, over one and a half million rifles have been produced, and now we have an improved version out, the Mark Two. We also get our percentage on that model, as our rifle was its prototype. That would have made us wealthy in our own right, but I was determined to reassure the earl that I did not marry his daughter for her money and title. So, I arranged for the monies earned from the rifle to be paid into the earl's estate account. It was fair to say that he was against it, stating that we should reap the rewards, but I was insistent. There was plenty to go around, and I felt comfortable sharing it with the family that had lovingly excepted me as kin. Besides the earl had recently upped Bella's allowance to afford me fifteen hundred pounds a year; that was an enormous amount of money. You could say my father-in-law had pots of dough, and with the sales of the rifle, we made even more.

When Bella and I visited London to negotiate with Lord Winter, we took the opportunity to see the queen up close and personal as she walked from her royal train. I was lucky to be in the right place and time to prevent some nasty buggers from shooting her as she climbed into her coach outside the station. Being tall, I had spotted the sods and got into them well before they could do any damage. For my effort, Queen Victoria knighted me the next day. Of course, once this happened, I was the flavour of the month. Before this, people had struggled communicating with me as my accent and manner was mystifying to them, and they had great difficulty trying to pigeonhole me. After saving the queen's life and earning a knighthood, it somehow didn't matter anymore. On gaining the queen's favour, I was suddenly inundated with invitations from all and sundry.

That is when Aharon Hyman from Selkirks, asked me to become a director. Now, that did turn a few heads—a Jewish firm asking a gentile bloke to be a director? Little did many people know that I had struck a deal with Aharon back in Scotland not long after I had first arrived. I had stopped in his father's shop in Portobello to buy underwear, and what they had to offer was absolutely ridiculous. They had presented me with one thing after another, but you would not have caught me dead in that stuff. Goodness knows why I felt that way.

So, I asked for pencil and paper and drew a quick sketch of what my idea of men's underwear should look like. Aharon's father applauded as he immediately saw the practically of the drawings. It wasn't long before he organised production of my designs, and it didn't stop there. Later, a woman's bra was created, and when Bella displayed this to the ladies in Aharon's family, it took off like a forest fire. They were so impressed with my efforts that I was rewarded with 2 percent of their underwear sales, which continues to this day. It appears that what I designed was ahead of its time, but everyone come across mentions that, regarding most of my suggestions.

These outlandish thoughts just come to me. I

have no idea from where. But all the clothes I had come across were much too itchy, cumbersome, and far too hot to wear. I felt they were most definitely not what I was used to. Even now, concepts will pop into my head for no apparent reason, although most of my suggestions seem to work. One of the things I am most grateful for is when I first came across Selkirks. It gave me the name I had been looking for. Samuel Mack had been written on my army documents, but to be quite honest, the name grated on my nerves, so when I saw Selkirks, it caught my eye and felt right—like family, and I grabbed it. I dropped the 's,' and I have never regretted it. I sometimes daydream that if my memory comes back, maybe somewhere will be the name Selkirk on my family tree.

Another of my life's triumphs was, of course, our children. Bella gave birth to twins in 1864, a boy and a girl. We named Bernard after his grandfather, the earl, and our daughter was named Mary after my unknown sister, in recognition of that missing part of my life.

The twins grew up quite different in both personality and looks; we loved them both to bits. Bernard is the thinker and has auburn hair like his mum, and Mary is a fiery wee thing with red hair that was just like mine had been, or so I am told. The shock I received from my head wounds removed all the colour from my hair, leaving it steel-grey, but Bella recalled my hair was Mary's colour when we first met on the HMS Esk.

In 1866, we were blessed with another daughter, Margaret, who we named after Bella's mum the countess. Like Bernard, she has her mum's hair colour, is studious, always reading, and of course, bright as a button. Last in our line of Selkirks came Samuel, born in 1869 and named after yours truly. He turned out to be a lot like me, a big lad with red hair. He also loves the solitude of the bush and would find every excuse in the world to be out in the forest, doing his best to avoid socialising. As he grew older, he became a crack shot and could shoot the eye off a gnat at one hundred paces.

I'm happy with the life I've led and am so very proud of our family—each and every one of them. However, sometimes when I think back, I still wonder who the hell I am and where I came from. I don't think as much about it as I used to, but in quiet times, I have this deep longing inside me that one day I'll remember my life before all this.

CHAPTER FOUR

Shadymore 1894

We planned for all our children to have a good education as I felt it was paramount in making your way in the world; however, this belief tended to be generally out of step with other well-to-do families. Initially, we built a schoolhouse in Brittermore, and they attended along with the villagers' offspring and most of our employees' children. I was determined that my kids live healthy lives, become accustomed to mixing with people from all walks of life, and not set themselves up as being above other folk, which was often quite apparent among the gentry.

The school grew quickly along with the village and soon had four classrooms with teachers. From there, the boys moved on to a prep school in Shrewsbury. For the girls, we chose a new girls' school that had recently opened not far from the boys', and just up the road from Bella's old school for young ladies. The young blokes flourished and went ahead to eventually receive their degrees at Oxford. On the other hand, our girls were unable to enrol at a university as women were not permitted to attend. This angered me because they were as clever as the boys, but the colleges wouldn't listen to reason.

By the time our eldest twin, Mary, was eighteen, she showed a desire to become a nurse like her mum. Of course, it was frowned upon by the upper classes because it was thought to be well below their lofty station. However, that did not stop us and off she went to the Nightingale Nurses College, with our blessing.

As Margaret was a different kettle of fish altogether, being a mere nurse was not good enough for her. She wanted to be a doctor. Naturally, that put the cat among the pigeons as women were not accepted into medical college, not here in the UK. So, I put the feelers out and found a university in Dunedin, New Zealand, that allowed women to study medicine. We were advised that it was one of the better medical schools in the Southern Hemisphere and was at the leading edge of universities to consider including women as students: far ahead of the UK at the time.

By the time Margaret was twenty, we had arranged for her to sail to the other side of the world to study. Because the degree was for five years, it took a bit of forward thinking to arrange for her lodgings. Luckily, by chance, I met up with Moshe one day and mentioned about Margaret's plans to be a doctor. After explaining the whole story, I told him our latest problem of obtaining accommodation with an acceptable family. Moshe said to leave it with him because he had friends living there, and they might know of a family she could board with. A week later, after receiving a cable, Moshe called around to the estate and told us his friends would be only too happy to have Margaret stay with them. They had two grown-up daughters. One of them studied law at Otago, and both still lived at home, so one more would not make a difference. They lived up on the hill not far from the university, and as long as Margaret did not mind living with a Jewish family, they were happy for her to be part of their household. I sent my gratitude to them for opening their home to Margaret. Cables went back and forth, and presently, the requirements for an extended stay were sorted.

Next, we were faced with the problem of finding a suitable companion to accompany her on the journey. Fortunately, a friend knew Lady Julia Readman, a spinster in her forties who was keen on the adventure. She sounded perfect for the job, and I later heard that afterwards, she remained in New Zealand for nine months; she returned full of enthusiasm for the country as a whole. The last thing that worried me was it was too far for Margaret to come home between semesters, which meant she was going to be without a familiar face in all that time. We put a plan into place, so each year, part of the family would visit her in turn.

By the end of December 1887, what we had been dreading was upon us, and it was with a heavy heart that we watched as she walked up the gangplank in Southampton for the long journey. It was expected she would arrive in New Zealand in the middle of February, at the height of summer, in time for the start of the academic year.

Bella knew Dunedin well as she had spent time there thirty years ago when she helped with a cholera outbreak as a Nightingale nurse. Back then, the population was only five thousand. But as it was the closest city to all the gold mines discovered in Central Otago, that had changed. Now it was thriving, with over forty-five thousand people living there, and the area continued to attract even more from all over the world. Of course, I had misgivings about Margaret going. She was a good-looking kid, and I felt certain that sometime during those five years, someone would inevitably sweep her off her feet. On the other hand, I knew I couldn't protect her forever. She was a grown woman and had a mind of her own. I could only hope that if she was to find someone, she would choose wisely. As it happened, our daughter thrived down in New Zealand.

Our eldest son, Bernard, is an outgoing bloke, and like the rest of our family, seldom needs an excuse to escape out into the forest. Nevertheless, he did well at university, gained a degree in accountancy, and was soon promoted as our manager for both the trust and the estate. He diligently kept his finger on the pulse, so he didn't have as much spare time as the rest of us to get away. I would only have to ask, and he could tell me where every penny went, or was saved. Because of his upbringing, people from across the board found him very approachable. He's a natural leader and is a favourite with all the staff, tenants, and other folk from different walks of life.

His twin sister, Mary, can also get on with all and sundry, and I'm proud to say she has become an excellent nurse. She always was at the forefront to nurture whenever she tended the sick and loved working with children and old folk. However, her nature is quite different from Bernard's and is more like her mother—strong willed. You have to watch out if you cross her as she can fly off the handle if things don't go her own way: certainly, a force to be reckoned with. Notwithstanding, she's more independent than Bella ever was and determined to make her particular way in the world.

Then there's our youngest, Samuel. Right from his early childhood, he took a keen interest in the forest and all of its wildlife. His best mate, John, our Warden, Toby's, second son, was the same. They were always reading books on natural history and various animals from around the world. I swear these boys were joined at the hip and continued on to university together. I trolled all the universities throughout the UK, hunting for any offering a curriculum involving the environment or conservation, to no avail. I was quite disappointed and found it hard to believe because it would have suited them both. So, they chose subjects they enjoyed other than their preferred forestry studies. Sam chose music and history, and John took English literature and art. He had some talent, but his mum, Eliza, encouraged him as she was an artist of some renown herself. Recently, we were delighted when she had been commissioned to paint the queen as we already had many of her paintings on the manor house walls.

Once Samuel and John had their degrees, the first thing they did was to vanish into their beloved bush for weeks on end, where they meticulously planned for their initial trip to Yellowstone National Park in the USA. After that, they delved even deeper into books, studying the flora and fauna of many places around the world, from Africa to New Zealand. Over the years, they came back from their trips with some fantastic ideas about the welfare and care of endangered species that we have implemented. This year, they plan to visit Margaret in Dunedin and intend to have a good look at New Zealand's first national park. I'm proud to be Sam's father and a surrogate uncle to John because they are extraordinary men. I like to think it was my love of the outdoors that I instilled in my family right from the very beginning as being the start of all this, and why all the kids grew up loving wildlife in its natural habitat.

Their Aunt Amy, Bella's sister—extremely clued up in animal healthcare—has also encouraged the family's love of the subject. She has her own veterinary clinic and animal hospital, operating behind her Shrewsbury home. When the children were young, they would stay with Amy and Angus during the holidays and spend hours in her hospital tending the animals. I feel this is what inspired Mary and Margaret to turn towards the medical profession. Of course, it was already in their blood as their mum is an ex-Nightingale nurse; they just began with birds and animals and worked their way up to people.

I first met Angus McDonald on the HMS Esk on its trip home from New Zealand, and we got on like a house on fire. Even though he was wounded like me in 1863, he can still recall the incident when the Maori attacked Auckland, though he is not supposed to talk about it. I wish I could recollect what happened, but so far, it's not to be. We had invited him down from Scotland as our architect to create our first school not long after I had married Bella. That's when he met Amy, or Lady Amelia Margaret Gale as she was known then; she was eighteen. When Amy turned twenty, they were married at St Chad's in Shrewsbury, and I was his best man. The earl and countess finally were able to put on a big wedding for at least one of their daughters, as Bella and I had married quietly in Scotland two years earlier. Although Angus was not titled, his parents did have money, so the earl and countess were very satisfied. Besides, he is a cracker bloke.

Before long, he had set up his own architectural business in Shrewsbury and became the man to turn to when we wanted designs for all our buildings in both Sledgemore and Brittermore. He created some fantastic architectural ideas for us. After he completed the school, he designed the lodge up on the lake, all the staff accommodation houses, the new pub in the village, our new church, and so many more of our buildings. His firm is always kept busy. In fact, he often has to turn contracts down. The family were very enthusiastic about our collaboration and soon put him on the park's board of trustees.

Not long after they were married, my sister-in-law wanted to set up her own veterinary practice, but there was some concern that she didn't have a degree to put up on the wall. Fortunately, she was able to earn her certificate of competence with the help from one of Angus's friends who was a lecturer in veterinary science. He visited them from Scotland and turned up with all the exam papers she needed, in his briefcase. Amelia completed the review over the weekend, and he then watched over her as she completed her practical. The tutor was impressed by her results as she received a 96-percent pass. She set up her clinic out the back of their home in Nursery Cottage, which was originally the earl's Shrewsbury residence. When she had to take time off to have her two boys, Angus and Bernie, she found a young vet to help her out, who continued to assist her whenever she needed it. Her practice is very popular, and she hasn't looked back.

Then there's Bella. She has been my love, my best friend, my anchor and our supporter throughout the years. What would we have done without her? She has practised great understanding, dealing with a man ignorant of his past. While thinking about her, I'm smiling, as it took me back to when she first set up the village school. She included basic nursing for the girls and then enticed me to teach a music class because I could play five different musical instruments. Luckily for me, she later employed a part-time music teacher, John Clough, to let me off the hook, that is until he emigrated to New Zealand not long after he married. We then employed a full-time teacher who included music as one of her subjects, and she also organised a pretty good school band.

Toby, our ranger, instructed bush-craft classes at the school. He was the obvious choice because he is an excellent bushman. Not long after I appeared on the estate, Toby and I caught a poaching ring. That was quite an adventure; I can tell you. Anyway, Bernard was grateful and offered Toby a new position he had created as our forest warden. For the past thirty years, Toby has continued doing this and loving every moment. It turned out the blokes we apprehended that day were Toby's wife Elisa's father and her siblings. They were not only poaching from the earl, they were stealing gold from his mine, so they got hefty sentences. Her old man died before completing his thirty years, and the boys got twenty. They must have been released about ten years ago; we don't have a clue where they are now. However, I'm sure they are aware that if they ever set foot back in the county of Shropshire, they will be hung.

Another memorable day I must tell you about was when our eldest son, Bernard, was twenty- four. He married Lady Catherine Williams of Adfa. She comes from an old Welsh family who farmed cattle and sheep just over the border from our place. In 1888, our first grandchild, Samuel, was born, and boy, did we spoil him. A couple of years later, Bella was born, then came Catherine, and last to arrive was another grandson, Bernard, in 1894. The manor house is full of young children once again, and Bella loves it.

As I write this, I'm looking at the forest and daydreaming, thinking how far I have come for a bloke who was 'born' into this world at around thirty years old. My most difficult, recent memory to come to terms with is when Bella's father, Bernard, unexpectedly passed away in 1889. We all felt his passing keenly. He was our rock. I was devastated as he was like a father to me, and we were very close; I still miss him immensely. Before he died, unbeknownst to us, Bernard had petitioned the queen. He secretly disappeared down to London one day to visit Her Majesty. He kept it all very hush-hush, and it wasn't until after the funeral and the interment in our wee churchyard, that Bella and I were summoned to see the queen at Windsor. We had no idea what it was about, but of course, my mother-in-law, the countess, did.

We travelled across town from our hotel, buffered by the wind and rain, but once we entered the palace, the hushed atmosphere was a welcome relief. Before long, we were ushered into the queen's private chamber, and the memories flooded back. The last time I was there was twenty-six years ago in 1863 when she knighted me. I had then met her eldest son, Edward, and we have become good friends over the years. This time the queen didn't dally at all and got right down to the reason of our summoning. She spoke about the time the Earl of Shadymoor had visited her nearly a year ago, when he had formally requested if she would permit the earldom to be passed on to me. I was stunned and stared at the queen with my mouth gaping, not knowing what to say. She explained that usually when an earl dies, with no sons to carry on the title, the earldom becomes redundant through the lack of direct heirs. However, as she was entitled to do, she was going to make an exception. I stood, gobsmacked, while she made it clear the reason was that I had saved her life. She went on to say it was for what I had done for the country, for Shropshire, and for her personally, and because of that, she was more than willing to pass on the earldom to us both.

She rose and spoke ceremoniously. 'From this day forward, you will be known as the Earl of Shadymoor, and you, Lady Isabella, will be the Countess of Shadymoor, and your mother will assume the roll of the dowager. From this day forward, your eldest son will inherit your title and will continue to follow through the first-born male line.' She then addressed me.'Lord Selkirk, I believe awarding you this earldom is a just reward. Your father-in-law, sir, must have been very proud of you, and for him to ask this on your behalf, it shows one the high esteem he held for you. This has been the easiest decision I have ever made as it has been thoroughly deserved. You have built schools and proceeded to educate your villagers. You have established the first cable car and have utilised a hot springs for the good of those very people. A first of its kind in my kingdom, you have turned a forest into a nature park. When your rifle became the finest gun in the world—and still is, I might add—you created munitions employment for my nation. I must also make mention of your knack for designing clothes that bring much comfort to my subjects. My dear lord you have not let power override you, and I see you are not too proud to be humble. For this, you are a shining example to my people, and for all your accomplishments, I thank you.

'So, Count and Countess of Shadymoor, I expect more amazing things from you both. I have sent a cable to your mother, Countess Isabella, and by this time tomorrow, the kingdom from one end of the empire to the other will know of your new title and deeds. Your daughter Margaret is in New Zealand, I believe. She will be thrilled with the news, I'm sure. I still find it incredibly thrilling that within minutes of sending a cable to a country as far away as New Zealand, an answer will be received virtually straight away. Now you must excuse me as I have a full list of engagements this day, my son. The Prince of Wales will see you to your coach.' With that, she turned and walked out with both of us bowing and scraping until the door shut behind her.

We stood looking at each other, blown away by what had just happened. I couldn't find the words to express how I felt. I saw a tear in Bella's eye. 'Oh, Sam, I know Daddy loved you so much, but I didn't expect this.'

His Royal Highness Prince Edward entered, smiling as he approached us and patted me on my back. 'Well deserved, my dear Samuel.' He shook my hand then chatted comfortably as he escorted us out to our coach. He told us the most splendid thing he had ever done was to take the waters at the spa lodge and continued on to enthuse about our whole project. The prince and I were good mates and got on well. In the past, he had often confided in me the sorts of things which would have made his mother furious.

We drove back to the London summer house in silence. I was still in shock and felt what had happened was like a dream. The next day, by the time we took the train to Shrewsbury, I realised it was real, all right, as our news was in all the papers. As we arrived in Shrewsbury, the church bells were pealing, and crowds were gathered in the street, some standing three deep, waving at us as we drove out to Shadymoor. There was even more fanfare as we arrived at the manor, as all the servants were lined up on both sides of the entrance, and my mother-in-law stood at the top of the steps.

As we approached, she smiled broadly and announced in a loud voice for all to hear, 'Welcome home, Lord and Lady Shadymoor.' Thinking back, even after all these years, I still recall how mind blowing it was for me to receive the earldom. Not a bad accomplishment for a bloke like me. I would like to think that my own parents, if I were ever able to find them, would be pleased with what I have accomplished. Our eldest son, Bernard, was a bit overawed with this unexpected occurrence, but he is a level-headed man, so I feel quite confident that when the time comes, he will take over the title with the same flare as his grandfather. Our daughters have now become ladies, but I thought it bizarre that the boys would continue to be addressed as just mister.

I thought it was a good time to go out and visit our eldest daughter Mary in Africa. We had visited her there before when she was nursing in South Africa, but she had since had a transfer to Rhodesia. She's pleaded with us to come out for quite a while now, and as a result of Bernard and Sam taking over more of our duties, there would never be a better time to visit. After all, we are not getting any younger.

CHAPTER FIVE

South Africa 1894

We caught a liner from Southampton on the thirteenth of March and after twenty-nine days arrived in Capetown. As a nurse, our twin daughter was sent where she was needed, and on this occasion, she had been transferred to Bulawayo Rhodesia. With Christmas and New Year behind us, I was looking forward to escaping the cold English winter. Cape Town was coming to the end of its summer season, but it was still warmer here than a hot summer's day in England. The scenery was stunning, the bay was a deep sapphire blue, against a baby blue sky with white puffy clouds hardly moving, and of course Table Mountain dominated the scene. Quite a change from when Bella and I first arrived from New Zealand in 1863. We couldn't see Table Mountain that day as there was a howling southerly blow, the wind driving the rain chilling us to the bone.

A lot of water has travelled under the bridge since then. I have fond memories of Cape Town as it was here where I found out I could play the piano. This was one of the most positive things that could have happened to me after my memory loss. It gave me something to cling onto from my past. How and why I knew how to play was irrelevant. The fact I could, helped me to achieve some normality in my life. I recall that it was here where I discovered my determination to preserve the native wildlife. I didn't believe in hunting for sport, so I never killed unnecessarily, only to cull if the creatures were a menace or overcrowded. Where these thoughts came from, I had no idea, but these beliefs followed me all of my life.

All those years ago after the weather had cleared, Bella and I had taken the opportunity to climb to the top of Table Mountain. But, on this trip, we don't have the time as our train is booked for first thing tomorrow. Of course, we were much younger back then and I was still reasonably fit, and so to was Bella. Maybe we would give ourselves more time to look around on our way home. I would love to check out if there has been any progress since our last visit to the Cape.

It was going to be a long slow trip to Rhodesia, but we are excited and looked forward to seeing Mary again. She had been out here for two years now so it had been a while since we had a catch-up. The rail had only extended from the Cape as far as Mafeking, and that part of the trip would take around twenty-four hours, as long as there were no hold-ups. We would rest one day there before we continue on by coach to Bulawayo on Monday. That section was the longest and will take about six to seven days. So, it's a good week from the Cape, I would have thought, if everything went okay that is. I rubbed my hands in anticipation for the adventure, and I was especially hoping to spot the native animals in their own habitat.

We had heard through the grapevine that there was a bit of rumbling with the local Matabele, but nothing that the British South Africa Company could not handle. I found it strange that this huge country was run by a company. But I thought it advisable to just keep an open mind, to see how it would pan out while we were here. After all I don't know this country's history fully. The prospect of travelling through the mountains and the African plains gave me pleasure but I felt excitement rush through me at the expectation of seeing the wild herds of Cape buffalo and springbok, all types of antelope, lions, and elephants to I hope. It was everything I wished for, I hoped we would be rewarded. We both had our rifles with us just in case. I had the latest Enfield fitted with the most recent scope. This was an upgrade from the rifle I had with me over thirty years ago, it had made us a lot of money and still does. Bella had my original rifle. We had them mainly for protection and didn't intend to go hunting with them. I guess I'm a bit out of sync with other folks. I am all for preserving wildlife, while the majority want to have a stuffed head on the wall.

I've been warned that there's a bit of political unrest simmering, and to keep my eye out. Apparently around the beginning of the year Jameson, an Englishman under the orders of Rhodes, chairman of the British South Africa Company, crossed the border into the Transvaal with six hundred men and weapons. I was told in passing and didn't take much notice at the time of what was said, but I gathered that the soldiers were sent in to restore order and protect the English settlers living under Dutch- African rule in that corner of the world. It turned out that it was a smoke screen and in fact an illegal invasion. The Boers captured the invading force, and the instigators were sent back to the UK for trial.

After hearing this I searched through the newspaper hoping to find out more. I soon realised that Jameson's true intention to cross the border was the gold and diamonds mines. They used the excuse of unrest to annex this part of the country. This was all done in the name of our Queen Victoria, creating another red dot on the map of the world. I came to the conclusion that it was really only the greed of the company, itself, who wanted the mines, and bugger the Dutch whose country they invaded. All in all, it was just plain theft. Jameson was forced to surrender, and Rhodes had to resign as chairman of the company. No doubt a lot more was involved, but a consequence of all this caught up with Bella and I at a place called Mangwe Pass.

Just before we left the Cape, we received a cable from Mary in answer to ours. She was looking forward to seeing us both, that she had some exciting news to tell us, and she would explain when we arrived. I wondered what it could be.

We chose a sleeper on our trip north, and by the time the train pulled into the railhead at Mafeking, we were quite relaxed. We needed to be as the coach trip ahead of us was a five-hundred-mile haul through to Bulawayo. It wasn't a cheap trip either as they charged us one shilling for each mile. Our daughter was worth every penny, and as this was the only way to see her, we had to grin and bear it. As this stage was non-stop, we would have to sleep on the coach, making for an uncomfortable journey I'm afraid. There would be breaks every ten or fifteen miles to change the mules and an hour stopover for a meal at both Palapye and Tati Hotel. Then we would travel through the Mangwe Pass toward the final destination of Bulawayo. I wasn't looking forward to this part of the trip.

The vehicle run by the Zeederburg Company was a big four-wheeler stagecoach, pulled by ten large mules. They chose to use mules because over the past year, there had been an African horse sickness which wiped out a significant number of livestock, so making the old nag a premium price. Besides they were cheaper to buy and could still do the job, but the animals looked like brutes. The coach could carry up to fourteen passengers, this time there were only be twelve of us including the two drivers. Even so, stuck inside a stagecoach with ten other people for a week was not my idea of fun. But it was all there was, so we had to accept it. So, there would be eight inside and two up top sitting on the baggage, with the driver and his offsider in the driver's seat. It was looking like it would be a wee bit cramped.

The passengers congregated at the departure point outside the new telegraph office. We stood looking at each other until the driver jumped down and introduced himself. He told us his name was Arjen Van Der Burg, and his offsider was Freek De Ven. His accent was broad Afrikaans and I had difficulty understanding him at first. He indicated that we load our belongings, and we threw most of the baggage up on top as the boot couldn't accommodate it all. He then explained what to expect on the journey. The mule team would be changed frequently over the week, giving us about fifteen minutes at each stop to stretch the legs and use the privy. The changeover on the third hour would supply food and drink that we could consume on board. At Palapye way station there would be an hour long rest, to have a sit-down meal and to freshen up. And, again, at Tati hotel, that was before we headed through the Mangwe Pass, after that we continue onto Bulawayo. He advised us to make every stop count, to exercise when we could, even to walk while eating, as it was a long tiring trip. He also would appreciate if the men would give the ladies a bit of room to stretch out now and then, he did not mind a few of the younger men sitting on the roof. 'We take turns driving', he said looking at his offsider, 'and we sleep out on the baggage. So, sleep when you can, as we will be,' he laughed. I was the oldest male, but I still intended to do my stint on top. He then mentioned that as we were to spend a lot of time together over the next week, it would be a good idea that everyone got to know each other.

A look of concern crossed his face as he grunted, 'Evidently the locals believe the stories of native unrest were only rumors, that they were just making noise with nothing to worry about. But you are permitted to keep all your weapons close at hand, just in case'. Our driver then pulled his pocket watch out and announced, 'Right now, ladies and gentlemen, you need to step aboard. We will be away in five minutes.'

On board we introduced ourselves to the other passengers. Eliza Clark, a young mother travelling with her three-month-old baby Gertrude. She had been given the call to join her husband in Bulawayo. He had bought land there and had just completed the building of their house. Lily and Ernest Williams, a middle-aged couple who had a menswear shop in the town. The American Silas F Bolton was last to climb inside the carriage, an ex- miner in his middle thirties.

Three young miners in their twenties, John, Thomas and Herbert, chose to climb up on top, allowing the seven of us to have a bit more room on the first section of the journey. The driver yelled out, 'Gaan, gaan,' (go, go) flicking the whip. The mules took the strain, and slowly we pulled out onto the street heading north.

All of the women sat together on one side, the men on the other. I positioned myself opposite Bella and Silas was next to me. We sat around yarning, getting to know each other for the first hour or so. Bella and I were going incognito under the name of Mack. I did not like the limelight and avoided it whenever I could. It was good to be just us once again. So, I reverted to the name I was originally called all those years ago when I was shot in the New Zealand Wars back in 1863. I didn't like the name, but I didn't want every Tom, Dick or Harry to be all over us because of our title either. I bit the bullet, and for this trip, our surname name was Mack. So, we introduced ourselves as Bella and Sam Mack, farmers from Shropshire, England.

After we had talked a bit, we settled back and took in the views as we headed towards our first mule changeover. We changed sides then until the next way station. The stagecoach jolted and swayed like a ship at sea over the rough tracks and clay roads. It was like being on a boat, and a couple of the ladies felt a little travel sick. It would take some time to get used to the swaying. After the second change we started to relax into the journey as the conversation went around the cabin. On the third change, all the men moved up top as young Eliza had to feed her baby. Either that or the other option was to throw a blanket over her. Now there were six on the roof, and the driver made room for me next to his mate for the next hour or so. Slowly the day came to an end. Our conversation slowed as each of us dropped off to sleep, waking up with a start as we hit a pothole. I found it quite tiresome. I must be getting old.

On the third day, we came to our first hour long stop, where we could strip off and have a good wash. Being cramped up for so long you could smell the body odor drifting around the cabin. A decent scrub was well overdue, and a sit-down meal was a real bonus. An hour was not long enough, but we all felt refreshed for a while and looking forward to the next hour stop thirty-six hours away.

We had come to know Silas a wee bit by then,

and when he was explaining why he was heading up to Bulawayo, there was shocked silence on both Bella's and my faces. He had sold his diamond mine to the Rhodes Company and found an interest in the development of the horseless carriage or automobile. He thought he would take this idea back to the States as he was friends with the Duryea brothers, and with his money, he believed that this was an incredible opportunity.

'You know I have met this nurse in Bulawayo. She is fantastic, and at every opportunity I travel all this way to see her. I have been courting her for nearly two years now. Actually, I'm on my way up there again, but this time is different, as I plan to ask her to marry me,' he stated with a big grin on his face.

'That's nice, I was a nurse once,' responded Bella, wondering if she should ask her next question. 'And what is the young lady's name?'

'Mary Selkirk,' he replied.

We had somehow anticipated this answer, but it still took us by surprise, and we sat there with open mouths. I stammered, 'But...' Before I could continue, I got a kick in the shin from Bella with a shake of her head.

He looked at us. 'Are you both all right?'

'Yes,' answered Bella sweetly. 'It just reminded me of how I met Sam.'

'Interesting,' he said. 'She is from your neck of the woods to. Have you heard of her?'

I jumped in with, 'The name rings a bell, but I don't think we've met the family.'

Silas continued, 'I think she is well off. I actually don't really know. She has kept that part of her life close to her chest. For me, I don't care. I have all the money I want, and it's not important anyway. I would swim to England for her if I had to.' I look of tenderness crossed his face as he thought of her. He chatted on to us keen to let us know his history. 'Both my folks were from the deep south in the USA, but they died back in the Civil War. I was just a baby when a Yankee officer rescued me after finding me hidden under some clothes. He took me home to his wife and they became my ma and pa. I was lucky as they brought me up pretty well. Yes, I have a lot to thank them for. My Pa is an engineer, and I got the thrill of building and adventure from him. My sister Jane is a writer of children's books, and my other sister Mabel lives in Washington and is married to a politician. So that's my story. She knows that I'm coming, but I sure hope my lovely lady accepts me.' he added wistfully. 'We love being together, and we have so much in common, so I have my fingers crossed. I don't really think I have to worry.' he frowned. 'Boy, I have to say she is some woman, small and fiery. She sticks up for herself and will put you in your place if you do her wrong, but that's what I love most about her. You can't deny she is her own woman. I would like to think of her as a modern woman for the coming twentieth century.'

Bella and I were speechless. Was this the news our daughter cabled to us before we left—not a scrap of information has past her lips about all this. This was so typical of Mary. She was as Silas described, an independent woman—and she did what she thought was right for herself. A small smirk touched my lips. This young bloke, well not young really, as he must be in his thirties, was tall, blonde, with wide shoulders and rough hands. I could see he was used to manual work and wasn't afraid to get his hands dirty. I had heard about the new invention of a horseless carriage, and the word car whispered in my mind when I had read about it. Most folks presumed it would be a passing phase, but I didn't think so. Bella kept catching my eye, and when we arrived at our next mule change, she was out like a shot, taking me around the back of the stalls.

'We have to say something, Bella. My God, he wants to marry our daughter, and we have had no idea.'

'Look Sam, let's leave it until we arrive at our destination and sleep on it, in a nice bed. Then we will take him aside and have a talk. I don't want to embarrass him among all these people on the coach, and we won't have the opportunity to talk privately to him before then.' She looked up at me. 'This brings back so many memories of our meeting.' She laughed. 'The poor man is going to be horrified that he was in the presence of his future in-laws. He'll be wondering if he put a foot in it, saying something out of place.'

A voice bawled, 'Boarding.' We rushed back and clambered into the coach. Looking ahead twelve hours until our next one-hour meal break, then from there it was on through the pass, after that was the last section the run into Bulawayo.

CHAPTER SIX

Rhodesia 1894

I felt the next twelve hours were the longest in history. After all these days travelling my bum was so sore from the constant rough road, that I found it hard   to crawl down when we came to each stop. By the time the pub at Tati came into view, I was blissfully thankful for at least an hour's break and a decent wash. I could smell my own body odor, and everyone else's, for that matter. Somehow, the women on the trip seemed to adapt to the discomfort of the long haul better than us men. Bella was a box of birds, even assisting young Eliza to take a break from the baby. We could all see she sorely needed a bit of shut-eye. The blokes on the roof had not bothered to come down into the cab, and Silas spent a fair bit of time up there with them, talking, playing cards and sleeping.

We pulled up outside a large wooden house, with an enormous veranda, and sighed as we climbed down for the last regular one-hour stop of the trip. Washed, fed, and feeling so much better having some warm food inside of us, we headed on towards Mangwe. I was starting to count the stops for mule changes as my mind, by this time, had slipped into neutral, which was a word I had not thought of in years. I figured it had something to do with a car. Silly thoughts. Another word to add to the list I still had hidden in the draw back home. At the fourth staging post from Tati, called Murray's, the wrangler informed us before we left that the telegraph cable had gone down and his offsider had gone out to check it, but had not returned.

'Be careful,' he called out to the driver. 'There have been a few Matabele around: more than usual that is.'

Freek gave us a quiet warning, 'Make sure to have your guns and ammunition at the ready, just in case. I'm not thinking anything will come of it,' he offered. 'Probably just a lot of posturing and wind.' Still I was a little apprehensive as we drove out heading towards the last stop before Mangwe Pass.

A couple of hours out as we rounded a knoll, we saw black smoke lifting into the late afternoon sky in the distance. Arjen pulled the mules to a halt and asked if anyone had any binoculars. Silas jumped down from the roof saying he had a pair in his carpetbag, retrieved them, and passed them up. The driver stood up on the coach seat searching the horizon for any clues that told him something was wrong.

Arjen swore forgetting that ladies were present, 'Bloody hell. The staging post is ablaze, and it looks as though all our replacement mules have been slaughtered.' We quickly gathered around him anxious to hear his solution to our dilemma. 'I think we need to turn around and head back to our last stop at Murray's. Something funny is going on, and if the Matabele are stirred up, we are in grave danger.'

We all agreed. He was a local with all the knowledge, and I did not want to have Bella near any danger, or any of us for that matter. We returned to our seats, and as we were settling in there was   a rifle shot. The driver did a forward somersault   off his seat onto the backs of the mules. That frightened them so much that they shot forward heading towards the burning staging post in the distance. I stuck my head out the window to see what was happening and saw his sidekick trying to grab the team's reins. I noticed he was only able to reach with the help of one of the blokes on the roof hanging onto his legs. Before we knew it Arjen, our driver who was shot fell from the mules back falling under the coach. There was a lurch as we ran over him, and the coach careened down the trail. Lily Williams gave a squawk, started to sob and Earnest rushed over to do his best to console her.

Eventually, Freek the co-driver got the team under control. Next John one of the miners, gave us a shock when he stuck his head through the window, the others on top must of held his legs. With the coach rolling as it was it was a bloody dangerous move, and he had to shout to be heard over the noise of the racing mules. 'Keep your weapons handy,' he screamed. 'We can see a lot of movement up ahead, so we intend to go straight through them and make for Mangwe Pass. If we do make it that far, we'll try to reach the fort. It's only three and a half miles farther on. So, hang on folks, and be prepared to use those rifles.'

His friends pulled him back on top as Silas climbed down the other side coming in through the window. He carried a Winchester repeating rifle and two American six-guns. As the Williams and Eliza had no weapons Silas gave his six-shooters to Ernest and Eliza. Lily was a basket case and continued blubbering until Bella lent across the seat and shook her. Then she sternly hissed, 'We don't need all this crying; that's not going to help; we need to be strong for each other.' The shock on Lily's face was a picture, but the action worked, as she stopped, giving us a chance to think about our predicament.

Bella asked Eliza if Lily could take care of the baby, so she would have her hands free to use the gun if necessary. Eliza recognising the practicality of that placed Gertrude into Lily's hands. Bella, speaking softly to the woman, 'Lily, your job is to protect this wee dot. If we have to start shooting, you get under the seat with her. If things don't improve, we may need all the firepower we can get.'

Feeling embarrassed now that she had recovered her senses, Lily nodded and hugged the baby tightly to her chest. Her husband never said a word. As the coach raced down the trail it swayed like a drunk, inside we could at least brace ourselves, but the boys up top would be finding it hard to get a purchase. Then as we came up out of a small gully, a mob of fearsome-looking Matabele, gathered with a menacing manner on the road ahead. Our driver whipped the mules harder, and the Matabele opened like the red sea. I spied a few ostrich feathers as they flashed past, but more importantly I noticed that they all carried a variety of firearms. They fired at us as we sped through them, and we returned the fire, only managing to point and shoot. A minute later we were out the other side. No one was hurt, not even a scratch, but it worried me as I considered how long our mules would run before packing it in. We were supposed to change them here, and our replacements had been killed, lying back there in the dirt. Now we had fifteen miles to travel until we arrived at the fort. Those mules will be stuffed even if they could run the distance, and honestly, I thought that was a pipe dream. Would the fort hear the gunfire or see smoke and send out a patrol? I didn't know the answer to that question.

Silas stuck his head out to see what was happening behind us, and yelled above the noise, 'They are following us.'

'Oh bugger,' blurted Ernest. 'The Matabele can run all day, and if the mules falter at all, they could catch up with us. The animals can't keep up this pace, we need to get some distance ahead before they run out of steam.'

John stuck his head through the window once more.

'Freek told us the mules won't get us to the fort, but there is protection at the pass and some natural rock formations where we will be able to protect ourselves and make a stand. So, make sure you have the basics with you when we stop, as we will have to run for cover up the hill. There will be no time for personal gear, just rifles, ammo, and ladies. If there is water or food, bring as much as you can carry.'

I looked at Bella, and she held out her hand. 'We are together, Sammy. That's all that matters. Now let's get ourselves organised.'

Slipping, sliding, rocking, it was like being tossed around in a storm, but we managed to find what we required among our gear in the cabin with us. The boys up top had passed down food and water plus baby stuff. Most significant of all was firepower. I filled my carry-on bag with as much ammo as I could. Without warning a shadow of rock flicked past the window and then there was a squeal as one of the mules collapsed in a heap, completely spent. Then others smashed into one another until there was a mass of dead and dying bodies in a heap. How the coach stayed on its wheels was beyond me. Freek came down quickly.

'Hurry! Hurry up. There!' He pointed up to a saucer-shaped hill. 'It's a natural dish and will give us ample protection. Now, go go go!' he yelled. 'I will stay here with John and give you covering fire, until you are all safe, if necessary. Now, go!'

Silas grabbed the baby and all its gear, and we took off as fast as we could. Bella and I, not as young as we used to be, were a bit slow. Thomas stayed with us just in case we needed help. When Silas was up and over the top with Eliza, he came back down to help Lily, then returned for Bella. By the time I fell over the ledge, there was rifle fire down at the coach.

The Matabele had caught us up. Freek and John poured fire into them, and the Matabele just melted into the scrub. The five of us with rifles at the top gave the others covering fire as they made a break for the upper rim. That was until a big warrior materialise out of thin air and stabbed Freek in his back with his assegais. Thomas was next to me and let rip. I thought the Matabele went down, but I was not certain as I had focused on John, who was running in a zigzag movement up through the rocks. There wasn't a Matabele in sight, then just as we thought John was in the clear, the sound of four rifles rang out. John lurched and fell back, not making a sound. Thomas was beside himself. 'He is my friend, you bastards,' he cried out. Silas and I had to hold him back.

'He's gone, mate,' I reasoned. 'Let's look after the living; we can't do a thing for John now.'

He calmed down, tears in his eyes. 'We had gone through so much together.'

Herbert, the other miner, shrieked out, 'They're burning the coach.'

The flames lifted high in the still air topped with black smoke. They then proceeded to slaughter the few mules that had remained alive.

The saucer was only about ten feet in diameter and backed up against a rock face. Nine of us were left, including the baby. Everyone had a gun except Lily, who had the responsibility of the child. At the back of the saucer was a small overhang, so we piled up stones so Lily could crawl inside and be protected from all sides. The baby's mother was an excellent shot, and she stated as long as her child was protected, she would fight with the men. We set our defenses. Now we had protection from the rear, and with all of us spread out and laying down, we could just about touch each other, so we felt confident that protecting each other would be relatively easy.

'Do you think they will attack through the night?' I asked no one in particular.

Thomas offered his opinion. 'Be prepared, I think they might attack soon to try us out, and if they find it too difficult, they will probably lay off until first light.'

Silas checked everyone to make sure we each had enough ammo. Then out of the blue, our attackers seemed to materialise out of the ground. We had no time to think. We pointed and fired repeatedly. Bodies piled up below us until one warrior got close enough to stand up and fired down at us as he came over the lip. Bella and I turned together and fired simultaneously, he fell back, but he had shot Thomas through the head. Everything was a blur, and we kept firing until we could not hear a thing, then they just vanished. Their bodies, thirty or more, left where they lay. We were exhausted, thirsty, and tired.

I called out, 'Is everyone okay?'

There were some missing voices. I turned to see Silas standing over Eliza, who was not moving. Bella went to her and turned her over. She had gone, shot through the neck. I was going to move her, but Silas suggested, 'Leave her where she is, I don't like to do it, but it looks as though she is alive, and it will give them the impression that our numbers are still the same. We need to be sensible.'

We did the same to Thomas as well. Herbert had a small wound on his arm. Bella came over to me looking grim. 'If they do a concentrated run at us, I don't think we will hold them.'

'I know, my love,' I replied. 'If we do survive, we must do something for the baby as she has no mother now. I wonder how far this rebellion is reaching. For all we know, the whole country might be in an uproar.'

Silas built up the lips of the ridge adding more rocks for protection. Lily climbed out of her hidey- hole, distraught that Eliza had been shot, but more determined to be brave for the child. Herbert was on picket as we managed to eat and drink, then we relieve him until the night closed in. Bella moved around us doing what she could for both our deep wounds and superficial cuts. It was a long night. We could hear bird noises most of the evening. I whispered to Bella, 'They are talking to each other.'

Eyes wide, we lay close together, with my arm draped around her. As morning drew close the darkness lighten, and she looked at me, 'If this is our last day together, I would not have missed what we have done together for the world,' she whispered as she leant over and kissed me. Her smile and green eyes still the same as all those years ago.

There was silence as the sun lifted over the far

horizon, then they attacked.

The Matabele came out of nowhere, as they threw everything at us. All I saw was a wall of black bodies with their anklets of fur, armbands, and necklaces of teeth, all shouting their war cries, with the overpowering smell of animal grease in the air. They screamed their defiance at us with a screeching noise that was paralysing, it sounded like 'chee chee'. Some had rifles, but others used the traditional assegais and spears.

Lily hid the baby in the small cave so she could be with her husband. She had never fired a gun, but she made a lot of noise. The Matabele fell back only to attack repeatedly until they broke through, this time killing Herbert and Lily in the process. That left only four of us. We fought like lions. Silas was everywhere. Just as I thought we had pushed them back again, a big bloke with an ostrich plume came up over the top. He had a scar down one side of his face and the whites of his eyes were bright, as were his white teeth. His mouth was wide open, as he screamed at us. He stabbed down with his assegais right into Bella's back. At that moment, time stood still. Bella didn't make a sound. She died so quietly, without a murmur.

The huge Matabele pulled his spear out of her with a triumphant look in his eyes. Rage surged through me, and my temper flared as it had never done before, I went berserk. Silas told me months later that it awful to behold. First off, I stood up and shot the bloke in the head. Then I screamed at the top of my voice, 'I'm a Taniwha; I'm going to eat you.' I cannot remember a thing, but he said I jumped from the lip of the saucer with the dead Matabele's assegais in one hand, rifle in the other, and attacked them all. I was completely crazy as I slaughtered them. With spittle coming from my mouth I screamed about being a Taniwha, and that I was going to devour them all. I stabbed and shot in a frenzy before finally running out of ammo. Then using the rifle as a club, I went at them again and again. He told me bodies piled up all around my feet. The Matabele, no doubt thinking this bloke was mad, cringed in terror from me, and started to fall back. Then a warrior came up from behind me with a knobkierie and whacked me. The first hit only made me stagger a bit, but the second and third laid me out. Silas shot him in the back. He was now alone as only he and the baby were left alive. Everyone had been killed.

'I tell you, Sam, I thought I would be a goner as well, but a chief, he must have been a chief, turned up and stopped the attack. He looked down at you, said something, and they all pulled back and disappeared as quickly as they came. I rushed down to check and found you only just alive. I had to half carry and half drag you back over the lip, but I managed to get you back under cover. God, you are a big man to pull around.

Then ten minutes later, a patrol found what was left of us.'

I discovered this story months after the outcome as I was knocked senseless and not coherent for ages. All this time, I was unaware that Bella had died, so when I eventually came out of my stupor, I went into mourning for the love of my life. That left me with months of depression, which Mary helped me through. Even now, I just wish I had died alongside Bella. She was my whole life, and now I have no reason to live.

CHAPTER SEVEN

Rhodesia

I had survived with Silas and Eliza's baby Gertrude, the only passengers on the stagecoach who did. By all rights, we should have all died on that hill, but we didn't. We endured.

The three of us were taken back to Fort Mangwe. The fort had been cut off from Bulawayo and the surrounding district for several months. No information could get in or out as the cable wire had been cut. Later we found out that the cable from Bulawayo to Mafeking had never been cut. My daughter had searched for the three of us, Silas and Bella and I, but the last news she received was only that we had left Murray's post.

I cannot imagine what was going on in her mind, not knowing whether we were alive or dead. She sent a cable home, and our youngest son Sam, came straight out. I gathered he arrived a month after the relief column from Mafeking. By the time he had reached his sister, Mary had found us both, but of course, their mother had died.

I was a mess for days on end, in and out of consciousness. My head wound from the three smacks to it, had left me senseless, and they speculated that I would eventually die. But I was made of sterner stuff. Slowly and steadily I pulled through, though during this period, I was a dribbling fool. Silas was my constant companion he sat by my bed and talked and read to me. After I came around, he informed me I would say unusual things like, 'That's nice, but I need to fly to London,' and 'The flight is twenty- three hours,' and 'No time to talk right now.' Then I'd drop off to sleep again. Later I would regain consciousness and mix him up with someone else. 'Is that you, Brill?' I would say. 'Is the surf packed?' and then I'd drop back off to sleep.

When eventually I did regain consciousness for longer periods, he told me what I talked about, but I could not remember a thing about it or comprehend what he said to me. Of course, he passed on all of our conversations by cable to Mary, it had been fixed by then. It had come as a complete surprise when he found out that she was my daughter, and that I was an earl. He couldn't get over it, to find out that his girlfriend was a titled lady, and I was had a peerage. Still it did not change his attitude towards either of us, just maybe left him a little overwhelmed. He continued to spend more time helping me and was my faithful companion. I wondered if he was trying to make an impression, but after deliberating I came to the conclusion, nah, he was just a good, genuine bloke.

When Sam arrived, I begun to recover slowly. I was so happy to see him, but by then it dawned on me that my Bella had died, and I was not even there when she was buried. Only Silas was there. They buried all the passengers from the coach up on a small hill overlooking the fort, the day after the attack. When I was well enough, I was taken up there frequently, and I would sit and look at Bella's grave. Just a wooden cross with Bella Mack carved into the wood that even now was starting to fade. I could not accept she was gone, but after a while, my memory recovered, and I began to recall the attack up to the point when I was whacked from behind. But depression was like a dark cloud enveloping and gripping me in its clutches. They wanted me to go through to Bulawayo, but I refused. I wanted to be near to Bella. Sometimes I would sit all day by her grave, talking to her and not giving a bugger what others thought.

My children were worried. Mary cabled Bernard, our eldest son, and asked him to find my old journal. She gave him some words to write down that I had spoken of. Flying, Brill, the surf, and other words I had mentioned in conversation. She thought that might help my recovery or even jog my memory from the past. However, she mostly wanted me to go home, and as I didn't want to go, it was taking a lot of effort on her part. In my mind, I was not going to leave my Bella. Eventually it was my youngest Sam who came up to the graveside, and spoke all day, including Bella as if she was there.

'Look, Mum, talk to the old man.' He had picked up on the way I talked years ago. 'He needs to move on. You know he cannot stay here looking at your grave. We are all aware you are not there but looking down on the family from above, and I bet you a penny to a pound you are not happy with Dad.'

He turned to me, 'Do you think Mother would be pleased with you, Dad? Do you? She would be horrified to see you sitting all day looking at a piece of dirt and asking what are you are doing about that wee dot who now has no parents since her dad was killed when his farm was attacked. Would Mother just accept that? Of course not. She would be running around getting that baby into a home or taking her home with you. She would not be thinking about herself. She loved you, Father, and for her to see you like this would make her so unhappy. We need to celebrate her life with our family, not drown in sorrow. I miss her so much, as does Mary. You are not the only one; we need to mourn together as a family back home.'

I remember looking at him with tears in my

eyes. He looked so much like me at his age, just a little bit older than I was when I first met his mum. 'I cannot help it, Sam. I just want to die. I don't think I can live without her.'

'Dad, we all loved her. She was the sun and the moon, my inspiration, and I want to remember her like that, not a faded wooden cross in a far-away land. I think we would all be better off if we all were home in our own environment. I'm looking forward to seeing the paintings of her in the hall. It will bring her alive again the way we both remember her. Come on Dad, let's all go home. Margaret is coming home from New Zealand with that young bloke she is keen on, Adam Fenton. Mary has Silas, and Bernard and Catherine are genuinely worried about you. Our family is growing, Father, and you have to be around to see your grandchildren grow up, for their future. Think of them. Come on, Dad, it's time to go home.'

He stood up and offered me his hand. Looking up at him, I could see he was determined, and logically he was right. I was still in two minds and about to argue when a sunbird flew out of the tree and perched itself on the cross on Bella's grave. I just looked at it with tears pouring down my face.

'It's a sign, Sam,' I muttered. 'When your mother and I arrived in South Africa the first time from New Zealand, we spent a day walking up Table Mountain. As we came off the mountain at the end of the day, a sunbird flew over us. Your mother was so happy. She told me that was good luck at the end of a perfect day. I think she is telling me to go home.'

I lifted my arm, and Sam pulled me up as I turned to watch the bird fly up into the air and disappear into the distance. We ambled back down to the fort. I was still reluctant to leave, but Sam pushed me along.

Mary was thrilled as was Silas. 'I'll arrange everything, Father. You just rest. I have taken time off from the hospital and will come home with you. Silas will also come back with us, and of course, Sam. We are all here for you. Would you also like to place a proper headstone on Mother's grave? I can arrange that before we go.'

'Yes, I would like that: just the name Bella. That, for me, says everything.'

Within two weeks, it was done, tickets were booked for the trip south on the coach, though Mary insisted we would take longer and stay each night in the pubs on the way down and get a new coach every day. They had started a continuous service once Bulawayo had been relieved. So, it was going to take longer but more relaxing. The wee baby had been adopted out to a woman who had lost her own child at childbirth, so we knew she would be well taken care of.

Before we left, we visited the headstone made of black granite and there carved in the middle was the name Bella. I placed flowers on the grave before leaving for the final time. Mary had organised that flowers would be placed there every week for the next few years. Money was put into the account of the carver of the tombstone. They had a bit of trouble pulling me away from Bella's grave as deep down I thought I might never get back to see her again, so I dragged my feet.

Mary booked cabins on the latest steamship, the SS London Town, a twin-funneled, twin-screw liner. She cruised at fifteen knots and could take two hundred passengers. She was heading back to the UK after having some work done in South Africa, so there were only eighty-odd passengers on the home trip, taking about twenty-three days.

With fresh sea air and comfortable accommodations, Mary hoped that by the time we arrived in the UK, I would be feeling better. We would be there at the end of the English summer. So, it proved, but I was having bizarre dreams and still not quite with it. I would stare at the horizon for hours in a trance-like state then come out with things like, 'Keep the speed down, Bob; it's only fifty through here.'

Sam would ask what I meant, and I had no idea. Then our conversation turned to the army in South Africa, and that there could be war in the future with the Dutch. Unexpectedly my thoughts turned to the subject of Afghanistan.'I got a couple of medals from serving there, but I'm not allowed to talk about it.'

Mary replied, 'Father, you were only in the army in New Zealand, and you cannot remember that. Has something come up from your past?'

'Ah, no.' I frowned. I was confused, and so were my children. Poor old Silas was not sure what he was getting himself into. One night at dinner he mentioned the horseless carriage enterprise he was going to invest in again. 'Don't you know it's real name is a car or automobile,' I declared. 'Do you know, at the time when I came through the mist, there were a billion cars on this planet, and all together they generated a greenhouse effect, which was causing significant problems for the future.' The three of them looked at me stunned, you would of thought I came from another world.

'Mist, Dad?' questioned Sam. 'What mist? Can you remember?'

I sat in a daze not saying a thing, all I could do was shake my head.

In the distance I heard Mary say to Sam, 'He is doing that more and more each day. It's like his memories from his past want to come through, but when they do, they are all jumbled. He is getting better, but I need to write down what he says. I think it is important. Furthermore, it is good if someone is with him all the time when he is awake. I'm sure he will not hurt himself, but I just want him to know we are with him and love him. He has taken Mother's passing very hard, and we don't want anything happening to him.'

Three weeks later, we arrived in Southampton and caught the train that had been booked for the trip north to Shrewsbury. The old coachman, George Cotton, was there to meet us. Hell, he was older than me and should've been retired. He was dressed in black. He came over to take my bag and looked at me. 'We are so sorry, my lord. The news of the countess passing has shaken us all to the bone. Please accept our deepest condolences.'

Bella was loved by everyone she came into contact with. She had done so much to enrich the lives of the people around her. She was going to be missed, and the family were not the only ones to have a large hole in their lives. We drove in silence all the way to the manor house. I sat mesmerised looking into the forest, the same forest I saw all those years ago when Bella took me home after we had married. I watched as the railway workers working at the track were pushing a spur line through to our village of Brittermore.

The coach road was not coping now, and

people all wanted to ride the cable car up to the lake to take in the hot springs. It was decided that a train would be the best form of transport, and it was not far from completion. I felt different somehow. I was not really that interested, yet prior to seeing Mary in South Africa, I was excited to see the railway progressing towards our village. Actually, I was not interested in anything at all at this time, not even the bush. My whole purpose for living, died with Bella. All I wanted was to be left alone, so I could just remember my wife in my mind, and to hell with everything else.

I was a real worry for my kids because for all their lives, I had been this big, strong bloke who was fazed by nothing. I loved life and the forest we lived near. We had built up our place to be a world-class conservation park, and for them to see me like this, as an uncaring, mindless husk of a man was distressing them. On the trip back I seemed to be improving, but the blackness came over me as I got closer to home, and that is what really scared Mary. She had a difficult job getting through to me as Sam had. I think, she was hoping that our daughter Margaret, a newly qualified doctor, might be able to help, as poor Mary thought she was losing me. She was getting angry at herself, and at me for not trying.

Bringing me home, was turning out to be a complete flop. Of course, they put it down to the whack on my head. But when I was coherent it seemed funny to me. I thought, heck, I was shot in the head three times in Auckland and now whacked three times around the head in Rhodesia. Why does everything happen to me in threes when it comes to injuries? Even so, at the back of my mind, I knew I was not the full quid, and I should have been trying harder to reach out to them. They were doing their best to get me right and I was not helping anyone.

Even once we arrived home, and we had the memorial service, I was cold and uncooperative to all concerned. In spite of that, my friend the Prince of Wales was there. But I hardly spoke to him. Margaret had arrived home just before us and as a doctor now, she felt it her duty not to leave me in a depressed state. So, she checked me from head to toe, telling Mary that physically I was fit as a fiddle, but my state of mind was a mess. She then went on to explain that there had been a breakthrough with this type of malady called psychology, and Margaret knew of a London doctor, who had studied under Wilhelm Wundt in Germany. She thought that he might be the man to help.

So, she sent out a cable to her acquaintance John Smallbridge, who arrived a couple of weeks later from London. He took one look at me and asked if I was prepared to accept his treatment. Honestly, I was in two minds, but even I knew there was something wrong with myself, and so I agreed.

The doctor then explained his procedure to me. 'Sam'—I had insisted he call me by my first name—'the mind is a complicated machine, and I think I can help you, but you must be prepared to work with me, for if you don't, then there is nothing I can do. Do you understand? I don't care what you've said or have done in the past; this is to help you. So, if you're saying things that we don't understand, that is fine. It's all about speaking what's on your mind. I'll write everything down, and the next day we will go over in-depth, what was spoken about the previous day. It will take time, but as long as you want to continue, I'll be here for you. This science is new, but it has been proven in Germany and the USA, and eventually it will happen here in the UK, so we are in this together? If so, we start tomorrow morning at ten a.m. Does this suit you?'

What could I say? My mind was telling me I wasn't well, and if this helped me even a wee bit, I needed to go through with it. I nodded. 'Yes, John, I would like to try.

The sessions started the next day, and for a month every day for two hours he would just talk to me—no medication, just talk, and slowly I began to respond. One of the things that came out of these sessions were tiny pieces of my old memories before I had been headshot in New

Zealand. Even though I could remember only some things, and I still did not understand them, it was the start of the mist slowly clearing from my mind. However, it was something that would cause a headache for my children in the future.

CHAPTER EIGHT

Shadymore

This new form of treatment was in its infancy when John started with me. Usually, most doctors would take one look at you, diagnose you as insane or incapable of rational behaviour, and stick you in a lunatic asylum. Though, in my case, being an earl, they would have made sure I was locked up in a comfortable room before throwing away the key. John Smallbridge was a liberal thinker; he believed that the majority of people in these places could be helped back to normality, then be sent home to live normal lives with their families.

The next morning on the dot of ten, sure enough there was a knock on my door. The butler announced, 'Dr Smallbridge, Your Lordship' as John walked in. In his hands he had my old journal from 1863, the one I wrote all my thoughts and sayings and things I could talk about but could not remember. John had gone over this book, and I gathered he was impressed with what was written. In addition, John had a smaller journal that was from the time in Rhodesia up to the present day. So, he had a lot of information to work with, and he told me that this was unusual as most people lose touch entirely. He began his sessions slowly and took care to make sure I was fully relaxed. For the first time since Bella's death, I found I could talk about her and with his gentle persuasion, I was able to talk about what was on my mind, and soon my hidden memories started to emerge.

A few weeks into the sessions, my depression started to lift from a blackness to more of a grey. John expressed his pleasure, 'The light at the end of the tunnel is not far. Sam, you are doing well.'

When I finally did come out of the grey into the sun, I think what I told the family had them all asking, is he going back into darkness again, but that was down the line. My first breakthrough happened an hour or so into our session during the third week. I was standing, hands in my pockets, gazing out the window and looking at the forest. John was sitting in a chair with a pad observing me when he heard me gulp. 'Are you all right, Sam?' he asked.

I turned and looked at him. 'You might need to write this down, mate. I think I have remembered my birthday.'

'Oh, that's wonderful,' exclaimed John. 'When do you suppose it was?'

I paused and said, 'Fifth of September 1984.'

He looked up, puzzled. 'I think that's wrong, Sam. Are you sure it's not 1884? No that's impossible as well, since it's 1894, and that would make you only ten years old. Why is that date in the future significant to you?'

'I don't know, mate, but it feels like my birthday. It's an intense feeling more than just strong.'

'Well, let me think about it, Sam, and we will talk about it tomorrow. In the meantime, sit quietly, and see what else comes to light to improve on this memory. This is a real breakthrough, and even if the date is wrong, your mind is now processing information from the past: it is a positive sign.'

I could not remember why I thought of the futuristic date, but the memory did come back much later. The weeks slipped by, and I was becoming more rational with each passing day. However, I could now think about Bella without going into deep depression and I was starting to accept her passing. But I still missed her so much. The manor or park still held no interest for me though. So, I was fortunate to have my son Bernard carry on with all the duties that were usually my domain. The way I felt, I could not be bothered. Though I was inclined to like being by myself I was now holding my own in conversation with everyone. Memories began to slip into my mind, slowly at first, then it was like a freight train under full power. Too much information like that switched me off for a while, but I always gave John some snippet each day to keep him happy. Afterwards, I started to mention the odd name, like Brill, and I said this name over and over. Brill, who was Brill? My memory released Bob, then Kydd.

'Bloody hell,' I yelled, scaring Margaret when came into the room one morning. 'Bob Kydd, he was a mate.'

'Father'—she hugged me—'that's wonderful; we have the name Kidder in the journal; would this be him?'

I frowned at that. 'I'm not sure. Kydd seems right to me. I have no idea why Kidder would be there? That's a mystery, Margaret. I think this Bob was also Brill though. Once again, I'm not sure how that works. Somehow, I feel happy with this name; he seems close to me. Does that sound funny?'

'No, that's normal, Sam,' replied John. 'If this friend is close, then your feelings would be warm towards him.'

'Yes, well, I have another name as well, and he is in the journal also. The name is Shane Langton, but once again it is written as Lang. I'm not sure why that is.' I looked at them. 'My memory is slowly returning, and I'm afraid, Margaret, that there is a big mystery about New Zealand that seems to be pulling me back there. I cannot put my finger on it yet, but I'm getting there. I also have this deep feeling that when my memory returns fully, there are going to be some shocks, and I don't want the past to harm my family.'

'That will never happen, Father; we are with you together as a united family. Not under any condition will you embarrass us. Just continue as you have been doing, and tell us the memories as you remember them, and we can sort it out together. We are all here for you, Father.'

I thought that was all very well to say that, but I had this niggling feeling that I was going to blow the lid on something. I didn't know what, but this memory was just there trying to peek from behind a cloud, and it worried me.

Another few weeks slipped by, and arrangements were now under way for the weddings of both Margaret and Mary. They had decided to have a double wedding, so the place was filled with future in-laws. I had agreed, as I felt much better and happier about myself. Through these preparations, I continued the sessions with John, but my focus was more on my daughters' weddings.

It was a lovely autumn day. Bella would have been overjoyed. I was there to walk them both down the aisle at St Chad's in Shrewsbury at the beginning of November 1894; it was a big occasion for the County of Shropshire and for all of us at Shadymore. The girls and I had a family hug. More than a few tears were flowing, and we were all thinking about how much their mother would have loved the weddings. We tried to be positive, but sometimes it was hard to be strong, so behind closed doors we let our grief flow, and the girls had to rewash their faces.

The manor was full to overflowing for two weeks, and you could hardly move. Bernard, my eldest son, was my strength. He took over all the organising, and that left me to step back from a lot of my duties, so I was quite relaxed and at ease. With the weddings over and both my daughters away for three weeks on their honeymoons, the place emptied, and I was again with John for more sessions, feeling more relaxed and with an anticipation of what my mind would come up with. I knew in my heart, if anything came up that was important, I would not say a thing until I had all my family around me. So, for the next three weeks, it was a slow work in progress.

I suppose the relaxed atmosphere and my state of mind were the right conditions to open up my memories. Oh, I had had truckloads before, but they were all quite confusing. Now they were coming in a sequence, and I could even hear voices of people talking in my mind. I did not feel like I was losing it. 'Just a standard procedure of the mind coming to terms with the lost memories', John told me with confidence. I still had not had any recollection before 1863 as yet except the date I believed was my birthdate. I was starting to put together bits and pieces about my life just before the time of the attack in Auckland. This was when my memory gave me a shock: I remembered Adam Fenton from my time in Auckland.

Adam! I would like to work on that piece of information, but I needed to ask him some questions.

They were due back from their honeymoon in a few days, so we mutually decided to stop for now, and when Adam and Margaret returned home, we would all get together for a meeting. However, I was still a little disappointed that no memories of my parents and my unknown sister Mary, had surfaced yet. But John was quite convinced that I was progressing well, and it would not be long before there was a major breakthrough. 'You are doing well, Sam,' he kept saying.

So, we waited patiently until Margaret and Adam returned. Mary and Silas arrived home a day later. She still had a contract to finish and had to return to Rhodesia. They would leave by the end of December. Margaret and Adam would go with them and carry on to New Zealand. Adam was keen to get home to set up a medical trust fund with Margaret for their scholarship at Dunedin University medical school. They all planned to go via New York as Silas had a business meeting with the designers of the automobile manufacturer.

Everyone was moving away, and I hoped that most of my memory would return before they all took off. Margaret was happy with my progress and thought that I had recovered enough not to be a hindrance to myself and others. 'You are back to your normal self, Father,' she said, 'so come out to New Zealand this summer, and it doesn't matter if it's late summer; just come and spend time with us.'

I thought that might be a good idea. I didn't want to go to Rhodesia as all the memories would flood back and Mary would keep an eye on her mother's grave. So, it was decided. For the first time in a long time, I felt a little bit excited about venturing out. We discussed that it would be a good idea to bring Sam along. He was keen as mustard to return to New Zealand again, last time he was there, he checked out their first national park. I would leave the manor in the capable hands of Bernard.

The afternoon of the second day, that Margaret and Adam were home, we gathered in my office. Well, it was an enormous lounge really with plenty of seats to sit on. It was here that I asked Adam about his early days.

'Adam, I know this might sound funny, but please bear with me. When I first met you, your name triggered a memory in my mind and just before you were married, your name became clearer to me. Then the other day my recollection spat something else out, which I wanted to put to you. Let me tell you a story that I remember, and will you say if you can recall it, or anything at all about it for that matter? This will help me immensely. I'm sure of it.' I thought for a minute. 'First you lost your mum to fever or something. Your father, Sydney Walters, was shot a year later in New Zealand. Then a bloke by the name of Stewart MacSomething took you to Dunedin, I think. How does this sound? Is this correct?'

He looked at me. 'How! How, do you know that, my lord, er, ah, Sam? Yes, my original name was Walters, and my father was shot in an ambush between Papatoetoe and Otahuhu, in New Zealand.'

Before he could go on, I jumped up. 'Yes yes, I remember now.' Rubbing my hands through my hair and pacing the floor, I continued, 'We were attacked by Maori, and your father was the driver's offsider.' Now I was mumbling to myself, I turned to them, and I could see worried looks on their faces. 'No, don't worry, it's all coming back. It was a terrible day, pouring with rain.' I was frowning, thinking hard. 'Yes, we were under the cover of a tarp in a wagon. There was the sound of rifle fire, and a horse went down and another shot that must have killed your dad, Adam. I'm so sorry, mate. I remember he was given a full military funeral at the Otahuhu Anglican Church.'

'That's right. I was told later, when I was older, that was where he was buried. I have visited his graveside,' Adam replied.

'I have something else; a canoe comes to mind. Were you given a Maori canoe by, I think, a Maori woman?' I was concentrating hard now. 'Yes, Tui, she was married too.' I stopped and looked into the distance. 'Bloody hell,' I blurted. 'Shane Langton. He was a friend of mine. Oh hell, Shane and Bob Kydd were my mates.' I was choked up with emotion, but I continued, 'And there was cake, and your brother Noah would not come out behind a woman's frock.'

'My God, Sam, you must have been there to remember that,' replied Adam. 'I was only five, and my brother was three. We were taken by Stewart McInnes and Sofia McFarlane to Dunedin. I don't remember all that much; it's a bit of a blur, but I do remember the trip down on the ship. That was exciting stuff for a five-year-old.'

'Okay, that's fine, Adam, but can you remember anything about the people with me?'

'Well, we were adopted by my parents, Mary and Thomas Fenton, and my brother, and I took their name. Of course, as Mother was Stewart's sister, he was always Uncle Stewart to us, and it was funny the way things turn out. As Sofia married our mum's older brother Angus, and she became our aunt.'

I looked at him, Angus, and Sofia. Now, those names were ringing bells in my head. Why would that be? 'To be truthful, Sam, when I first met you, I felt you looked familiar, just like my mother's family. Is that possible? You are bigger than them, but the characteristics are there. I did not realise you were a redhead until Margaret told me, and both my uncles, Stewart and Angus, are redheads. You look so similar you could be related.'

'Yes, Adam, there might be something there, but it's not clear as yet,' I confessed. 'Can you think of anything else that might help me?'

'All I can remember is what I told you. I was only a young fellow,' but wait a minute.' He was frowning in concentration. 'There was a Maori man with sergeant stripes, and I think they called him Bill. Uncle Stewart told me he was a printer or something like that. Does all this help you? I cannot believe that we crossed paths so long ago, and for you to now be my father-in-law, it's quite unbelievable. Uncle Stewart has not been at all well lately, but when I get back, I can ask him about the incident of when you both met up. That might help bring forth more memories. He had kept that part of his life close to his chest.

'Mum did say he was dragged into the army to fight in the Waikato, but his friends helped him get back to Dunedin. We are not sure if he got his discharge papers, so maybe that's why he never talks about this part of his life. My brother and I treat him like a father. If it weren't for him, we would never have had an education, or have excellent parents. They are looking forward to having our second wedding in Dunedin. A letter came from Mother the other day to say the arrangements are going well.' Turning to Margaret, he grinned and added, 'There are not many couples who can say they got married twice to the same woman within a matter of months. This really suits the family and saved them from all coming out to the UK. As I said, some of the older members are not well, and the trip would have been hard for them.'

'Thanks, Adam. I would appreciate you having a yarn with Stu when you return, but remember he would have known me as Sam Mack. I'll look forward to catching up with him when I come out to see you and Margaret. I hope by that time my memory will return enough to recognise him. Right, time for a break. I'll catch up with you all in a few moments; I need to think about what I have remembered and what Adam has disclosed to me.'

They all plodded off while I sat back down to get my thoughts in order. I had a lot to think about. I now had names: Sydney Walters, Shane, Tui, and Bob, all their last names. I had Bill the Maori bloke, who was with me when we were attacked in Auckland, though Bella had told me about him years ago. I didn't know he was a printer. Stewart and Mary, their oldest brother, Angus, I remembered the attack between Papatoetoe and Otahuhu, though not the circumstances. That's more than enough to go on with. My memories were coming back, but the day of the attack in Auckland was still a blank, then there was how we got to be on that wagon when we were attacked in Otahuhu. We were getting there though, and I felt elated.

CHAPTER NINE

Shadymore

Now that I remembered snippets about my two mates, Shane Langton and Bob Kydd; my thoughts threw up the name Robert. So, there's a good chance that Bob's name might of been Robert Kydd, but with the nickname of Brill. I'm uncertain of the significance of that name. Where I had met them or anything about their families, I have no clue, just their names and now and again unconnected bits and pieces came to me.

When thinking of Shane, the word grunt came to the fore, whatever that meant, I had no theory. When concentrating on his name a young Maori woman, Tui, came to mind. I had a vivid flashback of being under attack, and she was slashing out with a Bowie knife at anyone who got close, from under a wagon covered in mud. This recollection jogged my memory and gave up the name Sidney Walters and Stewart McInnes. I think Stewart and I had a close connection, but I could not work that out. Hell, he felt like family, but why? In addition, Bill, the Maori sergeant with us at the time. I told my family that this was the most information I had

had from my past before I had met their mother.

Then I had this mental image of a large river, a fort, and a Maori village with black faces, though the faces could have been from Rhodesia; my memory was a bit jumbled. This was confusing as I also remembered soldiers tied up and marching through the bush. This vision gave up a face of a rugged Maori with half an ear and a scar on his left cheek. The unusual part of this, was that I was leading, ahead of this bloke, and the ones tied up were behind me. It begged the question, why was I with the so-called enemy, and why were these men bound? I'm uncertain the significance of this, but I'm sure it will come to me. I'm positive of it.

Another interesting picture that came through strongly was of me playing in a band. I believe that my mates and Tui were there also. Soon small chunks of my past came to me every day. Well, I think it was my past. According to John, I had broken through my block. He suspected the knock on my head had helped me start the road to recover my missing years. So the injury might have ended up being the best thing that could have happened to me.

But I would have rather had no head knock, and kept my memory loss, if Bella was still by my side. I found it painful without her. I still had a way to go as I had not recalled any element of my youth or my parents, but I was getting there.

There was one vivid vision that stood out. I had planned not to mention this to my kids, but it was too powerful a memory, to not confide it to them.

'You might think I'm reverting back to the way I was, and that couldn't be further from the truth, but I believe this is important. Remember I mentioned the word chopper in my journal? Well, I recalled having been in one; it had a large blade.' I frowned, concentrating as I spoke, no, four blades above me and a blade at the rear. I think the four blades gave this craft lift. I recollect that I was given earmuffs that let you hear the pilot talk, as the machine was very noisy'. I had their attention now; they all leaned forward in their seats so to hear every word.

'The pilots both sat in the front, I think there were two of them. I was in the back in the main cabin with two blokes that I assumed were my mates. We were flying well above the ground and looked down at a dormant volcano. Remember that map I have from all those years ago? I believe it was drawn from the air, because I saw it laid out like that.' It was a powerful image. 'I'm finding it difficult to comprehend, but I was flying.'

'Now don't jump to the conclusion that I'm having a relapse. I'm all right, and no doubt John will be able to put this into perspective for me. I figured it needed to be mentioned as this was a memorable impression. Let's face it; I could not have been flying that's impossible, but the memory is persistent, and my mind chucked out for some reason. I'm certain it means something, but unsure exactly what. I believe this is part of my previous life from before I met your mother, so it is important not to just shrug it off, just because we don't understand it.'

Margaret came over to me. 'Father, I must say, I'm so pleased. Well, we all are, to see you getting back to your old self.' She hugged me, pulled away, held me at arm's length, and then looked into my eyes. 'You don't know how much we have been worried about you, and to see you now like this, is wonderful. However, I'm concerned that we are leaving you before you are fully recovered. I feel we are abandoning you, Father. I will stay if you need me.'

'Don't be silly, Margaret, and you too, Mary,' I replied. You are both married now, and your married life is only just starting. You both have places to go and things to do. I still have Bernard, Catherine, the children, and of course, Sam. You have to do what you need to do, and please don't worry about me. I'll be visiting you for your summer, so we will see you all again very soon. Besides, I'm quite positive I'll be a box of birds by the time Sam and I come out. So you go and do your thing. I'm sure that you will make a name for yourselves; I'm convinced of that.'

A few days later, we all went down to South-ampton to see them off. It was another sad time for everyone, as it will be some time before we meet again. We waited as the liner slipped its moorings, turning its bow seaward with four of my family members waving madly from their deck until the ship disappeared from sight. I was quiet heading home. Well, we all were because it will be quite a while before Bernard saw his sisters again. We were a close family and had done so much together, but life had to go on. Now they were gone I felt a desire to get back to work, and to restore my memories with John's help. I was sixty-three and it was important to me now. Surely my mind would give up its mysteries of my past life before my time was up. Well, I hoped so as it has continued on for too long.

Somewhere at the back of my mind there was this niggle, even if I did reclaim my memories of those years, my parents could well be gone. They would be at least in their late eighties or nineties, and my sister might only be a couple of years younger than me, making her at least in her sixties, and no doubt, a grandmother. All the years that have passed in which I had been out of their lives amounted to quite a while, a life-time in fact. I would be just a fleeting memory to them all. Was it fair to just turn up and rake over old coals? I think if I were in their position, I would not mind. Let's face it, after all, we were family. Thinking seriously, I'm sure time would not at all be relevant if I found them. After all, if they were still alive, it would be a celebration. I was going to hold on to that thought.

John and I settled back into the sessions. For the next few weeks nothing happened, I'd hit a brick wall and I found it frustrating. We celebrated the Christmas of 1894 with the remaining family, and as usual the staff Christmas party was enjoyed by everyone. Then on a grey, wet day, after Boxing Day, the butler knocked on the door. On the plate was a letter, as he announced in a monotone voice, 'A letter from Buckingham Palace, your Lordship.'

I thanked him, and he retired. Frowning, I looked at the letter, undoubtedly from The Queen as it had her seal on it. I wondered, what's this all about? It had been a while since I had seen her. I had had a condolence letter from the royal family after the death of Bella. Then at the memorial service here at Shadymore, Edward, the Prince of Wales attended. But I had not met The Queen to speak to since she bestowed the title of earl on me. I was not into all that pomp and ceremony stuff. I was however good friends privately with her eldest son, Edward, who would be the next king. Her majesty was getting on now and didn't get out and about like the old days, so Edward was preforming quite a lot of her duties. I wondered if this was from him. I slipped a knife into the seal, cut the envelope, and pulled out the letter. Nope, it was from Her Majesty. I read it through then read it again. Blast, I cursed to myself, I didn't want to go to this reunion. John and I were only halfway through our daily session, and was still sitting in his chair waiting for me to explan the interupation.

'I hope I don't sound impertinent Sam, but by the look on your face, I gather the letter brings bad tidings?'

'No, not really, John. Here, take a look, mate,' as I passed him the note. 'I suppose it is relevant to my state of mind and where I am at the moment.'

He opened the folded letter and began to read.

Your Majesty commands Lord Selkirk of Shadymore and one family member to attend Windsor Castle on the fourth day of January in the year of our Lord 1895 at four p.m.

To be part of the official party, to meet and greet a delegation of New Zealanders, who are here in my United Kingdom to petition Her Majesty on their grievances of land confiscation. All officers who were present at the time of the hostilities are summoned to my residence to welcome and receive their former foe. After the delegation has met with their queen, there will be a reception in the main dining hall of the palace.

By my command, Victoria.

He looked up. 'Sam, this might be the best thing for you. This might be a rare opportunity for you to meet with all these people who will be there. It could be a chance for you to remember something from your past. In fact, I'm sure you will—we are so close, so very close. This might be all you need for your mind to open up.' He handed back the letter.

Well, that was sharp and to the point. I was not going to look forward to this do, that's for sure, but there was no way I could get out of it. I could not remember much at all about my time there and placing people will be difficult. This was a waste of time at the moment, I thought. John, nevertheless, was of a different opinion, and said that the chances that this gathering jogged my memory was just too good to miss.

'It would not do any harm, and there is a very good change it would be helpful. It has come at just the right time, Sam. We are a bit stuck, so this is an excellent opportunity.'

So, I did my best to be optimistic about the meeting. The same day I received a cable from my brother-in-law Angus McDonald. He was my best man at Bella's and my wedding in Scotland. He had married Bella's sister Amelia and lived in

Nursery Cottage, Shrewsbury. It was a long cable stating he had a letter from The Queen to attend a reunion at her residence. Of course, he was taking Amelia with him. But if I had received one as well, he suggested that I bring Sam my youngest, and we could all   go together. I felt sorry for Bernard, my eldest for missing out, but he was weighed down with the running of the manor. After saying that, I realised that he did thrive on it.

Angus could remember the attack in New Zealand quite vividly, after all he had lost part of his arm that day. Whereas in my case, I was still a fizzer. Amelia was Bella's sister, and she was like a young sibling to me. She also had a rough time when the news hit her that Bella had died out in Africa. They were very close, but she was made of the same tough stuff as Bella and came out of her mourning much better than me.

The Brittermore train track had been up and running for at least a month, so Sam and I took the train from there. We changed in Shrewsbury where we caught up with Angus and Amelia. You could see Amelia was excited with the prospect of actually meeting some Maori from New Zealand. The first thing Angus asked was, 'Did you bring your medals with you? Her Majesty will expect it,' he stressed.

'Yes.' I nodded. 'Sam made me bring them, as he wanted to see me wear them.' I hadn't worn them since they turned up in 1869.

'They look good on you, Dad,' Sam said with pride. 'The New Zealand Cross for bravery and the New Zealand campaign medal is nothing to sneeze at. Uncle Angus, your campaign medal looks good on your uniform jacket.'

Amelia gushed, 'It is only right for both of you to be recognised, and I'm so proud of the two of you,' she smiled, squeezing our arms. 'I have booked the Windsor Hotel not far from The Queen's residence, so we have no excuse to be late. I'm hoping Her Majesty will have her Arabian stallions on display. I would so love to get close to them,' she beamed.

I rolled my eyes. 'Excellent. I have been the laughingstock to everyone in Shropshire with my riding habits. You can bet a penny to a pound that that bloody horse would bite me if I got close.'

They laughed. 'At least you can drive,' Angus piped up. 'That has to account for something.'

The trip seemed to fly by as we yarned all the way to London. Before we knew it, we were pulling up to London's station in a cloud of smoke and sparks. A couple of porters removed our luggage for us and hailed a cab. We asked the driver to take us to the Windsor Hotel, arriving just in time for dinner, leaving us no time to change, so we headed straight to the dining hall to eat. Later we took a walk up to the palace gates, wrapped up like an Eskimo as it was so cold.

Afterwards, it was back to the hotel for a bath and an early night. Even though the bath relaxed me it did not stop my mind from tumbling around all over the place. I was anxious about what the next day would hold. Would my memory be given a jolt? I had hoped so as it had been much too long. Then I started to worry that, if I did remember, how would I react, and that this might turn out to be a problem for me in the foreseeable future. My mind still had not settled as I climbed into bed, eventually slipping off to a restless sleep.

CHAPTER TEN

London 1895

I woke to a fine winter's day red eyed and tired. The sparrows were sitting on the window-sill making a hell of a lot of noise as I washed and dressed for what I thought might be either a stressful day, or if this thing with my memory came to a successful conclusion, it could be a successful one. I dressed warmly then I strolled down for breakfast.

I caught up with Sam, who had arisen early to walk around Alexander Park. He was so much like me at his age, taking advantage of any opportunity to head out into Mother Nature. Well, here in London, there was not much of that, but they had some excellent parks, and that's where Sam went. He was waiting for me in the dining room. A few minutes later, Angus and Amelia wandered in. Amelia had arranged for a cab to pick us all up at 3:15 p.m. that afternoon to take us to the palace. We had most of the day to fill. Sam and I took a walk around The Brocas, and Amelia and Angus went shopping. Looking at Angus's face, I thought he would have rather been with us.

It was nice just the two of us, and Sam told me how well I looked after my so many months of depression since his mum had died.

'There is colour in your face, Father. You don't know how worried we were. You actually frightened us. The family could not contemplate losing you as well.'

'Yeah, Sam, I'm feeling so much better now, son. The only thing is I wish I could connect all the dots. My memory is coming back but in a way that leaves me unsure, but it is, at least, starting to return slowly.'

He laughed. 'Now that's a saying I haven't heard you say for a while—connecting the dots. I remember when we were at school, I used to copy all your sayings, and it was always funny to watch how people would react to them. I would receive some strange looks. John Cotton and I used to say them just for a reaction; it was good fun. We could not get it right sometimes as we had to mimic your accent, and it never came out as good. You have never lost your accent, Dad, and I'm pleased you didn't; it's you, and your sayings make you unique. It would be nice, though, to find someone else who has your accent, then we might be able to pinpoint where you are from. We can only hope.'

Returning to the hotel and all through lunch, I was nervous about what the day would bring forth. Having my family with me I felt supported, and I knew they would be there if I went to pieces. Of course, I didn't want that to happen. I didn't wish to make a fool of myself, but I had to be prepared as this was new territory for me. Coming face to face with people who knew you, and if it wasn't reciprocal, it could give you a little bit of anxiety, so naturally, I was nervous.

Sam sympathised, 'Well, if nothing else comes of this, at least we will have some good food and wine.'

I snorted. 'You love your food Sam. You are so much like me, I could never get enough: not so much now though. But like you, I used to burn it off with all my tramping, and never put on excess weight. 'We yarned the afternoon away until it was time to head out to the cab that arrived on the dot of 3:15 p.m. We wrapped up, as the day was cold. The cabby was spick and span, dressed up for the special occasion of driving to the Palace. He did not often get the excuse to drive inside the castle grounds. We climbed aboard for the short trip. I was quiet and full of apprehension the closer we crept towards the palace gates.

Amelia smiled at me. 'Sam, why don't you ask the Prince of Wales to come up to the manor. It's been a while, and I have heard he has been a bit off colour lately, so this might be a good opportunity for him to get away from London for a few days.'

'That's a marvellous idea, Amy,' I replied happy that she was doing her best to take my mind off my concerns.

I like to think the prince and I are friends. After I was knighted, he came out to our place with his new wife to take in the waters. We hit it off and tried to get together as much as possible. I felt a bit sorry for him because his mother didn't treat him well and chastised him for a lot of his indiscretions. Oh, I knew he liked the ladies and was unfaithful to his wife, but for his mum to blame him for most things that went wrong, on a day-to-day basis, went against the grain with me. So, I had an open offer for him to come and stay whenever he wished. The thought cheered me up a bit. The gates of the castle opened as we moved closer, and I could see a queue of cabs in front of us and more behind as well.

'It looks like there could be a crowd,' I ventured. 'A lot of your mates, Angus, as I can see tartans climbing the steps,' I remarked.

Angus looked splendid with his medal pinned on his military uniform. My medals were fixed to my jacket as I was in civvies. Amelia flung out the word dapper to describe the three of us. It took longer to drive from the main gate to the foot of the stairs than it did to drive from the hotel. Eventually, we came to a halt, and a footman in all his regalia opened the door, pulled out the step, and helped Amelia down.

'Good afternoon, Lord Selkirk. Please walk to the top of the stairs, sir. There will be an escort to take your party to the dining hall.' As we started the climb, I heard him say to the driver, 'Be back here at six pm, my good man.'

I walked up the stairs with my fingers crossed hoping that I won't make a fool of myself, I only have two hours to get through after all. At the top of the stairs, a young lieutenant of artillery was waiting. He saluted us and said, 'Follow me, please, Lord Selkirk.'

We could see a stream of people in front of us all with their escorts heading down the long hallway to the dining room. It was years ago now that Bella and I walked this very same hall with her hand tucked into the crook of my arm, I smiled as I thought of her fondly. That was after the occasion when Queen Victoria had knighted me back in 1863. They invited us to The Queen's residence afterwards. Then once again in 1889 when she bestowed the earl's title on me.

Moving down the hallway, I noticed a variety of unfamiliar army uniforms everywhere, and a lot of pomp and ceremony. I was starting to sweat, so Sam passed me a hanky to wipe my forehead. 'Take it easy, Dad, and just relax. The worst that can happen is you won't remember a thing, and after all these years, it will be par for the course, but if you do remember something, it will be a bonus, so again, just relax. We're mates; I got your back.'

I had to smile at that, So, for him, I took a big breath and did my damnedest to relax. We arrived at the entrance to the dining hall and looked down from the top of the stairs. There must have been about a couple of hundred people milling around. It was a very colourful scene, with all the ladies in their new gowns and the many different coloured uniforms dotted around. Everyone had a drink in their hand, and mingling. A doorman announced our names as we entered.

'The Earl of Shadymore, Lord Selkirk; his son, Mr Samuel Selkirk; and Mr and Mrs Angus McDonald.'

We walked down a couple of steps to the floor of the hall. I don't remember a glass being placed in my hand; it just materialised. Faces turned towards us. I had not expected to be announced, and I stared at a mob of unknown faces and gulped. I heard Sam whisper, 'Big breaths, Dad. They are only people.'

I shook myself out of my trance and slowly walked farther into the room then stopped dead when this voice rang out.

'Lieutenant Mack, Lieutenant Mack, is that you?' A little bloke in an infantry uniform, with the rank of major general, slid into view after barreling past subordinates who had to move out of his way. He pulled up, and looked at Sam.

'Lieutenant Mack, you haven't aged at all.' Sam was a bit perplexed.

'Ah, I understand,' he grinned. 'I think, sir, you have mistaken me for my father,' and stepped to one side. 'Major General, let me introduce you to the Earl of Shadymore, Samuel Selkirk.'

The major general was frowning. 'I do apologise, my lord. I thought your son was an officer I had met out in New Zealand; he looks so much like him, but the name was Mack, not Selkirk. My name is Robb, my lord, and I was an ensign at Alexander Redoubt at the time.' He was peering at me intensely, then he exclaimed, 'It's you, sir, it really is. You were Lieutenant Mack. You have changed your name. Oh, my lord, it is indeed wonderful to meet up with you again!' He grabbed my hand, shaking it madly.

It was then, looking at him, I had a faint recollection of who he was, and there was another ensign with him at that time, Smyth. Good old Sam rushed in, 'Major General,' he explained, 'my father was wounded back in New Zealand. He had wounds to his head, and his memories from the first thirty years of his life are missing. So, sir, my father might not remember you. One of the reasons, for being here, besides being ordered by Her Majesty, was mixing with people he knew back then with the hope they might trigger some lost memories and regain his past of thirty years ago.'

Robb turned to me. 'My dear sir, come with me, and I'll explain how we met. Something might jolt your memory.'

I followed him over to a corner table. My mind was racing; yes, those names Robb and Smyth rang some bells in my head. Amelia and Angus didn't make it to the table because they were swamped by fellow officers from the Scottish regiments. Only Sam and I pushed through the crowd with the major general ahead of us. We sat down, and another glass of wine was placed into my hand.

'My name was Mack back then, Major General. I only knew that as there was a document in my pack with it on. I did not like my name, so I took the name I have today, Selkirk. You are correct in this instance: I was Lieutenant Mack.'

'Yes, my lord.'

'No, just Sam, Major General, just Sam.'

He looked at me. 'My name is Peter,' he replied with a broad smile.

'Hi, Peter, this is my son, Sam, named after me, so I can understand the confusion. People say he looks like me back then though. Like him, I was a redhead, but with the wounds to my head, I turned grey overnight. I cannot remember myself having been red but looking at my son, sometimes it's like looking in a mirror.'

'Take it from me, Sam. Your son is the spit-

ting image of you. Hell, man, you were imposing to a very young sixteen-year-old ensign, who
had no idea how to be a commander, or anything
really. You sir, changed that, and all these years
I have wanted to thank you, and now the opportunity has arrived. Can you remember anything
at all?'

I looked at him. 'Since we have been talking
with you, the name Smyth came into my head.
'Yes, that's right, Charlie, well, Charles Smyth.
He was left in command of the redoubt when
the colonel and the colour sergeant went to
the meeting with General Cameron in Drury. I
was second in command, and looking back at
that time, I was absolutely bloody hopeless—no
skills whatsoever. You and your other officers,
now let me think, Captain Kidder and Lieutenant Lang then yourself. The Maori woman was
Tui, I think. She was Lieutenant Lang's wife, and
Sgt Hohepa, and a man by the name of Mac something.'

'You have a good memory, Peter.'

'Yes, it was the only skill I had at the time. As
I was quartermaster, I had a lot to remember.
Your son, Sam, here, looked just like you when
you arrived at the redoubt, jogging my memory
of you when you brought in those prisoners, the
ones who illegally attacked the village of Pukekawa. You, sir, turned round my life, from a naive
ensign to who I am today. Before meeting you,

I had never admitted to anyone that I not ever mixed with boys my own age or with men for that matter. And there I was second in command of a garrison, admittedly, only temporary, while the colonel was away. So, when you gave me a few home truths, I had a long, hard look at myself. I was unquestionably wet behind the ears. Is anything coming back yet?' His eyebrows rose in query.

I shook my head in the negative.

'Well, you dressed me down good and proper when I rubbished the way you all spoke. I was not used to your easy-going manner, and I did not understand your comradeship. When you told me to my face what you thought about me, well, Sam, you scared the living hell out of me. You towered over me, and you certainly gave me the message. It feels like only yesterday. This was after you had arrived with the missing patrol in tow. They, under the direction of Sergeant Router and Corporal Smith, decided to cross the river into forbidden territory for a bit of argy-bargy with the local population.

'If it weren't for you and your companions, the war in the Waikato would have started much earlier, and we were just not ready for that. More lives would have been lost. Charlie and I sent out patrols until you arrived on the banks of the river with the men under guard, and you also had some Waikato warriors with you.

If I remember correctly, this incident mucked up months of reconnaissance of yours, and no doubt, the governor would have been unhappy with the outcome. We have a lot to thank you for. Can you remember anything I have talked about, Sam?' He was looking at me intently.

'Smyth—he was the older bloke?' I looked at him frowning. 'You gave us some money as we had none,' I divulged.

'Yes, that's right, Sam. Well done. I was the paymaster those days as well. I also sent more money to you the day you left. We found a wallet under Lieutenant Lang's bed, and I dispatched a private to catch up with you with extra cash as I believed I had not given you enough. He caught up with you before Drury and gave the wallet to the lieutenant and money to Captain Kidder. The captain gave his report to the private to deliver to our colonel about the incident with our patrol. We never saw you all again, though the money we advanced to you came back after the incident in Auckland. You know even today we are still not allowed to talk about it. This is where you received your head wound, I gather.'

Sam looked at me. 'How are you feeling, Dad? Are you okay to continue with this?'

'Yes, I think so, Sam. The major general has gotten me thinking.' I turned to Peter. 'Can you tell me anything about how we found your patrol?

This is blank to me at the moment.' Then before he could reply, I interrupted him. 'I just remembered something: I went into the mess kitchen and bludged some more pie, coming back into the mess, yelling you needed to promote your bloody cook: he was superb, and it was then that you figured I was uncouth?

The major general grinned. 'Little did I know,' he said, 'that was when you dressed me down. You told me to treat all men by their deeds, not by how they looked, spoke, dressed, or how educated they were. That even the lowest on the totem pole could be the best man in the squad, and that I could learn from everyone. I hadn't any concept of that at all, it hadn't even crossed my mind. My parents had too many children, paid for my commission, and hoped that I was sent to the ends of the earth—out of sight, out of mind. Well, I was at the ends of the earth, and you, sir, were the only one who bothered to talk to me like a person. I apologised to you the next day, well, to you all. From that moment on, I changed my way of thinking and took an interest in my men. Then I collected all the non-commissioned officers and asked them for their input. Now people are falling over themselves to be under my command, all because of you, and once again, I thank you. I was so hoping you would be here today, and here you are.'

'What happened to Ensign Smyth?' I asked.

The smile left his face.

'Charlie Smyth was killed at Gate Pa in the Bay of Plenty in April 1864, I'm sorry to say. He was such a good fellow, a better man than I was. At the time, I was just learning my skills. The day of the attack after the barrage, we attacked. Charlie's company was the first to go through the breach, but the Maori had come back into the trenches. We lost a lot of officers that day and a lot of good men. I was lucky, but Charlie died at the breach. I was not far from him when he died. He was the first and the only friend I had at the time, and I was devastated. I still think of him. Look, I think I have more to tell you. Why don't we meet up tomorrow in a less-inhibiting place, and we can nut it out together? I want to help, and we can privately have a drink and just talk. What do you say? Where are you staying?'

'The Windsor,' I replied. 'Make a time that suits.'

'How does eleven am. sound?' I decided.

'Perfect. I'll be around tomorrow. I'll pay for lunch; you pay for the drinks. Now that cannot be all that bad.' He got up from the table.

'Lovely to catch up with you,' he said, shaking my hand, 'and I'll see you both tomorrow.' With that, he turned and was swallowed up in the crowd.

CHAPTER ELEVEN

Windsor Castle

I sat at the table staring into space trying to piece together the memories that had now come to the surface, when there was an announcement from the entrance: 'Mr. Abraham Metcalfe VC of Auckland, New Zealand and the Reverend Henry Talbert VC of Wellington, New Zealand.'

Everyone turned to look at these two men. Only thirteen Victoria Crosses had been given out in the New Zealand Wars and to have a couple of them here was exceptional. I stood up to look at them as they slowly came down the stairs into the dining hall. I was pleased that Sam and I were a lot taller so we could see over most heads. I studied these two as they wandered around the room, shaking hands, smiling, then moving on. There was something about them that I couldn't put my finger on. I grabbed Sam's arm and whispered in his ear. 'I-I need to meet those two blokes.'

'All right they are headed this way; I'll waylay them for you.'

I watched as they were surrounded by men and women alike as everyone wanted to shake the hand of a VC winner. Then a realisation hit me. Sweat covered my forehead and the room swayed. I grab the back of the chair for support, and Sam, who had been about to leave me, grabbed my arm.

'Dad, for God's sake, are you okay? Look wipe your brow.' He handed me his hanky again.

I looked down at the floor, which was still moving, took a deep breath and everything stabilised.

'Yes, I think I'm right now. I had a flashback, seeing those two over there, and it threw me. Would you believe, it just dawned on me they were with me in New Zealand.'

I looked over there again as they broke away from the crowd. Now the taller of the two, what was his name? They had announced it as they came down the steps. Abe, that was it—Abe and Henry. Henry's head turned my way, and he did a double take. He pulled on Abe's coat and pointed in my direction. A big smile covered Abe's face and he said something to the men around him, then made a beeline for us both. It took them a while as they continually got caught up with people wanting to talk to them.

My memory was having a field day. Flashes of white horses with lather on their flanks, and the rain driving into us horizontally. We were attacked by some Maori and I sheltered under a wagon covered in mud. Tui, I hesitated, bugger me. Yes, that's right, Tui, I remember, she slashed out with a Bowie knife, and I fired at the same time. A voice in my head yelled ten o'clock, Sam and a body slumped down in front of us. There was so much noise and confusion going on. A bloke used the dead horse as protection, strange, he looked a lot like my family, and a body lay beside him. Shane, I screamed watch out there's more coming.

The recollection was so vivid it overwhelmed me, and I sat down with a thump. I can't believe I went through all this, and for over thirty years I had not remembered. Sam came in beside me, with his hand on my back.

'Are you okay?' he said with concern.

'Yes son, I'm fine. I have just recalled bits of the past that have eluded me for years. Seeing those two blokes has triggered those memories.'

I recognised Abe's grin immediately as they came closer. I rose from my seat and held the back of the chair, still feeling wobbly. He had aged well: big calloused hands, brown face, not as tall as Sam and I, but still a solid muscular man for his age.

'Bugger me,' he said, stretching out his hand to shake mine. 'Sam Mack, I do believe. Lovely to meet you again. Do you remember this bloke next to me?'

I looked at Henry. 'I have only just remembered your names now, for the first time in thirty years. Henry, how are you?' I shook Henry's hand. 'Sit down, fellows. This is my son, Sam.' They each pulled up a chair.

'You look like your old man, Sam,' Abe said. 'He'll never die with you around. So, tell us... what have you been doing for the last thirty-odd years, mate?' Abe asked.

'Would you like me to explain, Dad?' Sam asked.

I nodded.

He turned to both men. 'My father was head wounded in Auckland all those years ago, and he has lost his memory. Up until now, he has only remembered a few things, as the first thirty years of his life had gone. Only lately in the past few months, snippets of memory have been returning. Now when he saw you blokes, much more has come to mind and it's been quite a shock for him.'

'Oh, Sam, we are so very sorry, mate. Let's sit down and maybe we can help you out. Tell us what have you just recalled?'

I thought about the attack on the road. 'We were in a wagon.'

'Yes, that is right, I remember that.' Henry beamed. 'It was the first time we had met you all. What say I take you through it and see if we can squeeze more out of that head of yours? Abe, more drinks, my good man.'

Abe turned to me. 'Henry still thinks he is in command. He keeps forgetting that I was the officer, and he was the private.' He laughed. 'Everyone thought it was funny Henry being a Wesley minister in the Calvary, but it worked for us. Of course, few of us left now; just us two and Bill back home in New Zealand.'

'Bill,' I remarked. 'We had a Bill also,' I said, scowling in thought.

'Yes, you did. Bill Hohepa, he died in Auckland with—oh cobblers. Sam I'm sorry he was with you that day. My God. Oops, sorry, Henry.'

'No, no, God was there that morning. Otherwise, Sam would not be here today.'

'Drinks! I can think better with a glass in my hand. Do they have beer? This is gnats' piss,' Abe announced, waving his hand madly to get the attention of a waiter.

A moment later, a waiter slid up to us. 'Have you beer, mate?' he asked.

'Yes sir,' was the reply.

'Can we have four tankards, please, or whatever you bring it in at this beautiful establishment?'

I laughed. 'I'm not sure the queen would be happy with the palace being called an establishment.'

The waiter reappeared quickly with our drinks in tall crystal glasses. Abe thanked him, took a sip, and remarked,

'Now, that's a better drink. Where were we? Right I'll start from the beginning, I think.' He frowned, his mind thinking back thirty-odd years. 'We heard shooting as we came in at a hell of a rate, it was a lousy day, visibility was poor, with the mist and then the rain pelted down. We came upon you as your captain appeared from behind the wagon, and pointed in the direction that the attackers had disappeared in. We chased after them but never found any survivors. This was our first encounter with the war, the English had not invaded the Waikato at that point, so hostilities were not all that frequent. The Maori were a rebel group that we later found were trying to extract utu for the attack of the English soldiers on Pukekawa.'

'You were at Pukekawa, Sam.'

'I cannot remember. Sorry, Abe, but I was talking to General Robb just before you came in, and he also jogged a few memories. One was bringing those soldiers as prisoners back to the river and fort. I do not know why, but this reunion is helping a lot.'

'That is superb, Sam,' Henry replied. 'Well, we escorted you back to Otahuhu after we buried the Maori, who had attacked you. Then we had the funeral for Sydney Walters, the driver's offsider who was killed, at the Anglican Church. Do you remember that?'

'Vaguely,' I replied. I thought for a moment. 'Was this the same church with the wedding?'

'Yes, it was the same day Shane married Tui. He had a Maori wedding at Pukekawa, but I suggested he have a church wedding, and Tui was euphoric with that. You, my friend, were his best man, and Bob gave Tui away.'

That evoked the memory of sitting around a big fire singing and then it was announced there was to be a wedding. My memory was returning, in bits, anyway. I recalled that Bob was worried that Shane would not come home with us. Frowning and thinking to myself— what did he mean, where's home?

'Do you know why we were at Pukekawa?' I asked.

'No, sorry we were not privy to that information,' Abe replied. 'We gather you were on a secret mission and weren't allowed to talk about it.'

'Oh well. My mind releases memories all over the place, so I'm confident they will return, I recall a lot more now than I did before I arrived here.'

'That's good, mate. Well after we escorted you all to Newmarket the next day, I'm afraid that was the last time we saw you, Sam. We heard you were wounded, but so were we when the Maori attacked Auckland that night, and we never had a chance of catching up with you. I last saw Bob and Shane as I was leaving Albert Barracks, that is the army barracks, to go home. I was sent home to Whangarei, and as I was driving out to catch the boat, they were walking into the barracks. I managed to say hello and asked after you, but I had to rush off as the ship was about to leave. That was the last time I saw any of you again, but I must admit you all left a lasting impression on us.'

'Henry here, recuperated, was discharged and was sent to a new Wesley church in Wellington. We have kept in contact over the years, and when we found out that a Maori delegation was going to petition the queen, we got in touch and offered our help to the representatives from a European perspective. The Maori have been treated poorly, and land has been taken from them willy nilly. The greed of the settlers is to behold, and the government buckled under their demands. So, we are here to put our tuppence worth in, in favour or our Maori friends, our people. We have just been in with Her Majesty before coming down here to the hall. I'm not sure how it will go. I won't hold my breath, but she is our Queen, and the law is for everyone, but I think the moneyed folk will win the day.'

It was then I remembered something significant, and it popped out of my mouth before I could hold it in. 'The tribes will eventually receive compensation, fellows, and by 2024, the debt will be paid back. Some of the tribes will have vast amounts of money, and they will have business in commerce, housing, and education for their children.' I stopped when I saw the shock on their faces, including my son.

'Twenty twenty-four, Sam? Why that date in the future?'

I closed my eyes. 'That's what I was thinking of. I must have the dates mixed up, but I'm positive that compensation will be paid out but not in your lifetime.'

'Shouldn't you have said in our lifetime?' Abe grinned.

'Yes, you are right, our—a slip of the tongue.' But I was quite certain their lifetime was correct. What on earth was I saying? I thought to myself.

'Can you tell me anything personal about myself or the men I was with?' I inquired.

Abe looked at Henry. 'You might be the best one to answer that one Henry, as you got quite close to the blokes. What with the marriage and the funeral?'

'Yes, let me think,' he offered. 'It was so long ago.'

He sat for a minute or two then continued.

'Well, Bob—or Robert—Kidder came from Inver-cargill. Even now, I haven't been that far south, and I never ran into him again. Bob was and an organised man, a thinker, and an excellent officer. Shane and Tui Lang, well, Shane was a big man like yourself. I think Shane was an engineer, but he was army. He knew his business, a lot like you, Sam. Tui was released from her bonds because of what she did for her mistress at Pukekawa. Shane fell in love with her the same day, he told me. They were married twice —one European wedding and one Maori. She was a fiery wee thing but educated and could mix in all circles. You, Sam, were the tracker and bush-man, and surprisingly educated. I don't mean that disrespectfully, just that I didn't expect it. One of the things that caught our eye was your weapons. You did try to hide them from us, but we saw that they were so different from what we had. Funny, the weapons today are like what yours looked like back then.'

I smiled at that. 'Yes, that was because when I returned home to England, Enfield copied the weapon, and what you have today is taken from that rifle of mine.'

'Home, Sam. You are from New Zealand, not from the United Kingdom, born in Dunedin. You told us yourself.'

I just looked at him. 'What are you talking about?' I asked, though in my heart I regularly wondered if I was from New Zealand. The pull was constantly there.

'You told Abe and me when we were together that day.'

I mentioned Bob.

'Yes,' replied Henry. 'He was from Invercargill. Shane was from Kaitaia, though he lived in Wellington, and you were from Dunedin.'

My son looked at me. 'Dad, that's marvellous. All these years you have wondered where you were from. I remember your words, saying you had this pull to New Zealand and now this. You were born there, and Margaret is living there, and so are your lost parents, and your sister Mary, if they are alive. All your family might be there. Margaret is my sister. She is a doctor now living in Dunedin. We are going out to see her during your summer. This is fantastic news. Maybe we could ask Margaret to try to locate your parents. I'm sure they would be thrilled to know you are alive and well, Dad, though a bit old now.'

It was a bit much for me. I stammered, 'Sam, I still don't remember them or my sister. Let's talk about this later tonight.'

'Have we been of any help to you, Sam?' Abe asked, just as a footman came up to me.

'My lord, the Prince of Wales would like to see you in the west wing, the Blue Room, before you leave. I'll wait for you at the dining room entrance and guide you to him. Your son can wait here, my lord, and I will deliver you back to him and then escort you both to your cab.'

'Thank you.' I smiled as he moved on. 'My lord?' Abe chirped, puzzled.

'Ah, sorry, Abe. Yes, I'm the Earl of Shadymore, and my name is Samuel Selkirk.'

Now they looked stunned at what I said.

'Earl, bloody hell, how did that happen, my lord?' 'No Abe,' Sam said. 'Even after all these years, I find it difficult to accept the title.'

'How did you happen to become an earl?' 'Do you remember Bella, the nurse?'

'Oh.' Henry chuckled. 'Who didn't? A lovely, wee thing with green eyes and a no-nonsense attitude. Yes, we both had our wounds checked out by her.'

'Well, she looked after me all the way back here on the Esk. She became my wife and Sam's mother.'

'Where is she now?' they asked. I hesitated. Sam was looking at me carefully.

'I have a daughter who is a nurse like her mother, in Rhodesia. When we were out there visiting, our coach was attacked by the Matabele. Bella was killed.' I could say that now without breaking out in a sweat or have a fit of depression.

'We are so sorry,' they murmured. 'Our sincere condolences.'

'Yes, thank you. Well, Bella, unbeknownst to me, was a titled lady when in Auckland. She went under the name Bella Wrightson. Her proper name was Lady Isabella Dowett Gale. Her father was the earl, and her mother was the countess. Anyway, Bella and I married in Scotland without her parents' consent. We had to convince them I was a good bloke, and I must have been. The earl, in the end, treated me as his only son. He had lost a couple of boys in infancy, and he petitioned the queen to ask if the title could be transferred to me when he died. She did that with her blessing.'

'My God, Sam, that is unusual these days.' 'Yes, well...'

My son broke in, 'Dad did save the queen's life. You might have read about it when those three men tried to assassinate her at Windsor Station back in sixty-three.'

Abe's mouth dropped open. 'That was you, Sam?

And that's why she passed the title on to you?'

'She knighted me the next day after the assassination attempt, so looking back, she was grateful, hence the earldom.'

We sat there mulling over what was said until my son spoke.

'Dad, you know what amazes me, all my life I have listened to you talk, with the casualness of the way you speak and act, and I wondered where you got it from. Now, hearing you mixing with these two men today, they are the same as you. Your accent is very similar, and you have this identical way of speaking. You all fit together comfortably as though you're good mates, yet you haven't seen or spoken to each other for years. Dad, I believe this is the evidence of your origins. This is where you are from.'

He turned to Abe and Henry. 'I want to thank you gentleman for what you have done here today. My father, up until a few months ago, was sick. The loss of our mother was too much for him to take, and it has been an effort to get him to come around. All our lives he has struggled to remember where he was from, and now today with the general, and you both, you have helped him immensely. So, on behalf of our family, we thank you.'

'We are only too pleased to help. I wish we could do more.'

'No,' I countered, 'you have done enough. I can tell you from the bottom of my heart, I'll need all night to work on all the information that has come to me today. The best thing is it has opened the door to remember more.'

'That's very good, Sam,' Abe replied. 'You know you might have more reminders coming, very soon. The Maori delegation has not yet arrived, and I think they might drag some more memories out before the end of the day.'

'Look, my lord, er, Sam, let's catch up after all this palaver,' Abe concluded.

'A good idea, tell me Abe, where are you blokes staying?'

He laughed. 'Nothing grand for us. The Thistle on Fort Street, a bit rundown, but we are all staying together and have been for a while.'

'Both of you, including the delegation?'

'Yep, mate, all in together. We are a bit cramped as there's a dozen of us all told.'

'How long until you head home?'

'Not sure. It might be longer than we anticipated. We need to hear the result of The Queen's decision, and money is getting tight. We'll get by, but we have to be careful.'

'Okay, so why don't I send a cab around, and we will meet in a couple of days for a beer and a chinwag. Bring all your Maori friends. I'll work it out and get back to you.'

'That will be fine Sam. Look, we'd better get back to mingling. We will see you before you go.'

We all stood up.

'Wonderful to catch-up again. We will see you soon,' I voiced as Sam and I watched them wander back into the crowd.

CHAPTER TWELVE

Windsor Castle

My eyes followed them until they vanished into the crowd.

'Dad,' exclaimed Sam, 'this is the best information you have been given. I meant to say, before your memory loss you had no idea where you were from, and now they tell us you are from Dunedin, New Zealand—this is absolutely incredible. This explains why you talked so differently with your unusual accent. After all this time we finally know you were not born in the United Kingdom after all. Father, are you listening to me? You are drifting off again. Maybe we could ask Margaret if there are any Macks in Dunedin.'

Sam's excitement was bubbling to the surface. I turned to my son. 'Sorry, Sam, I was just thinking, and not reverting to the dark old days, if that's what you are implying. There is just so much to take in; I cannot believe it myself. We will have to wait until we get to our hotel so we can think about what I have been told, and and maybe go over what I have remembered since I've been in London. Yes, let's cable Margaret in

New Zealand, and see what she can find.'

'There must be relations there, Father; there absolutely must be,' Sam remarked.

'To be honest Sam, deep down, though I'm happy with what I have found out about myself. The name Mack. I just don't know; it does not feel right.' I shook my head. 'It still niggles at me after all these years, and I have had this feeling that it was not my name even back then. Could it have been changed and if so why? I don't know, but in my heart, I'm not a Mack. Heck, Son, that is why I changed it in the first place when we returned to Scotland all those years ago with your mum. So, I chose Selkirk as my name because it made me feel happy. There has to be some reason with that.'

I continued, 'Yes we will sieve through all the information over the next few days, that Peter, Robb, Abe, and Henry have given us. I'm excited, Sam. I really think we are getting there, though the information we are getting, is all out of sequence. But it is good that it is coming in, more than ever before. I wonder if it was the smack on the head that did it?'

'It is good Father, we seemed to have cracked a hole in your amnesia. I still worry about you though as the rest of the family do. We need to go through what we have learnt and put it in some sort of order. After all, two heads are better than one. Then there's the Maori delegation to come, I do not think they have arrived yet. So, they may pull some memories from you as well.'

'Hmm, I can't see them helping that much Sam, not really. The Maori here today will surely be high ranking. I mean, even if we had helped them take the prisoners back to the fort, I would not have thought we would have met any high-ranking chiefs.'

'Don't count your chickens, Dad. You will never know until they arrive, so keep an open mind.' He smiled and placed his hand on my arm. 'My father is a New Zealander now that will take a bit of getting used to.'

The noise of the crowd was getting louder as a lot of alcohol had been consumed, and you could hardly hear yourself think. 'Do you want to mingle, Father? Sam inquired.

'No, Sam, I'll just sit here and take things in. I don't recognise many anyway, except the general and the two New Zealanders. Where are Amelia and Angus do you know?'

Sam pointed over in the general direction of the windows as Angus broke away by himself, leaving Amelia talking to some Calvary blokes. It had to be about horses. Angus came over smiling. 'I've met a lot of fellows that I have not seen for years, it has been a pleasant surprise to see so many. How about you, Sam? Any luck on the old-memory front? I saw you talking to the colonial chaps. Did you know them?'

'They brought back a few memories, Angus. I intend to catch up with them in a day or two.'

'The wee general was quite gushy over you, too, Sam. It looked like you made an impression there as well.'

'Yeah, we are going to meet up tomorrow for lunch. It's all helping Angus. It really is. I'm further down the road, and I'm pleased I came.'

'Uncle Angus,' Sam commented, 'Father is not letting on the true extent of what happened. I have been watching him as he was talking to the New Zealanders. He relaxed with them, and you know how casual Dad is. Well, these men were exactly like that. Their speech is very similar, and the big news was they told Dad he was born in Dunedin, New Zealand.'

'That is terrific news, Sam.' He turned to me. 'You know, old man, all those years ago aboard the Esk, I had thought, well, we all assumed you weren't from Scotland. But because you had a Scots' name, they bundled you on board. I know it was a hospital ship, but it had no intention to leave Auckland at all. We should have realised that you were not a Scot. Anyway, now we know. You are a bloody colonial, my friend. Blow me down'—he grinned—'and might I say the best one I have met.' He laughed.

Suddenly the room went quiet with only a light murmuring of voices, as an impressive Maori of nearly six feet entered the room. Walking behind him was a woman who could have been his mother. The footman announced, 'Te Ruru and Rita Maniapoto and the Maori delegation from New Zealand.'

Suddenly I came alert, something, maybe a passing memory, made me focus on the pair as they stood at the top of the stairs gazing at the crowd. They looked like proud, intelligent people. The man had a straight back, tall with a brown face, piercing eyes, and big hands. His nose was not flat as I thought it would be but pointed, though not as pointed as a European. He didn't look out of place in European clothes with a top knot in his hair that was as black as the ace of spades. There no beginnings of grey creeping in, and a feather had been placed in the knot. There was a tattoo on his face and a scar on his cheek, making him look like a formidable, hard man. Later, I recalled the tattoo was a moko, and he would have been in his middle fifties.

He turned and supported his mother, Rita—well, I think it was his mum—down the steps. She was slightly built and bent with age. White hair to her shoulders and a wrinkled, brown face with an open smile. It was her eyes that I gazed at as she stepped slowly down the stairs and looked around the room. They were piercing as though the woman could see through to your soul, and a shiver went up my spine. To complete the look, she had a chin and lip tattoo, once again a moko, and she also looked imposing. She was an elderly lady well into her eighties, at a guess. She also didn't look out of place in European clothes, and I felt she would be dignified in any form of clothing, in my mind, anyway.

The UK was a long way for a person so old to travel from the ends of the earth to see The Queen. They slowly reached the floor, and I saw Peter Robb go forward and hongi Te Ruru then next the woman, pressing his nose to hers, their foreheads together. Hongi. The name jumped into my mind without even thinking of it. Subsequently, as Te Ruru moved into the room they were lost from sight for a while as I concentrated on the rest of party coming down the steps. One bloke caught my eye as I thought I had seen him before. He was a stocky bloke around my age, but hell, he looked healthy and robust. His hair was grey, half of an ear was missing, and his hands were large. There was no facial tattoo, but with a scarred, brown face, he looked quite fierce. and I would not want to meet him on the field of battle. He gazed around the room as he came down the steps and smiled as Abe came up to him and whispered something in his ear. I saw his head come up as he looked around the room, then his eyes settled on me. His eyes lit up, and he roared.

'By Jove, it's my old friend Bob Kidder's friend,

Lt Mack.' He then made a beeline for me, clearing a passage for the rest of the group following behind. As he reached me, the Maori chief spoke, and we all turned to listen.

'Tēnā koutou, tēnā koutou, tēnā koutou katoa.'

'We welcome you all here to meet with us at the invitation of our Queen Victoria. His voice was deep and clear, his English perfect. This was an educated man. I had heard from a few fellows speaking before the delegation arrived that he was an ignorant savage. They were clearly mistaken; he was most definitely chiefly.

He went on saying, 'Our enemies of yesterday are our friends today; we come from The Queen's farthest country, yet in her arms, she drapes the flag around us with good wishes. We are privileged to meet with our Queen to discuss our situation and our grievances. Like a Queen, she listened intently to our grievances, as a mother who loves a child. Her decision will be announced in the next few days. We were impressed and are convinced she will help us work through this difficult situation. Being here today among the army and navy personnel and their wives, it is a pleasure to meet you all again. There are so many of you. How we ever held out all those years ago against a mighty force, who have more personnel than

*fleas on a kuri (dog), I will never know, but we
did until might overcame us. Today we are now
whanau (family), and I say to you all, long live
The Queen.'*

Everyone politely clapped and chorused 'Long
live The Queen.'

Then everyone raised their glasses, and voices
called out, 'God save The Queen.'

As the drinks came down, I watched him
look around the room. He saw me, and his eyes
widened as he saw the Maori standing next to
me, taking his mother's arm. He propelled her
towards Sam, Angus, and myself. Amelia slid in
beside her husband to be closer to the conversation.

He arrived to stand in front of me, stared into
my eyes, then he smiled. 'It is good to see you
again, Lt Mack.' He leant towards me and instigated a hongi, then turning towards his mother,
he spoke something in Maori, then swiveled
back to me. 'I remember you well. I just wanted
to check with my mother the exact words that
you spoke to me all those years ago at Pukekawa. You challenged me when I asked the question about where you were from, and you answered that you came from the bottom of Ngai
Tahu Country, where the snow falls, there's ice
on the ground, and where a brave Tainui warrior
would cry with the cold. I had to smile at the

challenge as you looked like a person from our mythical past. I called you a red-haired fairy of the bush who played the flute to entice our warriors away. After you had given me your answer, I smiled inside. A brave man, well, you all were, as was I at the time, wanting utu on the men who violated our village. Your captain was a good orator and convinced me to let all the prisoners go, and we met once more. Wonderful to see you again lieutenant.'

He came forward and instigated another hongi, which took me back a bit, and in the process, I could feel my eyes begin to water. I felt I was home. It was then that his mother spoke to me.

'I'm Rita Maniapoto, and this is my son Te Ruru.' Her name sounded familiar to me. 'I believe you have lost your memory, is that correct? I can see it on your face and in your eyes and I noticed that you had to concentrate hard when trying to remember. Come, let's sit down and talk. These old bones have been standing for too long.'

We moved tables together so there was room for everyone to sit and talk in comfort. I looked at them. 'You are right. I cannot remember anything from the time of the attack on Auckland. It is only now that my memory is slowly returning after thirty years, so maybe with you all here, you might be able to help me. Before we do that, my name is Samuel Selkirk. I changed it years ago. This is my son, Sam, sister-in- law, Amelia, and her husband, Angus.'

Rita looked at my son. 'Yes you are like your father. The last time I saw him, he was a big red-headed man with blue eyes, a man of the bush, like you.'

Sam was taken a back. 'How do you know that, madam?' he asked.

'I know,' was all she said.

Te Ruru stood up. 'I must mix with these gentlemen,' he stated, waving his arm towards the crowd. 'I'll leave you with my mother in the meantime as she needs to rest. We will talk later.' He turned and strode off with most of his party to meet the men he fought against thirty-odd years before.

'Could I trouble you for a glass of water,' Rita asked. Sam jumped up and went to fetch her one. 'He looks so much like you,' she quipped as he came back with a glass. She looked at me. 'You are out of place my friend, out of time.' Her eyes bored into me, it felt as though she were looking into my soul, and it gave me this weird feeling. 'You are not from here, Sam, you are still trying to find your way home.'

'Well,' I replied, 'As a matter of fact I was just told by Abe and Henry that I'm from Dunedin, in New Zealand. It was a revelation as I had not known.'

'Yes, that is true, but you are out of time, my friend.' Goosebumps rose up over my arms.

'What do you mean by that, Rita?'

'There is a place where I lived not that far from the village of Pukekawa. The kainga (village) has gone now, but this area has many secrets and mysteries. It is tapu (sacred) to our people, as strange things happen there. Mist, and light sometimes, are seen there from a distance. We believe, it is the home of the Taniwha (supernatural creature), who, if he desires, can take whanau (family) to another place. I think you came from this location—you and your two friends all those years ago. The Taniwha and God brought you to us in a time of need, but God lost interest in what he was doing as there were more important things to do, and you did not get to go home. Your captain did. You must talk to Peri.'

I looked at her. 'I don't understand a word of what you have said.'

'That is fine. I have sown the seed. It will eventually come back to you. It is near the time for you to complete the circle. It does not mean anything to you at the moment, but it will, and your life will change.'

'No, please explain, I still don't understand your meaning.'

'Peri,' she said, turning to the Maori bloke, the one with the half ear and facial scars, 'can you add to the conversation?' Peri studied me.

'Is this the right place, Rita?' he asked. 'It could take an age.'

He had this upper-class English accent. How did he learn to speak like that? I thought. She raised her eyebrow to Peri, indicating to keep talking.

'Well, my good sir, we met at Pukekawa after the renegade English soldiers attacked the village. I was with the Hapu (group) that arrived the next day with my chief, Te Ruru. After he decided to spare the perpetrators from utu (revenge), you and I led the party of prisoners out to Alexander Redoubt. I was impressed, my good man, with your tracking skills, though not as experienced as me, by jove, but good enough to impress me. You and your two friends were different from other Pakeha. You spoke entirely unlike anyone I had heard at that time, and yet now I can hear your accent creeping in the way the gentle people from our country speak today — not completely but close. Do you remember Sgt   Router and Cpl Smith? We extracted utu on them at Camerontown the same time we attacked Auckland.'

'No, I cannot remember them. You were in that Auckland assault?' I questioned.

'Of course, old fruit, would not have missed it for the world. Yes, I remember it clearly as if it were yesterday. I lost some good friends that morning, and to make matters worse, I was captured to boot. Silly me, I did manage to escape, and I fought with Rewi at Rangiriri, then captured again, but thanks to your friend Bob, I was released into his care. I guided him to the place that Rita told you about, a cave where the Taniwha lives. Of course, I did not get too close. I left Bob at a marker, and he had about a three- to four-hour walk to the place under tapu. This was, he said, where you came from. Your friend Shane had marked the trees to take you back to the cave. My good man, that place is not a fit for a man of my disposition to go near, so I wished him well. There is more, good sir, but like Rita said, you are not from here, and the time to return home is near. I'll leave it there for now. I hope I have not upset you as that would not be cricket.'

My mouth dropped open, I did not know what to say, none of it made sense at all. But there was no reason at all for them to lie. Hell, we only just met not even an hour ago, and there was no way they would have known I was going to be here today. So, I guess I had to try to accept what they were telling me.

'Excuse me. I must reunite with my chief.' We will talk again later. He stood up and walked away towards Te Ruru who was surrounded by army personnel.

CHAPTER THIRTEEN

Windsor Castle

About thirty minutes later, Peri arrived back laughing.

'Te Ruru is talking tactics with the general, a bit over my head.' He looked at Rita with a worried look on his face. 'Are you kapai (well), Rita?' he asked.

'Thank you for your concern, Peri Nepia. Yes,' she replied, 'I'm getting old and tired, that's all. A nap would do nicely at this moment.'

I focused on them both as I waited until Rita looked more comfortable, 'I'm sorry I didn't get the full gist of your story. You were in Auckland, then, Peri?' I asked.

'Yes, a lovely little battle. It started out fantastic, but the rain gods decided to arrive. By the time we were halfway up Queen Street, it was hard to light the ti kouka leaves. We smashed windows and threw in our fire sticks until we arrived at a music shop. We just had broken that window when we were fired upon from the Union Hotel. One of my companions went down, and the rest of us jumped through the window, only to be shot at from a couple of men barricaded against the wall. Three of my friends were killed. All I had time for was to fire at the flashes with my shotgun. I was hit and ended up not quite myself, stumbling everywhere. But at the same instant when I fired my gun, I realised I had fired at a Maori warrior. Then I immediately, I recognised the man behind him.'

He looked at me with sympathy in his eyes. 'I'm afraid, my good man, it was you. I was the cause of your memory loss. I have not thought about it for years but seeing you again has brought it all back. My dear chap, I'm so very sorry, and the Maori chap with you was Wiremu Hohepa, a lovely man. The place we were attempting to burn was Wiremu's employer's shop, he was a printer by trade. I bet you a shilling to a bag of eels, he was there solely to protect his employer. If my memory serves me correctly, my good man, Wiremu died that very day. I found that out much later. You know he saved your life that morning. The fortunes of war are always hurtful to the survivors.

'As I said, I was wounded oh, only a flesh wound, but I ran from the building dazed. I slipped, fell, and hit my head on the corner of a water trough and knocked myself senseless. Oh, what a silly chappie I was. I was found later by the English soldiers and they incarcerated me in a shop somewhere on Wellesley Street. The nurses attended to my wounds. One of them stood out, a lovely lady, Bella, as I recall her name. She attended to all the captives with a smile on her face. I had never met anyone with green eyes until that moment. She left a lasting impression on me, old sport. After I was thoroughly checked out and left to my own devices, I managed, with a couple of my friends, to break through the rear wall and escape. We found our way back to Rangiriri, dodging all the army patrols.'

I looked at him with an amazed expression. 'You met my wife, Bella?' I blurted out.

'Oh, did you marry her? What an attractive couple you both would have been. Where is she now, old chap?'

'She was killed in Rhodesia, this year,' I croaked.

'My dear man, my heartfelt condolences. She was a lovely woman and a skilled nurse. I am concerned kind sir, that what I have told you might be a little too much for you to take in, all at once. Are you alright?' I nodded. 'I am heartbroken that I was the instigator of your memory loss. Had I known you were both in there, we would have bypassed the shop. We can't have friends shooting friends even in a time of aggression. I do hope your life was not too inconvenienced by the affliction I caused you. I give you sir my sincere apologies,' he lent forward and hongi-ed.' I was touched by his sincerity.

'It amazes me that sometimes something bad, can turn into a good thing. What happened did enable me to meet my wife. We certainly had a good life together, in fact a remarkable life, and were blessed with both children and grandchildren. No, my life has been splendid. The only thing that has been worrisome to me is this black hole hiding my early years, but you cannot have everything.' We spoke a little longer, then he smiled as he looked back on better times. 'My dear sir, I remember for a Pakeha, your tracking skills and bush work were top notch. Also, I was quite taken with how you articulated and used the correct pronunciation of our bush and bird life. Yes, you are right, no matter what happens, we always have something good to look back on.'

Dinner was called as we watched servants bringing out even more food, enough to fill the tables to overflowing. As it was a stand-up affair, we were each given a plate and were expected to fill it as we wished. Everyone mixed well, as we mingled among the crowd of uniforms with their ladies in their elegant attire, and the well-dressed Maori. Each person seemed friendly enough. I suppose, given the circumstances, this was the palace, after all, you couldn't cause a ruckus here; you would never hear the end of it. I moved over towards Te Ruru and Rita, who stood against the wall. She used a carved walking stick for support.

'Would you like a chair?' I asked and she nodded. She looked very uncomfortable and frail. Sam had heard me ask and returned with a chair under his wing.

'There you go, Rita,' he announced.

'Kapai' (thank you), she answered ever so quietly, smiling up at him as she sank into the chair. 'Thank you. I'm feeling my age, and it is near my time. I wish to be home when my time comes to be with my whanau.'

I muttered, 'You have years yet surely.' She just smiled.

'Not long now, Sam, not long at all.'

Once settled and nibbling at her food, I took the chance to question her, 'When do you all leave? I would like to catch up with you all for another yarn.'

'Well,' Rita admitted, 'we are at the convenience of The Queen. Once we have her answer, we can go home anytime. Though the earliest is at the end of the month as there are no sailings until then. We have been delayed as The Queen had been sick for a few weeks, leaving us to eat into our funds. We can hold out, but we will have to be very careful with our money. We didn't expect to be here quite this long.'

'Abe and Henry are with you, so is there a

dozen of you altogether?'

'Yes,' she affirmed. 'They were so helpful. There are a lot of Pakeha like them, especially the ones who are born in Aotearoa. They call themselves Kiwis: an excellent name for all of us.'

I went all goosey again. I really needed to get back to the hotel and think everything through. The delegation had at least three or four weeks before they could leave, and being such a large group, they might run out of money before then. This was not on as far as I was concerned, and I pondered about their predicament.

I turned to Rita. 'Look, Rita, I have plenty of room at my place. Why not give me a couple of days to organise for you all to come and stay with my family and myself. Please don't think of it as charity because there is a purpose in the offer. With you installed in my home, it might give me a chance to gather even more of my lost memories. If you do this for me, I will pay for your return fare home to New Zealand in style. I'll send you all first class.'

Rita just looked at me with shock on her face. 'You would do this for us,' she asked in a surprised voice.

'Of course. I have the money, so that is not a worry. I feel drawn to you all, and the longer I'm in your company, the more I believe I'll find out about myself. This day has opened up some significant gaps in my life. You and your people might help to bring me those last recollections. I can only hope.'

'I will need to see our chief. Even though he is my son, it will be his decision,' she said formally.

'Yes, that is fine. In the meantime, let's get the ball rolling.'

'Sam'—turning to my son—'will you get things started for me? Cable the manor house and let them know we will have a dozen guests—eleven men, and Rita is to have the stateroom. Book the trip for in two days' time, on the train. Ask for my special carriage to be attached, and we will take it right through to Brittermore. Book a state or first-class cabin for them all on the next liner out to New Zealand. Do that as soon as you get back to the hotel. I'll catch up with you then?'

'Okay, Dad, will you be all right?'

'Yeah, Son, I'll be good as gold. I have Amelia and Angus if I run into any problems.'

'Should we not wait for the chief's response?'

'Nah, Son, I'll talk him around; you get going now.'

Sam pushed his chair back and stood up from the table, saying as he was doing so, 'Lovely to meet you, Rita, and I will look forward to catching up with you on the train home.'

He turned and found an usher who guided him

out to catch a cab.

'How can you afford this?' Rita inquired, watching Sam disappear into the crowd. She had previously sent Peri off to talk to Te Ruru and advise him of the offer. 'Wait for his reply and return with his answer,' she had said. In the meantime, it gave us a chance to talk.

'Oh, Rita, I was knighted soon after I arrived here for saving The Queen's life. Furthermore, unbeknownst to me, Bella, my wife, was a titled lady. Her father was an earl, and when he died, he somehow managed to convince The Queen to let me take over the title, and so it has happened. I'm the Earl of Shadymore. Money is no object, and it would be an honour to have you all stay.'

Te Ruru came back himself. 'Sam that is a generous gift to us. We would need to do something for you in return. We cannot expect to have you do this for nothing.'

I scratched my head, 'Well you could talk to the school children about your culture. Why not give a few lessons in Maori, and how about showing the children how to carve? I like those'—I was pointing at his chest, and the word tiki came into my head—'tiki around your necks.'

'Good, then we will accept your kind offer. God does move in mysterious ways, my friend.'

Abe and Henry came up to me later, 'Is it true?' they asked, 'Are we staying with you?'

'Yep, with you all there, you might help me immensely, and Henry, you might be able to give a service at our church. I do not think the Reverend Toogood would mind.'

'That would be admirable, I would enjoy that, Sam.'

A trumpet sounded, then an announcement came from the door. His Royal Highness, the Prince of Wales was entering the room. Folk gathered on both sides of the hall bowing as the prince passed them. He stopped and spoke to a few here and there. He was a keen military man, and any excuse to talk military matters, he would talk for hours.

Eventually, he walked up to me. I bowed. 'I would like a word, Lord Shadymore, after this gathering has finished. My footman will escort you.'

I bowed. 'A pleasure, Your Royal Highness.'

He wandered off to circulate, then about fifteen minutes later, he turned and on behalf of his mother, formally thanked the Maori delegation for coming.

Then he walked out of the room. The party started to break up. Everyone was soon escorted out, to catch their cabs. I told Rita, that we will arrange for a coach to pick them all up from where they were staying at the Thistle Hotel, for the trip to the manor house. And I would be in touch with her when I knew the time.

Amelia and Angus where waiting for me.

'Well Sam, that went off pretty well.' Amelia declared. 'I found the this afternoon most interesting, has anything come back to you at all?

'Yes, I think so, Amy, but I need to go back to the hotel and put my thoughts in order. I believe inviting the delegation to stay with us will be a plus. Every time Rita spoke, I felt there was something there, something she was not saying. Then Peri... I felt he held back something also. I believe it is to do with the place he mentioned—the cave with the Taniwha. There has to be something there, or why would Bob go back there? There is a niggle at the back of my mind, Amy. It's right here,' I said, patting my forehead.

Angus grinned. 'We noticed how you were reacting to those colonials and the Maori people. You seemed much more relaxed than we have seen you in ages. Furthermore, your speech was slipping back to the way I remember when I first met you.

Personally, I think having this group come home with you will be the catalyst. We are so pleased for you, but I must admit, Sam, it makes you wonder what Rita means by "out of time"?'

'I have no idea, Angus, but I think it is significant. We will be able to work on it when I'm home. The word tiki came to me when I was talking to them, so the more I'm with them, the further I believe I will remember. I'm meeting General Robb tomorrow, maybe he can fill me in on that time period of my life as well. Then Abe and Henry, I can catch up with at home now. I believe it begins at Pukekawa, and the time before that is around that cave. It's a feeling hard to explain. Rita affirmed we came from that cave; that is the pivot, and I will have to work on that.'

I looked up, and the room had emptied. A footman was waiting at the door. He must have been waiting for me. I turned to Amelia and Angus. 'His Royal Highness wants a word with me, so you head back to the hotel, and I'll catch up with you both for supper tonight.' I kissed Amelia on the cheek and shook Angus's hand.

'Thanks for being here today. Your presence has helped me, and I appreciate that the two of you were there for me, it gave me strength.'

Amelia slipped her arm into Angus's, who touched my arm.

'We will see you soon,' she whispered, and they left me to wonder what the hell the prince wanted.

CHAPTER FOURTEEN

Windsor Castle

As they left the room, a footman seemed to materialise next to me, out of nowhere. 'Would you follow me please, Lord Shadymore. I will escort you to his Royal Highness's apartments.'

The Prince of Wales lived at the other end of the castle, so after a good five minutes of fast walking, we finally came to his door. The escort gave a discreet knock, then without a word, opened the door, bowed and announced, 'Lord Shadymore, Your Royal Highness.' He then backed out of the door as I walked in. I always admired how the staff were able to do this, it was a skillful maneuver. To be able to achieve this and hardly be noticed in the process is impressive.

The prince stood by the window looking out at the grounds, Bowing to the prince, 'The Earl of Shadymore, at your request,' I voiced.

He turned, 'Lord Shadymore, welcome.' He seated himself in a high-back chair and indicated I take the seat opposite. 'Please sit down, sir.'

With the formalities over, I smiled. 'How are

you, Edward?' I asked.

He had worry lines on his forehead and he looked uneasy, not the easy smile he usually displayed whenever we were together. Something was definitely on his mind.

'I'm in a pickle, my dear Sam,' he retorted. 'Of all my friends and acquaintances, you are the only one who I can actually trust to help me out of this dilemma.'

'Of course, I'll do all I can, Eddie,' I pledged.

We always spoke casually together, away from the ears of the general public. Ours was an easygoing, relaxed friendship, that comes from being friends for thirty years. I just liked him as a mate, otherwise I wouldn't have been here. But I never abused my connection. It was as simple as that. So, if he needed a trusting friend, then I was it.

The prince poured two drinks and handed me one. 'I'm in a crisis, Sam, and God knows what I'm going to do about it; I don't know where to start.' He wiped his hands on his legs as he talked, his mouth turned down at the corners and the frown on his pale face deepened, more than I had ever seen. He was in such a state.

'Look Eddie,' I advised. 'Just relax and start at the beginning; I'm sure talking about it and getting the problem off your chest will be helpful. We bottle things up too much, and the next thing you know, we're blustering fools. My friend, we cannot have the future king in a situation like that. So, start from the beginning.'

I guessed it would be about women again. It was common knowledge he played around and had had a lot of affairs in his time. But this did seem out of proportion to his usual manner, so it must have been a biggie. 'Let's take it from the beginning, Ed,' I said.

Before he started, he rang a bell and a servant opened his door. 'I do not want to be disturbed at all. I'm indisposed even to Her Majesty until after Lord Shadymore leaves.' The footman bowed out the door. He sat down again and took a big breath.

'What I'm about to tell you, Sam, is known only to the Archbishop of Canterbury, the Secretary of State, and a French priest who has since died. No one else—no one,' he emphasized.

He sounded so nervous; I had never seen him like this before.

'The priest died only in the last month, and I can tell you my name is "Mud" at the moment.'

I thought, Oh no! someone has found out about one of his flings, and the girl was in the family way. I sat there quietly waiting for him to relax into his story.

'Right,' he said. 'How do I start?' He looked apprehensive and sat for a moment gathering his thoughts. He took a sip of his drink, stroked his beard, then looked up at me.

'It all started back when I was twenty, before my marriage to Alexandra. As you know, I used to get around a bit in those days, especially in France. This one particular time, I took a young lady with me, Lady Blanche Proctor. She was a pretty young thing, and we had so much fun together to the point that I fell in love with her. If my memory serves me correctly, she was friends with your late wife, Isabella, and her sister, Amelia, at the school run by Mrs. Rowden in Shrewsbury. They were, I gather, quite close until this incident. Even though your wife was a bit older, and your sister-in-law was younger than her.'

'I have never heard of her. No both Bella or Amelia, never mentioned her,' I pointed out.

'Yes, after what I have to tell you, your wife and her sister would not have seen nor heard from her again,' the prince replied. 'Where was I? Oh yes... in love. When you are in love—that moment when the world is seen through the eyes of the young, and nothing you do is silly or pretentious—your mind is numb, and you don't think. You just focus on one thing: the woman in your heart. One afternoon in a small church outside Paris, I married her.'

He stopped talking to let that sink in. I looked at him as the penny dropped, then my mouth dropped open, and I said, 'Poo.'

'Yes, precisely,' he blurted out. 'Shit is the correct word.'

'How the hell have you got away with this?' I burst out. 'For God's sake, Eddie. You had a state wedding, you were married by the archbishop. The whole bloody world was there, and now you are telling me it was a bigamous marriage?'

'You can see my dilemma, then,' he conceded. 'Oh but,' he muttered, 'there is more to come. She became pregnant and had a son, and of course, this is where it gets complicated. He is the true heir to the throne.'

'Double shit,' I broke in. 'Does your wife know?'

'Of course not, old chap, not this one anyway. There's repercussions everywhere you look.' He held his head in his hands, and rubbed his hands threw his hair. 'It is so complicated, and my actions have been abominable.'

'Why has it come to a head now?' I asked.

'Well when we arrived home as the happy couple, back in 1862, her father thought his daughter might have a claim to the crown,and told the archbishop.The Secretary of State, at the time, under the instructions of the, then prime minister, and unbeknownst to the queen, took her parents aside and explained to them that the marriage never happened. That it was a figment of the girl's imagination, and that the young lady was delusional. Then the marriage certificate was destroyed, or so they thought.

We both had copies, but it now appears that Lady Blanche, was very clever and had another copy made, and that was the one that was destroyed. My certificate had been confiscated years ago. That's where my problem is, she had a son, my son, and if this gets out, he will be the rightful heir to the throne of England. Now the powers that be are not happy.'

'What about the priest? He is a witness, and he would not just disappear?'

'He is dead now, Sam. By unusual circumstances I would say. His church in France was robbed and burnt to the ground, all the silverware was stolen, and all the written records were destroyed. The priest was still inside the church at the time. Of course, they never found out who the perpetrators were, but I have a sneaky feeling that our government got rid of any evidence about my marriage. I'm to blame for an innocent man dying. I hope God forgives me.'

'What about Blanche? I responded. 'Where has she been all these years?'

'Yes, well, that's another element that I'm not proud of. Since 1862, she has been in a lunatic asylum, locked up and the key thrown away, and   I did nothing—not a thing—to stop it. I'm quite disgusted with myself. How could I let this woman just rot away because of her love for me?' He jumped up and started pacing the room.

'She had our son in that asylum. My son was born there, and I had no say—no say, whatsoever.'

'What happened to the boy?'

'Yes, that's a good question. They bundled him off to the colonies under another name. He was adopted out, and I was not told any of the particulars. They said it would be better that way.'

'Do you know what country?'

'No, but I have an inkling he was adopted by people from Shrewsbury, who immigrated to New Zealand. But I cannot be sure.'

New Zealand again. It sure came up all the time, I thought.

'Getting back to the woman in question. Why now?'

'Well, she was being moved to a new establishment. She is now in her middle fifties, and they decided to put her in a private home for the gentry. The institute where she was incarcerated before, was an improvement on the regular asylum. It was more like an apartment with a servant and a walled courtyard garden. I gather she is a voracious reader and has read everything from poetry to survival in distant lands, and she is not afraid to speak her mind either. She must be a strong, determined woman. Because how she has coped so long like this, I can't imagine.

'Now, the reason this has come to the fore is because she has escaped while being transferred to her new place of incarceration. The government would not have generally minded. Blanche would be looked upon as just a senile woman talking rubbish, if she said she was married to the Prince of Wales. Some authoritarian would capture her again and put her back inside, but she has the original marriage certificate, and according to the Secretary of State, that makes her a danger to our country.

'I'm also worried about my son, wherever he is. They might just get rid of him even though he does not know his background or his birth parents. I would not put it past them; the government can and will be quite ruthless. If they catch Blanche, they could do away with her as well, then next in line will be the boy. Well, he will be thirty-three now. I'm at my wits' end, Sam, and that's why I asked you to see me.'

He stopped talking then announced, 'I need another drink.' He got up and walked to the cabinet and poured a large whisky.

'Do you want another, Sam?'

'Yes, thanks. I believe I need it after that story, Eddie,' I replied with understanding.

He slowly walked back, passed me my drink, then took a big gulp from his glass and shuddered.

'So, my friend,' he said, 'what are your thoughts?'

I had deliberated throughout his whole story wondering where I come in. 'I will do anything you want me to do, Eddie, but I have no idea what? If she has just vanished, how do you think I can help? I don't know the woman, and she doesn't know me, and let's face it, she is getting up there in age. Surely the authorities will find her, and when they do, she will be put back under lock and key. I mean she would have no money or clothes. How will she cope? Where did she escape from?' I asked.

'They were taking her from Longnor to Shrewsbury. As the coach turned onto Shrewsbury Road, a wheel broke, and while the guards were fixing it, she just vanished into your forest. They never expected that to happen. I have wondered if she had been planning this for years, as a chance to get away. You know how thick your forest is, and there are all those cabins you have built for your ramblers. So there will be accommodation for her if they are empty at night. Furthermore, there is food in the cabins. She could steal clothes, and disguise herself. She is a very resourceful woman.'

Ah, I thought, she is near our place, so that's why I have come into the picture.

'We have some good trackers, and we could quickly pick up her trail.' my mind raced, going through the possibilities. 'All we need is her place of entrance. But sir, and it is a big but: what do we do when we find her? If you think the government might harm her, what should I do with her?'

'Keep her safe, and notify me, Sam, and I'll work out something. She is resourceful as she has already been gone over a week and has not been seen once. I believe she will survive, but for how long is in God's hands. The people I have spoken to, who have seen her recently, think she is still an attractive woman. I would not know her now, as I haven't seen her for a long time. There is a possibility she might not know about the passing of your wife and try to make contact with her or her sister. That is all I can think of at the moment.'

'If that's the case,' I said, 'we haven't had any reports of break-ins or thefts. So, she must be living rough, off the land, but there is plenty of wildlife up there. Once I return home, I'll get a few of my experienced staff, including my son, to search the park. I won't tell them the story, naturally, but I'll have to let them know they are looking for a woman in her fifties. Is this okay by you?'

'Yes, marvellous. I really want you to find her before the government, and if you do, Sam, don't tell them you have located her. Hide her away until you make contact with me, and then I can sort out what to do.'

'I will do that, Eddie. I would not like to see

a woman put in danger through no fault of her own. She might even know where your boy is, and if that's the case, it might pay to get her out of the country. Can you convince the PM that she is harmless, just an older woman wanting some quality of life in her later years. Surely, coming from you, that has to help?'

'I gather, Sam, that this PM does not know a thing about Blanche. I have to go through the Secretary of State. I don't like him at all, and he is the one running around trying to find her. They don't consider me as trustworthy, Sam— too many women, too many affairs. I will try, naturally, but we might have to protect her some other way. I'll have a good think about it, but please put on your thinking cap also. When you find her, please cable me something about the weather. Say "fine" if you have found her, and that way I'll know she is in your safekeeping. Alternatively, "rainy weather" if you cannot locate her.

'Well, Sam, I have bared my soul. Thank you for your help in this matter. I do wish you the very best of British luck. I'm absolutely confident that you will find her, that is if anyone can. Please be gentle with her if you are lucky. She has had a hard time of it and will need handling carefully.'

'I'll do my best, Eddie,' I said as I climbed out of my chair and shook his hand.

'Good luck, Lord Shadymore. I'll look forward with anticipation to our next meeting and cable.'

'It has been a pleasure, as always, Your Royal Highness,' I replied as he rang his bell, and the footman opened the door.

'Escort Lord Shadymore to his cab, please.' We both bowed as the door closed. Turning, I followed the servant down the hallways to the main entrance of the castle. My mind was in turmoil, what with my memory loss and now this. Climbing into the cab, I thought I would cable my son Bernard and get him to contact Toby, our ranger, to have a preliminary look around. We would be home in a few days, so I hoped the lady in question will survive the outdoors until we can find her. The government was keeping this under wraps and would not want to be seen running through our forest with packs of dogs. Besides I would not have allowed that at all anyway. I have come across some government agents in the past, and a few I would not trust with my daughters, let alone a vulnerable, older woman. They look like rogues, the lot of them, so we must do this quietly for our future king's sake.

CHAPTER FIFTEEN

London

When we arrived back at the hotel, the first thing I did was to send a cable to my son Bernard, telling him to very discreetly have Toby, our ranger, search for a woman and to check if there had been any break-ins. I didn't want her to be detained, just to check things out and wait until I got home. I suggested he start at the Shrewsbury end of the estate. I emphasised in capitals, to just look—that's all that is required, and as soon as I returned, to have Toby meet me at the manor house.

Sam had completed all the bookings I had asked him to do. He had cabled Bernard, and a reply had already been returned. He looked forward to the Maori delegation coming to stay and hoped they would be with us for at least a few weeks. The carriage was booked and would connect to the regular service to Shrewsbury, and a steam engine there would be used to take us through to Brittermore. From there the delegation would be driven up to the manor house.

The telegraph was such a neat invention. All the bookings were done from one place, saving so much time, though after all these years, I still was reminded about my iPhone that was still wrapped up in my pack at home. Communication could be quicker, but there was no infrastructure, I did not understand what that meant, and I was at a loss about how I came to have one of them in the first place. I mean the word was not known, so it was confusing.

The telegraph was the usual way to communicate, and that was still a newish invention. A ship out to New Zealand was booked for my New Zealand guests in first class. At least they would travel home in style. It was due to leave in the middle of January via the Suez Canal. A new ship, the SS Rangitoto, was a luxury liner with state rooms, first class, and steerage passengers. The first port of call was Lyttelton. That meant the delegation would be that much longer getting home as they would have to wait a couple of days before the ship departed for Auckland. Sam pencil-booked both of us as well, unbeknownst to me. We were going out to see Margaret sometime this year, so he decided we should make use of this ship. He was sure he could talk me around and decided on his own bat to place a booking on my behalf.

I was looking forward to catching up with my daughter and husband in their own environment. Sam had been out there, and he described it to me as having a pleasant climate, much warmer than England. I could understand why she loved it out there, as there were mountains, bush, excellent fishing, and plenty of room to move around. The people were more relaxed there, apparently a good place to bring up children, and everyone had a bit of colour in their cheeks. The problem was I could only remember bits of it from 1863. I could never get a clear picture in my head, but I was determined to summon it to mind.

As far as Sam was concerned, the sooner the better, and I was in for a surprise in the near future when I found out. With dinner finished, I suggested we all head up to my room and go over the day's activities. I needed to analyse everything into chronological order, and to do that, I wanted everyone with me because if I missed something, they would bring it up.

Amelia was the first to speak up. 'How are you fairing, Sam? I must admit since Bella's passing, this is the best I have seen you, and you look more alive. I'm pleased you came to The Queen's residence; it has been good for you.'

'Yes, you are right, Amy. It feels as though I'm closer to the answer of my lost years, than I have ever been. I just wish Bella would have been here at the end. She would have been thrilled. I'm really excited about what I've learnt today, I seem to have had a bit of a breakthrough. Since then, snippets of other memories are returning to me. So, all in all, I have to be happy.'

Sam piped up. 'Dad, from what I have made out it looks like the village of Pukekawa is where it all began. That's the point of reference—the start. From there, you can go forward. The memories from before are not as easy to come by, but going forward, seems easier. Can you describe the village?'

I sat for a minute thinking. 'I'm not sure, Sam.' I then had a vision of a meeting house and smaller huts on either side of it. I recalled something and explained what I saw. 'Bush up close to the back of the village with a stream, and a big cooking fire.' Oh heck, the more I was talking, the more it came back. 'Gardens full of kumara, that's a sweet potato.' I stopped talking and frowned. 'There were muskets firing.' I waited for a moment longer. 'No, nothing else as of yet. So where do we stand up to this point?'

'Well, Father, that is progress for you after all these years. See, it was a positive move coming here to this reunion.'

'Yes, Sam, but why were we there? That is the major issue. Let's hope that part of my memory will return. I hope so. It's over thirty years since all this has happened, and if I do get my memory back, will it really clear things up, or make matters worse? In the end, my biggest concern is to know about my family and friends that I left behind. Henry explained that my friend Shane had a Maori wedding. That must have been in that village at Pukekawa.'

'Yes, and he went on to say she was released from her bonds, whatever that means,' Amelia added. 'Let's face it, the information you have received has been excellent, Sammy. I'm sure this will help you immensely once you can sit quietly and put it all together.'

'Well, I can ask Rita when we see her later. I'm sure she will tell me. I must admit I vaguely remember Tui under the wagon when we were attacked, so it must be in my memory somewhere.' Sam came back with, 'And by the sound of it, your friend hardly knew the girl. I mean, you arrived at the village, and the next thing, he was married to her.'

In the back of my mind came the words 'gone in a day.' What the hell did that mean? Then I had this vision of a big, bearded bloke sitting on the ground with a Maori woman kneeling in front of him. Her hands were holding on to his beard, pulling his face towards her. I could hear the words in my mind. I want you. In my mind's eye, I saw my other friend. It must have been Bob sitting there with his mouth wide open just looking completely dazed at what was happening. Then Shane—it must've been Shane— uttered, 'I will marry you.' I looked down and saw a harmonica in my hands. Shit a brick, it was coming back. Subsequently, the voice in my head said I'll do my bit, and I could hear my reply, no, mate, it is your wedding night; we will sort it, or words to that effect.

I opened my eyes and peeked through my hands, I hadn't even realised I had lent forward and must have been rocking back and forth with this memory.

'Are you okay, Dad?' Sam asked in a troubled voice. He had bent over and was holding my arm, gazing at me intensely. Everyone had a concerned look on their face. I pulled myself together and looked at Sam and the family.

'Yes, I'm all right. I had a vivid memory about the village that is all.' My God, it was coming back, and I went on to explain the recollection. 'That is why Tui was on the road with us heading to Auckland, and Shane married her at that village. Hell, after all these years I remember that —'

'Hmm,' Angus interrupted, 'how do you feel about the Maori man, what is his name, Peri? He was the one who caused all this pain and anguish for you. Do you feel any animosity towards him, Sam?'

I looked at Angus, shaking my head. 'No, it was a war situation, and anything can happen, as you know. I was in the wrong place at the wrong time. Let's face it; I had just shot three of his friends, and if it wasn't for Peri, I would not have met Bella. So, everything is for a reason. He is a good bloke, and I like him.' And I laughed. 'He speaks better English than some I know. I wonder where he got that upper-class way of talking, I'll have to ask him.' I smiled. 'Let's call it a day. I'm quite tired, and a bit of quietness would be nice now. It has been a full-on day.'

Everyone stood up. I kissed Amy on the cheek, shook Angus's hand, and gave Sam a hug. They shut the door as they left my room. I went over to the table, took out paper and pen, and sat down to write the sequence of events that I had remembered.

I woke with a start. I had fallen asleep with my head down on the table. I pushed myself up, went over to my bed, undressed, and piled into the pit. My mind raced as I lay there looking at the ceiling. Pukekawa was predominate in my thoughts. I was pleased with the idea I had to invite the Maori delegation to the manor. I'm certain Rita had a lot more to tell me and Peri also. I was convinced they both were holding something back. At this time, I had no real proof, but I felt it in my bones: there was something, and I was determined to find out what it was.

I had a restless night and I woke early. I dressed and went for an early morning walk in the park. I caught up with my son, and we ambled around the lake. We didn't talk; we just walked with our own thoughts, father and son content to be together. There was hardly anyone around, which to me was a bonus. Most gentry don't rise until ten or eleven in the morning, and to my way of thinking they had wasted the day. As we turned to head back, I asked Sam if he would come with me this morning to see Peter Robb, as two heads were better than one. He smiled. 'Father, wild horses would not keep me away.'

At 11 a.m. we sat waiting for Peter and in walked the general. A little bloke, but he carried himself well. Straight back, confident, and purposeful raced through my mind as I watched him. He looked around the room, spotted us, gave a wave, and headed over to our table. I had a vision then of a sixteen-year- old boy unsure of himself and very nervous. Looking at him as he weaved his way towards us around the tables, I thought he had come a long way, and not the same young fella at all.

'My dear Lord Selkirk and Sam, lovely to see you both again this beautiful morning. I thought I saw the two of you over by the lake. I am always up early, army habit. If it was good enough for the men to rise at dawn, then it's good enough for me.'

The waiter was hovering. 'Tea for three, my good man,' ordered Peter.

He sat down, and we talked small talk until the tea arrived.

'Okay, Peter, a question. Would you please tell me all you know about what happened all those years ago even if it is second-hand information? It might trigger other memories for me. Is that okay by you?'

'Of course, Your Lordship.'

'No, Peter. Like yesterday, just call me Sam.' 'Sam.' He grinned. 'Right,' he said, placing his cup in his saucer. 'Where to start.' He frowned in concentration, then he explained, 'The first time we had contact, it was from a booming voice across the other side of the Waikato River. Our patrol had gone missing, and with no senior officers, we were in a bit of a dither. Your party changed that. You had found the patrol, incarcerated them, and brought them back along with a few Tainui warriors. So, that was the beginning when we first met. Of course, there were consequences to all involved. Charlie went over to collect them, and I gather that Peri, the Maori warrior from yesterday, was there also, though I had never met him. I was left to look after the redoubt while Charlie was down with your group.

I read the report your captain left after the commanding officer returned. It appeared that the patrol attacked the village of Pukekawa for no apparent reason, and your party was over on the Tainui side of the river spying for the governor. This incident made you come out into the open, so to speak, when you saved the village. The patrol killed two old men who were working in the kumara garden, and a warrior was shot, but you did a medical procedure on him, and he survived.' He stopped to gather his thoughts.

'Ah, yes, Shane's wife, Tui, who had been a slave, was released from her bonds when she saved her mistress from rape that day, by the then Sgt Router. It was just after this, I think, that Shane married her in a Maori ceremony. I heard later that they married again in the Anglican church at Otahuhu. We also heard of the attack on your party on the way from Papatoetoe to Otahuhu.'

He stopped and ordered another tea. Once in his hands, he went on to describe the village. He had been there when things were more friendly with the inhabitants. 'I must admit,' he said, 'Maori are a bit different from a lot of other natives around the world. The women would fight just as hard as the men. The fit younger women would become warriors, and the older women would look after the children. They were a formidable foe. Incidentally, Sergeant Router and Corporal Smith, who led the attack against Pukekawa, were killed in Camerontown when Riwi attacked months later.'

It was then I started to sweat. In my mind, I could see us attacking the patrol with a Maori bloke behind us whacking them as we drove over them. I saw a woman with a moko; yes, it was Rita with Bob. Bugger, yes it was Bob. He yelled not to kill them, and Rita indicated they would tie them up then. I went a bit pale, and Peter waved over to the waiter. 'Whisky, old chap, as quick as you can.'

As soon as it arrived, he thrust it into my hand. 'Drink this, Sam, straight down.' I felt it hit my gut with a bang.

Sam was asking, 'Father, are you okay?'

Slowly, colour came back to my face. 'I do apologise, Peter. When I remember something, I go a bit funny. I'm all right now.'

'Thank God, Sam. I was not sure what it was about, but I noticed your son was not unduly worried.'

'Yes,' Sam said, 'Dad has been like this for a while now, and then the trauma does move on, though whisky is a good remedy. Usually, when it happens, he has a breakthrough when another piece of the overall puzzle comes out.'

I coughed and wiped my forehead with my hanky.

'Yes,' I stammered with a sickly smile,'I remember a little bit more.There was Bob, Shane,Tui, the Maori sergeant and one other—McInnes.' I had a shudder; that name sent goosebumps down my spine. 'He was kept out of everyone's way, so he must have been important.'

'Funny, that,' Peter replied. 'For us, we lost one man. He hadn't been with us long, but I thought his name was McInnes. However, the paperwork got lost with all the to-ing and fro-ing, still I might have been mistaken. We never found McInnes again—a bit of a mystery. Anyway, by the time the commanding officer arrived back, he was not a happy man. He gave everyone involved a dressing down. The men from the patrol were given six months' hard labour. The sergeant and corporal were whipped and given six months' hard labour and night duty in Camerontown. Both men, as I said, were killed there in the attack by Riwi. That's about all I can give you, Sam. I do hope it has been a help. Let's have luncheon, and then, my friend, I do need to get on. The army waits for no man.'

We had a pleasant lunch, and as Peter was about to leave, he passed his card to me. 'Do try to keep in touch.' He left with a wave, and I let out a big sigh.

'A positive morning, Sam,' I voiced.

CHAPTER SIXTEEN

London

That afternoon, I received a cable from Toby, my forest warden. He had located the woman in question and had left a couple of his rangers to keep an eye on her. Then while she was out foraging for food, they had restocked the supplies in the hut. They hoped she would think this was a typical occurrence, as they did not want to spook her. They planned to keep their distance until I arrived home. Toby went on to say they had stopped taking bookings for this hut, and a mile from the turn-off, they had installed danger signs so no one would inadvertently go there. His men would also keep trampers off that track. Thank goodness for Toby. I sent him a cable: 'Well done, and good thinking. See you in a couple of days.'

The next couple of days slipped by quickly until we caught up with the Maori delegation once again. I had sent a coach to pick them up and bring them to the station. Amelia and Angus had left the day before, so it was only Sam and myself there to meet and greet them. Then we all boarded my own private carriage, for the manor house in Shrewsbury. We spent the rest of the day eating and talking, until we arrived at Brittermore. There we had three buggies waiting to take us all to the manor. As we trotted up to the main house, the Maori were intrigued by our forest. People out and about would stop and stare at our passengers, but when they saw Sam and I, they would raise their hats and wave as we went past.

We arrived as Bernard and Catherine came down the steps to greet us all. The staff were lined up as a grand entrance for the delegation. A few of my staff found it daunting seeing these brown natives from New Zealand, with their fierce looking facial tattoos, entering the house. That is, until Te Ruru wished everyone a good day and thanked them for their hospitality. Once they realised he was well spoken and not a savage, they visibly relaxed.

We found them wonderful guests. Toby took them through the forest and up to the hotel, where the Maori showed the hotel staff how to cook in a thermal pool. They were a big hit at the schoolhouse where they demonstrated their carvings to the children, and taught them Maori songs, and children's games. Then Henry gave a rousing service at our wee church. I enjoyed all of their company and with them being with me most of the time I was able to recover more of my memory. I couldn't get over the feeling that when I was with them, it felt like home. Of course, the familiar way Abe and Henry talked also helped. Then I would notice Rita look at me and smile her secret smile.

When it happened, I'm not too sure now. But out of the blue, a huge chunk of my memory returned in a burst of colour. It was after I had met with Blanche, Prince Edward's legitimate wife, who was now a runaway prisoner of the state. I had sent a coded cable to the prince as he had requested, and we kept a careful eye on the woman. She had made herself quite comfortable in the hut. We came to the decision that I would contact her, but I was concerned as I did not want to scare her. So, I was careful to make a lot of noise when I approached, to warn her that someone was coming. By the time I arrived, she had hidden in the bush to watch from behind the ferns.

I entered the hut and made a pot of tea, then went outside and sat down to drink it. Eventually, she came out of hiding and quietly snuck up to the hut. I had seen her, but I did not let on. When I did catch her eye, I slowly got to my feet. 'I'm so sorry. I thought this hut was empty. I must have booked the wrong accommodation,' I apologised. She relaxed a bit, but was vigilant. She was a slim, grey-haired woman, in her middle fifties, with a touch of still dark at her temples. She had a wide mouth, a fresh complexion, and blue eyes with the start of crow's feet at the corners. She was only about five feet, five inches. I found her easy on the eye, and when you consider she had been incarcerated for the last thirty years, she didn't look too bad at all. She looked up at me, and I could see she did not trust easily. I had to win her over, otherwise, she would bolt.

'I've just made a pot of tea. Would you like a cup, madam?' I asked. There was no answer, but she accepted the cup when I handed it to her.

How do I start? She sat down making sure she could take flight if needed. 'You used to know my wife, Isabella?'

She jumped to her feet. 'I'll never be captured again,' she yelled as she prepared to take off.

'Blanche,' I said softly, 'I'm not here to capture you, but to help keep you out of the government's hands. The prince asked me to help, so here I am. I'm Samuel Selkirk, and you are safe on my land with my family and me.'

'You are Lord Selkirk?' she questioned. 'I am. Have you have heard of me?'

'Who hasn't?' she replied. 'I'm not going back, my lord. I would rather die first.'

'Please sit down, Blanche, and call me Sam. No, you are not going back, and I think I just might have an answer to your problem.' She sat down but was still wary. 'Look Blanche, at this present time I have a dozen New Zealanders at the manor house. They are due to head back to New Zealand in a week. What say we send you clear out of England, with them. Then you could spend your remaining days on the other side of the world where no one will ever know you? There is an old woman in the delegation, and I believe she can disguise you so you will blend in with them, she has done this before. Of course, I'll have to ask her, but we must try.'

I stopped talking and thought. Why did I say that, when was this done before? Then it came to me, Rita had used her camouflage skills on the Scottish bloke Stewart McInnes. He was disguised to prevent the army from recognising him. Hell, he was part of the patrol that attacked the village, but he helped get the children out of harm's way. Was he from Dunedin, I wondered?

She looked at me. 'Are you in good health, sir? You seem a little lacklustre?'

'I'm sorry Blanche. My memory was lost during the New Zealand Wars. I'm just starting to get it back, and what I said to you about the disguise, well, I just remembered this very same woman helped my friends and myself in New Zealand do exactly that.'

I took a deep breath. 'We can do it. I'm sure they will help you and you will be safe with them. However, if she cannot, we will think of something else. Anyway you will be free from danger at the manor house. Come with me, now, Blanche. My rangers have been keeping an eye on you for the last week or so, to make sure everyone was kept away. No one knows where you are, except us and the prince, and he will not tell anyone. I can assure you of that.'

'You have been watching me?' she continued to be suspicious. 'I've seen no one.'

'Yes, they are pretty good at staying hidden. They have also restocked the food so you would not have to forage every day. You have done well out here, but it's time to move on. Come home, Blanche. You can catch up with my sister-in-law, Amelia, have a hot bath, and we will sort out some fresh clothes.' Her clothes were un-ironed, but she looked clean, all in all she looked a box of birds.

'A bath would be lovely,' she murmured. 'All right, Sam. 'I'll come with you. I feel you are genuinely a kind man, and that I can trust you. Besides it will be lovely to catch up with Bella again.'

'Oh, Blanche, I'm sorry but Bella died recently in Rhodesia when we went out to see our daughter.'

'Oh, dear me. I'm so sorry to hear that, Sam. I always remember her as a bubbly girl.'

'She was that, and I miss her dearly. Look, you will find some men's clothes inside the hut, I had them delivered with the food. Pop back in and dress yourself in those, so no one will see a woman coming back with me. We will pick up the wagon with the other men, and you will be just one of the boys.' She did as I asked and pulled the hat down on her head, so unless you got close, you wouldn't think she was not a man. We walked out to the waiting wagon on the main track, then piled aboard with the other rangers and headed home.

Once back at the manor house, I introduced Catherine to Blanche and asked her to be take care of her, while I went for a yarn with Rita. I wanted to ask her if she would disguise Blanche for me. I found her out in the sunroom in a comfortable chair, soaking up the winter sun.

'Rita,' I asked as I walked up to her, but felt alarm as I noticed she had fallen slightly forward. Oh hell, I thought, rushing up to her. Is she okay? I gently pushed her back into her chair. Her breathing was laboured and she looked sickly with a pale face. I checked her pulse and discovered it weak. I picked her up and took her inside, placing her on the bed then wrapped her in a blanket. I rang the bell that was next to her be and waited until a maid came. 'Pass on a message to Mr Bernard, to cable the doctor please, and ask Mr Te Ruru to come to his mother's room.'

Te Ruru burst into the room, took one look athis mother, dashed out, and a few minutes later was back in the room with his medicines. In his bag he had crushed manuka bark, which he told me was a sedative that would relax her. 'This has happened before, Sam,' he said as he dribbled the liquid into her mouth.

'As she has got older, she has had this problem with her breathing. I think Europeans call it asthma. Now these kumarahou leaves need to be placed in a bowl of boiling water. Would you do that? Just throw them into a pot of water, and bring it to the boil, then come back.'

I rushed down to the kitchen. The cook had the boiling water on, and she took the leaves and placed them in the pot. We watched the water start to simmer then boil as she sieved off the liquid into a jug, which I took back up to Rita's room. Te Ruru lifted his mother to a near sitting position and little by little let her sip the liquid. We sat and watched her for ten minutes, then her eyes blinked as she slowly became wakeful. Bit by bit the colour of her complexion came back to normal, and her breathing became regular.

'Thank you, my son,' she said, 'and you also, Sam. I need to start my journey home, but time is not on my side.'

Relieved, Te Ruru bent over his mother. 'Rest, Mother. You will be home before the next great journey.' By the time the doctor arrived, he was not needed.

Te Ruru worked on her as the delegation prepared for the trip home. I called on her each day, and much to my relief, she soon came right. I wanted to ask her that question about Blanche, but left it until she was stronger.

Not long after that, we had a couple of strange visitors, government men who asked if I had seen a woman that had escaped captivity. They suspected she was in the area and were sure they would find her. 'Be careful and contact the government if you do see her.' one of them said, producing a card. 'She is quite mad and will say anything to avoid capture.' So, they were still hunting for her, and I was told they had been looking all over the kingdom. We will have to be prudent, I thought. I did not like the look of those blokes at all. Toby had told me there were some unusual people booked in at the park, and had noticed some of those fellows were armed. He told them straight, in no uncertain terms, that guns were not allowed unless it was an organised cull.

'They didn't like it, but they left their rifles behind. I still think they may have carried handguns though, so that is a worry.'

'Keep me informed, Toby. Follow them discreetly and find out anything you can.'

It was at this time that The Queen sent a cable to say that she had to delay her answer to the delegation, it would have to be another month. The Maori were greatly disappointed to put it mildly. So, they prepared to return to New Zealand without a solution in their pockets. They had hoped to return with good news, but it was not to be. Abe and Henry said they had not been expecting much, there are too many Europeans in NZ now, and the Maori population had dropped dramatically. They were not coming from a place of strength, but they had to try and will continue to do so in the future.

'We have to have faith in the law, and The Queen's message might still turn out favourable. Anyway, you have to be optimistic,' expressed Henry.

He went on to say that by the time they get home, the cable maybe waiting for them.

By this time, Rita was up and about. I went over to her, 'Do not worry Rita, if the cable comes through earlier, I'll wire places like Suez to let you know the outcome.'

'That's splendid of you Sam, but your son Bernard can do that, as you will be coming home with us.'

'Don't be silly, Rita, I have things to do here. I am sorry but there is no way I'm going to New Zealand with you. We will not come over until Sam and I head out later in your summer, as we hope to see my daughter Margaret in Dunedin.'

'Mark my words Sam, you and your son will travel with us, and you my friend will be whole again before the weeks end.'

Was this some kind of joke? Thirty years had gone by, and I still had a way to go before I was completely healed. Now, with just the say so of an old Maori woman, I had to believe that I would be whole again, with my memory returned, with a click of the fingers... 'Nah, I don't think so, Rita,' was all I said.

She looked at me with knowing eyes, giving me goosebumps again. 'Yes, I believe now is the time for you to talk with Peri.'

Like a kid, I did as I was told, and I went off to search for Peri. Everyone who had heard to her words scratched their heads and wondered what she had been getting at, including me. With luck, I might get some answers from Peri, though it worried me what might come to light about myself.

I found Peri out in the forest, leaning against an old oak tree and I could see the pleasure on his face. He gravitated there whenever he could as the bush was where he felt at home. With the sun on his face, he smiled to himself. The cold winter days did not seem to affect him at all. He had looked asleep when I approached him and had plonked myself down on nearby fallen tree trunk, his eyes snapped open.

'Ah, kia ora, Sam. Did Rita send you?' I could still not get my head around people who seemed to know what was going on before it had happened.

'Yes, she told me it was time to talk to you, whatever that means,' I replied.

Peri smiled, 'What I say might feel strange to you, but in your soul, you will know I speak the truth. It was a long time ago when I last spoke to your friend Bob Kydd, that was before I left him near the place of the Taniwha. Which, incidentally old chap, is exactly the same as it was over thirty years ago. Even the Pakeha don't dare go there.' I looked at him with anxiety tying knots in my stomach. 'You know your friends' names were Kydd and Langton, not Kidder and Lang?'

I nodded my head. 'I only found out recently about that, but why change them?'

'The name you went under was Mack.' He looked at me intently, and I started to get tingles up my spine. 'Well, old fruit, Bob told me your name was Samuel McInnes.' My eyes filled with water as I put my head in my hands. He touched my arm. 'It will come back, Sam. Rita is never wrong, my friend.'

'But that bloke who was with us was Stewart McInnes.'

'Yes,' replied Peri, 'the connection between you both are years apart. His brother Angus was your third great-grandfather.'

'Oh, what the hell are you talking about, that's a load of rubbish. No way!'

'I'm only telling you what your friend Bob related to me. Tell me, can you remember the mist?'

'No,' I snapped, 'but you are going to explain it to me, right?'

'No Sam, that will come back to you in its own time. When it hits you, you will have a complete memory recovery. All Rita and I are doing is creating the trigger. Your mind will do the rest. However, I do have more to tell you, your mother's name is Mary, and your father is Wayne. Your sister Mary, I think, if I'm correct, is twelve years younger than you.' My mouth dropped open, and my eyes stared at him. This felt unbelievable, but it had to be true. You just didn't pluck those facts out of a hat.

'Bob had a sister, Sasha, who was a captain on a fishing boat with her father. Bob told me he did not work with his father as he would get sick walking through a puddle on the road. Then there were Shane's parents, Mona and David. They have two daughters, but their names, I have forgotten. I'm sorry to say. It's not like me to forget.'

'How do you know so much? How can you remember all this, Peri?' I asked mournfully.

'Well, to begin with, old chap, our language was only verbal until the coming of the Pakeha, and nothing was ever written down. So, we would pass on stories of all our births, marriages, deaths, battles, and whatever happened in everyday life, only by the spoken word. Because of that you end up, my dear friend, with a memory that you can recall at any time. We are losing this now as our children are educated and can read and write. Today they just write everything down on paper.' He smiled. 'In my case, I still use the old ways, but I might be the last, then another part of our history will be gone forever. Rest for a while, Sam. Let the sun work its miracle of warmth on you. Let yourself sleep, then afterwards I will finish off my story. Your mind, my friend, has been given a huge shock, when you recover a little, I'll explain more. Just know you will soon be whole again.' I closed my eyes as I thought this was too much to take in. I suddenly felt drained, and I quickly dropped off.

CHAPTER SEVENTEEN

Shadymore

I woke with a start. It was cooling down, yet the sun was still shining on my face. 'How long have I been asleep, Peri?' I asked.

Looking at the sun, he said, 'About an hour or so. Do you feel relaxed, old boy? We can carry on later tonight if it suits, my good man, but I believe we should get this over with now, and let your mind access this information while you sleep this evening, and you will be the better for it. Do I have your approval, old chum?'

'Yes,' I replied in a small voice. I was feeling better, and I did want to know. Heck, I now knew my parents' names for the first time in thirty years. 'So yes, full steam ahead, Peri.'

'All right, now. Where was I? According to Bob, your parents, more specifically, your mother, was a teacher, and your father was an accountant. He told me your sister, from an early age, always wanted to be a doctor.' I looked at him amazed, like a fool my mouth opened trying to fathom this information. 'A bit much to take in, my old fruit, but it now is out there for your mind to accept.

'This next part is quite weird to relate to you, and I had trouble trying not to laugh when Bob told me, but I have a feeling that in the future, it's not going to be that farfetched. He explained to me about flying in a thing called a helicopter... I think I have that right. I figured he was a silly fellow at the time, but he was so serious. Bob also told me you had a degree in conservation at Otago University. I am not sure about what that degree was used for, but I have been aware of a few people who use that word now. Oh, and you were born in 1984.' I went silent, stunned at the repercussions of what he had said. He continued on, unconcerned, to tell me that I played rugby. 'I wouldn't be surprised by that, as it is a common game all over Aotearoa', he added.

'I took Bob back to the spot where he said the three of you came out of the mist. And we exchanged gifts, I had carved him a tiki for good luck, and he gave me his light with no flame; he called it a torch. The light has gone now, but it is in pride of place at my whare back home. He entered the bush, and that was the last I ever saw of him. The thing is, my good man, Bob knew our future, he knew it all. They spoke of him at Pukekawa, as a powerful tohunga (spirtual healer), but Rita and I think he was much more than that. He was aware of our future to the point of telling us specific things years in advance of their time, for instance how the war would end. His knowledge was remarkable.

'Everything he disclosed has come to pass. He confined to me this fact from all those years ago. The three of you went into the mist in the year 2015, and it brought you back to our time as it was then, in 1863. You must return to your own time, my good friend. Bob will be looking for you. He told me he would never give up. He also requested that if I was ever to run into you or Shane, to suggest that you place a letter in a bank vault, wherever you are, to be opened in the future.'

'Hang on. My mate Shane, he never went back with Bob?'

'I don't know, old fruit. I have never run into any of you again until now. Another thing, Bob told me to pass on the information, that when you return home, to make sure you have some sort of resources waiting for you in the future. He suggested bank notes, stamps, gold, silver, or take shares out in established firms. He did mention the Bank of New Zealand was still going strong in his time. To me, my friend, I thought he was going potty, but now I don't know. So now it is up to you to find your memory and get home.'

I felt panic rising in me, and I sat there gasping for air as my eyes filled with water. Then I started to gulp, until Peri rubbed my back vigorously. 'Take one big breath, man. That will do it, good chap,' then he finished with a whack on my back. I did as he suggested, and it calmed me. My trouble was, all that he had said, I somehow felt was truth. How, it didn't matter. It felt as though Peri had touched my soul.

My head spun with all the consequences of the things he had related to me. If this was all true, and if this nonsense with the mist was correct, I could go forward into my so-called time. If this was right, when would I arrive? Would it be thirty years into the future from the time I left? Would I get back in time to see my parents, and Mary?

Peri spoke again and took me away from my thoughts. 'Sam, all your life you must have wondered about why you talked the way you do. Then there was the equipment you had with you, including your rifles, and all your clothes. They were so out of place, much too advanced. Bob didn't say that much about our future, only to say that land compensation would be paid in full by 2024. A long way off, but he was enthused that the tribes in his time are doing very well. I hope in my heart that this is true. Would you like me to go and find your son, my friend, for whanau at this time is important.'

'No thank you Peri, I need time alone. Will you go back and tell the family that I want to spend time out here by myself and to reflect about all that you have mentioned?'

'Good Oh, old chap, I'll take my leave and catch you on the morrow.' I watched him stride down the track heading for the manor house. I collapsed against the oak and the last thing I remembered before my mind switched off again, was that Rita had not been wrong.

Bird noise broke into my sleep. I tried to roll over, but the trunk of the oak tree inhibited me. It was not quite dawn, and the night animals were heading back to their lairs. My head hurt, my mouth was dry, my eyes gummy and I had a migraine. I felt as if all the years had caught up with me—it was as if I was an old man. Sleeping rough was a young man's game. All I could remember was Peri leaving, then bang, and I woke up. I had slept through the whole night. It was bloody cold, bugger, it was winter, I could have frozen to death. What was I thinking? No doubt my family would have presumed that I would have shacked up for the night in a hut, not under a bloody tree—I shivered. I was lucky the foxes didn't have a go at me.

The first thing I thought of was how good a cup of hot soup would be, to take the chill away... to take the frost from my bones, now that is what I needed, a good old soup in a cup. It wouldn't take much to heat, just pop it in the microwave, and... and... hang on a minute—a microwave? There are none of those here.

Then like a lightning bolt, I saw my mum in my

mind, then my dad, and my little sister. She was about twelve. My early life had returned. I could not believe it, I was able to recall those missing years. I sat up and lent against the trunk of the tree, and tears ran down my face. It was hard trying to stop crying once I had started, but thirty years of buildup, would not be calmed so easily. Eventually, I staggered to my feet and walked a hundred meters or so to a stream. My God, I'm back to thinking in metric, I splashed water onto my face. Shit that's cold, I thought, washing away the gumminess in my eyes. Reflected in the pool I saw myself, bugger me, I looked like hell. I needed to get home and have a damn good hot bath, and throw some hot food into me.

Then unexpectedly I remembered my mates. University, the army, fighting in Afghanistan. Then of all things, being offered a contract to play rugby for Otago. It came in full colour, and the years fell away. I thought of my parents, I so wanted to see them. I focused on my family, the camping trips, the birth of my wee sister, and taking her under my wing. I saw Mum and Dad at my graduation and how proud they were of me. Oh, how I have missed them so.

That did not take away the bond I had with Bella's parents. They were wonderful, and I loved them to bits. But my mum and dad— I craved to see them; it had been so long. Now maybe I just might be able to find them. They would be old by now, most likely passed on, but I had to try. I hugged myself and rocked back and forth, repeating the words, Mum and Dad, over and over. Then my mind jumped, as my childhood flashed through my mind, primary school, intermediate, then high school, playing junior rugby, all of my mates' families, and the girls in my life. My attention continued onward to the point when we flew up to Ruapehu National Park to start the cull for the Department of Conservation.

Then in my mind's eye, I saw the mist. Oh my God, there it was swirling about us, and it wasn't till the day after that we realised we had gone back in time. Oh poo, I searched through my memory bank and it was all there, including Stewart, he was my third great-uncle. How confusing. The memories flooded in and I cried like a baby. This is how Sam found me when he came looking.

'Dad, Dad,' he called out with concern, as he rushed towards me. 'Father, are you okay? I brought a rug, here, let me wrap it around you. You must be cold. Bugger me, Father, you look like hell. Come on, let's get you home to a warm bath and put hot food into you.' He put his arm around me, and taking my weight, he half carried, half walked me back to the manor. Bernard heard from the servants that I was in a state, and he was out like a rocket to help bring me in.

Everyone fussed over me, and eventually after a warm bath and hot food, they tucked me up in bed, and I dropped off to sleep.

I slept the whole day, so when I finally woke, it was night. I went for a pee, shot down to the kitchen, and made a leftover chicken sandwich, then went back to bed and slept until dawn. When I woke, there was no sign of my headache, my mind was clear, and my memory was still intact. I sat in my chair looking out over the manor, contemplating my course of action. In the back of my mind, I had already made that decision. Once I left my home here, there was a significant possibility I would never get back, and that meant I would never see my children or grandchildren again. Was it selfish? I don't know, but I had this drive to see my parents and my sister, that is if they were still alive. Also, there was the possibility to catch up with Shane and Bob.

First, I needed to explain all this to my children, Amelia and Angus. Then I needed to, as Peri had suggested, work out some sort of resource I could take with me, so I would have money. That is if I could get back through the mist. Now what was the exchange rate when we left? I thought it was two dollars to the pound or close enough. Shares would be the thing, old notes would be another, and postage stamps. I had a few... well... quite a few, old penny stamps still attached to their envelopes. They might be worth a few dollars in the future. So, I could take them as well. First thing's first though, I needed to tell my kids about what was happening. What gave me some unease, was would they believe me? I think Peri and Rita, should be at the meeting, as backup.

I dressed and wandered down to the dining room for breakfast. My family looked up from their plates, they were all there waiting for me. 'Father,' Catherine called, and jumped to her feet, and rushed over to kissed me on the cheek. 'Well,' she said, as she stepped back and looked up into my face, 'I must say, you are looking the chirpiest I have seen you for a long time.'

'Yes, I'm feeling the best I've felt for ages,' I answered, looking at them all. 'My dear family,' I announced, 'could we all meet in the drawing room before lunch? I have something of paramount importance to convey to you all. Would you, Rita, and Peri, come as well, please?' I went over and gave my grandchildren a kiss.

'Are you sure you are okay, Father?' asked Sam with worry in his voice.

'Yep Sam. I am. Let's wait until we are all in the drawing room, and then we will talk.'

I sent a cable to Angus to request their attendance. The reply said they would catch the train immediately and would be here before lunch. All I needed to do was get myself in the right frame of mind. I went up to the old attic and rummaged through my old pack and found the map. After all these years, I finally understood it. My journals were there to, and I quickly read through them wondering how it didn't twig I wasn't from here, But I guess your memories would only come back in their own good time. I searched through the pack for Mary's note I had tucked away. Oh, Mary, I thought. Dear sister— I have thought of you for all these years. There was my old phone, still wrapped in paper. Lucky if that worked again, I took out the SIM card. It would still have photos of our time on it, but after all of these years, I wonder if it would be corrupted?

By the time I gathered my thoughts I went into the drawing room. Everyone was expectant, waiting for me to explain what was on my mind. I looked around the chamber. 'Before I explain the purpose of this meeting, I want you to understand that I'm not reverting back to the dark old days. I'm as coherent as anyone sitting in this room. Now to all who were unaware, after talking with Peri and Rita, my memory has returned in full, and children, it is not what you think. No one will believe what I have to say, except these two Maori people from New Zealand. But I want you to know from the outset, I speak the truth.

'As you know, right from the beginning, I have been quite different. My language and accent were not from the mother country. I was at a loss for all these years as to who I was and why I was here. I've talked about things not even thought of, let alone invented. Right from the very beginning, I always felt I was out of place. Well, it appears I was. My name is Samuel McInnes. I was born in Dunedin, New Zealand in September 1984. I have a degree in conservation, and that is why even with my memory loss, I was intent on preserving our forest that we have here today.

'I stopped and waited for them to start to rubbish what I said, but they just sat with an astonished look on their faces. They had not expected this.

'My parents, your grandparents' names are David and Mary. My sister, Mary, was twelve when I disappeared with my mates into the past.' Still not a sound. 'That's right. We came through the mist into the past. How or why it happened, I have no idea, but we did. If my parents are still alive in their time, they will be in their nineties, and Mary will be fifty-one.

'Remember my stories about flying, well, it is normal in my day. In 1903, a New Zealander flew the first fixed-wing flight, but the Wright brothers from the USA will be recorded as the first manned flight. That map that has been in my pack all these years with that date 2014—that was the year of printing and manufacture of the map.

Bernard jumped up, disturbed by my words.

'Father, I think you might have been on the whisky. This has gone on too far; it is just too far-fetched.' Peri rose to his feet.

'Bernard, what your father says is true. His friend Bob told me years ago about everything that your father has just explained to you. That was when I took Bob back to the place where they had originally arrived. For years, there were stories of people going into that area and never coming back. So, you have to accept that your father and his friends came through the mist into our time, old chap. Now to put things right in his mind. Sam needs to pop back to see if his parents are alive.' They turned and looked at me.

'Oh no, Father, you cannot even think of it,' Sam cried. 'You are not doing this by yourself.'

'I have to, Sam. 'It is a driving force in me, I must do this. If I'm able to see my parents before they die, then I have to try. Peri will guide me back to this place where he dropped Bob off thirty years ago. Won't you Peri?'

'Of course, old man, but no farther, as I stated to your friend it is the place of the Taniwha.'

Angus was thoughtful.

'At the beginning Sam, you used to say many things we did not comprehend,' he said, racking his brain. 'Ah yes, remember when we got to Sydney you asked where the harbour bridge and opera house were.'

'Yes, I did,' I replied. 'In the twenty-first century, they are there, like the Auckland Harbour Bridge, Sky Tower, and a million other things. On the planet there are millions of cars, trucks, and planes—it goes on and on. Look you are my family, I know it is hard for you all to believe me, but this was my life.' Shaking my head in wonderment, I continued. 'I remember meeting the young lady, Sofia, who helped Stewart take the children to Dunedin. Well it turns out, she married Stewart's brother, making her my third great-grandmother. Now here's another one for you, one of those very children, Adam, married your sister Margaret in Dunedin. I tell you it's confusing all round.

'Then there's our name Selkirk. Long ago I took that name because it was familiar to me. It turns out Selkirk was my grandmother's maiden name, no wonder I found it so comfortable. The genealogy of our family today is going to be all over the place, but children, family, and friends, I feel in fine fettle—a box of birds—so don't worry and I hope you will support me in this. I will try to return home to my era, but if I can't, I'll endeavour to come back to the manor, and to you all. But I must try to find my sister and parents. Please bear with me. After thirty years, it is a blessing to have my memory returned. I don't want to leave, but the pull is too strong. I need your support even if you don't agree.'

Catherine was the first to speak. 'Well if it were me, I would want to go myself Father-in-Law. You need closure on this. Do not concern yourself we will still be here when you return.'

Rita had sat quietly while we had talked, until she stood up to go, then said, 'When you get home, Sam, be sure to catch up with Bob and Tui.'

'You have that wrong, Rita. You mean Shane and Tui.'

'No, Sam, it is as I say. Now I must lie down. We leave in a few days, so I must gather my strength.'

Bernard shook his head, 'Father, are you really sure?' I nodded. 'In that case, I will not allow you to go unless there is a family member with you. So Sam is going with you.'

'Okay, Bernard, I guess I put you in charge, so you are the boss. Sam,' I asked, 'are you up for this?'

'I really don't know about this Father. I just don't know. It's so unbelievable. But where you go, I will also. I guess someone has to look out for you.'

I was touched by their loyalty. I looked at all my family and said, 'Thank you.' The dice had been thrown.

'One thing I failed to mention Father,' Sam piped up with a grin on his face. 'You have already been booked on the ship south with Rita and Te Ruru. I had this feeling we were going with them.'

CHAPTER EIGHTEEN

Shadymore

As the family broke up, and headed out to continue on with their day, I sat and watched them muttering to each other. Angus, I believe, was the only one who really understood what happened to me, but I found relief in knowing it was all out in the open. Angus was with me from the very beginning on the Esk, when I first came out of my coma. He knew I was different from the norm, but from the future, that might have been a bit hard to handle. At least he had an open mind, but the rest of the family were sceptical.

Who could blame my family though, for thinking like that? I mean, if the story I related to them, was told to me cold turkey, I would have laughed it off as fantasy. The only difference was, this was my family, so more than likely, they would give me the benefit of the doubt. I only hope if I do get home to my century, and I took Sam with me, that he would be able to make the transition. Even I may have problems going home to my era, after all time had moved on thirty years, and technology would have moved on along with it. Not much sense worrying about that now. Of course, all of this was supposition, as I hadn't a clue of how much time duration had past in the future. Heck, we might end up on the same day my mates and myself came through the mist. So really, I had to be prepared for anything.

In the meantime, I had things to sort out before we headed off. We will take Blanche to New Zealand with us, so she will need to be in disguise. The idea I had of asking Rita before, was put on the back burner, as she was sick then. But she looked much stronger now, so this might be my best opportunity. Back in 1863, Rita had disguised Stewart, changing him from an English soldier to a Maori, the turnround was amazing. I bet you, a penny to a pound, she would be able to modify Blanche's appearance, with only a little bit of effort.

I walked up to her room, lightly knocked on the door, then opened it slightly. A voice deep inside called, 'Come on in, Sam.'

The wonder of how she knew it was me, always gives me the chills. She sat in the sun focused on the gardens below, she looked so much better. 'Hi, Rita,' I said.

'Kia ora, Sam. Have you come to talk about Blanche?'

'How the heck did you know that?' I asked. She turned and smiled at me.

'Well yes, I was wondering if you wouldn't

mind disguising her as a Maori woman for the trip out to New Zealand? I remember years back, you did a great job on Stewart, changing him from a solider to a bushman. If it is all right with you, I'll send Blanche along so you can weave your magic. Maybe, as your cabin on board is large enough for two, you could even share with her. That is, as long as you don't feel it is an imposition on you. I have just found out, that it appears Sam and I will be coming out to New Zealand with your delegation, after all. That means I will be able to keep an eye out for her also, though I know she would be in safe hands with your people. By the way, tell me how did you know about her? We have been trying to keep her presence quiet as she is in a bit of a bind with the government.' I knew I was babbling. Take a deep breath, I told myself, give her a chance to reply.

Her eyes were closed as she spoke. 'Come to me Sam.' As I did so, she asked for my hands, which she held with a firm grip.

'Of course, I will help you, my friend. But you must be vigilant as there are dangerous people who will try to stop her. Listen, the four of you are bonded, although I'm not altogether certain, but I feel it includes—your son Sam and my friend Abe, it has been written my friend. And Sam, Blanche will never find her son, that in a way might be a good thing. He is safe, but not where she, or the authorities think. Once you're back in Aotearoa, the time will go swiftly, and there will be no time at all to search.'

My mind raced. What was this about bonding the four of us, supposed to mean? How the hell did she know that and why? I just didn't understand this supernatural link she seems to have. Rita continued that she would make time on the trip out, to teach Blanche a bit of basic Maori.

'I cannot say any more, Sam. Indeed, I have said more than I should.The future should look after itself, but in your case with you being out of time, I feel a helping hand is necessary. But once in Auckland, you will have to move, there is to be no wasting of time, as people will be watching you. So, don't worry Peri will return you to the place of the mist, but I cannot emphasise the urgency of speed.' She opened her eyes, gazing out past me through the window. 'Time is short for me, Sam, this will be my last journey, as my time is near. I need to be home for the final part.' she admitted with a smile. 'Send Blanche to me, and you will not know her when I have finished. Now, I have to have ingredients for the dyes, could I ask you to send up a young maid to assist?' I felt the chills again as I left her room. I had a lot of time for that old woman, but I had to admit, she could be downright spooky.

I thought about what would happen if the authorities found out that Blanche was staying here. But I was lucky with my staff, I know that not one of them would say a word about her, their loyalty was never questioned.

I knocked on her door. 'It's me, Blanche—Sam.'

The door opened slowly to reveal an entirely different person from the one I had transported from the forest hut. It was amazing what warm food, a bath, and clean clothes could do for a person. She looked strong and confident with her light grey hair. For a woman in her fifties, she looked fit and clearly able to cope with what lay ahead.

After all the years she had been imprisoned, I would of thought she would have been hard as nails, and look like a bag of old rags. This woman staring up at me was not like that at all. She had soft skin, blue eyes, a little nose, and a full mouth that smiled as she said, 'Come in, my lord.'

She ushered me to a chair. As I brushed past her, I said, 'Oh just call me Sam.' She adjusted her dress as she down and gave me her full attention.

'Now, what can I do for you, Sam? she asked. 'Though, of course, in my predicament, I doubt whether it will be very much at all.'

I asked had she thought through the possibility of travelling out to New Zealand. It was something we had spoken about while in the forest hut? It would be so much safer for her, than to be trapped here in England, and over there she had a chance to live a normal life without harassment. She stared at me with a rather unladylike, open mouth, so I went on to explain to her the discussion I had had with Rita.

'You might need to change your name, but you will have time to think about that on the trip out. My son and I are going out as well, so we will be there to protect you. Furthermore, you have the Maori delegation that are staying here at the moment, heading home on the same ship. I can vouch that they will not let any harm come your way.'

This time I paused and waited for a reply. Her eyes opened wide and she looked stunned unable to speak. Finally, she got herself together, 'You Sam... You, and your family would do this for me? My God,' she said from behind her hand that moved up to cradle her face. 'You hardly know me Sam,' she said, peering between her fingers with moist eyes. No one has ever done anything nice for me since I was locked away all those years ago.

'Blanche, I don't like injustice, and in your case, what the government has done to you is definitely not going to happen again on my watch. Even so, I am breaking the law, and there are a lot of people trying to recapture you, but the Prince of Wales wants you safe, and that my girl, is what is going to happen. We will have to be very careful, hence the disguise. No one will touch you. I promise you that and you will have a new life, in a new country. Heck Blanche, you have a lot of years left,' I grinned. She peeked from behind her hands, then held out her hand to me.

'Sam, I just don't know what to say. I cannot thank you enough for your help. I really had no idea what would happen when I escaped from the wagon. I had no plan at all. Maybe hoping for a few hours of freedom was all I was after. Bella was a lucky lady to marry you, and I'm pleased you found me. Yes, it would be wonderful to have the freedom, without having to look over my shoulder all the time. Have I got that many years left, I do not know? But surely you must know a woman doesn't talk about her age Sam.' She grinned with a twinkle in her eye. 'I am in my middle fifties, and I know, all I do have is hope.'

'I'm pleased you see it that way,' I said with a smile. 'Excellent. Well, Rita is in her room, so pop down and see her, and I can tell you she will transform you into a woman who even you will not recognise.'

'Just one more thing, though, Sam. I have no money. I'll never be able to repay you.'

'You don't have to worry on that score, Blanche. I would not leave you destitute. I'll set up a bank account when we get to New Zealand in whatever name you decide, so you won't need to skimp and scrape. That's a promise.

Okay, kiddo, you pop down to Rita's room: the blue door down the hall.'

I spoke as I headed to the door, when I turned back to her, she was right behind me. She put her arms around me and on tiptoes kissed me on the chin. Well, that's as far as she could get without me leaning down. Tears were rolling down her face.

'Thank you, Your Lordship,' she said as I slipped out. I could hear her sobbing behind the door as she slowly closed it behind me, at least I thought she was sobbing with relief. Anyway, I'm sure it would have done her good to let it all out. I walked down the hall rubbing my chin. That's the first time since Bella died that a woman outside the family had kissed me, and I felt guilty.

My next port of call was my son Sam. I asked him to book another Maori woman passenger onto the boat. Then I thought he would need a name for the booking.

'Call her Moana, Sam, and do that as soon as possible.'

I had explained to him previously that Rita was going to disguise her, so not even her mother would know her. Sam went to do as I asked. What's next? I thought. I needed to take cash or something with me. It didn't matter what era I turned up in, I needed ready money. I had a few envelopes with the black- penny stamp on them. I thought about four of them, and I was pretty sure they would be worth a bit in the twenty-first century. Moreover, I had some mint one-pound notes. I collected all these together. I came across a couple of red-penny stamps as well, though not in good condition. Looking at them, I decided to take them anyway, and a few sovereigns.

I came across some stamps from New Zealand on letters from my daughter Margaret, who was in Dunedin, and a few stamps on letters from my daughter Mary when she was in Rhodesia. I was pretty sure these would be worth something in my future time, but to be on the safe side, I had my son Bernard buy one thousand pounds worth of shares in the Australia and New Zealand Banking Group. When we arrived in the twenty-first century, well, if we did arrive, they would be worth quite a bit. I hoped so anyway. I also had arranged a bank draft in the ANZ bank in New Zealand for five thousand pounds, and this would allow me to put money aside for Blanche, and help to keep us in the style that we were used to. I laughed to myself. So, on the money front, we were set.

Then I collected my old backpack, which was still in good order after thirty-odd years of being hidden away. I went to the mantelpiece and took down my sister Mary's kiwi pin, with a silver fern attached, that I had mounted all those years ago. Then I gathered all the money, stamps, and coins I had, and placed them in an old leather wallet I found. I wrapped the whole lot in a canvas waterproof and placed that in the bottom of the pack. Next was my rifle. How it survived the fight in Rhodesia, I had no idea as at that time I was out to it, but it did. I placed that on the table with ammo. Once that was completed, I sat down and thought, what's next.

I recon a lot of change would have happened in Auckland since 1863, but would I be able to communicate in some way with my folks or my mates? I remembered we had placed a letter to be opened in 2014 in the ANZ bank just before I was shot, all those years ago. The original letters would still be there in my time. I wondered if it worked, if our families received them down the line. Maybe they did, in that case that's what I'll do again. I needed to give it a go, at least to let them know I was trying to get home. But who should I send letters to? Mary would surely be married, and after thirty years, everyone most likely had moved on, but I had to try somehow. I was hoping Mum and Dad would be alive, but there was a chance they would have passed on by now. So, I decided to send a letter to Bob's old address and also to Shane's. I should try the parents, but I didn't think they would receive It. But if it did turn up at their old address, someone might remember my parents and send it on to Mary. Subsequently, I thought no. I'll just send it to Bob, and if I don't make it home, then my parents will not be disappointed. Let's face it, this was going to be a hit-and-miss journey. I had a plan of sorts.

I sat down and started to write a long manuscript to Bob. I explained what had happened in my life, it took a while. Well, I spent a few days on it, but then I didn't finish it. At least it was a start, I'll finish it on the boat out. I sat back and read the letters and the start of the manuscript. I thought if they didn't know who this was from, they would prefer to believe that it was from a nutter. I was determined to place these in a vault in Auckland or Christchurch when we arrived, to be opened after 2020. I did not know when I would get back, so it was all going to be pure luck. I was sixty-three now, born in 1984. If I found my way back, and time ran parallel, it would be 2044. That sure made my brain hurt, or would I return around the same time I left? If it was 2044, that would make Mum and Dad's age around eighty-five to ninety. Bummer, don't go there, I thought. I placed the letter with the stamps in my bag.

Another thought entered my mind. I remembered Bob saying there was a possibility we might go farther back in time, and this was a risk, of course, we had to take. Heck, we might even go farther into the future, I didn't know. Peri said, once he left Bob at the start of the trail to the cave, he never saw him again, and of course, Rita mentioned Bob and Tui. What was that all about? I had no idea. So, one had to be positive, and we would play things by ear.

I must admit I was a wee bit apprehensive, and even selfish, leaving my family to find my sister and parents. I had everything to live for here and now, and my grandchildren were here also. Sam and I might never see them again, and it tugged at my heart strings. You keep telling yourself thirty years is a long time to be lost in your mind, and making contact, or trying to, with my folks was important, and if it turned out impossible, then I'd work hard to come home, but at least I would have tried.

I sat down with Bernard, my eldest, heir to the title and my daughter-in-law Charlotte. 'Give me seven years,' I said. 'That's how long it'll take for me to be presumed dead if I'm not back by then. You can declare me lost on an expedition to New Zealand's Fiordland. Then you can officially take over the title, Bernie. You have complete control of the estate, and I know it will be in the best of hands. I have written out letters to our solicitors, so everything will be in order. Don't look at me like that, Charlie.' I always called her that when we were by ourselves. 'It is not as bad as all that.'

'But Father, you are talking as if you are going to die, and none of us want that, and what about

Sam? He is going with you. We could lose both of you, and that is not fair, not fair at all. Even though I've said I would agree with what you want to do, now I'm starting to have a change of heart.'

'I know, Charlie, Bernard, but Sam does not have to come. He is his own man. Let's face it; I'm getting on. If I don't do this now, I'll never do it and will surely regret it to my dying day. Your mother, Bernard, would be with me all the way.'

'Yes, I know, Father. It just seems like you are chasing a dream.'

'Well, if it turns out farfetched, then look at it as a holiday for Sam and me, and when we get back, we will celebrate with a family party. Look, kids, I will do my damnedest to come home. I'll keep in touch through letters and cables so you will know where we are, and we must also remember I have Blanche to look after and to make sure she gets a new start. Remember, I love you all, but this is for me. It might be selfish, but I need to do this, and I hope eventually you both will understand,' I grinned. 'The recent cables I got from the girls, they think I'm swinging from the lampshades.'

Bernard laughed. 'Yes Dad, I got one also from Mary, to ask me to put you in irons and to stop this foolish escapade. You have made your decision, Father. Go with our blessing and be safe; always stay safe.'

'Thank you, son, Charlie. You will never know how thankful I am that I leave with your good will. Let us have a special meal before we head off.' I stood up. 'Yes, a spot of music before we leave will brighten the place, uplift your spirits, and we will leave on a high note.' I kissed Charlie and hugged Bernard. My family will always be with me wherever I go.

CHAPTER NINETEEN

London 1895

On a sleazy back street in London, a meeting took place in the room of the man the government referred to as the Controller, his real name was Sir Anthony Purcell. He was tall and skinny with a balding head, pointy nose, and grey, unblinking eyes. When he spoke, his thin lips would hardly move, and his glare made the two men with him nervous.

He was head of a government organisation that did sometimes Illegal and particularly dirty work, on the unsuspecting public, for the Secretary of State. Even the prime minister and his caucus had no idea what these men were up to. He recruited far and wide for his group, from all areas of society. In this case, one of the fellows with him this day, had done twenty years in Her Majesty's Prison for poaching and stealing gold. He was in his late forties, early fifties, a skinny man of around five feet, six inches. One wrist had been broken over thirty years ago and never set right, so his hand was twisted at an unusual angle, looking as though it was still broken. He was resourceful and quite capable of anything the controller put his way. Although he was a violent unpredictable, slimy person, when in the presence of of the Controller, he always felt uncomfortable, as his boss scared the hell out of him. He stood in front of him with his cap in hand and head bowed.

'Davis,' the Controller spoke with a rasping voice, his unblinking grey eyes piercing him, 'this is the most important task you will ever undertake.'

Sir Anthony swung his gaze to the little man next to Davis. A short, fat fellow of five feet, five inches, but his size and looks were deceiving. He was unpretentious, and barely noticeable. He had the ability to move quickly and silently, and to blend in, whenever he needed. His name was Ethan Simms. He was the brains of the pair and excelled with a knife, which happened to be his weapon of preference. A Yorkshire man, who all his life, had been robbing and killing until a few years ago, when he was caught and sentenced to hang. The Controller had seen his potential, so the hanging was aborted, but to all and sundry he was hung, conveniently making him officially dead. Now, he was Sir Anthony's man, and he thanked his lucky stars he was. However, in the back of Ethan's mind, he would run if the opportunity presented itself.

John Davis was a different kettle of fish. He was sent to prison along with all the males in his family, all on the same day, though at various prisons around the kingdom. He had been caught poaching on the Estate of Shadymore. The Earl of Shadymore's son- in-law also discovered the gold they had stashed as well. His father died in prison. Of his brother William he had no idea, not knowing if he was alive or dead. He hadn't seen Willy since the day they were sentenced thirty years ago. He had a sister in Shrewsbury, the only soft spot in his make-up. She was married to the earl's forest ranger, Tobias. He was with the earl's son-in-law the day they were all caught. His sister Eliza had done well for herself, and for once in his life, John, who normally was a complete bastard, didn't plan to rock the boat there. It was the least he could do for his sister. The only kind thing he had done in his entire life was to not make contact with her at all.

Besides if he returned to Shrewsbury, and got caught, the hangman would be waiting. The magistrate had plainly emphasised that, when he had said, step into this Shire, and you hang. John still harbored dark thoughts about the earl though. Oh yes, he knew that Sam Selkirk was the Earl of Shadymore now, and if he spotted him and got a chance outside of Shrewsbury, he would do him for all the years of anguish he had been put through.

It was Samuel Selkirk who broke his wrist all

those years ago, and even though it had been fixed at the time, twenty years of hard labour had its effect, and it never knitted together properly.

The rasping of Sir Anthony Purcell's voice held their attention. 'We have a very grave problem, and it is up to us to rectify it,' he snarled. 'This is the background. Listen carefully. Straighten up, Davis. Don't slouch,' he spat. 'Have I got your attention?'

'Yes, sir,' they said in unison.

'Right, now this is of national priority. A woman by the name of Lady Blanche Proctor has escaped from captivity, and she has to be found. There is no need for you to know the whys and wherefores. You have to stop, and silence her at all cost. This is of paramount importance, do you understand? I have cables going out to all operatives, it is that important. Every country in the British Empire is on the lookout. If we do not succeed, this will cause an international incident to the effect that our beloved queen and country could be at risk. We cannot allow that to happen. Have I made myself clear?' The two men nodded. He glared at them through hooded eyes. 'Do you?' he snapped.

'Yes, sir, but...' Ethan said meekly, 'deposing of a high-rank person will not be easy, sir.'

Sir Anthony looked sharply at Ethan. 'There will be no repercussions for you to worry about.

You have my full backing, that is how important this is, but do it discreetly. You find her, then get rid of her. All operatives have the same orders. Now the government will be very thankful when this deed is done. So, a bonus of one thousand pounds each, goes to the men who complete this assignment. That is... your reward will be twenty years' pay for the one job. This huge amount of money shows how important it is to national security.' Both men gasped: one thousand quid. All sorts of exciting things went through their minds.

'Now, the lowdown—she had a son who, years ago as a baby, went out to New Zealand. Once again, you don't need to know the ins and outs. She was never told so she should not have any idea that he is there, but there is always a chance she might have knowledge of him. It won't do her any good though, he disappeared years ago. God knows we have hunted ourselves and cannot find him, so it will be a dead end for her. In saying that, if she knew that he was sent to New Zealand, there is a chance she could try to stow away on a ship and go out there. There is one leaving in a few days for Auckland via Christchurch, New Zealand. I want the two of you to watch that ship twenty-four hours a day.

'If she is spotted, I want you to cable me at this address.' He handed them a piece of paper with the cable's address written on it. 'Memorise that, then burn it in the grate. If she is seen boarding the ship, we have tickets for you both just in case they are needed. If you follow her aboard, cable me before you leave, we will use a code-word "leaving2". Then you will have to do your duty on board. There is a cable station at the wharf entrance, and keep in touch at each port of call. Cable when the deed is done, send the word "Sunshine." All this is hypothetical as the chances of her getting to London and even boarding the ship is a long shot, but we have to have contingencies for every eventuality. We do not want her to show-up overseas at all, so it is imperative that she disappears. In your case get rid of her at sea. Understand?' The two men nodded.

'She was last seen escaping into the Shadymore forest. We have been told, in no uncertain terms, that the earl will not give us permission to venture into the park with dogs or guns. We have men cautiously surrounding the estate watching and waiting, and up until now, she has not been seen emerging.'

'Does she know the earl, sir?' Ethan asked.

'No, she doesn't, but in her early years, she was at school with the earl's deceased wife and her sister, so there is a possibility she might make contact. We have had men on the estate incognito and around the villages asking discreetly about a grey-haired woman in her fifties.'

He handed them another slip of paper. 'This is her description. At this moment, the earl has a Maori delegation from New Zealand staying with him. They will travel back by ship to New Zealand in the next day or so. Watch out for this woman and let's hope she does not turn up with this group.'

'How many women with the Maori party, Sir Anthony?' Ethan asked.

'Only one, and there are eleven men, including a couple of white colonials. I'm afraid if any of the them get in the way, they will have to be dealt with. Nothing is to stand in the way of silencing this woman. So, Davis, Simms, make sure your handguns are in working order, and get the deed done quietly whenever you get the opportunity. Mind you, we don't want a shoot-out anywhere in public. I hope I have made myself clear. I will not tolerate a cock-up. We will clean up any mess, but if you are seen, you are on your own, and I'll have my department get rid of the both of you. It is not to come back on our doorstep. Do it properly, and you will be rich. Muck it up, and you're dead, there is no middle ground.'

We have booked you a room at the hotel Royal Spar in Royal Pier Road. It's close to the wharf from where the ship leaves.' He handed them a folder. 'These are the tickets if you have to board the ship SS Rangitoto. We have booked the only small two-berth cabin in steerage, with meals.

That will give you some privacy. We don't want you mixing too much with the other passengers. As I have said, it most likely will not come to this, but if you have to leave in a hurry, you have the tickets. If you have to board, there is fifty pounds for your allowance, you can use it for bribes, as well. Now sort yourselves out and get to work. I want no slip-ups, you hear? I'll emphasise it again: Do it right, or you're both dead meat. If you don't see her before the ship leaves, cable me with the word "Unseen," and then meet me here a day later at midday. Right leave here fifteen minutes after I have gone. Burn everything and lock the door on the way out. 'He turned with no parting words, shut the door, and left.

John could not get over his excitement. 'A thousand pounds Ethan, a thousand, imagine we can do what we want, and go wherever we want.'

Ethan was quiet. He thought, I don't trust that bugger, Sir Anthony bloody Purcell. If we do this woman, what's to say he won't get rid of us the same way. Now I have this idiot with me who will shoot before thinking, so I'm going to have to have a bloody good think about all this before I make up my mind. If this woman does catch this ship, there could be an opportunity for me to vanish as well, and I'm bloody sure I'll get rid of this sneaky, scrawny shit next to me. It's a big ocean out there. They burnt all the papers in the fire grill as they were ordered, and fifteen minutes later they left making sure the door was locked behind them.

'We will head down to Gravesend after we pack our gear. If nothing else, we will have a week in a pub with an ale or two all on the government,' Ethan bragged.

The Royal Spar Hotel was two hundred yards from the entrance to the wharf where the ship was berthed. John sat in the bay window and had a complete view of the loading and passenger entrance to the ship. Ethan headed down to the gate and become as inconspicuous as possible. This was Ethan's speciality, he could mingle unobtrusively. They settled down to watch and wait.

Sir Anthony walked briskly away from the meeting. A thought went through his mind. The things I do for this country. If ever the prime minister or his colleagues find out what I actually do, I'll have to skedaddle out of the country. There will be no pension coming my way. A tight grin came over his face. What am I worrying about, he thought as he turned into the mall, hailing a cab. I have plenty of secrets on my files that would make the government very embarrassed. Besides there is no way that anyone knows what the Secretary of State and I do for our country. Most of the PMs are soft, and their cabinets are a waste of time. There is always room for people like me to keep the country safe, through being vigilant and ruthless. Feeling justified, he changed tack, yes, dinner I think would be appropriate. 'The Navy Club,' he stated as he climbed into the cab with not a care in the world. Not knowing the operation, he outlined to the two men, Davis and Simms, would change the lives of so many people in the future, including his own.

CHAPTER TWENTY

Shadymore

The music of the piano played softly in the background as the large group tried to enjoy their last evening meal together. But the enormity of what Sam and I were going to do made everyone just a little bit depressed. A dinner with music, seemed a good idea, but in the end, it just fizzled out. Blanche had excused herself an hour before, faking tiredness, but in reality, she was embarrassed and felt the family should be by themselves on this last night. Rita had done an impeccable job with the alteration of her appearance, and I hardly recognised her. The colour of her hair was now black and much shorter than the long grey hair she had had before her disguise. Her face, arms, and I was told, legs were now brown, and a light moko had appeared on her chin, also her lips were a darker shade of blue. At first glance, she blended in well with the group of Maori. The only way you could tell she was European was to stand up close and scrutinise her face and her eyes, as they were clearly blue. Overall, she would blend in and pass muster. The rest of the party soon made their excuses as well, leaving only the immediate family looking at each other over their glasses of wine.

A cough. 'Do you want me to continue playing the piano, my lord?' the new music teacher from our school whispered.

'Oh, sorry, Mavis,' Bernard replied. 'No, you head off. Thanks for the time and effort.' She closed the lid as she turned to go.

'Safe travels, Your Lordship.' With a sniff, she slipped out the door.

By ourselves now, we attempted even more to show a happy face, but it was quite impossible. The family were going to split, like they never had done before, and there was an excellent chance that Sam and I—their father and brother —might never return home. A last-minute flurry of cables from the girls in New Zealand and the USA, pleaded with Bernard not to let us go. I had replied to both of my daughters, explaining once again that I had to try, but I was sure that my return cable fell on deaf ears. In my heart, I knew Margaret would meet up with us in New Zealand and try to put a stop to what she believed was a childish endeavour. I know she would do anything in her power to stop us from completing our journey. Until then, I would have to put more thought into how I would counter her and be a bit more persuasive with her when we docked in Christchurch.

Tomorrow was a 6 p.m. sailing, so we needed

to be away by 8 a.m. as it was a long trip. With this in mind, I turned to my family.

'It's time for bed I think. A busy day tomorrow.'

I was not looking forward to our separation. I had convinced the family to say all their goodbyes at the manor house. It was a significant effort to move fifteen people from the manor to the station along with all their gear, then again, onto the wharf. If the family had decided to travel down to London with us, it would have been chaotic. Sam and I had already said our farewells to his mate John and to his parents, our forest warden, Toby and his wife Eliza. Also, we said our goodbyes to all the staff. There were a lot of watery eyes, and I would rather that be the case at home, and not on the wharf among strangers. So, with a hug and kiss on the cheek for all the grandchildren, and to Catherine, I turned to my boys. 'I'll see you both in the morning, fellows.'

I left the room and slowly climbed the steps to my bedroom. Was this the last time I would do this? My thoughts were dark, yet I was determined to go through with this plan to find my parents and sister.

A light snow had fallen overnight, and morning arrived dark and cold. I climbed out of bed, and washed and dressed in the room, probably for the last time. I could feel Bella's presence.

No doubt she would be saying, 'Don't be silly, Sammy. Go and do what needs to be done. The children will be fine, they are grown adults. All your life you have been your own man, so this is no different.' I smiled to myself, yes that would be Bella. I dressed and walked downstairs to breakfast. I left my luggage outside my bedroom door. I had decided to only take my pack and a suitcase for on board, as I had wanted to travel as light as possible. I convinced Sam to do the same. If we managed to slip back to my century, our clothes would only be useful to a museum, so they would have to be replaced anyway.

The manor was a madhouse with the Maori guests coming and going with all their luggage, and staff were everywhere, doing their best to assist. It looked like organised chaos. I found the family and our friends at the table for the first meal of the day. I could see that Sam was on edge and my grandchildren were hanging around their uncle like ducklings on a pond. When I sat down with them, the children rushed over to me. They were young, but they sensed something ominous was going to happen. They knew Sam and I were going away, but that was all, and as far as I was concerned, that was all they were going to be told. Later, it would be up to their parents to explain. It was a solemn breakfast, to say the least. Even our guests were hushed.

With breakfast over, our visitors thanked Bernard and Catherine for their kind hospitality. Bernard had done all the work, and it was, as far as I was concerned, his right. From now on, he would be the bloke responsible. I was proud he was such a capable man. They all headed down to the waiting coaches. Our gear was already packed on board for the trip into Brittermore. All that was left to do was to say goodbye. Our Maori friends slowly sorted themselves out as I watched Blanche and Rita step into the first coach followed by Te Ruru, Abe, Henry, and Peri. A couple more jumped up top, and the rest went into the second coach. I yelled for them to be off, that we would meet them all at the station. Toby's wardens had scouted the park and had reported no unforeseen problems, or any strangers lurking.

Sam and I were wrapped up for the cold, and boy it was cold — freezing, in fact. About the only thing I was looking forward to was being out of an English winter. I mentioned to Bernard, 'We will cable the family at every opportunity and keep you all informed.' I noticed Bernard's eyes were moist.

He grabbed and hugged me. 'Just be safe, Father. Just be safe and come back home to us.' He then turned to his brother. 'You have an enormous job, Sam, looking after our father. Keep him out of harm's way, and yourself to, and please return home also. No foolishness. I want you both home after this little adventure. I'm already counting the days.'

We hugged them all. Catherine was openly crying, and the children were now crying because their mother was crying. Sam was visibly upset, and he turned to them looking at the children. 'I'll be off, then; I'll tell you about the big adventure Grandpapa and I had, when we get home.'

He turned and strode quickly down the steps to the waiting coach, jumped aboard, and slammed the door. Catherine threw her arms around my neck, crying into the front of my coat. 'We will always be here for you, Father-in-Law,' she said as she reached up, pulled my head down, and kissed both cheeks, then turned and scooped up the children and rushed back inside.

Bernard grabbed my elbow. 'Go with God, Father.' He turned and followed his wife inside. My chin rested on my chest as I ambled slowly down the steps and climbed aboard the coach, and with a flick of the whip, and a 'gee gee' from the driver, we moved off, and headed towards Brittermore.

We were quiet in the coach, deep in our own thoughts, and I felt like hell. Sam never spoke or looked at me all the way to the railway station, I was aware he was unhappy with me. He was not alone—I was sorry about it all as well. Why the hell was I leaving my family for a dream? There was a significant chance I'd never get back, or end up in some other place and time, but I had to try, this urge in me was so strong.

For thirty years, I never knew who I was, and now I do. It was as simple as that, and it was time to find the lost part of myself, and my family. Stop beating yourself up I kept saying to myself; this is for me. In my mind, I could hear my sister Mary say that you can always go back once you have found us. Yes, I thought, if I can find them. I could find my way back or die trying. It is not the end of the world, I told myself. I needed to keep an open mind. I felt better.

The rest of the group had a pretty good idea how we were feeling and left us alone. I had no misgivings about Blanche as she was tucked in beside Rita and her son, with Abe positioned opposite her. There were no worries on that score, and it left Sam and me to brood with our dark thoughts. The trip down went without a hitch. We both slept until we arrived at London Railway Station at 3 p.m, then we transferred straight onto a coach that delivered us to the ship just after 4 p.m.

We milled around outside the main gates, and smelt the salt air in our nostrils, along with all the fishy smells and coal dust. We could see the SS Rangitoto docked, it looked spick and span. Five hundred and fifteen feet from nose to tail, with a fifty-two-foot beam, draft-wise, I was not sure. She had twenty- four first-class state rooms with their own dining room. She carried four hundred and eighty first-class passengers and seven hundred in steerage. Though on this trip, she was nowhere near full. She was five decks high—a modern ship of the line. The purser collected all-state and first-class passengers together and began to usher us up the gangway into the inner midships.

'Straight through, ladies and gentlemen, please. My assistants will give you your room numbers, and there will be stewards to take you to your rooms. Your baggage will be with you shortly.'

The smell of fresh varnish and new carpets gave the ship that brand-new feel. Everything was spotless and well appointed. I kept my eyes open to see if anyone was taking an unwarranted interest in us. Sure, there were a few, as it was not every day you saw a group of Maori clambering aboard a ship, but nothing or no one stood out, and darkness was closing in. With the English winter and the sun vanishing just after 3:30 p.m., twilight was on us before we knew it. So, to spot Blanche as she boarded would have been impossible, I thought. The trouble was sometimes it didn't matter how smart you were. There were folks out there much more intelligent than you would have thought, and that caused a bit of a problem on the trip south. As I wandered up the gangway to our state rooms, I could see the other walkway with people in second-class steerage boarding. These people where the new immigrants going out to New Zealand—some for Christchurch and others for Auckland. Some were indentured, and others paid their own way. I think the purser said there were only one hundred and eighty of them. There was no way we would be able to mix with them. They had their own deck and promenade plus a dining hall, and the gate between the first and second class, was manned twenty-four hours a day, and was solid steel.

The men and women were then segregated below decks. We mustn't have the lower classes getting above their station, must we? Absolute hooey was my way of thinking, but my mind had now reverted to the twenty-first century way of thinking, not the nineteenth. A bit harsh I thought when I remembered the P&O cruising in my future time and everyone mixing and having a good time. However, it did leave me to believe that we would not have any problems with some of the unsavoury characters from second class, doing their best to harm Blanche. Well, so I thought, it was funny how wrong you could be.

Among our state cabins, there was our group of fifteen and only two other couples, and they looked like they could not fight their way out of a paper bag, so I felt confident that we should have a pleasant trip out. However, we needed to have our wits about us as there were one hundred and fifty passengers in first class.

John Davis sat and stared out of the bay window of the Royal Pier Hotel. He had watched the coaches pull up outside the gates to the wharf, and even though twilight was setting in, he took particular notice of the Maori who were slowly walking up the gangway as they made their way inside the ship. It was hard at this time of the day to pick out faces, though that did not worry him as John knew that Ethan was much closer to the passengers.

He saw an old Maori lady supported by another Maori woman on one side and a tall Maori warrior on the other, walk onto the ship. John thought that the towering Maori might have a tattoo on his face, though at this time of the day with the evening closing in, he could not be sure. He gazed, subconsciously counting them as they disappeared inside the ship. Thirteen, he thought, unlucky for some. How many were there supposed to be in the group—twelve or thirteen? Bugger, who was that? He lent forward to get a better look. He saw the earl and his son. It had to be his son as he looked the same build from this distance. Shit, I would like to fix that bugger, he thought—so close, yet so far. As his mind was taking revenge on the earl, the penny dropped. There were only twelve in the delegation that saw the queen, ten Maori, and two white blokes. Thirteen went on board. The slimy buggers had disguised the woman—it must have been her. He jumped down from the bay window, ran downstairs out the door, and made a beeline for the departure gate. Ethan was nowhere to be seen as he ran up to the gate. John was stopped by the gate official.

'You cannot go any farther, sir, unless you have a ticket for the ship.'

John looked around nervously wondering what to do, when a shadow slid past him. 'Follow me, and don't look around you, numbskull.'

Ethan was ahead of him and slipped into a closed dark alley.

'What the hell are you doing? Ethan spat. 'You are drawing attention to yourself.'

'Yeah. Maybe, you little fat bugger, but I counted thirteen in the Maori group, and there was only supposed to be twelve. What the hell were you doing letting her get past you?'

'What, I was looking for a white woman, not a darkie. Are you sure?'

'Of course, I'm bloody sure. I definitely counted thirteen,' John snapped. 'There were two women walking up that plank.'

Ethan looked at him. 'Right. If you're positive, I'll send the cable and meet you back here, you get our luggage and tickets.'

John turned away with a parting shot, 'Not like

you to get it wrong, you little prick,' he mumbled as he rushed back to the hotel.

He grabbed all their gear, and checked that the tickets were in his pocket, he then raced downstairs with both bags. They had under an hour to get aboard, and they did not want to miss the boat, so to speak. Ethan arrived at the gate at the same time John turned up. 'Got everything?' he asked.

'Yes, here are your bag and ticket.' Passing them over to him, they made their way over to the official at the gate. They handed him the tickets, and the official checked them against his list, then pointed to the second gangway.

'Don't muck around, sirs. The gangway will be closed in thirty minutes.'

The two men walked swiftly to the entrance, once again presented their tickets and were ushered up through the ship's door to the second-class purser. He gave them their room number. Well, it was the only room in steerage and a map of the ship with their cabin marked in red, with the toilet and bathroom in blue. No inside conveniences for them. The times of meals were printed at the bottom of the diagram, the purser mumbled, and left them to find their own way. They found their cabin—steerage one—and by the time they had thrown their bags onto the bed, they could hear the gangway being pulled away from the ship.

Ethan sat on the bed, looking around—two separate single beds, a wardrobe, a mirror, an electric light over each bed, the first he had seen, a jug of fresh water, and a porcelain basin to bathe your face. If you wanted the bathroom you had to walk down the end of the hall. It was not much, but he had lived in worse. On the plus side, there were three meals a day, all the tea they could drink, and they had enough money for ale, not too bad when you thought about it.

He looked up and grinned at John. 'Well, Johnny, old boy, that was the easy part.'

He looked down at the map on his lap and placed his finger on it to show John. 'On this map here, there is a gate between first and steerage class. We will need a plan to get through to first class. We have time on our side to work on that one. Bribery is always an easy way, but a knife in the gut helps also. All we need is the key to unlock the door. A lot of water has to flow under the keel before we reach New Zealand, and quite honestly, I would like to do it as quick as we can, so we can enjoy the rest of the trip.' He frowned, 'We'll think of something,' he declared. 'We always do, and the best thing is, they will not be expecting us at all. In the meantime, we have a few hours to fill in until dinner, so a quick nap is the story, I think. Time to relax and then formulate a plan for the near future,' he said as he lay down with a smug look on his face.

CHAPTER TWENTY-ONE

SS Rangitoto

I walked into our state room, a large well-appointed room. Around the walls were comfortable lounge chairs, and a round coffee table, close to a writing desk. Paintings lined the wall, and there were two large portholes. I noticed they hadn't scrimped on the up to date features like the many electric lights. There was one in the centre of the ceiling and even more around the corners of the room. There was even an electric buzzer if you wanted room service. To top that off the thick carpets were plush. On the left was a separate bedroom, that had two single beds, with bedside tables including lamps, and also a double wardrobe was tucked into the corner. Everything was spick and span with a full-size mirror and complimentary dressing gowns. On through the bedroom was a bathroom with its own shower and bath plus a toilet. I smiled at these modern facilities; it will make our long journey much more pleasant than I expected.

I sent off a cable to Bernard to let the family know that we had arrived safely on board. I had been told by the purser that if I ever wanted a cable sent, there were cable forms to fill out in the desk. If we were at sea, they would send the signal on, either when the boat docks or if they come across another ship expected to arrive at a port quicker. So, we might be able to keep in contact a little more with the family.

Sam sat on the bed and looked around. 'I think this will suffice, Father,' he said with a smug grin. 'Much better than those poor folks in steerage, I should think. Look I'm buggered Dad. If you don't mind, I might just have a quick nap before dinner.' He kicked his shoes off and lay down on the bed. 'Quite comfortable,' he mumbled, 'wake me for dinner,' and promptly dropped off to sleep.

I decided to pop down to see if Rita and Blanche had settled in. I knocked on the door and heard Rita answer. 'Come on in, Sam.' Once again, how did she know it was me, I shrugged my shoulders and entered.

I walked in and announced, 'Just checking, ladies, to see if you are settling in okay, and if you're happy with the accommodation.'

Rita beamed, 'This is kapai, Sam.' She sat in one of the lounge chairs positioned to look out the porthole at the activity on the wharf. 'It is very comfortable thank you, I think we will be happy here for the trip home.'

Blanche smiled at me. 'Sam, I have to pinch myself. I've been expecting a policeman to come and drag me away. I cannot believe this is happening at all. I feel sure I'll wake up at any moment and still be incarcerated in my old room. For me to smell the sea, and to be free, I did not think it was at all possible.' She took my hand. 'Thank you.'

There was a shudder as we all felt the engine gain power, then a slight movement as the ship gently pulled away from the wharf. We were away. We looked out the window and watched as the lights of Gravesend slowly disappeared, as a shower of rain obliterated the town. Then the heavens opened up, and all we could see was our own reflection in the porthole. By morning, we would be well out into the English Channel, and plough down the French coast at fifteen knots.

'Will I ever see England again?' muttered Blanche, mainly to herself.

Rita heard her. 'No, Blanche, you will never come back in this time. Your destiny is to live your life in New Zealand, free, but in a way, that you have no concept about it as yet. You will be happy though, and that is the main thing.'

I looked at Rita. There she goes again being mysterious, but I let it go. I had come to the conclusion that delving too deep into what Rita said could leave you with lots of question marks. Just let things pan out, I thought. I looked down at Blanche, and she was still holding my hand; she realised it as well. 'Oh, sorry, Sam. That is so forward of me and I do apologise.'

'No worries, Blanche. It's marvellous to know we are friends, and you feel as though you can do that. With no one in your life, I'm sure this is all new for you. It must be good to have friends again after such a long time, and now, at least, you can count all of us in the party as mates. So, if you need to hold hands, I'm sure any one of us will not mind.' Rita looked up at me pointedly and gave her little smile. What the hell is she thinking now, I thought to myself. 'I think,' I said, changing the subject, 'for a start, we need to keep an eye posted on your room to watch for any unsavoury characters that might take a particular interest in you. I'll work it out with the boys. If, after a couple of days, no one is interested, we can just make sure that your door is kept locked at all times. One good thing Te Ruru and Peri are just next door to you.'

As it turned out, everything was as it should be, and we all settled down to on-board life. Whenever Blanche went for a walk or to a meal, there were always a couple of people with her, we didn't take any chances.

From the cold days of the English winter, the weather started to change to the warm, balmy days of the Mediterranean. Eight days into the on-board routine, and the only incident we heard of, was that the gatekeeper in steerage had lost his keys, but they were found twenty-four hours later, not far from where the guard had been sitting. We didn't think of it as a concern for us. I wish we had, but it seemed so insignificant at the time. It was around this period that the purser told us that we would be docking at Port Said before going through the Suez Canal. The captain wanted to top-up with coal even though he had enough for the trip south. He was a cautious man.

'So, we will bunker there, and it will give you a day to explore the port. I expect the ladies will enjoy it as there are a lot of markets to browse,' he informed us. 'No steerage passengers will be alighting,' he went on to say. 'Only first class.'

What a lot of rubbish, I thought. They treated these people like criminals. This class system really got on my nerves. All my life I had tried to make   it easier for the people who worked for me, but it was hard to break through the barriers as it was so ingrained in every one's beliefs.

I found it hard to accept, that in Egypt we were still on home soil and under English law, as still it was an English protectorate. So, to my way of thinking, there could be folk out here who might know about Blanche. We would have to be on our toes.

Once we had docked in the industrial part of the port, I made a decision that there should be at least four of us to escort Blanche at all times.

Henry as a Wesley minister was intrigued about the mosques and with Hemi, who was a lay preacher, they decided to check out what they called the competition. The others didn't want to wander round, so the escort job turned out to be Sam, Abe, Peri, and me.

We did not have to wait for transport as we expected, as the touts all come out of the woodwork and their donkey carts stood in line, while their Arab owners screamed out their fares. In the end, the five of us clambered on one for three Egyptian shillings for the whole day. As we looked around, we noticed unsavoury stuff floated on the surface of the water, and we could smell the unpleasant mixture of coal dust, donkey poo, and dried kelp. It all penetrated our senses as we drove out of the wharf area towards the main bazaar. I looked back, and could see tiny boats, like bees around a honeypot, had surrounded the ship. Vendors shouted up to the confined steerage passengers, tempting them with their wares. It looked chaotic as they manoeuvred themselves as close as they could, pushing and shoving each other out of the way.

Farther out towards the dock entrance, stood the Port Said lighthouse, the first building in the world to be built with reinforced concrete, and it was impressive even from a distance. I read somewhere years ago that it was fifty-six meters high. I hoped I would have a chance to have a look at the building, that is if we had time on the way back. We had to be back on board by 5 p.m. We waved goodbye to Henry and Hemi, as we took a left turn out the gate, and they continued straight ahead in their own cart. We settled back with a cloth over our mouths, as it was a dusty ride to town.

Ethan had used his time diligently; he had gone over every inch of the map he had been given and had noticed a small security lapse where he thought he could move unseen from steerage to first class. In the meantime, John Davis started up a friendship with the guard on the gate between first class and steerage. Casually, he would turn up and offer him a ciggy and chat about football and why he was going out to New Zealand. Slowly the guard got used to him being around, and soon he opened the gate so John could come and sit with him to play checkers. They spent hours together.

Their opportunity came when the guard, Able Seaman Roger Sawell, took short. He hunched over holding his stomach, 'Can you look after the gate, mate?' he said. 'I need the heads.' He took off like a scalded cat. John had observed before where the keys were, and grabbed them, then passed them to Ethan, who had arrived with his large bar of soap. But there were too many passengers around, so Ethan had to return to his cabin, where he pressed the key into the soap to imprint the exact outline.

When Roger returned, John inquired about his health, then excused himself as he shuffled to his side of the gate. The absence of the keys was not noticed until the guard change. They looked high and low and could not find them. Roger was taken off guard duty and stuck on latrine chores. John worried about how to return the keys back to the other side, now they had no use for them, without anyone knowing. As luck would happen, a passenger, a single girl in steerage took sick, and the doctor on board asked for the woman to be brought through to his surgery. Ethan had heard this and offered to help. A matron accompanied her, and Ethan was there for his stocky strength, since they were both of the weaker sex, as the girl may faint or suffer some other female problem on the way. Most males thought women were prone to do this fainting thing at the drop of a hat. So, the gate was opened with, of course, the spare keys from the captain's quarters, and the three went straight through to the doctor's dispensary. On their return journey, Ethan deliberately tripped not far from the gate, he fell onto the matron, who supported the girl. Everyone went down in a heap. The guard ran up to assist. 'Oh dear, are you all right miss, missus?'

As they pulled themselves up, Ethan quickly slipped the missing keys behind a locker not far from the gate. He apologised to everyone. 'It was so silly of me; I was keeping an eye on the lass here and not watching where I was walking. Are you all right, miss?'

'Thank you, sir. Yes, I'm fine.'

'And you, madam?' he asked the older woman. 'Yes, I'm fine, but you need to be more careful. You could have done yourself and us an injury.'

'I will certainly do that next time, but as long as you are all right, that is the main thing.' He thanked the guard and helped the two women towards the door of the women's quarters then rushed back to his cabin.

'Did everything go to plan, Ethan?' John asked.

'Yes, the keys will be found, and they will put it down to either falling out of the guard's pocket or off the ring. I have started on the wooden duplicate, it is only to be used once or twice at the most, so it will be good enough. I have done this before, and it will work. A bit of fat in the lock when we're ready, to make it turn easy will be all that is required. Right, John. I have also found another way to get out of here into first class. Though it can only be used sparingly. There are two doors at the back of the kitchen so the stewards can connect between decks. Even though first and state decks have their own kitchen, some of the stewards still have to carry food between these decks.

So, my friend, when we dock, I want you to cause some minor disruption in the kitchen to give me enough time to slip through the door. I have stolen a steward's coat and should, with luck, be able to use the same door to get back here. A market is a good place for me to do my work. I'll bet you your last penny that they will go there, and if so, I will follow them. I'll steal some Arab clothing to blend in. With me at the market mingling among the crowd, they will not see me, or suspect. I'll just be another bloody Arab. If this doesn't work, then it is onto Plan B. On the next moonless night, you will use the key to go through the gate, and I'll go the kitchen way again, then we will pop up onto the top deck. I have been talking to a steward who says the toffs and the Maori all like to take a turn out on deck before turning in, so that's our second plan. Okay, my friend, let's prepare now to make our thousand quid.'

CHAPTER TWENTY-TWO

Port Said

When the ship had docked, a large crowd of second-class passengers came out on the deck to look over the port and to strike up a deal with the boat vendors. The frenzy of the rowdy crowd was distracting, which made it the ideal conditions for Ethan and John. So, they snuck into the busy main dining hall. As Ethan headed towards the kitchen door, he noticed stacks of plates by the buffet, he said over his shoulder, 'Make as much noise and mess as possible to distract the buggers.'

John picked up a dozen plates and moved down towards the galley area when he staggered. His plates were thrown forward over the serving staff, as he fell against the counter. Plates rolled and smashed to bits over the food in the servery, and John howled as though he had been hurt. The chefs came running out of the kitchen, some through the door that Ethan was standing by. As they did, Ethan quickly moved through into the kitchen. He shrugged on the stolen steward's jacket, over his walking-out clothes, as he walked on with intent. He grabbed a plate with a silver cover on it and moved toward the rear door of the kitchen, which was opened by a steward who had just returned from first class. The steward stood back and held the door open for Ethan.

'You'd better get in there,' Ethan explained with a flick of his head. 'Someone has fallen over; it's a bloody mess.'

Ethan then shot up three floors, coming out into the first-class kitchen. From here you could look over the lavish dining room. Ethan with the confidence of a person who was at ease in his duties, walked straight into the dining room, and placed his dish on a vacant table. Behind cover he slipped out of the steward's jacket and shoved it behind a large flower arrangement attached to the wall, then headed towards the ship's departure exit. The purser was distracted, reading his clipboard. 'Morning,' Ethan said as he walked past.

'Have a nice day, sir,' the purser replied, without looking up. He stepped out onto the gangplank and headed down to the swarms of Arabs waving and gesturing at him to take their cart.

First thing's first, he thought as he watched the earl's donkey cart head off towards the market. Seated in the middle amongst the men, he studied the woman they were after. Cunning buggers, you have to admit that, it was a good disguise. Just as he was about to choose on his own donkey cart, a poxy-faced young man and a tall, thin man approached him. The tall man asked. 'Are you Ethan?'

Ethan's hand flicked, and a knife appeared from the pouch of his inner arm sleeve. He crouched ready to pounce. 'What if I am?' he snarled. 'What's it to you?'

'Don't worry, friend. Put that knife away,' the man said as he stepped backwards out of range of the weapon. He looked around quickly. 'Careful you will draw attention to us. We have a mutual acquaintance—Sir Anthony. He cabled us to catch up with you if the ship docked here. He gave us your description, and we have been watching the ship since the first passengers disembarked. We are your backup. We were wondering how you would get ashore, as steerage never are allowed to get off here. But if you work for Sir Anthony, you would be a resourceful cove, and so here you are.' He looked up towards the ship. 'Is she still on board?'

You didn't last long in his business unless you were careful, especially if you worked for Sir Anthony, so Ethan was cautious. 'I don't take things at face value' he said with suspicion, 'what does he look like?'

'Well, it's been a while,' the tall bloke said thoughtfully. 'He was tallish with pointed features and narrowed grey eyes with no emotion in them. A scary cove, he would cut you down without even a blink.'

'Yeah, that's him all right.' Ethan slipped his knife away. 'So, what are your names? You know mine.'

The tall one replied, 'I'm Jonna, and my partner with the scared face is Paul. We are here for support. We have heard you were good with a knife, and I can see now, how quick you are,' he said with admiration. 'So, is she nearby?'

'Yes, she just left on that last cart,' Ethan informed them.

Paul said, as he shook his head, 'We saw no white woman.'

'No, she is disguised as a Maori woman.'

'The cunning bastards,' Paul remarked. 'I saw a brown woman climb on board the cart and didn't take a second glance. She had a tattoo on her chin. Some of the women down south at the beginning of the Nile have the same markings. Well, Ethan, now we know. We had better get a move on; the market will be crowded. We have arranged to pick up our Arab disguise at a small house on the way. It's important to blend in as much as possible, for the love of God, we have to do the job properly. If we get caught, they will hang you, or stick you away in an Arab prison for a long time. Us whites don't last very long in their prisons.'

They clambered on board a cart, and with a

flick of the whip, the donkey slowly walked towards the town. It was only a ten-minute drive to the house, and they pulled up in a back alley behind it. It was an uncared for hovel, small, whitewashed, and broken- down. As they entered the door, the smell of decay hit Ethan. With faeces on the floor mixed with bird droppings, the place stank. Ethan took a deep breath. On the table were three sets of Arab garments that were loose fitting and not that clean, still they went with the general smell of the house, if you could call that smell a name—it was stink. There were also three flat top skullcaps for their heads. They quickly slipped them over their ordinary clothes. With a bit of mud rubbed on the face gave them a rough, unclean look and moreover took away the whiteness of Ethan's skin.

Jonna grinned. 'You'll do. At a glance, you will blend in. From here it is only another ten-minute drive. We should be able to spot them quickly enough, as two of the men with the woman are tall.'

'After you have done the job, we are going to cause a lot of noise by shooting that large, grey-headed cove. He is our target. Yours, of course, is the woman, but if things go belly up, we will lend a hand. With us making a lot of noise, it will give you a good chance to hightail it back to the ship, in the confusion. I'll send the cable to Sir Anthony once the job is done. I know the code

"Sunshine." Are you satisfied with this, Ethan?' The locals tapped their pockets to check their weapons. Each had a revolver with a six-shot barrel. 'A few extra rounds never go amiss.' Jonna laughed.

'Yes, that's fine, as long as I can get in close as she has four men with her.'

'Don't you worry. We will take care of them, and let's face it, all except one, are all old sods, so it will be easy to do our job. You mark my words.'

Ethan gulped. 'This place is starting to make me feel sick. I need some fresh air away from this stink. Let's go, then, I would like to be back on board for lunch if I can hold it down after this muck.'

They climbed onto the cart once more, pulled out from behind the building, and continued down the dusty road to pass camels, goats and the occasional cow. They approached the first stalls, and the crowds were light, but as they went farther into the bazaar itself, the street closed in, with alleyways off to the left and right, and Ethan realised this was not going to be so easy after all. Everywhere he looked there were hundreds of people all calling out in different languages. Vendors sold products from clothing to fowl and he thought the smell of the place was disturbing, to say the least. It could have been even worse than the hovel he had collected his clothes from. Jonna looked at him sensing his unease. 'You will get used to the smell and the crowds after a while,' he smirked at his discomfort.

The cooking fires of camel dung, poop on the road, and beggars in filthy clothes, holding out their skeleton hands asking for alms, made Ethan pull back. 'Bugger, this is even worse than I thought,' he remarked to no one in particular.

Jonna leant forward, tapped the driver on the shoulder and ordered him to stop. 'We will walk from here; it will be easier than the cart.' He tossed the driver some coins as they jumped off.

While shouldering bodies away from themselves to clear some breathing room, Ethan placed his foot into some fresh cow dung that just happened to be deposited from the cow in front heading down to the slaughter pit. 'Shit on a blanket,' he growled, while up to his ankle in the stuff.

'You'll get used to it. This is a good day, when they drive the whole herd through, you are swimming in the dung,' Paul sneered.

They moved off as Jonna bellowed at the bodies in front, in the language of the people, to clear out of the way. Ethan couldn't help but be impressed by Jonna's fluency in their language. Then he stopped at an old beggar and asked if he had seen a few large European men. The elderly man pointed down an alleyway crowded with people. Jonna tossed him a coin, and the three villains headed towards the alley, searching faces as they passed. Eventually, they came out onto a small square with a water pump in the middle, and brightly coloured canvas awnings covering the stalls around the edge. A water boy shimmied up to them and asked if they would like to drink, offering them a tin cup. Ethan paid his two millime to the boy and looked around.

'Well, they are not here. We are not making any progress at all, it's already taken us an hour,' Ethan moaned.

Paul whispered, 'Steady on, matey. This is one of the central squares; it's small but most people find their way to it as the food is edible even for us whites, and the locals do congregate here.'

He pointed. 'Look, now there is a money changer over on the left who's fair, by Egyptian standards, and when there's an honest money changer, people flock to them.' He smirked. 'Have a bit of faith. We know this area well; have another cup of water.' Ethan didn't like being told what, or when, to do something. He was always a loner. Ethan liked his jobs like that, and quite honestly, he would have preferred not to be with John Davis either, and now here he was reliant on more outsiders. This was not to his liking, not at all.

He grabbed another cup from the water boy, drank, tossed his money into the cup, and settled down to wait. The other two moved away to keep an eye on the entrances to the square. Five alleyways, like the spokes of a wheel, lead to this area.

Ethan stood under a canvas roof trying to ignore the bartering and the noise, shooing away everyone with a wave of his arm as his mood became black. Another hour slipped by. Bugger this, he thought, we are not making any progress. They must have gone elsewhere. Then he caught sight of the earl as the group came into the square. Being short, he had to move to make sure. Yes, it was them, and the woman in question was still in the middle of the four men for protection. Ethan, slowly, little by little, slipped into the shadows and started to follow the group. He was entirely focused on what he was going to do. He watched the five of them pause at a stall, then luck happened to come his way as the four men separated a little from the woman as she stopped to browse through some materials.

Ethan surveyed the group as she fingered the cloth. The seller said, 'An excellent fabric for a lovely lady.' Ethan could hear her speak with an English accent and knew he had the right woman. He moved up to the stall and started to run his hands over the cloth as he inched closer. She turned and stepped up to the next vendor, who sold fruit.

She picked up an orange and gave it a gentle

squeeze, and he heard the seller say in broken English, 'Freshly picked today.' The white bloke —it had to be one of the colonials—was at her back looking over her shoulder, but not that close, as his body was not touching hers. Ethan made a decision; this was the time to strike. With a slight twist of his hand, the knife that was sitting in his arm pouch slipped neatly into his palm.

The blade glinted in the sun, and all Ethan's focus was on the killing stab. He brought his arm up in an uppercut when a voice exclaimed from behind, 'He has a knife, Blanche.'

In that split second, the white colonial appeared where the woman had stood. Ethan plunged the knife into him just as he saw the man push the woman as hard as he could into the fruit cart.

Ethan pulled out his knife and stabbed again, but the bloke had moved ever so slightly, and the knife entered under the arm. He heard him grunt, and then the injured bloke brought down an elbow to hit Ethan hard on the bridge of his nose. So hard, in fact, that he thought he heard the cartilage crack. His eyes started to fill with water and blood poured from his nose. The fruit cart crumbled, and fruit rolled over the road. Ethan with the fruit moving under his feet slipped, and his shoes still covered in cow dung gave him no traction. He had to wave his arms like a windmill to retain his balance. The white man had fallen hard against the woman who had collapsed into the vendor, and everyone fell into a heap.

Ethan was shocked. This had never happened to him before, and his mind was in turmoil as he looked for an out. He raced off up the nearest alley. He was unsure if the earl had seen him, but at this point, self-preservation took priority. He pushed and shoved past the locals, then he heard shooting. The crowd turned away in panic and starting to run from the commotion, so it became easier for Ethan to follow the throng, and to flee from the scene as fast as he could. He had no idea where he was going and heard more shots as he broke out onto the main road. Luckily there were plenty of donkey carts waiting for custom, so he jumped aboard one and bawled, 'To the ship wharf. Do you understand?'

The owner nodded, cracked the whip, and they were away. Ethan was a mess as the front of his clothes were soaked in blood. He ripped off his Arab disguise and wiped his face. Then tore at the fabric and chucked the bloodied clothing over the side of the cart. He rummaged through his pockets and found some Arab notes, so when they got to the ship, he could just jump off and slip aboard. He then settled himself and pinched his nose, held his head back and hoped that the bleeding would stop by the time he reached the boat. He was lucky there was not much blood on his English clothes.

The wharf was quiet when Ethan arrived. Most first-class passengers had either disembarked or had found other things to do on board. He jumped down and handed the notes to the cart owner who accepted them with glee. He had been paid three months' wages for that trip. With his head lowered, Ethan walked quickly towards the gangway. The guard's attention was caught, as he rushed to the entrance, but Ethan didn't stop. 'I've had an accident, my good fellow. I must get aboard and get it seen to.'

As Ethan had looked and spoken like a middle-class passenger, the guard didn't even suspect he was from steerage. He thought, what a god-send, as he belted up the gangway with no pursuer in sight and headed for the dining room. He stopped at the flower arrangement, removed the steward's jacket, and slipped it on as he walked towards the kitchen. Then with a quick look around, he let himself in through the kitchen door of first class. The kitchen was busy as they prepared lunch, so no one took any notice. He picked up a plate, with head down, he left through the rear door, he moved briskly with purpose as he descended to the steerage kitchen.

When he reached the steerage dining hall, he entered the men's convenience. There he ducked into a shower booth, stripped off, and washed himself down, getting rid of the dirt, grime, cow dung from his feet, and the blood from his nose. After thirty minutes, his nose had stopped bleeding, but it was left swollen, and his eyes had started to blacken. Now he had to breathe through his mouth, and this was causing him distress. He dressed just in his trousers and shirt, peeked outside the door, saw no one in the vicinity, and made a beeline for his cabin. God, how lucky are we to have a cabin, he thought. I can hide in here until the bruising has gone down. He opened the door. John Davis was lying on his bed and looked up.

'Bugger me,' he said as Ethan came in. 'You look like hell.'

'Yes, I am. The bloody job backfired. I got an elbow to the face, and I stabbed the wrong person. That white colonial bugger stepped into the space of that darn woman, and I jabbed him instead. I had her lined up to, but he did me an injustice, so I stuck him twice for the inconvenience, but he still managed to do this to my face. I've never fouled up before—never. Piss on them all,' he spat. 'So, Davis, I'm not sure if anyone saw me, but I will have to assume they might have. I will have to remain incognito until things quieten down, and it looks like I'll only be able to move around at night for the foreseeable future.'

CHAPTER TWENTY-THREE

Port Said

The smell of burning camel dung filled our senses with a pungent odour and made our eyes water. The four of us endeavored to push past people to view the goods for sale and were nudged a little apart. We drifted over to the fruit stall that was right next to a hot-food vendor. If you took a deep breath and forgot it was dung burning, the food didn't look too bad. Blanche had moved from the materials vendor and was at the fruit stall squeezing the oranges when the seller waved his arms, and in broken English claimed, 'Splendid. Very fresh, madam. All picked today.'

Abe hovered behind her at the fruit stall and we all completely ignored a short, rotund Arab who stood, and gazed at the fruit next to her. I was nearby at the hot food stall with Sam and sampled the vendor's wares. Peri hung to the rear a bit, a stall that had knives on display had caught his eye. But with him being back a couple of paces, he noticed something out of place. Out of the corner of his eye he caught a glint of steel appear right next to Blanche. The fat man had pulled out a knife. Peri screamed, 'He has a knife, Blanche.'

She turned sharply towards Peri's voice, only to have Abe step into her space and shove her with some force towards the vendor's cart just as the assailant swept his knife up in an under-hand swinging motion. The knife caught Abe in his armpit and was thrust yet again. Before he could think, Abe quickly jabbed his elbow into the attacker's face, it connected with the bridge of his nose, which surely would have brought tears to his eyes. Then blood flowed from Abe's upper body as he moaned and staggered into Blanche, who then fell face first onto the fruit vendor's cart, spilling the fruit all over the walk-way.

The seller tried to prevent his stall from top-pling, but with the combined force of Blanche and Abe's weight falling on top of it, the barrow crashed over onto the vendor. The canvas roof collapsed on top of the lot of them and hid them from the street. The wee fat man skidded on the oranges lying all over the ground and nearly lost his balance, but managed to wave his arms in the air to prevent himself from falling. With a look of panic on his face, he took off like a scalded cat into the fast diminishing crowd.

Only seconds had passed, and even though he

was dressed in Arab clothing, I saw he was European. I swung around to the sound of a handgun go off and saw a poxy-faced short man, in Arab apparel, practicality empty his weapon into what was left of the fruit cart, and the canvas with the hope of hitting someone underneath.

I prepared to run at him when my son Sam beat me to it. With his head down he charged into him headfirst. By now the bloke was nearly out of ammo, and used his last bullet on Sam. I saw Sam check for a second, then blood appeared at the top of his arm just as his head slammed into the bloke's stomach. As he a big man, Sam's weight, threw the second assailant hard against the hot food stall.

The booth collapsed and burning camel dung from the cooking fire covered the second assailant, and his hair caught fire. He dropped his gun on the path, and screamed in pain, his arms furiously rubbing the hair on his head, as he attempted to put the fire out. I grabbed a bubbling frying pan with both hands, it was still full of hot sticky goat stew. Then whacked him full in the face as hard as I could with it. He screamed even louder, moaned a bit, then screamed once again as the hot stew peeled away the skin on his face. With a bit of effort Sam, scooped up his gun with his good hand, when there was another shot from out of sight. The burning assassin stopped screaming and dropped stone dead with a hole in his forehead; his mate had killed him.

Sam and I both turned and dived for the dirt road and the cover of the materials cart as another shot came between us. Up until then, only about thirty seconds had gone by, but it felt like hours. Sam was wounded; Abe was also down. I could not see Blanche—and where was Peri, I thought.

I spotted the third assailant; he had his gun lined up on us ready to take another shot as we were attempting to roll under any sort of cover we could find. That's when we heard this Maori challenge being called out from behind the man with the gun. I looked up to see Peri, who had broken off part of a fallen stall to give himself a weapon. It was a bamboo pole, and he was using it like a Taiaha "a traditional weapon". He waved it around the top of his head then in front of his body, jumping forward then back, while the pole moved in very fast circles. The tall assailant was hesitant and unsure what he was confronted with. I could see him frown, another European dressed as an Arab, I noted.

The attacker lifted his gun as Peri stepped one foot forward. I suppose it was the constant motion of the pole that took away the concentration of the assailant, who seemed to be mesmerised by it. The tall bloke hesitated before bringing his gun to bear on Peri who, with all his strength, brought the pole down onto the assailant's wrist. We heard the bone snap with an almighty crack from where we lay. The attacker shrieked in pain, dropped his gun, and brought his broken wrist up tight against his chest. Then Peri quick as a wink, flicked the pole like a lance and jabbed the staff against the aggressor's throat with so much force that I think he broke the bloke's windpipe.

Blood gurgled out of the tall man's throat and he lost control of his equilibrium. With blood all over him he tried to regain his balance, then Peri hit him again in the stomach. The assailant began to topple forward, and in that split second, Peri smoothly dropped the pole and pulled out his putu "a stone weapon" from the waist of his pants. As the head of the assailant passed within reach of Peri, he swung his putu into the attacker's skull. The loud crack of stone on his head, vibrated off the walls of the square and then came a sound like a dozen broken eggs. The bloke hit the ground dead as a dodo, with grey matter spilling onto the road. It went deathly quiet, and you could hear a pin drop, then we all seemed to gravitate into action.

'Are you okay, Sam? I saw you were hit, son' I asked him in a worried voice.

'I think I'll be as right as rain, Father. It went straight through the meaty part of my arm. I'm all right. Well, let's hope I am. It's Abe who I think is in a bad way.'

I helped my son up as Peri came running over. He wiped his putu on the dead man's clothes. 'I never thought I would ever use this again in battle,' he proclaimed with fire in his eyes. 'We must see to Abe,' he stressed as he swiftly moved past us, and called out Abe's and Blanche's names.

Sam's arm had started to stiffen up, as I rushed after Peri to assist. We pulled back the canvas roof, and we saw Blanche covered in blood, busy doing all she could to stop the flow of blood that oozed from Abe's arm. We watched as she stuffed her petticoat into the wound.

'Are you okay, Blanche?' I asked.

'Yes, I'm fine,' she whispered, although Abe was completely out of it and unaware. 'This brave man took that knife intended for me. We need to get him back to the ship's surgeon.'

Peri took one look at Abe and said, 'We need a cart.' And he rushed off to find a couple of donkey carts for us all. I stayed to aid Blanche as best I could. I noticed the stall holder lay still, on our right, he had been away from the protection of his cart and looked to have been shot three times. The poor bugger, I thought, caught up in a conflict not of his doing. Two men were killed for the deed, but that is not compensation for this man's wife and family. Blanche had wrapped Abe around his chest and under his arms. When Peri returned with a couple of carts and drivers, I covered Abe with a piece of canvas roof, then gently lifted, and carried him out from behind the cart. I was distraught as he hadn't regained consciousness, and I placed Abe gently on the floor at the back.

'You go with the cart, Sam. The surgeon needs to look at your arm as well—you also, Peri. Blanche and I will take the other cart and follow you. Have you checked that gun?'

'Yes, but there are no bullets left, however the tall man, who Peri finished off, had a couple in his coat pocket.'

'Take that gun, and we will share the rounds just in case. We will be just behind you.'

Peri searched through the clothes of the dead blokes and found another half a dozen bullets underneath the dead man, that Sam had missed, but nothing else—no documents or identification. They were definitely European.

As we settled the two wounded men in the first cart, it was about to leave, when Peri climbed aboard as their bodyguard. The road was clear, and the market completely empty, though I saw eyes staring out from behind doors and windows. Then we heard running feet, and up the road came six men of the Egyptian constabulary. The officer was an English captain. All had their guns at the port position, presented at an angle across their chests, and would be ready to fire in a split second.

'What in the blue blazes is going on here?'

yelled the captain as the group performed a half-circle manoeuvre to surround us and came to a halt, only a few steps away from the five of us.

The officer stepped one pace forward with his hand on his revolver. 'You lot have a bit of explaining to do.' We must have looked a mess, with Blanche covered in blood and her petticoats ripped to buggery. Sam and I, after rolling around in the dirt, were covered in food, blood, and a mixture of cow and goat dung. Abe was wrapped up like a mummy, and Peri, on the other hand, looked quite the gentleman as he hadn't even worked up a sweat. What took the captain's interest was Abe and Sam, wounded on the back of the cart, and of course, the bodies on the street.

The captain eyed the mess in the street and the two dead men. He hadn't seen the stall owner as of yet, or the food and fruit all over the pathway. 'What's your story? Who killed these people?'

'We did,' I ventured.

'Well, you'd better come with me,' he ordered.

'Before we do, Captain, can I ask you to release these wounded men? The one lying down is in grave danger. We need to get him to the surgeon on the ship. Then I think you might like to hear our story.'

The captain went over and looked at the men. 'Right. This man looks seriously injured.' He spoke in Arabic to his sergeant, who jumped aboard Sam's cart. They took off at a fast pace.

'My sergeant will get their statements while travelling to the ship, he speaks English as well as we do,' the captain assured.

'Right, sir.' he turned to me, 'Now what has happened here?' he demanded.

'We are off the ship, The SS Rangitoto,' I explained. 'it is moored at the bunkering wharf. We only came into the market to stretch our legs, and we were attacked by these two men—and a third one escaped. These men attacked and wounded my friend with a knife and and shot my son. They were the injured you just released to the ship's surgeon. Peri, the Maori man, who went with the cart and this lady here, Moana, are from New Zealand, they helped save our lives.

'Furthermore,' I pointed out, 'that bloke over there killed the stall holder, we covered him with canvas. We don't know why this unprovoked attack happened, but all we did was protect ourselves. This man here,' I said, pointing to the one who I had hit with the frying pan, 'was killed by his friend over there,' pointing at the tall bloke with his brain leaking out onto the road, 'to stop him talking, no doubt. Notice they are both Europeans dressed as Arabs.'

The captain frowned; I could see he was thinking. This could go on for a while, I thought, and if we were to get away from here, I was going to need to tell him who I was. Otherwise there was a chance, we could end up remaining for a long holiday, and I couldn't afford to be stuck here in Port Said for weeks. I've never done this before in my life, but I was going to have to pull my title.

'Captain can I talk to you privately?' I asked as I took him aside. 'Sir, can I trust you to keep a secret?'

He looked at me. 'What are you trying to say?'

'Look Captain, I am the Earl of Shadymore, Sir Samuel Selkirk, I am here on a special mission for the Prince of Wales.' He looked pulled back with a start and studied me with a frown upon his face.

He looked at me closely, then took a step back. 'Oh God, you are him? I saw your photo years ago. My father kept it from the time you were knighted when you saved the queen's life. So sorry, sir. You go about your business. I'll sort all this out.'

'Captain, you don't know how much I appreciate this. There is one thing though. That poor bloody vendor's family will suffer because of what those men did.' I pulled some notes out of my pocket. 'If you can find his family, please give them this money. It doesn't compensate losing a loved one, but it will help them get by.' He looked at the notes.

'Bloody hell. Oh, sorry sir. But that will be a year's wages for them.'

'That's good, it is going to a good cause.' 'I'll see to it, sir. You can count on it.'

'These dead men, I think they thought we had money and were fair game, so I have come to the conclusion that it is a robbery gone wrong. However, Captain, no one must know that I was here. If you can keep that quiet, I will write a letter to the prince praising your effort on our behalf.'

'You don't need to do that, sir,' he said with embarrassment.

'I must. It is the right thing to do, what is your name Captain?'

'My name sir, is William Ross of Bedfordshire, now captain of the Egyptian constabulary.'

'Thanks, William. You will not regret this. I promise you.'

'Don't worry, your Lordship. I'll compose my report to show some unknown assailants killed a shop vendor and were killed by the mob. That is an everyday occurrence here.'

By this time, the driver of our donkey cart was getting a bit edgy. He wasn't comfortable with the dead bodies lying nearby. You could see the relief on his face when the captain whistled to catch his attention, and he moved the wagon up to us. In fluent Arabic, the officer told the driver to take us back to the ship.

We climbed aboard, and with a wave, he turned to his troops, and in both English and

Arabic the captain ordered, 'Let's get this mess cleaned up.'

The driver flicked the whip near the flanks of the donkey. He wanted to be as far away, and as quickly as possible, from the market. He turned, and we headed back to the ship. With all the excitement over, the reality and shock of what had happened settling in, and Blanche started to cry. I put my arm around her, and she cried into my coat. 'Oh Sam,' she blubbered, 'it is my fault that Abe and your son are hurt. It's all my fault.'

'Blanche, the only fault lies with those men who tried to harm you and the people who sent them. It has nothing to do with you. We must be more vigilant in the future. Otherwise, we may not be so lucky.'

'You were cautious, Sam,' she cried.

'That might be right, Blanche, but we should not have let them get so close.'

Blanche wasn't convinced and was still sobbing softly as we climbed the gangway onto the ship. Once I had delivered Blanche to her cabin I went straight down to catch up with my boy and Abe in the dispensary.

The surgeon's assistant attended to Sam as I walked into the surgery. 'I was lucky, Dad.' Sam grinned with a look of relief on his face when he saw me. 'The bullet went right through the upper arm, missing the artery.'

The assistant spoke to Sam, 'Mr. Selkirk, I'll give you a sling, keep your arm as immobile as possible, and we will look at it again later. You will be stiff and sore mind. But we hope your arm will be almost healed by the time we reach New Zealand.

Ah bugger that, I thought, he'll need a bit of physiotherapy before then. Abe was another kettle of fish. The knife had punctured a lung, and the surgeon had him on the operating table. The knife had also done a bit of damage to the chest wall, he was lucky to be alive. He would be incapacitated for the whole journey and most likely for at least six months after arriving home. He was a brave bloke taking that knife wound for Blanche, and I was going to make sure that he would not suffer financially for his effort.

Sam hopped down from the table with his arm in a sling.

'You will need these pills for the discomfort,' the assistant surgeon prescribed. 'They will help with the pain, and right now I believe you should go and rest. The shock will catch up with you, and your body will do better if you can get your head down. You will be sore for a while, but overall, you will be capital. Now, if you'll excuse me, I'll pop into the surgery. The doctor will need a hand with Mr. Metcalfe. I'll let you know when he is out of surgery and in recovery.'

Sam and I thanked him and went back to our cabin. Only two hours had passed since we had left it, but it felt like a full day, and I was shagged. My age was catching up with me. I helped Sam get out of his clothes, have a good wash, then get dressed again in fresh, clean clothes. I replaced the sling. 'Thanks, Dad.' He yawned as he lay down on the bed and instantly fell asleep.

I had tears in my eyes, to think I could have lost my son, all for this drive to find my other family. I started to have doubts that this idea of mine was a good one. After berating myself, I showered, changed my clothes, and lay on my bed for a kip.

I woke to Sam sitting at the edge of his bed with a glass of whisky in his hand. 'Well, this works,' he said through a grin. 'It takes the edge off the pain. Now, Father, before you go beating yourself up about what happened to me, remember I'm an adult. I make my own decisions. I decided to come out with you, so do not think you have to put a halt to what you are doing. We will continue on with this journey until it comes to its climax. If we find that mist, go through it and find your parents, excellent. If not, we go home. There is one thing, though, you are the only one who knows why Blanche has to be protected. Don't you think you should share that information?' He looked at me intently.

'No son,' I said. 'It's not that I don't want to.

It's if you know, then these bastards might turn on you. They shot at us today because we were in their road. If Blanche were killed, this would stop, and if they thought for one minute that you and the rest of our folk knew, they would try to exterminate the lot of us. I believe once Blanche is disposed of, they will have a go at me as I know the full story. After saying that, they also are quite aware I will not spill the beans to anyone. So for your protection, I will not share any information. You are here only to help me get Blanche set up in New Zealand, away from prying eyes.'

Sam looked at me. 'It is a dangerous situation, Father. If anything happens to you, I can tell you, I won't stop until I find the people who created this dilemma and stop them dead, and that, sir, will be the end of it.'

I had never heard Sam speak this way in my life. The way he said those words scared the hell out of me. In the future, if anything happened to me, it would be on the heads of those criminals.

CHAPTER TWENTY-FOUR

SS Rangitoto

The whistle blast was the last announcement that we were pulling away from the wharf at Port Said. Frankly I was quite happy to see the back of Egypt after all the trouble we went through. Our next stop, New Zealand was nine thousand nautical miles away, that meant twenty-seven days of sailing.

Late that afternoon, the weather was perfect as we maneuvered into the Suez Canal. It was quite a slow process, though. So, it wasn't till early evening when we finally approached our canal speed of around seven to eight knots. It will be around a fourteen- hour trip, so we won't be out the other side till morning. As we moved into the canal, it felt strange to have the landscape slowly moving past both sides of the ship, and there was the contrast as well—green on the port side, and desert on the starboard.

Thinking of the desert brought back memories of Afghanistan all those years ago. Though it was dark, I could still make out the outline of vegetation, but I would only be able to see what it actually looked like, in the early morning. I could make out buntings for the Diamond Jubilee of Queen Victoria, going up in all the small towns we passed. I found it incredulous that this was all English territory. The British Empire was at the height of its power, at this time, and had its nose in a lot of countries.

Once we settled into the run, down through the canal, I was requested to join the captain in his wardroom. I knocked at his door. 'Come in,' this deep voice answered. 'Ah, Mr. Selkirk, please come and sit down. Captain Malcolm Hirons was a short, robust man with a deep voice and long, bushy sideburns. His eyebrows covered his eyes making them look half shut as though squinting against the sun. His face was brown, and he had large, calloused hands. There was no sign of fat on this bloke, you could see strength in every fibre of his being.

I sat looking at him wondering what this was about. He smiled. 'I think, sir, you are travelling incognito. I do not want to presume that I should have been told why. However I knew, my lord, you were on my ship, and when I heard some dastardly fellows had tried to rob you, I felt I needed to summon you to see if everything is well.'

Bugger, I thought. I'm too well known. This being incognito wasn't working out the way I had wanted.

'Thank you, Captain. Yes, we were very lucky, but the culprits are dead, and I suppose I'm lucky, in a way, that the captain of the Egyptian constabulary recognised me as well. I believe we might have been in a spot of bother otherwise.'

'Yes, my lord, I took the time to look in on that colonial chappie. He doesn't look that good, but the surgeon has informed me as long as he gets the right care in the infirmary, he will recover. It will take time, I am afraid. A brave man that, to push that Maori woman out of the way and take the knife instead of the woman. He needs a medal that one, he surely does.'

'Well, Captain, he is a brave man. I have known him since the wars in New Zealand, and he already has a Victorian Cross from back then.' I didn't elaborate any further.

'A VC, you say?'

'Yes, and the minister, Henry, has one as well.' 'Then, sir, all my crew will be doubly vigilant that this does not happen again. We cannot have our empire heroes assassinated for a few paltry pounds.'

'Captain,' I inquired, 'I was wondering, has there been any instances that have been out of the ordinary since we left the UK? I have this impression that the assassin might have come from this ship. I cannot prove anything, but I have a gut feeling.'

He sat back thinking. 'Hmm, I've only had a couple of concerns that have upset the apple cart, but those sorts of incidents happen all the time on board a passenger liner.'

'What kinds of things?' I asked.

'Well, today, for instance, there was an incident in the steerage galley. One foolish passenger fell over the service counter holding a pile of plates. It caused quite a kerfuffle, I can tell you—dishes flew everywhere. It took a good ten minutes or so to clean the place up. No one was hurt though. Funny thing though, that passenger, why was he carrying so many plates? And then afterward he just returned to his cabin.'

'Oh, I didn't realise there were cabins on this ship in steerage.'

'Yes, only the one. Some obscure government department had one put aside, and it was taken up just before we left.'

Bells rang inside my head. 'You said a government department: how many in the room?'

'Just two men,' the captain replied.

'Can you do me a favour and keep a watch on that cabin? I have a suspicion that these could be the men who tried to rob us. There was a bloke, a short, plump man who might have been bleeding as he came back on board. I wonder if you would ask your pursers if anything out of the ordinary happened, when the passengers returned to the ship?'

He sat back. 'Is there more here, my lord, that I should know about?'

I looked at him. 'I'm sorry, Captain. I cannot say, but if those are the men, then the buggers are killers, and I would like to know just what they are up to.'

He scrutinised me. 'Of course. I certainly don't want my ship disrupted with criminal behaviour, but I do have a card up my sleeve. We always have one man undercover in steerage. So, I'll order him to step up and keep an eye on the cabin. I will tell him to recruit a passenger to help, as he cannot keep an eye on it twenty-four hours a day. They can pass along any information to the gate guard. Hmm, and that was the other incident I meant to mention. The gate keys went missing but were found the next day —very unusual for our men to be so sloppy. The keys turned up under a locker. I interviewed the crew member, and he said he had invited one of the steerage passengers to sit with him and play checkers. I didn't mind that as it is a tedious shift, but he took short and went off to the heads. When he returned, the passenger was on the steerage side of the gate. He explained to my man that he had a couple of things to do. It was after that when the keys were discovered missing, though they were found the next day.'

It could be nothing, I thought, but coincidences always raised the hairs on the back of my neck. 'Do these passengers have names?' I asked.

He got up and went to a cabinet and shuffled some papers. 'Ah, here we are,' he said. 'Yes, Simms and Davis.'

I never twigged about the name of Davis from my past, as it was common as hens' teeth. 'About that man I mentioned, with blood on his clothes, he might even have a broken nose. There is a chance he might not leave his room until his face comes right. One more thing, Captain. Is there any way, a resourceful person can move from steerage to first class without going through the gate?'

He looked at me with a thoughtful frown. 'Let's have a look shall we.' He rose from his chair, went to his desk, and rummaged around until he found the diagram of the ship. He spread it out on his desk and surveyed it.

'My God, of course it is possible. Look here, my lord.'

I walked over to the desk and said, 'Just call me Sam, Captain.'

He frowned. 'All right... Sam. There is a connection through to the first-class restaurant from the kitchen in steerage. For a clever chappie, that would be just the ticket.' Then he stopped with another thoughtful look on his face. 'The broken dishes might have been a diversion. Oh, the cunning man. See, you can pop up the stairs, and come out in first class, and from there it is only a hop, skip, and a jump to the pursers' station and out through the exit. You have to admire the chap's gumption. Right, Sam. First I'll interview the pursers and get a picture of any unusual comings and goings.'

'In the meantime, Captain, would you mind if I check the stairs to the steerage restaurant from first class? He might have left a clue. I know what I'm doing, I can pick up a spoor, as I've been tracking for years, and the old eyes are still as good as ever.'

'I'll get my steward to escort you, Sam. Report any findings directly to me. If it proves that they had something to do with the attack on your party, I'll incarcerate them in the brig until New Zealand. Oh Sam, on that note, I have decided we will dock in Auckland first. I thought the colonial chap should be in a hospital near his hometown. For me, it is six of one and a half dozen of the other. So, I'll leave you to let your party know.'

That was good news I thought, the quicker we left for my own time the better. We might be better off if, as soon as we arrived in Auckland, to get our plans for Abe and Blanche sorted quickly. Abe will need to be settled in hospital, where he can be cared for, and with Blanche, we will need to assist her to find accommodation and establish a new identity. Then we can hightail it to the bush south of Pukekawa, and wait for the mist to come, that is if it ever would. Margaret would be waiting in Christchurch, so I'd have to get a cable to her.

The captain rang a bell, and his steward popped his head around the door. 'Come in, Frost. Do you know the back way from the first-class restaurant to the steerage restaurant?'

'Of course, sir,' he announced.

'Good man. Will you take Mr. Selkirk down there? He wants to check a few things.'

I turned to him. 'Thank you, Captain. I'll be in touch.'

We walked down past the state-room restaurant and then to first class. I stopped at the pursers' desk. To the right was the exit door to the wharf. The steward pointed to the restaurant. 'The door you need is that door to the left, sir, behind the serving area.'

I slowly walked, searching the floor, though I wasn't expecting to see anything. Down the hall were large vases with flowers. As I stepped up to the last one, I observed that a few of the flowers had broken stems. I knelt down by it as I noticed some dark matter on the floor. That's when I saw a substantial gap behind the vase. I had a nasty suspicion that something had been pushed in behind the vase, it could have been why the flowers were damaged. I stuck my finger into the brown stuff on the floor and had a smell

—cow dung. This had to be him.

The steward escorted me through the door to the rear steps. The contrast to what I had come through was stark. There were no carpets on the floor here, just steel steps and grey-painted steel walls. It was quite bright also as all the lights were on. I slowly walked down, inspecting the steps. There was nothing until the last stair, where I found a few spots of blood, bingo. I found a couple more in front of the door that went into steerage. I was convinced that the little rotund bloke was in that cabin. Well, he wasn't going anywhere, but I sure as hell would like to get hold of the little bugger and wring his bloody neck.

I reported my findings back to the captain. 'Is that right, then we will have to do something about that. While you have been checking the stairwell, I have had both pursers in here and no one saw him go off. But a man by the description you had mentioned, was seen to return on board with a swollen face and blood on his clothes that he was trying to conceal. 'Right Sam, I think this is all the evidence I require,' he said. 'We need them out of that cabin quick smart. I think, Sam, I will take an armed escort down there, and throw them in the brig before any more shenanigans happen. If they turn out to be honest men, then I will apologise and upgrade them to first class, free of charge. If not, once out of the canal, I'll stop at Port Suez, and pass them over to the authorities. I don't want them on my ship all the way out to New Zealand, and I don't want the reputation of our company to be ruined by a couple of thugs. We will do it discreetly when most are asleep. I'm just thankful that the steerage cabin is well away from the main throng of the other passengers.'

The captain formed the plan and explained to me he would use six armed men. They won't give them a chance, and soon they will be in the brig.

'When we interrogate them, we will need to keep them apart to get a confession, you know play one against the other,' he informed me. It was settled. I had no further involvement until they were captured. I looked at the clock and decided to head out for a walk on the promenade.

Down in the steerage cabin, all was quiet, until a knock on the door caused a flurry of bodies. They jumped off their beds, with worried looks on their faces, but no one tried to enter. A note was slipped under the door. John bent down and scooped it up, and sat down to read the message. Ethan watched him go pale. 'What the hell's wrong with you?' he cursed.

'Read it for yourself.' He flung the note at him and Ethan studied it.

'Shit, the poxy buggers are onto us and there is no way to get off this tub. A plan is what we need as they are coming for us after midnight. The only good thing is that the informant, at least, came good.

'We gave him a year's wage; he should have,' said John.

'Enough!' spat Ethan. 'We have to formulate a plan.'

'Well, we could try jumping. We are close enough to swim to the sides of the canal. Because when they come and find us gone, they will search this ship from top to bottom, so there will be nowhere to hide.'

'Maybe,' Ethan suggested, 'we might try getting to the bridge and order them to heave to. It would be easier to jump if the ship were nearly stopped, then we could take a couple of hostages when we go over the side, it will put us in a better position.'

The more he thought about it, the more he liked that idea. The alternative was if they were caught on board, they would hang anyway, so he had nothing to lose. Up until this time, John was not sure, if all he had done was to break some plates, maybe he would've been able to talk his way out of it. But he had no time to think as Ethan threw things into a small bag, then placed over his shoulder. He checked his knife and revolver. 'Come on, man. Let's move.'

'Hang on. How are we going to get out of steerage?' moaned Davis. 'I think they probably will have an extra guard on the gate by now.'

'We'll go through the kitchen,' Ethan snarled. 'Now, come on, hurry.' Reluctantly, John followed Ethan out the door, and sneaked down towards the galley. Very few people were about, so they strode up to the door and stepped into the kitchen. There was only one chef who looked up as the door opened.

'Hey, you are not allowed in here.' He was a large bloke dressed in his white coat and chef's hat; he came around from the stoves rubbing his hands together. He stepped up to Ethan, 'Did you hear me, gaffer? Get out of here,' he yelled.

Ethan took half a step back and with a slight twist of his arm, his knife appeared. He stabbed the chef right in his heart. The big man collapsed without a sound and very little blood. John swore. 'What the hell did you do that for, you daft bugger? We have both had it now, you bastard.'

'Shut your whining. Grab his legs, and we will stick him in the cooler, so he won't be found for a while.' They dragged the chef into the cooler, closed the door, found a padlock, locked the door, and checked to see if there was any blood on the floor. 'Right,' Ethan said. 'all clear,' and off he trotted towards the door.

Taking a peek around the door, he said in a low voice, 'Come on.' They rushed up to the first-class restaurant. They ran through the kitchen and out to the promenade deck and disappeared into the shadows.

CHAPTER TWENTY-FIVE

SS Rangitoto

Once Blanche had recovered after the attack at the market, she spent many hours with Abe in sickbay. She held his hand, and every now and then would break down and have a good old cry. How could this man, Blanche thought, who never knew her until a few weeks ago, step in to protect her like that? It had been years since anyone had defended her. So, she talked and read to Abe, hoping it would help, but he was, for most of the part, oblivious in a coma.

People came and went throughout the night worried for their friend. Henry had been in at least a dozen times and had given Blanche Abe's background. He told her he had married in the 1860s, though his wife had died of a fever, he had no children, and he never bothered to remarry. He had sold his parents' farm in Whangarei when they passed on, and the money was shared between his five siblings. He had a farm at Mangere in Auckland, and ran a small dairy herd with cattle, pigs, and chooks for eggs. And he loved horses. His lovely home had excellent views over the Manukau Harbour and had a backdrop of the old volcano. He went on to say that he was well liked and had even been asked to stand for parliament. Abe had turned it down, as it was not his cup of tea.

Abe woke up while some of the conversation was going on. He looked very pale; Blanche immediately lifted his head and let him take a little water. He smiled. 'I have been awake a little while,' he admitted. 'Don't listen to Henry, he always paints me in a better picture than reality.'

Blanche went red. 'I'm so sorry to talk about you, Mr. Metcalfe, but as a person who saved my life, I felt I had to know something about you.'

'Please call me Abe. We don't stand on ceremony here,' he gave a wide grin.

'Are you hungry, Mr. Metc—er, Abe?' she inquired. 'There is some broth and bread for you, if you feel up to it.' Then the doctor arrived.

'Ah, you are awake.'

With the help of Henry, they propped Abe up, and the doctor suggested, 'A bit of food will make a difference.' Blanche went to the galley and returned with hot broth, then sat down and spoon-fed him.

He grinned between mouthfuls, 'I could get used to this,' he teased her. He dropped off to sleep halfway through, he never finished the bowl. Henry watched as she pulled up the blankets.

'Blanche, I think you need to get some food and fresh air. Take yourself off now. I'll look after my mate; you have been here all day.' Reluctantly, she touched Henry on the shoulder as she made her way to the door to be stopped by a couple of Maori.

'We are your escort, Moana—using her Maori name. You do not go anywhere without us.' They were tough-looking older men, but when they grinned, the years slipped off their faces.

'I think a walk first before dinner, would be a good idea, to clear your head. You have been with our friend Abe all day, and the sea and the scent of the land will revitalise you. Now we haven't met officially,' the taller one said. 'I'm Rangi, and my friend is Hemi.'

She noticed both had a putu stuck in their belts.

Hemi smiled at her.

'Don't worry this is just in case. You never know when we might need it.' They walked in single file until they reached the promenade deck, then on either side of her as they headed around to stand at the stern of the ship. The night was quite dark, but the light on the stern enabled Blanche to watch the froth of the propeller churning the black water below. The smell of the warm land and sea air helped to relax her as the white foam of the ship slipped slowly by. She released her hair to let the slight breeze blow through it, it made her feel so much better.

The three of them stood by the ship's railing enjoying the companionship when Simms and Davis slipped out onto the deck. Simms smiled to himself. Luck was on their side—shoot, stab, and over the side to freedom, and a thousand quid.

He whispered to John, 'It's her. We will move quickly. Kill those two darkies, and I'll shoot the woman—then over the side. Suit you, Davis?'

John was not so sure. The distance from the deck to the water was, to him, an awfully long drop, but what was the alternative? They had to get off the ship, and this was a bonus; they were just standing there, a flawless opportunity on easy targets. They came up behind the intake funnel, and Simms whispered, 'You go left; I'll go right, on three.'

They appeared from behind the funnel just as I came onto the promenade deck. I saw movement but nothing else, just shadows, and I shouted a warning. In an instant, Hemi had swung around and pushed Blanche behind him, and Rangi moved into the gap creating a barrier. Davis opened up firing at the threesome, hit Hemi in the chest twice, and as he fell, he took Blanche with him, and in the last moments of his life, he managed to cover her with his body.

Rangi jumped forward with his stone putu in

his hand and got nice and close to Davis before he could take another shot. He hit him on his right shoulder blade with such force you could hear the crack of the bone as it snapped. Davis dropped his weapon, and slipped to the ground, moaning. Simms fired at Rangi three times, as he collapsed, Ethan then swung around to turn his gun on Hemi's body. He fired three more shots at Hemi in the hope he would make contact with the woman underneath. There was a click, Simms had run out of ammo.

I had managed to get close to Simms as he concentrated on getting to Blanche, and I hit him on the side of his head with everything I had. The pain went right up to my shoulder as Simms dropped his gun and half collapsed onto the deck. He managed to hang on to the barrier railing for support. That's when all the lights came on. The crew must have heard the shots and turned everything on. It was carnage, blood everywhere, two dead, and Blanche had not moved. Davis sat on the deck, holding his arms to his chest, swaying back and forth, and Simms tried desperately to regain his footing.

Crew members swarmed out onto the deck and grabbed Davis just as I saw Simms start to slip over the side underneath the railings. I dived for him and somehow managed to grab hold of his collar before he slithered over. He wriggled like a fish on a hook trying like hell to hit me, but he had his back to the ships side, and he could not reach. I called out to anyone who was listening to give me a hand to pull him up. 'I can't hold him.'

Simms screamed, 'We have done the job.'

Then there was a tearing sound as the material ripped. The weight left my arm as Simms bounced off the side of the ship, all five stories down. He hit the water in a belly flop. The lights at the stern angled down into the water as we watched him being sucked into the propellers. Afterwards, a mass of redness coloured the water. He never resurfaced.

A crew member pulled me back and helped me stand. I still had the material from Simms's collar in my hand. I chucked it overboard then rushed over to see if Blanche was okay. How she managed to survive, I just didn't know, but she was not hurt. She stood up, the blood of Hemi all over her, and collapsed into my arms. Twice in one day, they had tried to kill her. It was too much for the woman.

'I'll take her to her cabin,' I told everyone within hearing range. She was out to it. I hadn't even looked at Davis, who was escorted away. Someone had gone to find Te Ruru, the Maori chief, to sort out the bodies of the two dead Maori. It's a shambles, I thought, as I pushed open the door into Blanche's state room only to see Rita staring at me with big eyes.

'I'm so sorry, Rita. Rangi and Hemi were shot; both are dead. It's a bloody waste.'

She didn't hesitate. 'I'll get someone up here to help clean up Blanche, Sam. Then I'll go and sort out our whanau.'

I placed Blanche on the bed, and a few minutes later, a young woman came in. 'I'll look after her, sir,' she said. 'Would you be so kind as to get the surgeon's mate to come up and give her a sedative once I have finished cleaning her up? The doctor will be involved with the man with the broken collarbone.' I looked up at her in surprise. 'Oh, news gets around fast on a ship, bad news even quicker,' she remarked.

So off I went. Once the mate was informed, I headed back to my cabin. My son was still asleep, and I gently woke him to bring him up to date with what happened. He sat on the edge of his bed with his mouth open, appalled at what I told him.

'This has got to stop, Father,' he stammered. 'It is too much, twice in a day, not only for that poor woman, but you are at risk also, and now we have another two friends dead because of something that only you know about. It certainly appears as though Blanche's disguise is blown also. I'm bloody mad. You have got to share this burden before more people are killed. Two heads are better than one. We need to do this, Father. I mean it. I have had enough of you placing yourself in danger. This has to stop now.'

I hung my head. 'You are right, Sam. It is getting out of hand. Look, son, I'll tell you, but it is so sensitive that you will never be able to talk to anyone about what I say to you, but I need help, and you are right—two heads are better than one. First, though, I want to see Te Ruru and offer my condolences. After that, I would like to interview that assassin.' I stopped and looked at my son. 'Then I will explain everything. Okay, Sam?'

'No putting it off, Dad. I'm coming with you to listen to what the bastard has to say.'

'Okay, Sam, that's fine by me.'

'Right, Father. Let me put my shoes on.' Sam had never spoken to me like this before in his life, and it was down to him being worried about me and what we had got ourselves into, that I felt relieved in a way and encouraged to share the burden. I felt quite exhausted, and my son would never tell a soul, and I must admit, this was a young man's game.

Once he was ready, I said, 'I am going to Te Ruru then onto the captain to inform him about what happened on deck, and we will need his permission to interview the sod we captured.'

Te Ruru was quiet. Losing his whanau was like losing his arm. 'We must be more cautious, Sam,' he whispered. 'I would like utu on that man who was captured, but I know that's unattainable, so we need to make sure that the woman is under our protection at all times. If she can make it through this episode, then I'll be happy, and my men will not have died in vain.'

We mumbled our commiseration. 'I'll talk again soon, Te Ruru. I'm going down to see the bloke later and see if we can get some answers.'

There was a sentry stationed in front of the captain's door when we arrived.

'One moment, sir,' he said to me. He turned and knocked on the door, sticking his head in and announced, 'Mr Selkirk and his son are here, sir. Would you speak to them?'

'Yes, yes, send them in, Townsend,' the captain muttered.

The door opened, as the captain slipped on his jacket. He looked up as we entered. 'A bad business, Sam,' he said. 'Appalling, indeed. I have arranged with the Maori chief to place their two men into a cool store for the duration of the trip, so they can bury them at home, according to their customs. I will hand over the prisoner to the authorities at Suez. So, I will like your written statement by morning, to hand over to the powers that be, and if possible, another from the Maori woman as well. Though I can understand if she is not up to it. My crew will write theirs, and with yours, sir, there is enough evidence to hang the blighter.'

'Would you agree, Captain, for me to have a

quiet word with the prisoner before you hand him over? I want to get to the bottom of this, and he is the only one who can tell us what it is all about. It is not just a robbery, they tried to kill the woman twice.'

'Yes, you do that, and write that up as well. The surgeon is with him at the moment.' he turned to address my son, 'How is your wound, young fellow? It's been a quite a day, hasn't it?'

'Stiff and sore, sir,' Sam replied, 'but I'm lucky as it could have been worse.'

He looked at us. 'Right, Sam. Find some answers, and pop back with your statement once you have talked to the man. Townsend, accompany these two gentlemen to the brig, please.' He sat down with a plonk. 'It's been a rough day all around,' he stated as we walked to the door.

Townsend uttered, 'Follow me, please, sirs.' He opened the door and headed out with a wave of his arm.

A couple of fully armed crew members stood outside the brig's solid steel door. It had an open grill, and we could see a weak yellow light shining in the cell to reveal silhouettes that moved behind the door. The doctor was just leaving as we arrived. He had an armed guard with him also, in case the prisoner decided to create trouble. The door swung open on lubricated hinges—not what I was expecting. What was I expecting—a squealing door like in a movie?

Movie, that word I hadn't thought of in a while. Another random term that I now understood.

The doctor took his leave, and the guard backed out of the cell slowly to keep an eye on the occupant. The doctor turned to me. 'Ah, Mr Selkirk, if you are going to talk to him, he won't give you any trouble. The New Zealander has made a real mess of his collarbone, and I will be surprised if he ever has use of that arm again. Though to be on the safe side, the guard will pop in with you. I gather that is what you are here for —to talk to him?'

'Thanks, Doc, we will be careful.'

The guard returned and entered the cell once again, with Sam, and I followed, I hardly heard the door close behind us as we looked at the figure on the bunk. He had crammed himself against the rear wall and had pulled his knees up to his chin. He didn't look a box of birds at all. The guard spoke to the man, 'Once again, Davis. If you move an inch, your guts will be splatted all over your bunk, comprehend?'

Davis nodded. His arm was strapped to his body. I noticed the other arm with the odd angle of his wrist. My eyes jumped to his face, and looked at him more intensely, then the penny dropped.

'John Davis,' I sputtered. 'What the hell have you done, John?'

'Ah, so you remember me, you prick,' Davis

snarled.

I turned to Sam. 'This was the bloke I found poaching and stealing gold from our place thirty- odd years ago. Eliza's brother, and your friend John Cotton's, uncle.' Eliza was my head ranger, Toby's wife. We caught the whole family doing this deed, and the last Eliza saw of her siblings and father, was when they were sent away for twenty-odd years in prison. We hadn't seen them since. 'You are a stupid bugger, John. Won't you ever learn. This deed now, is severe enough for you to hang? What the hell possessed you?'

'I haven't forgotten you, Selkirk,' he fumed, lifting his good arm with the angled wrist. 'You did this to me; it never knitted properly.'

'You should have thought about the consequences before you started your occupation of larceny, John. Twenty years in prison I would have thought that was enough for any man, but your old man said his sons were dumb, and I have to agree with the old bugger; you surely are. What's the story here, then? Killing is a step up from stealing. What the hell got into you to murder? Six people have died today—six!' I reiterated. 'That includes your mate, and for what? Trying to kill an innocent, defenceless woman, you miserable bugger. What brave men you both are. I hope they hang you from the nearest tree when we pull into Suez in the morning. What am I going to say to your sister? We saw you hang for murder in Egypt? What a lasting legacy that is to her.' I stopped and looked at him. He was in real pain and looked dreadful.

'Look, John, I might be able to help you get a reduced sentence if you tell me what's it all about. If not, you are on your own. My testimony will be enough to send you to the gallows.' His face was unnaturally grey, and even though he was in pain, he shook his head in the negative.

'So, not going to play ball, eh? It will be easy to get it out of you, John,' I said as I moved towards him. 'That shoulder sure looks very painful. I could give it a squeeze or two, but you might not like that, would you, John?' I ranted at him. 'Of course, if that's what it takes, I'll do it. I don't care a penny about you, so the more pain, the better, I'd say,' as I placed my hand on the wall just above his shoulder. I could see my son's face; he was appalled at what I suggested.

'You cannot do this, Father. It's not right to torture this man.'

'How many has he killed, Sam?' I snapped. 'He is not human and deserves the pain and agony for the loss of our two Maori friends. Then what about Abe? No, I'm going to squeeze this little sod until he pops.' My hand slipped down to lightly touch his shoulder, and John broke.

'All right, all right, I've had enough. What do you want to know?'

'Everything you know, John. Don't leave out a

thing.'

Then the words poured out of his mouth. 'It was a need-to-know operation. We had no idea what the woman had done, but Sir Anthony Purcell told us she was the target. Every operative in the empire is on the lookout for her so it had to be important. We would get one thousand pounds each to get rid of her, and when the job was done, we had to cable "Sunshine" to his Whitehall number. You nearly got her away, Selkirk, but I counted eleven Maori going on board when there were only ten documented. So, we had to catch the boat.'

'So, if we sent this code to the number you just told us, the hounds will come off the chase?'

'Yes, once he receives that code, then everyone will be reassigned to another job. If they don't get that code, there will be operatives waiting in New Zealand for you. Purcell is a sneaky bugger.'

'I have only met him once,' I told my son. 'Scrawny bloke and nasty. If we get home, I think I will have words with Sir Anthony Purcell.'

'Is there anyone else up top we should know about?' I demanded. John frowned. 'I think the Secretary of State. I overheard Purcell telling someone that the two of them were the only knights who were protecting the realm. I don't think even the prime minister knows.'

'Okay, John, as you have given us all this information, I'll do the very best I can for you. It might help you.'

'Oh, one more thing,' John muttered. 'Simms killed the chef; he is in the cooler. I had nothing to do with that. He came around and told us to hop it out of the kitchen, and Simms just knifed him.'

'Oh, heck,' I said, 'the poor bugger.' I turned to my son, and asked, 'What do you think?'

Sam looked at Davis.'John Cotton is my best friend, I cannot believe this low life is his uncle.' He shook his head, 'but I think he is telling the truth, Father.'

'Okay, let's get a statement up to the captain.' I called through the grill that we were coming out. The door silently opened, and we walked out with the guard backing out. The door closed, leaving a very sorry and sore bloke to mull over what he had done. I turned to the guard. 'Not a word about this. It is highly secret, and your life could be on the line if you talk to anyone about what you just heard.'

'I never heard a thing, sir,' he replied. 'I'm usually in the engine room and have hearing problems.' He grinned then winked.

'Thank you,' I replied. We sent word up to the captain about his chef and then headed back to our state room to write out the statement.

Once in our room, Sam grabbed me. 'You were going to torture him, Father. I could not believe it. That's not you.'

'No, Sam, it's not, but I had to convince him that I was, and your reaction really put the icing on the cake. Thank you. I would never have gone through with it, and if it hadn't worked, I didn't know what I was going to do, but it did. Now we have the code word and the number for White-hall. It was a gamble, but it paid off, thank good-ness.'

'My word, Dad. You had me convinced. I have come to the opinion, Father, that I don't want to know about Blanche. I find it hard to believe though, that our elected parliament condone murder, and this sort of secrecy. So, I will, with all my power, protect this woman till my dying breath, and when I get home, I will look for Pur-cell myself and give him a bit of his own medi-cine. To chase a lonely woman around the world and try to assassinate her, this is not the govern-ment I want in power.'

'A dangerous man, Sam,' I said. 'But as you know, I know people in high places who can put a stop to it, and you are right, this is outrageous and needs to be nipped in the bud.' I hugged my son.

'Thank God we have each other,' he said. I pat-ted his back.

'Come on, let's get the statements down, son. However, no mention of Blanche. They were just opportunists who went wrong.'

CHAPTER TWENTY-SIX

Suez Canal

The day promised to be a hot one as the ship approached the end of the Suez Canal and slipped into its berth at Port Taofk. As the plank went down, it was a hive of activity as sailors came out of the woodwork to do their allotted tasks. I watched as one sailor run off to what appeared to be the cable office on the wharf, though I lost sight of him among the buildings. Within an hour, a caged wagon arrived with six policemen and an officer.

When I first got up that morning, I had popped down to see Davis, and he was still in a lot of pain. The first thing he had said to me was not to tell his sister. 'I know I have been a cad all my life, and like the rest of the family, I mistreated her, but she does not need to know about this caper.' I agreed, if that was what he wanted, I would not say a word, and neither would my son. I went down to meet the officer and gave him my statement. On a separate sheet of paper, I had written a request for him to go lenient on Davis as he had helped with our inquiries. He added it to the other reports he had from the crew, who had been on deck last night.

'Open and shut case, sir,' declared the officer. 'He could be shot by a firing squad for this or could be sent away for a long time. It depends on how the magistrate feels today.'

'Today,' I said, taken aback.

'Yes, with cases like these, we don't like to muck around, especially since he is obviously guilty. We will cable the results to you in Auckland.'

As I stood on the wharf I watched as they, not so gently, pushed John Davis up the steps of the wagon, he did not look my way. His head was down, and he looked as pale as the white buildings around the area. The driver snapped the reins, and with an 'Abhhab, abhhab,' the horse trotted away with the six cops and the prisoner, inside the cage, and the officer up top with the driver. I wondered, as they disappeared behind the buildings, what would happen to him.

I put him out of my mind, as I needed to send a cable to my daughter Margaret, in Dunedin. She needed to know our ship was going to Auckland first instead of Christchurch, and if she wanted to see Sam and myself, she would have to be there when it arrived. I also wanted to cable my family at Shadymore, and another to Whitehall. I needed a walk so I found the local cable office by following the overhead wires. It was tucked away in a small run-down cabin in between a couple of warehouses, which surprised me, as it didn't seem to fit with modern technology.

I handed my messages to a young English bloke behind the desk. The third one, I told him, was government business coded with the just the word 'Sunshine. He counted the words I had written out. 'Two and sixpence, sir.' I paid him, and he sent the cables straight away. I didn't hang around for a reply but asked him that if one came through before the ship left, to deliver it to the purser for me. I thanked him and trotted back to the boat. I hoped this was the end of having to look over our shoulders.

When I returned to the ship, there were fully armed guards on either side of the gangplank. Looks like they weren't taking any more chances. The captain waved out and caught up with me as I came on board.

'Sam, I just found out that crew member who collaborate with those criminals, Jackson was his name, has jumped ship. I was going to discharge the greedy blighter—do anything for money he would. But honestly, he must have got wind of it when we docked, because he was gone. I wash my hands of him, the only good thing was, he forfeited his pay. I have reported him to all concerned in my cable to company HQ. He might find that he'll hit a brick wall in the future, and good riddance. We do not need men like him in our business. I dare say he'll get work, no doubt, on some crummy cargo ship heading back to England. Now, I'm just waiting to receive an answer to that cable to HQ, and then we'll be off.' Then he smiled, 'Sam, I hope you can relax now for the rest of the trip south, as I believe we have cleared the ship of all those unpleasant fellows, but we will still need to stay vigilant. Right, there is work to do.' He rubbed his hands together, as he was about to leave, then said, 'Come up to my cabin for a drink before dinner.' He touched my shoulder, 'I think a glass of wine to relax you would be the ticket.' He smiled again, turned and walked away, heading for the bridge.

I headed to Blanche and Rita's cabin to catch up. I knocked but there was no answer, until I heard a puffing sound coming from behind the door. Rita opened it, 'Oh, Sam, so sorry. It takes me a while to get around these days. I just was going down to have a small breakfast. Would you escort me?'

'Of course,' I said, taking her arm, then looking back into the cabin, 'Is Blanche around, Rita?'

'She left here a while ago for breakfast Sam, then I think she intended going down to sickbay to see Abe. The sleep did her a world of good and she woke up in good form this morning.

She is a fine strong woman, that one.

'I'm so sorry Rita, about Rangi and Hemi. They were such good blokes. I will always have good memories of them singing Maori songs to all the children at the Shadymore schoolhouse. I haven't the words to say how I feel. It's just a waste.'

'Sam, don't feel bad. It is the way they would have wanted to go to their ancestors, as warriors. They will be happy. Mark my words. More than happy that they saved Blanche. We are fortunate that the captain has given us the use of the cold store to protect them until we reach New Zealand. He could have just as easily had a burial at sea, and the spirits of our men would take so much longer to find their way home to Hawaiki. After I have had my breakfast, I'll go down to talk to them with my whanau, and tell them to wait for a few more weeks before they head off to their spiritual homeland. Spirits can be impatient, my friend, as they will find it easier to get there from Aotearoa.'

I escorted her to the dining room, sat her down, and a waiter came over. 'Just tea and a soft-boiled egg, young man.' She smiled at him and turned to me. 'Won't you sit, Sam?'

'I want to see Blanche first, Rita, if that's all right with you.' Rita reached out and took my hand.

'Sam, please do not be complacent, it's not over yet. You will have to watch yourself in New Zealand. Yes, it will be calm waters until we get to Auckland, but once we arrive, do take care.

There are still adversaries around who don't want you to finish your journey. They will want to stop the four of you from getting to your final destination.'

'Don't worry, Rita. My son and I will put our heads together and work out a plan. Right. I'd better get going. I'll catch up with you later.'

She patted my hand. 'I'll get a waiter to ask my son to take me to the resting place of our warriors.'

I left with this feeling of dread as I headed down to see Blanche and Abe. I stopped at the top of the steps when her words hit me. Rita had included the four of us when she spoke of our final destination. Hold on a minute—only Sam and I are going into the mist and try to get back to my century. What is she on about now? I turned to head back into the restaurant to clarify what she said, when I noticed activity on the gangplank. A policeman had run up the gangway and disappeared into the body of the ship. I wondered what the heck this was all about, then a few minutes later a sailor dashed up to me.

'Please follow me, sir, the captain would like to you see now,' he advised.' What the hell! Bugger me, more problems, I thought. My mind was in turmoil, as I followed the sailor up to the bridge.

We passed Sam as he headed towards the restaurant, and I said, 'I am wanted urgently by the captain.'

He turned and followed me. 'You're not on your own, Father, not anymore.'

The sailor knocked on the captain's day room on the bridge. 'Come in,' came the voice from inside. The crew member opened the door and ushered us in. He closed the door quietly as the captain came from around his desk. A policeman was standing to his right.

I looked at them both. 'What's going on, Captain?' I asked.

The Egyptian policeman said, in excellent English, 'May I, Captain?'

'Yes, go ahead Constable,' the captain replied.

The constable turned to us. 'We took Davis off the ship, as you know, and escorted him to the main jail. While walking him up the stairs at the back of the court lockup, two shots fired at us from a distance. Davis was killed instantly, and the policeman who was handcuffed to him was wounded as well. I'm sorry to say we have not apprehended anyone. We believe it was an assassination to prevent him from talking. I'm sorry, sir, but we thought that you and the captain should know before you sailed.'

'Can you explain what this is all about, sir?' the constable asked me.

'No, I cannot help you there, Officer. This is a complete mystery to me, and I have no idea why,' I muttered.

'Thank you, sir. It's another world, for these sorts of people, they implement things that ordinary citizens don't see or hear about. We believe it has to be gang related. Anyway, you know now, and we think it will be the end of it.' He turned to the captain. 'Thank you, sir, I'll let you get underway. Have a safe trip.'

As he left, the captain spoke to me, 'Well, I hope it's the bloody end to it.'

'So do I, Captain,' I said with real feeling. 'So do I.'

Sam and I left the captain's day cabin, and out of earshot, I whispered, 'I'm dumbfounded, son. How the hell did they know he was captured? They must have been out there somewhere watching the ship. God, they must have been certainly organised to get in front of the police wagon to shoot Davis. It must have been a spur-of-the-moment thing for them. Does that mean the authorities back in the UK now know that the cable we sent was fake? If so, we will have to be doubly observant when we reach Auckland. Hopefully, Sam, we will have a bit of respite until we get there, but once there we will have to formulate a new plan.'

'We will work on this together, Father regardless. It will have to be a watertight plan though.'

'You're right, Sam. We will need to get our thinking caps on.' We arrived at our cabin, and I plonked myself down in the chair near the porthole. 'Well, son, what now?' I answered my own question. 'I will need to see Abe and Blanche and bring them up to play.'

'You are still using your old words, Dad—up to play.' Sam grinned. 'Yes, I agree, a plan is what we need.'

We felt the ship give a shudder, and Sam and I looked out the porthole. It appeared that we were on our way once again. We watched the ship's head turn towards open waters then sat down quietly with our own thoughts. There was a knock on the door, and a sailor handed us a slip of paper: a message from the captain.

I read it out loud to my son, 'Sam, I have thought your predicament through,' it stated. 'We will be in Auckland for three days, so I suggest you and your party stay on board for this period and not leave till the last minute. We will be taking no passengers onto the ship except your family if they manage to make Auckland. We will tighten security, so no one we don't know about, comes on board. This will put doubts in any person's mind if they still are looking for you. Maybe you can turn this around, and you then become the watcher. I hope you find this a satisfactory idea. Don't forget that drink tonight before dinner.'

'Well, that's the start of a good plan. All we need to do is get Margaret on board, but that should not be a problem,' I claimed.

'This is good, Dad. I am a bit apprehensive about all these goings-on, and I sure hope you know what you are doing.' He ran his hand through his hair. 'What are we going to do with Blanche? Her cover is blown, and even now the people that have instigated this might have sent a cable to New Zealand.' Sam rubbed his head as though an idea would pop up. 'That is the big problem, it's tough not knowing who we are up against.'

'Well, son, we have three weeks to work on it. We need to bring in Peri as he is our guide back to the spot where I came out of the mist, and of course, there's Blanche. That is a another problem, but we will work it out. Once we get back to the bush, we'll be in our element. Then whoever is trying to follow, will have to be pretty competent to find us. You can bet your life that they will be town boys. If they do, Sam, I'm pretty good at ambushing the uninitiated. But I think we are jumping the gun. We must stay positive and hope we have sorted it out by then, in the meantime, we will plan for the worst-case scenario. Right. I need to see Abe and Blanche, so I'll leave you to it, son. Why don't you catch up with Peri and have a yarn, and see what his opinions are. I haven't been in New Zealand for thirty-odd years, so a lot would have changed. I should think that you would know it better; you have been out there twice.'

'All right, Dad, I'll give it some thought, and I need to pass on my condolences to our Maori friends.' I left him staring out the porthole as I went down to sickbay.

Abe was sitting up eating, considering it had only been twenty-four hours since he had been stabbed, he looked so much better with colour back in his cheeks. He glanced up as I came into the cabin. 'Hi, Sam, how are you, mate?' I studied him.

'More importantly, how are you?' I remarked. 'You had me worried, Abe. You really did.'

'Well,' he informed me, 'it will be months before I'm right, but I am determined to walk before we reach home port. Not sure about running the farm, but walking is a good starting point.'

'You cannot keep a good man down.' I grinned. 'And you, Blanche? I was so worried about you after yesterday, being attacked twice in one day. Are you all right?'

She held Abe's hand. 'To be perfectly honest, Sam, I'm feeling fine. The doctor gave me a sedative, and I slept all night. That was all the healing I needed because I woke refreshed. I must admit what happened last night, is a blank to me. Rita had to explain what went on and the outcome. I must go soon, and see Te Ruru and his men, to thank them and to pass on my condolences. It seems so little, just words, two more excellent people have died for nothing—it is despicable. I sometimes wish I was a man because I would want to have revenge on what they have done. I have to thank you, Sam, once again, but I think it is time to bring a few more into the story. It is not fair that only you carry this burden on your shoulders. Abe and Henry need to know and your son Sam to. I know, none of you would divulge my secret, especially Rita.'

She spoke her name with a frown. 'You know I sometimes think Rita knows everything. She sits and looks at me and smiles her secret smile, as though she can see my soul—in a nice way, of course.' She turned and looked at Abe. 'Don't you worry Abe, I am determined to see you walk,' she confessed. 'My whole existence, at the moment, is to work towards that goal. Now Sam, we have three weeks,' she emphasised, 'I want to be taught how to use a rifle and a handgun. I need to be able to protect myself.' She hesitated, 'No, not just myself—all of you. At the moment, I'm just a spectator. Well, that's got to stop. I know I'll be quite capable of defending myself, so I hope you understand. I don't care who teaches me, but I want to be able to pick up a rifle and know what end the bullet comes out.'

Abe grinned, 'Get me out of bed, and I'll show you.'

'You, Mr. Metcalfe, will concentrate on getting well.' Blanche said with authority, 'I have all the

Maori contingent to help, and there's Sam and his son, including Henry.' I had to laugh. Well, inside I did, because she was a wee packet of dynamite, besides it wasn't silly for her to know what end of a gun to fire.

'Okay, Blanche,' I said. 'We will work out some time to suit everyone.'

'Good,' she said. 'Now, Abe,' she whispered, gently turning to him, 'you need to rest.' She was still holding his hand. 'We don't want to tire you out.'

She stood up, tucked him in, picked up his plates, and left a glass of water for him to drink. 'I'll be back with your lunch.' She leant forward, and without embarrassment, brushed her lips against his forehead. Abe was asleep before we closed the door.

CHAPTER TWENTY-SEVEN

SS Rangitoto

Three weeks of normality was a real godsend, as we settled down to what turned out to be a voyage of tranquility. Blanche had explained to all of us what we needed to know of her story. I felt much better for it. I just hope the Prince of Wales accepted it when he found out. Then we got together as a team to nut out what we could do when we arrived in Auckland, so as to nullify anyone out there who had us in their sights.

It was a hard chore to come up with ideas, except to be watchful and stay on board until the last minute before the ship left for Christchurch. At least that might help throw a spanner in the works for the hoodlums.

It wasn't until around twelve days after Suez when Abe with a smile on his face, and the support of Blanche, left his sickbed and very slowly walked up to the promenade deck to sit in the sun. I was pleased as he looked like he had started to come right and seemed to get fitter each day. The surgeon remarked how amazed he was at how well Abe had responded to treatment.

He explained, 'I thought we would have had to lift him off the ship, but I've had to revise my prognosis.' Then he said with laughter in his voice, 'The way Abe is recovering, I'm sure there's a chance he'll race us off the ship when we berth.'

We were all there to congratulate him on his progress, as he came up to us, still holding Blanche's hand, when he came to a stop.

'Friends,' he announced, 'I might have found a solution for Blanche.'

'Thank God for that,' my son said. 'The situation has been a real headache,' he muttered with feeling.

Abe turned to Blanche, squeezing her hand. He spoke to us even though he was looking at her. 'I have asked Blanche to marry me.' She smiled shyly.

'And I have accepted,' she replied beaming from ear to ear.

'We will ask the captain to perform the ceremony. What this means is she will then have my name. We thought, to throw anyone off who might be looking for her, we would leave the ship via the steerage passengers' entry. We'll ask the captain to find a crew member disguised as me, to walk off with Henry, and the rest of our

Maori contingent. There is a good chance that anyone watching and counting heads will realise that Blanche was killed in Egypt. And that my friends might solve our problem. With most passengers alighting in Auckland, we will just mingle into the crowd. We will stay at the Harp of Erin pub, and I'll cable my sister to pick us up from there and take us out to the farm in Mangere. But we need to keep it quiet, we don't want anyone unsavoury knowing what is going on.' He stopped and looked at us. 'So what do you all think, of that idea?'

I smiled. 'Abe, this is splendid news and congratulations to you and Blanche. I think that just might do the job. I really do—a great plan.'

Everyone was happy for the couple, especially Henry.

It is about time, my friend. About time. This is fantastic news.'

Within a day, they were married. The captain was only too pleased to officiate the wedding, and Henry was his best man. We all crowded into the captain's cabin—Maori and Pakeha alike. Everyone was happy, though the look on Rita's face was happy but reflective. I slipped in beside her. 'Are you not pleased?' I asked.

'Yes, of course I am, Sam.' Then she grabbed my arm with a strength I did not know she had and pulled me down to her level, then whispered in my ear, 'Keep an open mind, my friend. Those two are not out of danger—not by a long shot. Well, none of you are. The plan will work for a few days, but things will change. I won't be there nor will my people, only Peri and some of his relations. Once you leave the ship, make sure you are armed and alert. Abe and Blanche will still need protecting.'

Oh hell, I thought. What the heck is she on about now? 'Henry is going home as well, isn't he?' I asked.

'Yes, but with Henry, there is darkness, and I cannot think why. Furthermore, Peri has an idea to put to you, and will meet up with you after the wedding,' she replied.

With the nuptials over, the captain gave the newly-weds a vacant double cabin, and the rest of us sloped off after shaking hands and kissing the bride. There would be no wedding breakfast for these two, except a special meal in their cabin—just for the two of them. Abe was still unwell and was in need of a great deal of rest.

I had begun to record my story from the time I had first boarded the ship. Now that I had a quiet moment, I sat at my table writing as I wanted to finish it before we reached New Zealand. It was getting quite large, and I figured it was going to end up a manuscript by the time I had finished. I planned to leave it at the Bank of New Zealand in Auckland and hoped it would be delivered to my mate Bob Kydd around 2020, in Invercargill. He might receive it, if luck ran my way.

The next day, Peri knocked at our cabin door. 'It's me,' he yelled. 'Kia ora, my friends.' He came in with his usual smile on his face.

I looked up at him and smiled. 'Ah,' he said, 'my good man, send my regards to your friend Bob, in your letter.'

How did he do it? He was as bad as Rita, but once again he seemed to be aware of what I was doing. He pulled a chair up and announced, 'Gentle people, I have an idea. My whanau are leaving from this ship with our dear departed and heading straight to the railway station. The captain, bless his soul, told us that we will dock at Queen's Wharf, at six in the morning. And it's only a three-minute walk to Britomart Station and the train leaves from there at ten a.m. What I suggest is, a few days later we do the same. We can take the train to Tuakau, then we can rent a wagon to take us to Pukekawa. From there, I'll guide you to the place I intend to leave you, where I left Bob Kydd. My friends, the bush is just as you left it all those years ago, so it may take some time to get you to the right area. If all goes to plan, it could be three to four hours, before I'll leave you on your own. As you know, we still consider this place as the home of the Taniwha, and the area is still tapu. So, be aware you are breaking the rules my good men, but sometimes this has to happen for good to occur.' He sat back on his chair and folded his arms.

'So, old chaps... what are your thoughts?'
'Trains run down to Tuakau?' I questioned.

'Oh yes, we have advanced splendidly in the last thirty years, my friends, you will notice quite a change around the townships when you are in New Zealand. The trains travel as far as Te Awamutu now. Rita and Te Ruru will stay on board all the way and will be picked up by the coach run by our people, to take them on to Taumarunui. However, you are all still in peril, and I do mean this seriously kind sirs, we cannot dally —no! I do not like to bring this up, but once we leave this ship, we will need to move as fast as we can, and to travel light. I hope you agree, my dear fellows?'

'You think they are still out there, Peri?' my son asked.

'To be truthful, Sam, I think so. I'm not one hundred percent sure, but when Rita says move, I always say how fast,' he gave a cheeky giggle. 'She is an inspiration that woman, and the last of her kind,' he said with admiration. 'The old days will never come back, and we need to adjust to this modern world. So does this plan feel satisfactory to you, dear chaps?'

'Well,' I said, 'it is the best we have heard so far, Peri, and I cannot think of anything better.' Turning towards Sam, I asked, 'How about you, son?'

'We need a backup plan, Dad,' he voiced. 'If there's a chance that someone will follow, then we need someone to ride tailgate for us,' he suggested.

'Yes, yes, young Sam. I have a plan for that, so you don't have to worry. You see, I have family now in Auckland and intend to utilise them. You will not spot them, but don't worry they will be there. So, it is no worries; no worries at all,' he grinned. 'And if there are crooks out there, they will get a shock of their lives, I can tell you.' He looked very pleased with himself, as he left our suite with a wave of his hand. 'We will talk again soon, gentlemen,' he said, leaving us a little perplexed.

I started to have second thoughts that maybe this wasn't right, and I began to articulate my thoughts to my son. He stopped me. 'Father, you have to go through with this now, or try to anyway. We need to be safe for a while, and if nothing comes of it, we may have to spend a month or two in the bush. Maybe things will have calmed down after that, but for now we need to be safe, so please, no more talk about backing out. We both want to get home in one piece, wherever home is, so let's just continue on and see how it pans out, okay?' he grinned trying to build my confidence.

It seemed to me, that the decisions were now out of my hands, and Sam had taken over with determination. Honestly, I was happy for him to do so. I was tired of all the goings-on, and it was time for someone else to take over. Sam broke into my pondering. 'Dad, there's a thought that has been going through my mind recently. Remember we have the election back home, coming up soon. You know the Conservatives have a good chance of winning, so as you know William Gladstone quite well. I have been thinking, would it not be prudent to send him a confidential letter when we arrive in Auckland. To explain what is happening, and to mention the attempts on Blanche and our own lives, not to mention the killings? That way if the government changes, hopefully a new broom will sweep clean, and Purcell might get a tonne of bricks falling around his ears. Honestly, Father, I cannot believe that our PM at the moment, Lord Salisbury, if he knew about it, would allow this sort of thing anyway. After all he is a very law abiding and idealistic man.'

He continued to explain, 'If Gladstone becomes the new PM, I'm sure he will be shocked at what you could tell him. On the other hand, the Secretary of State, at the moment, Sir James Holden, is another kettle of fish. I never did like, or trust him, when he last visited the manor. He was a sleazy man that I did not want to be associated with, and to think that Purcell is evil also. So, it looks like it could be a conspiracy, originating with these two gentlemen. I'm guessing the rest of the government might be in the dark about what's going on. If that is the case, with the letter you send to Gladstone, it might put an end to this caper once and for all.

I looked at my son. 'You know, Sam, I had never even thought of it. Yes, Purcell is an evil bugger, and you are right, Lord Salisbury is a good man, and so is Gladstone; I'll talk to Blanche and get her opinion. If she is agreeable, I will write the letter and send it off to them both, when we arrive in New Zealand. Of course, I'll have to ask permission from the prince first, but if I explain it the right way, I'm sure he will agree. No doubt it will be too long to send a cable, but I might be able to if it is at all possible.'

So, I not only had my message cum manuscript to Bob Kydd, my old mate, to finish. I now had a letter to a future PM and an ex-PM if this was the way the election goes. All this thinking was tiring me out. But it needs to be done. They both need to know of the dirty undercover work that is going on in the name of the queen.

Additionally, with the manuscript, I'm hoping this time-travel message will reach Bob before we get home, I don't want it to turn up unexpectedly on Bob's doorstep after thirty years. And there's another thing I haven't even thought about until now, what is my son going to think when we get back to my time. How will he fit in? Everything is going to be such a shock to him.

Take women's fashions for instance. It's going to embarrass him, coming from the Victorian era mentality, into the twenty-first century. He never saw much skin on a lady with all their finery, in the past, but in the twenty-first century, his eyes are going to be popping at the ends of stalks, and he won't know where to look. It is going to take some time to adjust to the information overload, he will experience. I could feel myself retreating to my old ways, to begin to worry about needless details again, when to get there in one piece should be my primary focus. I'm going to have to harden up a bit and revert back to my old army ways. If anyone takes a pot-shot at me, I don't intend to miss when I return fire. They will take us on, at their own peril as I haven't lost my touch, and Sam is just as good as I am. Of course, I mustn't forget that we have Peri and his whanau, as backup with us as well.

The purser informed me of some interesting piece of news when I came up on deck. He mentioned that the governor general spent a few months of each year at Government House in Auckland, and he was under the impression that he would be there when we arrived. I thought if that were the case, I might be able to send a private cable to the Prince of Wales through Government House. 'Who is the governor general?' I asked him.

'The Earl of Glasgow,' came the reply. Of

course, I thought—David Boyle; I had met him a couple of times before, he had travelled out to New Zealand in 1892. I should have remembered, but with my head injuries, I had clean forgotten. Well, if he is the boss, I thought, I will have no problem sending off a cable. The only issue is I'll have to be off the ship, but I'll work that out when we get there. I thanked the purser. Another problem solved, I thought.

We were in luck, the fine weather held right through our sailing of the Indian Ocean, around the bottom of Australia and into the Tasman Sea. The captain shook his head. 'In living memory, Sam, this has never happened before—calm waters the whole route.'

Slowly, we headed around Cape Reinga and headed down towards Auckland and the Waitemata Harbour. We approached Great Barrier Island then Rangitoto Island. I began to feel a wee bit overwhelmed. I was home, but in the wrong century. I just hoped that the mist still existed as a quirk of nature and enable us to return through it to my time. As we slipped into the port of Auckland the time had come for Abe and Blanche to leave us. By this time Abe, had begun to walk slowly with a cane, with her assistance. He had dressed in labourer's clothing, and Blanche, wore a plain dress and bonnet.

'We both cannot thank you enough Sam,' Abe said as we shook hands. 'Thank you for being a good friend to Blanche and escorting her out to New Zealand. Now I expect you will be able to have a few weeks catch-up with your daughter and be back in the old country for a late autumn.'

No one knew what Sam and I had planned, so for them, once Blanche was safe, we would not stay for long, then head home once a ship was available.

'No worries Abe, Blanche, please take this.' I handed a cheque of fifteen hundred pounds to Blanche to draw on the BNZ.

'What on earth is this, I cannot accept it, Sam,' she exclaimed. 'It's far too much,' she leant back as she shook her head.

'No, Blanche, it is our wedding present to you and the least I can do. I'll not see you both out of pocket because of Abe's wounds. Even though, mate...' I said, and looked at him, 'even though you can walk, you are a very long way off working your farm. This is to help out, and I will take it as an insult if you try to give it back. My son and I both want you happy and well.'

Blanche kissed me on the cheek. 'You are a good man, like Abe, Sam, and if you ever come out to New Zealand for any reason, our home is yours.' I shook Abe's hand once again, as did my son.

'We'd better go and mingle with the steerage folk,' he said to Blanche as they turned and walked down towards their exit point for what they hoped was safety and freedom.

CHAPTER TWENTY-EIGHT

The Home Secretary's Office England 1893

Sir Anthony Purcell paced the Home Secretary's office as he brought his boss up to date about their problem. He was furious about what had happened in Egypt.

'They were imbeciles,' he raved. 'I should have known that they would make a mess of it, but at the time they were all I had. Now both are gone, and even though we received the code word "Sunshine," can we believe it? If it wasn't for that lone operative, who kept watch on the ship when it docked, we could have been in a bit of hot water. To take the initiative to shoot Davis on sight has indeed saved our bacon. But did Davis talk that's the big question? I don't think we are out of the woods yet.'

The Secretary scowled, 'All right, Purcell. I don't want to know the details; I just want results. I'll leave it in your hands. I was, going to say capable hands, but this is a right muck-up, and you sir, will fix it. Next time we meet up, if it's not settled, I want your resignation in writing on my desk. Don't forget there is an election coming up, and if the PM loses, I'm out of a job, and you will also be out in the rain. So, sort it out. I don't want any repercussions coming back to haunt us. Do I make myself clear, Sir Anthony?'

Sir Anthony didn't like being spoken to like that, he was the one who normally did all the yelling and bullying. He seethed; he did not like it one little bit. 'Fine, but don't forget,' he hissed, 'we are in this together, so if it comes back to hit me in the face, your name will also come up. You might want to think on that, Mr. Secretary. In fact, if it does come to that, it might be advisable that we both find some sort of bolt hole to disappear into for a while.' he turned fuming and slammed the door as he left.

He was livid as he strode out of the building. Useless bugger, he thought. The amount of work I have done for him and the country, and I get no appreciation at all. My problem is there is no loyalty among the men I recruit. Most are blaggards, and once out of the country, I have to rely on their goodwill, which is only grudgingly given, if at all. If it weren't for the cash I offer, I'd have no one. It's a disgrace I cannot recruit from the army or navy, then things would be completely different.

He arrived back at his Whitehall office still enraged. He poured himself a brandy and sat at his desk to mull it over. If the woman had been dispatched, there was still a chance that know-it-all Selkirk, and his son, and no doubt, those two colonial fellows knew the full story of Lady Blanche Proctor. I'm sure, he thought that if this were the case, then in all probabilities, they would need to be silenced themselves, once they reached New Zealand. There was no other way. Of course, there still might be a chance that she lived, and that would be a double damn.

So, what to do; what to do? He tapped his fingers on the table. Who have I got in New Zealand that would be capable of doing this job? There would be four men to get rid of, and any of the Maori who got in the way, but I want it done professionally, not like the Davis and Simms fiasco.

He walked over to a filing cabinet and shuffled through the pile of papers until he found what he was looking for. Ah, yes, he thought. Jack Flower, an Irish bad penny, he thought with a grin. He would do the job adequately. Then another file popped up with another name. Ah yes, just the ticket. He picked up the file on a half caste Maori, Tane Hall. He had done good work in the past and was excellent with a rifle and handgun. He flipped through and came up with another file—on George Albert. Is that all? A bit thin on the ground, he thought.

Mind you Jack Flower had brought in men to help out in the past, and could repeat that now, as he would need at least three more men. He sat down at his desk with the files and started to write out a cable in code. He would send the instructions to Jack Flower, and a directive cable to the other villain's to all meet up at the Queen's Ferry Hotel in Vulcan Lane. It was nice and close to Queen's Wharf, where the ship would dock. It was also convenient to the railway station. They would need to keep an eye on the trains as one ever knew what the Selkirks were up to. In code, he wrote:

Terminate with haste.

Lord Samuel Selkirk and his son Samuel. Both are big men and stand six feet five inches. His son is a redhead, father silver haired. Cannot be missed. Also, Abraham Metcalfe from Mangere, five feet eleven, and his friend the Reverend Henry Talbert from Wellington, Wesley minister, shorter, stout, and grey haired. Any Maori that is associated at the time of dispatch must also be removed. There might also be a light grey-haired woman of five feet, two inches. First name, Blanche. Surname, Proctor. Eliminate with haste. Do this DISCREETLY, but do it quickly. Time is of the essence. Reply imperative, now and after task is completed.

A bonus of 200 pounds to each operative with the right outcome of assignment. Burn all correspondence.

The controller.

They will have about three weeks, for them to sort it out, he thought. He took the message down to his cable operator.

'Send this now, and as soon as a reply comes back, I want to be informed.' He returned to his office, pleased with himself. Another brandy, he thought as he walked over to his liquor cabinet.

Jack received their orders, in his dingy accommodation in Auckland. He replied, message received, and organised a meet up with his selected associates, at the suggested Queen's Ferry Hotel. But they found it too exposed and decided to head back to Jack Flower's flat on the hill in Ponsonby. They tossed suggestions around for an hour or so, well, two were. The third bloke, George Albert, was quiet, and he just listened to what the other two men said.

Jack Flower was of Irish descent. He had been caught up in a murder in Ireland, then recruited by Sir Anthony and sent out to New Zealand. He had no scruples at all. People were just a number to him.

'This is going to be too easy,' he scoffed. 'A couple of toffs that stand out. Two well-placed shots will do them nicely, then a cocky and a do-good minister. It is going to be easy as pie; mark my words.' He smirked. 'If we cannot get them that way, and I'm sure we can, well, if they take up lodgings in a pub, a small accident like a night fire will do as well. We can do the same at the cocky's farm, it will burn down quickly with him in it, no problem whatsoever. I have a few extra men in mind to give us a hand, if this is agreeable to you both.'

The two men nodded their heads in agreement.

'We will stake out the ship from the top floor of the New Zealand Insurance Company. That gives us a clear view onto Queen's Wharf. Furthermore, Robinson House is lower on the other corner, so we can place a man there. There's a chance they might take a train. Opposite the station is Talbert House, and that roof has a good vantage point right at the entrance to the post office and Britomart Station. We will also need two or three walkers on the ground, to follow and do the deed if they get an opportunity. I think that might cover all contingents. One more thing, there could be that woman the boss mentioned. If so, she goes the same way.' He looked up at Tane Hall. 'So, what do you think?'

Tane was part Maori, with a Maori mother and English father, though he took after his father's side of the family. He was an excellent shot and had been used by Jack a few times in the past. But if he had to go bush, he was bloody useless. A complete townie, he'd only been as far as Papakura on the train. He had never done a hard day's work in his life: soft hands, black hair, brown eyes, and a stocky build of five feet, six inches, and the only evidence there might be a hint of Maori in him, was a very light tan. Even though he was a good shot, he had never experienced anyone shooting back at him. But he loved to read the penny thrillers that were now becoming the rage, and he thought since reading these who done it's, he knew it all when it came to fights and ambushes.

This spiel of Jack's about the soft target, excited him. 'Superb ideas you have there, Jack.' He laughed rubbing his hands together. 'And I sure would like to be on that rooftop. It has a clear escape route as well.' He grinned. He anticipated it with eagerness. 'Have you got anyone in mind regarding the other blokes you will need?'

'Yep, I think so. It's been arranged, I'll talk to them tonight at the Thistle Hotel.'

He turned to George. 'You are quiet, mate.'

'Yeah, just listening, Jack. No need to make a noise if it is not called for.'

George was quite different from the others, a quiet, thoughtful man. A farmer, a large man with big hands, and he was only here because of what happened thirty years ago, at Gate Pa. He had been in the attack on the Pa, when he was spotted, by a young officer when he shot his sergeant in the back. The NCO had been a complete bastard and a bully to boot. The fact was, George did everyone a favour, but unfortunately, a young officer saw him do the deed, and kept it to himself. When this officer returned to England, he mentioned it to his cousin Anthony Purcell, who hid the detail away for future use. That was until he took the controller's job. Then he contacted George detailing all that he knew about what happened that day at Gate Pa. He was given a choice, either work for me, or face a hangman's noose. That's when George decided to work for Sir Anthony, though he always looked for a way out. He had been lucky up till now, as this was the first time in thirty years he had been called to do a job, but he was no killer—not like this. He was married now, with three children, and his third grandchild on the way, and he was mystified at what to do about it.

'One thing I'll put forward,' he said to Jack, 'I suggest that I look after Metcalfe, leave him to me if that's all right with you. With us both being farmers, we will think alike, and I'll be able to get him away from the house. Another thing you might reflect on,—the cable emphasised "discreetly"—and I don't think shooting people in the middle of town is prudent, do you? We need them out on the road or on a train, anywhere but the town. I'll fix Metcalfe my way, but let's be sensible. By all means, stake out the place, but do the job in a remote location.'

Jack grimaced. 'You are right, I'm letting my

enthusiasm get in the way. We will find a quiet place. Good thinking, George, thanks, for bringing it up. You fix the farmer; we'll do the rest.'

Little did they know that George knew Abe Metcalfe quite well, and there was no way he was going to shoot him. I need to warn him somehow, of what is going to happen, and to heck with the consequences. I'm no murderer, he thought. Well, once, maybe, but I wouldn't call killing that NCO murder, more an execution. In his mind's eye, George could still see the beatings some of the lads took from that shit of a sergeant. No, he thought, that was fair justice, and Abe will have a fighting chance as far as I am concerned.

Jack continued to plot, 'I have thought about escape routes if we do get a line of fire at the bottom of town. As long as our guns are not visible, we will be able to mingle with the crowd. All the tall buildings have fire escapes. So, if we finish the job in the city, we can be out of there as quick as hell. We will split up and head out individually and make our way to the old farm in the Henderson Valley until things quieten down a bit. I'll use the old-hat signal. When I put it on my head, that means the two men we are after, are next to me, I'll turn and walk away, so the shooters on the roof have a clear shot. If the weather is against us, we will get close with pistols. We will stroll up and do them; they won't be expecting that. You blokes on the ground will have the pistols, much easier to pocket. Any questions?'

'That doesn't sound like "discreetly", didn't you hear what I just said,' snapped George.

'Yes, yes, I heard you, but this is, just in case, if the situation arises.'

Not another word was spoken until Jack stated, 'Right. Well, I'll get away to meet with the others. You don't have to meet them, until it gets closer to the time. Us three will meet back here in a couple of days and run over everything again until we have it firmly in our minds.'

'Do you know what it is all about, Jack?' Tane questioned.

'Not a thing, and I don't care. Money's too good to let me even think about why. Remember, there will be over a couple of years' wages in this for each of us when the deed is done. The only problem I can see is, there will be police everywhere after this, so we will need to keep our heads down for a while. So maybe a few weeks at the old farmhouse, then clear right out of Auckland and pop down to the South Island out of the way. We can work on that back at the farm. In the meantime, no yakking to anyone and no getting pissed, Tane,' he emphasised. 'Leave that until after, we must keep our noses clean and do the job right. The money will be paid into a bank, I'll withdraw it and have it with me, to divvy up at the farm. Right oh, time to go. You go first, George, then Tane, five minutes later. See you in a couple of days.' Now it had become a waiting game until the ship arrived.

George Albert left, shaking his head. They didn't listen, he thought. These blokes were idiots. You can bet a penny to a pound that they will shoot innocent people, and he wanted nothing to do with either of them.

CHAPTER TWENTY-NINE

Auckland, New Zealand

The SS Rangitoto docked at Queen's Wharf on a wet, miserable day. The steerage passengers disgorged en masse from their exit, trying to avoid the rain as much as possible as it drove in from the east. People milled everywhere, and immigration officials directed them to various warehouses to organised them for their onward journeys.

Abe and Blanche, with their coat collars turned up, and hats pulled down tightly on their heads, walked slowly down the gangway, with Blanche protecting herself with an umbrella. Abe was much improved, though he had a walking stick for support. Instead of heading into the immigration office, they moved towards the exit gate. They had said their goodbyes to everyone, and Abe felt a bit down at the prospect, as he knew this was the last time he would see Rita. But she had patted his hand, hongied them both, and added a kiss on their cheeks.

She smiled with love in her heart, 'Enjoy your life together, you will see wondrous things. Take care.'

They headed out to the gate, where a convoy of cabs were parked waiting for their passengers. They climbed aboard, and the cabby threw their baggage under the tarp at the rear of the buggy. 'Harp of Erin Hotel, please, mate,' Abe yelled to the driver above all the noise from the crowds and rain.

'That's six miles, sir, at least five shillings.' 'Good as gold, mate. Just go, driver.'

He shrugged, 'You're the boss. But if it's okay with you, I would like half now before we head out.' Abe handed him half a crown.

'Don't worry, mate. I'm good for the rest.'

'Thanks, Governor,' the cabby remarked as he climbed aboard.

Abe turned to Blanche. 'We will cable my sister once we arrive at the Harp. It's out of town, and it makes me feel a wee bit safer, but just in case,' he patted his coat, 'my pistol here will be our insurance,' he said with confidence.

Across the road, three men watched the people alight from the ship. George Albert stared through the morning rain, not particularly concentrating, when out of the corner of his eye, he spotted Abe climbing aboard the cab. He said to the other blokes, who he had met only a few days before, 'I'm moving farther up the road to get a better view. You fellows stay here.' They just grunted as another downpour lashed the doorway, and they pushed themselves farther inside the door well. George walked smartly over to the cab rank and whistled to the driver. 'Will you follow that cab in front, mate? he asked. 'But don't overtake it; just hang well back. There's ten bob for you if we don't lose it.'

Christmas has come early, thought the cabby as he grinned, hitched up his collar against the rain, and with a flick of the reins, he pulled out into the middle of the road. Slowly he drove up Queen Street following in the ruts and mud of the cab two hundred yards in front.

The rest of the gang waited and watched as the immigrants shuffled to their appointed places, and then around nine am, the first of the Maori came down the gangway from first class. They carried the coffins of their deceased whanau to a waiting wagon. Jack Flower watched the passengers intensely, counting heads as he was doing so. He saw Te Ruru assist his mother. And a white man, he suspected was the Reverend Henry Talbert, help a man with a cane into a cab.

'There's the Reverend Talbert with Metcalfe,' he said as he watched the reverend support Rita and Abe up into a cab. The ride to the railway station would be all of a couple of minutes, but Rita was old, and her son wanted her dry and warm. Jack Flower turned to his men. 'Stay here,' he commanded, 'and keep a lookout for the Selkirks, while I sort this lot out.

Jack headed towards the cab and the wagon carrying the coffins. Visibility was poor when he arrived at the railway station's main entrance.The men on the roof will be at a disadvantage and quite useless in weather like this, he thought. He passed a couple of his men and Tane who, by this time, had decided he was ineffectual up on the roof and came down to see some action. Jack drawled, 'Follow me, Tane. The ones we want are in that cab up front,' pointing to Rita's cab as it pulled up in front of the station.

Henry helped Rita down then took her arm, and with Te Ruru, went through the entry into Britomart Station. Once inside the concourse, he passed her on to her son and stood back to watch the coffins being pushed down to the nearest guard's van. The bloke who was disguised as Abe Metcalfe slipped through a side door and disappeared.

Jack Flower watched the coffins as they were maneuvered along the concourse on a couple of trolleys. This left Henry Talbert by himself, well back from the others, so he sent Tane to stand behind one of the columns closest to Henry, out of sight from curious eyes. He took off his hat as a signal as the coffins approached the turntable. A voice called out, 'Mr Talbert, Mr Talbert.'

Henry turned around, but the concourse was crowded, he couldn't see anyone taking an interest in him.

'Over here, sir.' The voice called again, coming from the side of the large sandstone column to the right of the main walkway. Henry slipped around the column and walked into a short, light brown skinned male who gave a crooked grin. 'Ah, there you are, Reverend. You know, you should never get involved with things that don't concern you.'

He shoved a small handgun against Talbert's chest and pulled the trigger. Henry's clothes stifled the noise of the gun. He stumbled and made a grab for the column for support. Tane watched him with fire in his eyes and shot him again. Jack, who stood behind him by the column barked, 'Go on! Get out of here.'

Tane disappeared into the crowd, and Jack escaped through another entrance at the side of the station. A few minutes passed before Henry, severely shot, managed to drag himself into the main concourse of the station. Bedlam broke out as people rushed to him. A couple of young Maori were first on the scene. With waning strength, Henry grabbed an arm of the closest Maori. 'Are you Peri's whanau?' He coughed.

'Yes, Padre, we are so sorry. We were held up at the entrance by crowds.'

'Tell Abe.' Henry coughed, and splattered blood over the men. 'Tell Abe that he's not safe, and tell Peri they are waiting. He'll understand.

Go now,' he said. 'Just leave me to go to my God.' They lay him down. He coughed once more and died. People screamed to get the police as the two Maori men shot out of the station and disappeared into the teeming rain. They knew Peri was still on board the ship. So, one headed for the ship, the other caught up with another of his cousins. Information was passed on that Abe had taken a cab and needed to be followed.

'He is about twenty minutes ahead, and the cab driver I spoke to, thinks he overheard the Harp of Erin Hotel mentioned. We will go there now,' the cousin said.

Te Ruru and some of his party returned to see what the commotion was all about. When they saw Henry, they looked down at him in shock, they knew he had gone. Te Ruru went back to his mother and with an empty feeling in his gut, he explained Henry had been murdered. 'Mother, I'm going to send you back with most of our whanau, and I'll stay here and work out what happened, and if possible, I'll bring Henry back with us. There will be an inquest, look I know the chief inspector, so I'll see if we can get it over with, sooner rather than later.'

At that moment, the police had arrived and right behind them, a gaggle of reporters. 'I'll see you when I get home,' he leant over and kissed her forehead.

Her tears flowed, 'He was a lovely man. This is

the blackness I saw,' she whispered. 'Make sure everyone knows, son. They will have to revise their plans.'

There was a sharp knock on my cabin door. 'It's me... Peri,' he called out. His face was like thunder as he stepped into our cabin. 'The blighters have shot Henry,' he spat. 'They shot and killed him at the railway station. My whanau were too late to save him. My nephew came back to warn us, and the others are now following Abe to pass on the message. Henry's last words urged that Abe is not safe and nor are the two of you. We will have to revise our plans.' My son and I were stunned, and gawked at Peri, we found it hard to sink in.

'Henry's dead,' I stammered, and shook my head.

My son went wild. 'The buggers, Father! Henry was a minister of God, for goodness' sake, this is not right,' he blurted. 'We don't know how many are lying in wait, but we need to sort this out before anyone else gets killed—'

'Yes, young Samuel I agree,' interrupted Peri, 'I want revenge for Henry and utu on the men murdered on the ship. The only way I can think of how to do it quietly, is to make sure they follow us into the bush, south of Pukekawa, and to ambush them there. No one goes there, and they will never be found. You'll remember how thick that bush was, Sam, it took you ages to find that track from the cave you mentioned. Well, we will get them right into the thick of the bush and finish this off once and for all. That calls for a plan on how best to instigate that,' he stressed. We will need to be seen, as we sneak out, so they'll follow us. Then all we need to do, my good man, is to get there in one piece.

'That sounds like a good idea, Peri, my son replied. But Abe is a problem, how can we defend him, when we are hiding in the bush?' He turned to me, and added, 'Father, what do you say Peri sends a nephew of his, to catch up with Abe and Blanche, and discreetly suggest for them to meet us close to the track near Pukekawa. You know Abe; he will be careful, I know he will, and with Peri's whanau's help, they will be waiting for us. That way we will all be safer in numbers.'

What Sam said, triggered something in my mind, then it clicked. 'They'll have to come with us Sam, through the mist,' I uttered, 'and that means I'll have some explaining to do.'

I rubbed my face. Will they believe me, I thought, but I shouldn't worry about that at the moment. We need to concentrate on things now. 'Okay, Peri, can you send that message on to him?'

'All right, old man', he answered, as he walked to the door, 'I'll do it right away.'

'Thanks, Peri,' I continued, 'In the meantime, I need to get up to Government House to send that cable to the prince and the leader of the opposition, Gladstone.

'Don't you leave until I get back,' cautioned Peri. 'I want to be there to watch your back. Do you each have a pistol?'

'Yep, we are okay, there, Peri.'

'Good, my friend. I'll be back in fifteen minutes.' He opened the door and was gone.

Turning to my son, I said, 'We need a disguise, Sam. We can dress as sailors. This weather will help us, so we can wear long capes with hoods. Can you organise that with the purser, and I'll gather up all the cables I'm going to send, and my manuscript I'm to leave with the BNZ? If we can complete that chore as well, then we can think about how to get out of here sooner than we anticipated.' As Sam left to do as I asked, I sat down and wrote a cover letter to my mate Bob and popped it into the manuscript. I had my doubts he would receive it, but I had to try.

Thirty minutes later as the rain continued to pour down, and visibility got even worse, we sneaked off the ship dressed as able seamen. We wore long capes over our shoulders, with hoods covering our heads, and stooped somewhat to take height off our frames. To complete the deception, we carried large empty boxes in front of us. We clambered down the gangway and on into the closest warehouse. Peri gave us a few minutes, then followed suit. We never saw him again until we arrived back onto the ship: he was just a shadow in the dark.

We moved through the warehouse to the rear door and out into the adjacent warehouse that faced Custom Street. This store was filled with boxes to the roof, so we dropped our load and peeked round the door at the same time as a train shunted wagons onto the wharf. We managed to slip ahead of the steam engine just before it crossed Custom Street, and this gave us protection from any watchers. We were now out of the wharf area and into the bottom of town.

We entered through the rear side door into the Turnbull storehouse on the other side of the street. We walked smartly with purpose, and no one questioned what we were doing. We then popped out into the lane at the back, and slowly we advanced through town, using all the small, narrow alleyways. Eventually we made our way to Government House, which was situated on the hill between Waterloo and Princes Street, overlooking the city.

We jumped the back fence and crept up to the rear door of Government House. I looked through the window, and saw a young maid polishing the silverware, I knocked. She was taken aback to see two big men drenched with rain. Her eyes were wide, and her hand went instantly to her heart. Quickly, I said, 'My name is Lord Selkirk. Would you please deliver this note to the governor general? Tell him I'm downstairs.'

She didn't say a word but grabbed the letter, and whisked off as fast as she could, no doubt thinking there were two sailors playing tricks on her. Five minutes later, two marines came around the corner of the building.

'Lord Selkirk?' I nodded. 'Follow us, sir.' One positioned himself in our front and the other in the rear. It didn't look like they trusted us at all, but we soon arrived at the governor general's office. We stepped inside as the governor general pushed himself up from his seat behind his desk.

'Is that you, Sam?' he inquired. 'Yes, it's me, David. How are you?'

'It's been a while since we last saw each other. Come in, come in, my good man, and what can I do for you? Why are you dressed as an able seaman?' Once the marines had been dismissed, I introduced my son, and explained.

'What I want, David, is a loan of your cableroom operator to send wires to His Royal Highness, and the leader of the opposition, Gladstone, and lastly, the PM. I would like your operator to let me know when the reply comes back. Is this acceptable to you, David? I can hang around until it is answered.'

David Boyle, or to be precise, the Earl of Glasgow, was an astute man and never mucked about. 'That's fine, old chap. Come with me.'

He led us down to the cable station. When I handed the operator the cables, all he did was raise his eyebrows, I could see he was used to sending top- secret messages from his station. He immediately sat down and started to send them. The governor general turned back to the door. 'Come along, Sam. You and your son can sit by the fire and dry off until you receive your reply. It doesn't look to be a hot summer this year,' He laughed.

We left with the clicking of the operator's keys in our ears.

'I'll send in coffee. I need to get back to my desk, the paperwork I'm afraid is never-ending.'

Two hours later, we received an answer from the prince, Gladstone, and the PM, who I knew would be angry. All he said was, it will be fixed. Gladstone was quite forthright. 'I'll speak to His Royal Majesty this morning, and if elected, I'll fix those beggars, Lord Selkirk. You can rely on me.' There was more, but I was happy with his reply.

The prince's message was 'I'll talk to Gladstone and thank you for the protection of the lady in question.'

The governor general put his carriage at our disposal. 'See you back home, Sam. I'll make a point to call around to take the waters at Victoria Spa.'

We left with the marine guard at the gate, giving us a salute as we went through. The driver took us to the main entrance to the BNZ in Queen Street, where I rushed in with the cape still covering me, in keeping with my disguise. I found the bank manager, I told him my name, and as I had a large account there at the bank, I had no trouble placing the manuscript in the vault with instructions to be sent to Robert Kydd of Invercargill in 2020. He didn't even blink, which surprised me. You don't have people waltzing in and asking to look after a parcel for over a hundred years every day, surely. It was placed in a steel container and slipped into its own wall vault. We shook hands, and I was out the door and into the coach in thirty minutes. It was still pouring as we approached the ship. There was no way that anyone could have seen us as we rushed up the gangway into the ship, proper.

Fifteen minutes later, Peri brushed the rain off his coat before he entered the cabin. 'A good day to keep out of sight, and no one followed either one of you,' he gave a cheeky smile. 'A warm drink perhaps, my friend, will go down well. So now we will plan how to get to Pukekawa safely,' Peri informed us, as he sat down. 'According to Te Ruru, there is to be a coroner's inquest tomorrow for our friend Henry. Once that is over, he will take him south. It is a sad day for all of us, as we will not be there for his funeral, but he will be well looked after. Te Ruru has already cabled his friends and family in Wellington, that he will bring him home. As far as we know, the police are running around in circles with no leads at all. So, my friends, it will be left up to us to find these blighters.' He looked up as Sam thrust a large cup of coffee into his hands. 'Thank you, young man. Just the ticket.'

CHAPTER THIRTY

Auckland, New Zealand

Abe and Blanche arrived a couple of hours later at the Harp of Erin Hotel in Ellerslie. Even though the journey had been a quagmire of mud from start to finish, and the cab slipped and slid all over the place, they were both in a pretty good mood on arriving at the Hotel. The pub backed onto the railway line, and there was a racecourse on the other side of the line.

The rain poured down as they stepped from the cab, and they dashed as quick as they could, with Abe hobbling on his cane, to the main door of the forty-year-old pub. It was a two-story wooden affair with a balcony built around the second floor. This used to be a country pub a few years ago, but because of the railroad, Auckland had grown. Now there were only a few small farmlets around the area with houses being developed all over the place.

The driver brought in their cases and even went the extra mile, to help take the cases up to their room. They thanked him, and with the extra sixpence on top of the two half-crowns in his pocket, he left for the long slog back to

Queen Street. They tried to sit and chat on their bed, but the rain was persistent, with the noise like a constant drumbeat, and it was hard to hear each other speak. They had only been in their room for about fifteen minutes when there was a knock on their door. Ever wary, Abe had his pistol out, and Blanche quickly slipped behind the wardrobe door.

'Who's there?' he called above the noise of the rain.

'George Albert,' came back the reply.

'George, what the heck are you doing here, mate?' Abe demanded as he opened the door.

George looked like a drowned rat, and his coat was saturated as though he had been swimming in it. He looked miserable as his cab had been an open affair. He smacked his hat on his leg to remove the excess rain. 'Come in, come in. This is my wife, Blanche.' He introduced her as she stepped out from behind the wardrobe. 'Blanche, my friend, George Albert.'

'Please to meet you, Blanche,' George said with a worried look on his face.

'Hello, George,' Blanche answered, feeling a little confused.

'I'm sorry to intrude, but I have a story to tell you, Abe, and I think you will not be so happy to see me, once told.'

'Pull up a chair and get that coat off before you

catch your death,' Blanche ordered as she pulled out the towels and gave them to George. He hung his coat over the back of the chair, and vigorously rubbed his face and hair with the towel. Abe rang down for a hot pot of coffee. When it arrived, and the porter had left, George, with a cup in his hand, related his story.

'I apologise for complicating your lives by turning up here, but I followed you, from when you first piled into your cab,' he looked uneasy. His eyes glanced down at his shoes, then with a sigh, continued, 'You are both in terrible danger, my friend. They sent me to shoot you.' At the shocked looks on their faces, George lifted his hand. 'Abe, I'm not a killer, let me finish, mate. Look we all make mistakes, and mine was a beauty through the war that has come back to haunt me. But me a murderer—no way. I'm at my wits' end at what to do, so, I had to warn you. Let me assure you though, I know for a fact, that there is no way, that this rifle is ever going to be pointed at you.'

'We understand, George,' grunted Abe. 'If it weren't you, there would be someone else.' He looked away, feeling apprehensive, and squeezed Blanche's hand. What the heck are we going to do, now? he thought.

Sensing his unease Blanche reassured him, 'We will work this out, Abe. We have to. We cannot afford to look back over our shoulders for the rest of our lives.'

'Look, Abe,' George broke in, 'I don't intend to return to Auckland to meet up with the other men, so the least I can do is watch your back. I have met all those killers, so I can recognise them. We could create a diversion and maybe stage a fight, someone sees a body thrown onto a wagon, and that someone reports to the police, and then the gang hears about it. They might just think I had done the job. It could hold them off a bit. Though, mate, you won't be able to stay in Auckland or return to your farm in Mangere, as they know where you live.'

There was another knock on the door. George jumped up and stood behind the opening door with his rifle across his body. Blanche scooted around and hid, behind the wardrobe, as she pulled out a small handgun. Those hours of practice on board the ship just might pay off, she thought to herself. Abe slipped to the other side of the door, and cried out, 'Who's that?'

'Tamati,' came the answer. 'Peri's nephew, he told me to catch up with you.'

Abe opened the door to a good-looking Maori bloke, he was young with large brown eyes, dimples, and black hair that was plastered to his head because of the rain. He also looked like a drowned rodent. 'I have news Abe, and it's not good news,' Tamati announced as he stepped into the room. 'Henry was shot and killed at the railway station.' Abe stood stunned. George closed the door for him, after Tamati entered.

Abe brought his hands up to cover his face, 'My God,' he said. 'Not my mate, Henry. Those bastards!'

'I'm so sorry, Abe,' Tamati whispered, placing his hand on Abe's shoulder. 'He was a good man to our people. His last words were, that you and your wife are not safe anymore, and that you need to go undercover until things are worked out.'

Abe was in shock that this had happened, Blanche cried, and George looked crestfallen as he was part of this gang. 'I cannot think of what to do,' said Abe bewildered.

Tamati lent forward, 'I have an idea.'

Before he could utter another word, there was another knock on the door. This time everyone reacted in confusion. 'Who the hell is that?' George barked.

'Hemi,' came back the voice behind the door.

'It's getting to be like a railway station,' Abe burst out. 'Come in, Hemi.'

George opened the door, his rifle ready just in case it was needed. Hemi walked into the room, wet like everyone else, and combed his hair with his fingers.

'Peri sent me, I'm pleased I caught up with you, Tamati.' He turned to Abe. 'I have a message to give you. Do you know where Sam is heading?'

'No, he told me nothing about that, a bit strange I thought, but why?'

'Well, Sam made clear, that now he knows that you all are in danger, it will be safer to be together,' explained Hemi. 'So, he wants you to meet him just past Pukekawa, near the beginning of the bushline. Then Peri will guide you all further into the bush. Sam intends to take you to a place where no one will be able to find you. That is if you are agreeable, if so, I'll let them know.'

Hemi turned to Tamati. 'You know where I mean?' 'Yes, I do,' Tamati replied.

Well Peri suggested you travel quickly, to avoid being spotted, and to be alert.'

'What about Henry?' Abe sputtered.

'Our chief, Te Ruru, will look after him. I think he plans to wait for the inquest then escort Henry's body back to his family in Wellington. I'm sorry for your loss, Abe. He was a wise and kindly man to our people. Peri wants utu, so his murder will be avenged. It looks like the police have no leads at all. So, he is talking about Maori justice. I'll head back now and let him know, with Tamati guiding, you will wait for them near Pukekawa.' He turned to George. 'If you are his friend, he will need all the help he can get. Right, I'm off.' He opened the door, turned and said, 'Noho ora mai' (all the best), then closed the door behind him.

Abe felt discouraged, all this bad news had hit him hard. It was Blanche who took over in an instant. 'George,' she concluded, 'we need to work out this scenario you suggested, about the fake shootout. Then arrange for a covered wagon to take us to where we have to go. We will leave our suitcases here, so as not to draw attention to ourselves, we can pick them up later on. We will take only essentials. Will you follow us, George?'

'Yes! With Tamati accompanying us, that is the least I can do. We only need to head down to Otahuhu, and catch the train from there to Tuakau, and then we can pick up another wagon, to take us the rest of the way. No doubt your friends would have thought of supplies. What do you think, Tamati?'

'Yes, a definite plan. There is an evening train we can catch, so darkness will be our friend.' Abe sat there in a daze.

Blanche lent over Abe, 'Are you feeling, all right my dear?' she gave him a hug. He circled his arms around her waist.

'Yes, I will be fine. It is just a shock. Henry and I have been close friends since the war, for him to go like this.' He shook his head. 'This news has hit me worse than being knifed. I'll be okay, Blanche don't worry,' he patted her hand, 'and your right we do need to organise ourselves. You are doing a good job.' With that, he slowly stood up, and wiped his eyes. 'I do hope they follow us as I have a huge score to settle with them, if they catch up.'

At the same time, back on the boat, Sam, his son, and Peri worked on their own escape plan to get out of Auckland. Sam needed to be sighted, so a trap could be set down the line, but the trick mustn't be too obvious. Peri had seen that the villains still had watches out on the trains. Apparently, they hadn't given up yet. So, they came to the conclusion that they would catch the evening train, not from the central station as expected, but to jump aboard just before the tunnel, as it puffed its way up the incline to Newmarket. It appeared that Peri knew people who had contacts on the railway, and could persuade the driver to slow down more than usual, to allow the trio to jump onto the guard's van as it passed. The train left the central station at 8:30 p.m, so they would leave as soon as it got dark. The three hoped that the rain would hold to cover their escape.

That afternoon, a cable arrived from, Margaret to say she would miss them in Auckland, as she had to go to Greymouth, urgently. There was a severe breakout of measles, and all available doctors were expected to go. She had no idea how long it would take, but it could be for a month or two, and she would catch up when she got back. 'In the meantime, don't do anything silly, Father.' That part of the cable was written in capitals.

That was one worry out of the way, Sam told his son, 'I wasn't looking forward to facing her. She can be as determined as her mother was and would have done everything in her power to stop us from what we are going to attempt.' Then sadness hit me, as I realised that I might not see my lovely daughter again.

The day slipped by slowly and gave us time to sort through our gear. We only needed to take necessities and would pick up food supplies at Tuakau. Then Peri arrived keen to inform us on what he had heard. 'The police still have no clues about who shot Henry. Te Ruru is livid, he has called on all whanau for utu.

The authorities won't like it, as they insist that those days have gone. But I can tell you, Sam,' he affirmed, 'all Maori will be on the look-out, and if they find them, there will be no quarter, my good man—no sympathy at all. The blighters will be smote the Maori way.'

Settling down after that outburst, Peri admitted that he had arranged everything for us. The train driver would slow down as asked, and Abe and Blanche had been informed, and would catch up with us down the line. He also mentioned he had organised an extra couple of his family to catch the train at both Newmarket and Ellerslie Stations. They were there to keep an extra eye out. The main thing now, was to look as though we intend to go undetected, but to make sure they got a glimpse of us and followed.

Finally, it was time, we thanked the ship's captain, and sneaked out once it was dark, the rain was still pouring. We blessed the weather gods for their help as we dashed through the warehouse once more, then onward through the second one. There we waited for Peri, who was the lookout. Soon his all- clear whistle came, we peeked around the door then quickly moved out, and headed down Quay Street. We kept to the shadows away from the light of the gas lamps. Once out of the city, proper, we crossed onto the railway tracks and continued walking up to Parnell Rise. When we spotted a single manuka tree, we stopped to wait for the train to arrive. Eventually, the headlight cut through the rain and mist, and the coal smoke enveloped us as the train crept along at a leisurely pace.

'Be careful, Father,' Sam remarked, 'this is not a time to fall.' The engine chugged by, the smoke was thick, and the rain shielded us completely from the passing carriages with the dull glow of the gas lamps shining through the windows. Any passengers that looked outside would have only seen reflections of themselves in the windows. The guard's van came up to us with its gates open, and my son just stepped aboard. Peri had clambered on the other side, as Sam put his hand out for me, and heaved me towards the van's platform. As we arrived on the rear platform, the door opened.

'Ah,' the guard confirmed, 'you have arrived. Come on inside, it's warm and cosy in here, as the coal stove is going, and the kettle is on the boil. Will you sort yourselves out? I have to go through and check the tickets.' Once the guard left, we stripped off our coats and hung them out to dry. It took a while for our eyes to adapt as the guard's van had inadequate lighting. The kettle came to the boil and we poured out cups of tea then stood with our backs to the stove to let the warmth sink into our bodies. The smell of damp clothes filled the air, and I knew that our gear would soon dry.

Simultaneously when the trio were jumping aboard, a gang member, who had positioned himself two carriages from the front of the train, had seen shadows slipping onto the rear wagon. He was in luck as he had the impression that the men were quite tall. He chuckled to himself, they might be the ones they were after.

As the train slowed down at Newmarket Station, he jumped off and stood in the shadow of the centre doorway and waited for the guard's van to go past. A few people milled around as the train came to a steaming halt, and in that split second the weak light of the guard's van showed the watcher what he had hoped to see. A tall, red-headed man stood face on, as he looked out through the window with his back to the stove.

These are the blokes we are after all right, he smiled, pleased it was him to have sighted them. He walked smartly out of the station and crossed the overhead bridge into the main street of Newmarket. He caught a cab back into the inner city to inform Jack Flower that the men they seek were heading out of town. As he drove towards his boss, he went over what he had seen, it had to be them, the stature and hair colour and a vague shadow of another man, about the same size, stood next to him. Little did he know that in the same carriage was another of Peri's nephews, who noticed him jump off, then watched him intently, as he waited until the guard's van had passed his hidey-hole in the door frame, before he turned and walked out of the station. He walked back to the guard's van and reported to Peri, 'They had seen you and taken the bait.'

'The tricky buggers!' spat Jack when the news arrived. 'We need horses now. I don't care where you get them—just get them.' An hour later, the men came back with five horses fully saddled, taken from various stables around the city. 'Right, chums. We will follow the railway line, but we will have to watch at each station to make sure they didn't get off. I think they will probably want to get right out of town, at least to Papakura, Pukekohe, or even Tuakau as that is as far as the train goes. It's only a tiny town, but we have to be certain. Okay, let's ride.' They wheeled the horses out of the alleyway into Queen Street. The street was empty now, as it was close to ten in the evening. As the rain continued to teem down, they headed out of the city.

They made good time, and Jack's men arrived at the Ellerslie Railway Station within an hour. They noticed a group of men gathered across the road from the Harp of Erin. So, Jack told his men to stay put, and to keep an eye out. He trotted over to see what was going on. As he approached, he asked a man who stood by his gate, 'What's going on, mate?'

'There was a shooting. We heard the shots, and someone saw a couple of bodies being dragged onto a covered wagon, then it drove off at a hell of a rate. Now the hotel proprietor informed us that a married couple are missing. Abe Metcalfe, you remember him? He received a VC in the wars. Nobody knows what's going on, and the police haven't arrived yet. It's getting like a Wild West town, what with the shooting in Auckland and now this. We're not safe at all.'

Jack ambled his horse back to his men. 'It looks as though George did the job on Abe and a woman. I'd say all we have to worry about now is the old Selkirk bloke and his son. Right, no one got off here. Let's move out.' They turned their horses' noses south, with mud flying off their hooves, they headed down Great South Road. There won't be a wink of sleep for any of them tonight, Jack thought, not until they've caught up with their quarry.

CHAPTER THIRTY-ONE

Near Pukekawa

With it's usual smoke and steam wafting around the platform the train came to a stop at Otahuhu Station. I noticed four dark figures materialise from the shadows of the building and quickly slip aboard. I immediately alerted Peri and warned him to make sure that his whanau checked them out. Right away they recognised Tamati and told him where we all were. So, the four of them made their way through the carriages to the guard's van.

Abe looked depressed and overwhelmed as he joined us. His health had taken a toll, after losing his best friend, and his concern about Blanche's safety.

'I don't understand how can you help us?' Then he asked me, 'Where are we going?'

'I'll explain when we reach the cave, Abe. Please take my word, that as soon as we are there, I'll explain everything. You look beat, mate. Why don't you both sit and try to get a bit of rest before we arrive at Tuakau? We intend to have a bit of a tramp later, and I think that might tax you. So, it's important to get as much rest as possible.'

Abe plonked himself down on the bench seat next to his wife. 'I do feel tired,' he sighed. 'A rest is surely needed.'

The guard came back into the van and looked around surprised. 'Oh, I didn't expect my domain to be completely taken over. But as I'm doing this as a favour for friends, I'll do my paperwork in the first carriage. Thankfully there are few passengers on a night like tonight. Oh incidentally, the journey might be a bit longer than anticipated, there's flooding south of Papakura. It's not too bad apparently, but enough for us to have to slow to a plodding pace. So, we don't expect to arrive at Tuakau, until at the earliest, ten in the morning.'

I looked over at Abe and Blanche as the guard left. 'Well in that case, we have plenty of time to relate to you an account of why we are heading where we are. Please keep an open mind, as it's going to sound a bit weird to you both.' I spoke for an hour or so and when I'd finished, I got the impression that they thought I had lost the plot. I was favored to have my son to back me up, though, even he was not entirely convinced.

In the end, Abe spoke up. 'Time travel, Sam?' he shook his head. 'The only reason I'm with you now is I know in my heart you are honourable and trustworthy, so I want to give you the benefit of the doubt. Logically we are at least safer in numbers, and as we haven't got any other place to go, Blanche and I will go along with it, and see how it pans out. If you say there is a cave, then I believe you. At least we will have a roof over our heads.' He smiled, 'I think I'll try to have that sleep now,' he announced as he lay down on the bench seat and closed his eyes.

'Thank you for trying, Sam,' Blanched acknowledged. 'Anything is better than having to look over our shoulders every minute of the day,' Even with Peri vouching for my story, they were both very sceptical.

It was fortunate that the rain started to ease as we pulled into Tuakau Station. Peri rushed to off to arrange a covered wagon for us. I collected the supplies for at least two months, and Tamati, with his cousins, arranged for Abe and Blanche to have a hot meal in the pub. My son stood guard behind the front door with George. Then Abe hired us a room for a few hours, so we could remain out of sight until we were ready to leave.

The wagon driver picked me up at the store, then the rest of us at the pub, and by one in the afternoon, we plodded down River Street and headed for Pukekawa. My son sat up front riding shotgun, while the rest of us were concealed in the back of the covered wagon. While hidden, we worked to split our supplies, for when we hit the trail, so as to share the load. Once completed we rested, and the sloshing of the wheels on the mud road sent me into a deep sleep until Peri shook me.

'We are here Sam. From this place we hike.' George had stayed back in Tuakau to wait for the crooks to turn up, and to point them in our direction, then he would tag along behind them.

I looked at the bush. It was just as it was thirty years ago, but as I looked towards the river, I noticed it had been cleared for farming. A sadness hit me to see, that this once pristine forest had been ruined. We packed up our gear, thanked the driver, and asked him if he were questioned, to mention that he had brought only two men out here. He was an old bloke and knew Abe from the war and had no qualms about telling a few white lies for us. Peri took the lead.

'Take it slow,' I cautioned. 'Abe is still not one hundred percent, and we are not as young as we use to be.' Blanche had dressed herself in men's clothing, so at a quick glance, she looked like one of the blokes. We headed inland, and our speed diminished, not because of our age, but on account that the bush was so thick and wet underfoot after all the rain we had. How the hell did Peri know where he was going. For that matter how was I going to find the cave in all this. This thought kept running through my mind as I had no answer to it.

Late in the afternoon, we arrived at a small,

protected flat-grassed area. Peri stopped and made a decision that this was the right place to set up camp and to prepare an ambush. I looked at the surroundings, he was right, it was ideal as long as we stayed hidden in the bush and let them come to us. With the dummy bedding next to a fire, it will entice them to come straight in. I told Peri what I was thinking.

'Ah, my good man, I was thinking the same.' Peri responded with enthusiasm. 'They will only be looking for two people. We will build a small raupo hut, with an open side next to the fire, so the light will shine on the disguised bundles. There is plenty of cover for us to hide in, and we will leave the entrance to the track open for them. George told us that they have no bush skills, so if that is correct, they will see, what they think is you asleep and come straight in.' He looked at me intently. 'I want the man who killed Henry, so if the opportunity arises, he is ours, Sam. My whanau and Te Ruru have first dibs, my good man.'

'What will happen to him if he does turn up?' I queried.

'That will be up to our chief, but I will tell you it will not be pleasant. My family members have a canoe on the river waiting and will take him down to Taumarunui. No one will know, but we are determined to have our utu—you can be sure of that. Now, my friend, there is something I feel

I have to do for you. It does go against my way of thinking, but it needs to be done. If I can keep my nerve, I'll do my best to guide you as close to the cave as I can. This bush has gotten thicker over the years, and as it is tapu, no paths have been trodden for as long. The knife cuts that you left, on the trees, will no doubt have vanished with time. So, if I don't assist you, it will be too difficult for you to find your way. I have the directions all in my head, even though I have never been there, so I will find it much easier than you. Besides, it is my gift to Abe and Blanche to help them to safety. Do you find this agreeable?'

I gave him a wide smile. 'Peri, you are a great bloke. Between you and me and the gatepost, I was a tad bit worried about how I would get through this bush. It does seem thicker than I remember. Thank you for your offer. Now let's get some food into us, and plan tonight's entertainment.' I rubbed my hands together in anticipation.

Five horsemen thundered into Tuakau in the late afternoon. The horses were exhausted, with sweat on their flanks as they had been ridden hard. The five men skirted the railway station and headed down to the Tuakau Family Hotel on George Street. Jack climbed down and ordered Tony to feed and water the horses, while the rest of them were to ask around town if anyone had seen the Selkirks.

Just as they were ready to disperse, George Albert stepped out from the pub's main entrance and whistled. Jack looked up, smiled, then he wandered up to praise George, 'You did a good job back in Ellerslie.'

Before he could say another word, George said with menace, 'What the hell do you think you are doing? You waltz in as though you own the place, and I bet your bloody horses are stolen, you dozy bugger. They have a cable station here, and the constable will know to be on the look-out for five horses. Get out of here Jack. Bugger off. The Selkirks took the Pukekawa Road in a covered wagon. I have borrowed a horse and will hang back to see if anyone is following you. Now, get the hell out of here before too many folk see you lot.'

'Oh shit. Right boys,' he yelled, 'Saddle up, we are moving out.' Tane had hoped for a feed.

'What about eating?' he moaned.

'Later. We need to get clear of this town.' They all remounted, turned, and headed out towards the new bridge that spanned the Waikato, then took the road to Pukekawa.

An hour had passed before they approached a wagon coming in the opposite direction. They stopped and waited for it to catch up to them, then Jack kicked the sides of his horse, and ended up in the middle of the wagon's path. It creaked to a halt. Jack called out to the driver, 'Did you take a couple of blokes up this way?'

'Yep,' the driver answered, and spat tobacco juice onto the road. 'About an hour up this road to the bushline, you'll see where I have turned the wagon around.'

'What's the track like?'

'Not good,' the driver explained, 'but with them ahead of you, they would have left a clear path, I'd say.'

'Thanks, mate,' Jack replied as he pulled his horse out of the way and headed up the road. The horses were fully spent by the time they arrived at the wagon's turning point—over fifteen hours with hardly a stop. The men climbed down and looked at the track. The bush was thick with toi toi and massive tree ferns at the start, and as you looked further in, you could see the trees getting bigger and the bush more dense.

A few of the men started to have second thoughts, after all they were tired and hungry. Now they were expected to follow this track, knock off a couple of blokes, and then tramp back to the horses, before they had a decent meal in them. They were about to voice their opinions when George turned up.

'No one is following you, so you are clear,' he stated. 'It gets dark around eight tonight, so I wouldn't muck about if you want to catch them up.'

'Yeah, we are going now,' Jack snapped. 'Tell me, what did you do with the two bodies, George?' he demanded.

'None of your business,' exclaimed George. 'If anyone is caught, you cannot tell tales if you don't know, so I'm keeping mum. Look, Jack, don't piss about. I'll strip the horses, so at least when you get back, they will be rested. It will only take me about ten minutes or so, I'll be right behind you.'

Jack turned to his men. 'Okay, fellas, let's move.' Opposition melted away as the five entered the bushline on foot, some more reluctant than others. George watched them leave, then stripped off the saddles, walked the horses down to the river, and left them to forage for themselves. Thirty minutes later, he entered the bush and followed their tracks.

Once the sun dropped below the horizon, dusk closed in pretty darn quick. Tane was apprehensive, 'Do you think we should go back to the entrance and wait for them to come out?' He looked around for support. 'Look at us—no food, wearing only city clothes. We are not geared up for this, Jack.' he growled. There were a couple of affirmatives from the men.

They had stopped for a breather when Jack put his hand up. 'Can you smell that?' Jack asked eagerly. 'Wood smoke, they are not far ahead. We won't reach them tonight, but we will be there by morning. Think of the money. A couple of years' wages. All you have to do is spend one night out in this bush, and you will be on the pig's back.'

Unbeknownst to Jack and his men, eyes observed them from the bush. George had hung back and had seen Maori flitting between the trees. He gave the whistle of a tui and felt, rather than saw, a Maori materialise beside him; it was Hemi.

'They are like a mob of sheep,' Hemi grinned. 'You could hear them for miles. The trap is set, and it appears they will not make a move until first light.'

'Well,' replied George, 'I'll hang back here in case someone makes a break for it and tries to get back to the horses.'

The false dawn finally pushed the darkness of the bush back as Jack and his men organised themselves. With only a dry biscuit to eat and a sip of water, the empty bellies of the cohorts didn't bode well. But Jack bolstered them with reminders of the fortune they will make. So, they tightened their belts another notch and waited for his command. They resumed their hike on the track, and forty minutes later arrived at the grassy area where they could see a partly built raupo hut facing the warmth of an open fire. The hut was built so the heat would bounce off the back wall and give the men on the ground warmth all evening. The fire still burnt brightly and gave plenty of light before the full dawn. On either side of the fire were two prone bodies covered with thick blankets and hats pulled down over their heads. 'Look at them. This is going to be easy,' Jack whispered. 'It is like taking candy from a baby. Okay,' he pulled them together for a quiet word, 'Tane and I will take the right side; you other three on the left. Just empty your rifles into them. No one will ever find them in this bush, that's for sure. Once we clean up the area, the bodies will be gone forever. Right,' he commanded, 'let's do it.'

They split up and ran in. As they came closer to the bodies, they poured rifle fire into the blankets. Bullets twanged off the torsos of the sleeping bodies. But Jack's gang were too high on adrenaline to notice that the hits sounded wrong. It was as if the bullets were hitting tree stumps. They stopped when they had emptied their rifles. One of the hats had been shot off the head of one of the sleepers, and then it dawned on them that the bodies they were shooting at were not bodies at all.

They looked bewildered, when a bullet came out of nowhere and hit Tony in the head, flinging him back into another man. A split second later, another shot, and the bloke behind Tony was hit in the chest, and he fell into the fire. The smell of burning flesh and clothes filled the camp. The rest of the gang turned and ran in fright. As they did, there was the sound of another bullet that hit Tane in the shoulder, it spun him round to fall on his face, and the next shot took Jack himself, full in his stomach. He fell over a log and screamed.

It was too much for the remaining member of the gang, so he hit the path at full pace and disappeared back into the bush. A few minutes later, a distant shot was heard. Later George wandered in. 'I think that's the lot of them, Sam,' he shouted as I emerged out of the bush with my son Sam, Peri, Abe and Blanche who shoved another round into the breach of her rifle, just in case. Rifles at the ready, Blanche and Sam looked over the dead and wounded men. 'Thank God this part is over,' Abe then remembered his dead friend, and snarled, 'I have no sympathy for them at all.' Tane then managed to climb to his feet and was about to run off, when Tamati belted him just enough with his putu, to drop him on the ground, but not enough to kill him.

George pointed to the man with the stomach wound, who squirmed on the ground, 'That's the boss there: Jack Flower. It was all his idea.'

I squatted down to talk to him. 'Who killed Henry?' I spat. 'I can help alleviate the pain. Just tell me who killed our friend.' Jack's face had gone an unusual grey colour, and he started to spit blood.

'This hurts,' he moaned.

'We can help you,' I repeated, 'Who killed Henry?' As Jack spilled the beans, my son found some paper, and scribbled furiously.

'Tane did,' Jack cried out as another wave of pain gripped him. He then recounted his tale. He paused in agony when Sam pushed the paper towards him.

'This is your confession, sign the bottom,' Sam demanded.' With a shaky hand, Jack wrote his name on the document.

'Help me get rid of this pain,' he squealed as Peri came up to me.

'Did you get everything you need, my friend?' he asked.

'Yes, thanks Peri, he spilled his guts out in more ways than one. I cannot believe the twisted minds of some of the people in power.'

As I stood up, Peri pointed his rifle at Jack's head and pulled the trigger. It happened so quickly I had no time to react, my mouth fell open.

Peri noticed my reaction, and shrugged his shoulders, and said in a dismissive manner, 'This is utu. He wouldn't have lived, anyway. He was the leader of the gang that killed Henry, so there was no way he was going to live under our law. Besides he was an evil man.' He turned to Tamati and Hemi. 'My good fellows, grab this piece of rubbish', he urged, pointing to Tane, 'and take him down to the canoe, and keep him quiet.'

'Sam, take Abe and Blanche with you, and continue on in a westerly direction. George and I will clean this up. When we finish, no one will ever know that anything out of the ordinary happened here. I'll catch you up shortly.'

Still in shock we left them to it. It had been years since I had seen that sort of thing, and even though I felt they deserved what was dished out, I did not like killing in cold blood. Now we were caught up in multiple murders, and if these blokes were ever found, we would be in big trouble. But what could we do? They were hell bent on killing all of us. These thoughts raced through my mind as the four of us left the scene behind. The only good thing about it was, we had a written confession from Jack Flower. It will make a few high-ranking politicians' heads roll in the near future.

CHAPTER THIRTY-TWO

The Return Home

Peri eventually caught up and gave us the news that entire area around the site had been cleaned. He went on to say that George had taken the horses through to Tuakau, and left word that he found them wandering around by the river. 'There is no need to worry,' he reiterated. 'There is no sign of any hut or cooking fire, or even a fight. You are quite safe now. If push comes to shove old man, I will take complete blame for what has happened, so you can go with a clear conscience. Well, my good chap, it's time to get you to the cave.'

Our progress was slow through the undergrowth, as the bush was even thicker than before, and we had to cut and slash every step of the way, as we headed toward our destination. All this while Peri's eyes kept dancing here and there, and he got more apprehensive with every step closer. We walked up a small hill, and I stopped and looked carefully around at the surroundings. I turned to him, 'Peri, I can see this is making you too uncomfortable mate, but it's alright, I know where we are.' I beamed at him, 'you can drop us off here. I've recognise where we are, I'd say it would be most likely another hour, and we would be in the cave.'

'Thank you, Sam,' relief was written all over his face, 'I do not mind admitting that I am a bit scared, old chum. I'm not comfortable with anything magical or mystical, and to top this off, this place is guarded by the Taniwha.' He took my hand and dragged me into his face for a hongi. We will never see each other again, my good chap. I will miss you terribly; all of you in fact. I will mark the track for you on the way out. You never know, you might need to return. Give my best wishes to Bob,' he hongied each of us and with a mihi ki aku hoa (farewell my friends). Then turned, bent his head down, and disappeared back down the track.

'Okay, we are not far from the cave now,' I informed them, 'I remember this place, and I have been this way before, though a long time ago.' I took the lead as we moved on. Close to an hour later the bush became more sparse and the land rose up ahead of us. I could now see the entrance to the cave, we would only have to climb up a small bank to reach it.

Sam took the lead and was the first to cautiously stick his head inside the cave. A few minutes later he called out, 'It's warm, dry and empty, with water dripping in the back.' He came back down to help Blanche up, and then Abe and I followed. He later collected firewood, and it wasn't long before our shadows were flickering off the wall of the cave. I had a look round and discovered evidence that Bob had been in the cave, all those years ago. He had scratched his initials: RK on a calendar he had made, recording the days he was here. Then his scribbling stopped abruptly. It looked like he had stayed in the cave for a few months. Did he get home? I wondered...

For seven weeks, we sat, talked, slept and hunted for food, hoping for a storm with the mist that would, with luck, propel us back to my century. As each week passed, I could see them doubting my story, still the inactivity helped Abe to regain his full strength. As we waited I felt pleased that Peri had taken Jack Flower's confession with him, and I hoped, as he knew people in high places, that this would make it safer for us if we were unable to get home to my time.

A big southerly blow hit us at the beginning of the eighth week. It brought with it lightning, thunder, torrential rain and mist, and visibility dropped to a few meters. We sat huddled together wondering if this is what we were waiting for, when there was an almighty jolt of lightning right above us, and then thunder reverberated throughout the cave. Soon a golden mist materialised around the cavern, swirling in circles. The electricity in the air made the hairs on our arms stick out. 'This is it,' I yelled, and grabbed my gear, 'come on, follow me.'

We slipped down the embankment and headed south into the mist. 'It might make you nauseous,' I yelled above the thunder as Blanche vomited onto the bush floor. Sam complained of being dizzy, and then the mist and the storm rolled on by, it was over. We stood on a flat tussock area with the smell of sulphur surrounding us. I turned to my party. 'I think we have arrived.'

'Where is here Sam?' Abe asked.

'My time, I hope. Smell that sulphur; that's volcanic. We must be close to the central high country. We never noticed that odor in all the seven weeks we were in the cave.' We looked around. The nearby bush was not as thick as what we had come through.

Suddenly a voice called out from the forest. 'You are surrounded; please place your weapons on the ground.' My heart dropped to the floor. We stood rooted to the spot as we dropped our weapons and the voice came again. 'Can we have your names, please.'

I could not see where the voice had come from as Abe called out, 'Samuel Selkirk and his son Sam, Abraham and Blanche Metcalfe.There was quietness, then I heard a radio click, and a voice spoke into it.

'Rover one, do you read, over?'

'Confirmation,' was the reply.

'Rover one, this is Rover two. We have four subjects from page one, section A. Do you copy, over?'

Silence, then, 'Copy that Rover two, bring them into victor four, over.' I heard a double click. All the time this was going on, my group listened with open mouths.

'What's going on, Dad?' Sam asked with fear in his voice.

'They have radios, son.' I saw no need to try to put their minds at ease. 'A radio is a talking device to communicate between people.'

Blanche clung to Abe as a squad of army blokes approached us from out of the bush, right in front of us. They didn't seem aggressive to me. I could see the person in the front had the insignia of a captain.

'Good afternoon, welcome to the twenty-first century,' the captain remarked.

My mind switched right into neutral—all I could think of was, I was home. I heard Blanche say, 'That's a woman; how is that possible?'

I looked at the captain, and sure enough, their leader was a woman alright. I was certainly home, yet I felt as lost as the people around me.

The captain looked at the chart in her hand then addressed me. 'You must be Lord Samuel Selkirk aka McInnes, and the man next to you has to be your youngest son, Sam.' I was speechless. She turned and saluted Abe. 'Lieutenant Metcalfe VC. Welcome; it is not every day that we meet a war hero, and you ma'am must be Lady Blanche Proctor.

'No,' Blanche corrected her, 'I am now Mrs Metcalfe.'

'My apologies. I'm sorry my name is Rana Campbell. My men call me captain, boss or Ra, as they think the sun shines out of my bum. Oops, sorry folks, I apologise for being rude, you will not be used to our way of talking. We have no time for questions at the moment I'm afraid. We will escort you up to the hut at Victor Four where you will be, showered, issued with clean new clothes, then wined and dined, and tomorrow our commanding office, Lt General Flanagan, will meet up with you. He will then bring you up to date with necessary information, as this is only a need-to-know operation. So please gather your weapons, and we will be on our way. Sergeant, give them a heads-up at base that we are leaving now, and I'm sure this party require a good feed, and a bloody good shower to I'm betting. I don't mean to be rude, my lord, but you do stink.'

With that, she turned, and we followed bewildered and apprehensive.

We sat down for a meal, clean and dressed in fresh cloths. I felt it strange to wear jeans again, and Blanche, was a little confused with what she was given to wear. Women's fashion had come a long way since her time. I looked around and thought it unusual that there was no sign anywhere of a TV, and I didn't see one mobile phone in use. Maybe they made a point to not push technology into my group's faces,so making them even more confused. But there was a thought that nagged at me, how did they know about us, to have this all set up and ready—no doubt time would tell?

Then I found out that it was now 2026. That really rocked me, to think I had only been gone ten years or so in this period, yet it had been thirty, back in the nineteenth century. My heart leapt, that meant I would be about the same age as my parents and only twenty years older than my mates. I dwelt on that, then realised at least I would get to see them. It had been a worry that I would never have found them alive, and if things panned out, now I would. Hell, my sister Mary would only be going on twenty- three. These thoughts raced through my mind, as the four of us hit the pit early. It was wonderful to sleep in clean sheets once again; it had been a while.

The smell of coffee brewing drifted past my nostrils as I woke and rubbed my eyes. Sam was still out to it, as I shot into the shower. It was bliss, and as soon as I dressed, I walked into the kitchen to have the steward hand me a large cup. I was still at the table admiring the mountains, when the rest of the group filed in half an hour later. I hardly recognised Blanche as she approached, dressed in modern clothes, and I saw that someone had done her hair for her in twenty-first century fashion. We all chose our breakfast from the bain marie and sat down to eat. I reminded them that the General would fly in at around ten that morning to talk to us.

After they had had a good night's sleep and were slowly adjusting to the idea that they were now, indeed, in the twenty-first century, they could not hold back any longer.

'Fly?' they all asked in unison. 'Just wait and see,' I told them.

The noise of a chopper could be heard as it echoed around the mountain tops, and right on schedule it dropped down toward the landing pad. My three companions rushed to the window to see what the noise was, and were gobsmacked, as they peeked out at the spectacle in awe.

'Remember Sam,' I explained to my son, 'I had told you I had flown. Well, this is flying,' I said, as I pointed out the window, just as the chopper settled onto the pad. A grey-haired tall bloke with the rank of Lt General, climbed out of the passenger side. My God, it's Captain Flanagan, I thought, as he came inside. He came straight over to me with a huge smile on his face.

'Sam, it is great to catch up with you again,' he exclaimed, grabbing my hand and shaking it wildly. 'My God, man, you gave us a fright when you three blokes disappeared ten years ago. We searched everywhere for you, and it wasn't until Bob came back that we knew where you were. Looks like you have had an exciting life, but I'm afraid the experience has aged you, as you look so much older than your years, my friend.'

'Yes, General, in my time, I've been away thirty years, but tell me how did you know we would be back?'

'All in good time, Sam.' He turned to Abe, shook his hand and addressed him, 'Welcome Abraham, lovely to meet a VC holder, and you also, Mrs Metcalfe, and you to Sam, I'm pleased to meet you all. I gather you have had a bit of a tough time of it. First things first though, it has been arranged to fly you all to Ohakea airbase. We have a special area set aside, mainly so we can bring you all up to date with what's happened over the years, and of course our technology. There you will meet some government people and historians, who know more about you than I do. We have a big house there to house everyone, built around 1912, with eight bedrooms. It has a conference room, etc as well. We intend to get your parents up to you there Sam, as there's plenty of room. I will arrange for your mate Bob Kydd and his wife Tui to meet you there as well.'

Tui, I remembered Rita told me I would meet Tui, but I had figured she'd meant Shane and Tui. 'What about Shane have you heard from him?' I asked.

'Oh, he never came back, Sam. Lived his whole life in Dunedin.'

'My God, my daughter lives in Dunedin. If only I had known. I would have tried to see him.' I felt crestfallen, as I realised I had missed out.

'Hmm you still might, keep an open mind.' was all he said. 'Right, I'll have a talk with my people, then we are off.' he told us. 'Things have certainly changed since your day, and most likely you have a thousand questions. But leave it until you meet the historians and the government crowd, as I'm sure they will have answers for you also.'

Twenty minutes later, we were ushered into the chopper. My son, Abe, and Blanche looked terrified. 'Come on there is nothing to worry about. You are perfectly safe here—just enjoy the excitement of it.'

I reassured them, 'Look at it this way, you must be the first people from your century to ever fly, so you are pioneers.'

I grinned hoping to give them confidence, but their eyes popped out of their heads in alarm, as the sound of the rota-blade whirled above our heads, and the noise made it hard to hear. We were all given headphones, and it took them a while, until they understood, that the pilot was actually talking to them. We rose into the air and headed south, the look on the faces of my friends and son were a joy to behold.

Within forty minutes we were on the pad at Ohakea, where a van with darkened windows took us away from prying eyes, to our next destination at the far end of the base. Even the van ride was golden to my group, no horses, and Abe was laughing. 'This is marvellous,' he said. Blanche was just wide-eyed and speechless.

'Yes, we don't use horses for transport anymore,' I remarked.

When we arrived at this massive old home, the team from the secret service were waiting for us. They ushered us all into the conference room and made us comfortable with refreshments. Then they waited until the stewards departed and the room was quiet before they began their explanation on how they knew so much about us.

CHAPTER THIRTY-THREE

Home

There were only two government agents waiting for us in the room, and the one who took the lead was a young woman in her late twenties early thirties, Sarah Holdsworth.

She directed us to the chairs,'Welcome to Ohakea. Please take a seat. This will take some time, so make yourselves comfortable.'

We all gathered at the table and gave her our attention, and she smiled at us.

'Okay, let's start from the beginning she began. It all started when Robert Kydd came back through the mist,' she explained. 'He got the third degree as the authorities at that time suspected he had murdered you and Shane,' she glanced at me. 'It took us a while... well, a few months in fact to find out the truth. My compatriots back in the day were rather heavy handed with Robert, and instead of giving him aid, they threatened him, and told him to drop his search. Luckily, he is a very determined individual,' she smiled at me, 'and he went ahead anyway. He never gave up on you Samuel, in fact he is still looking for you to this day, so when we spring this on him, he will be ecstatic.'

'Did he receive my manuscript, do you know?' I asked. 'I deposited it in the bank in Auckland before we left there.'

She looked at her watch, 'It is due to be delivered as we speak by courier.' Sarah answered.

'Now one of your original questions was, how did we know about you?' she claimed. Well, you have to thank your eldest son Bernard for that, your message to Gladstone sent ripples around the UK. Then heads began to roll when Peri Nepia presented Jack Flower's confession. How he got it, never came to light.'

My gut clenched when she suddenly lent forward and looked me in the eye, 'Do you know what happened to him and his gang?'

I went clammy, and the lie slipped out easily. 'No. We didn't see them. Peri told us that it was this gang that had killed Henry Talbert.'

'Oh well,' she straightened and continued in a friendly manner, 'we had hoped that after all these years that the truth would come out. I gathered from the old records, that he was a nasty piece of work. So when the gang vanished, no one really cared that much. There had been a rumour, and that's all it was, that a part Maori bloke was cooked alive in a hangi in the King Country. However, there were so many unbelievable stories coming out of that area those days, that the authorities at the time, put it down to a myth to discourage people from the area.'

We all glanced at each other with poker faces.

'So, the authorities had Jack's confession, and the finger pointed directly at Purcell, he was under the wing of the Home Secretary at that time. Gladstone won the general election in 1895, and once he had settled into his new roll, he took the Prince of Wales aside to explain, and was given the same history the Prince had told you, my lord.'

'It's just Sam, Sarah,' I corrected her.

'Right, Sam it is,' she looked at me, then continued. 'So, Gladstone then had a quiet chat with your eldest boy, and Bernard explained what you were attempting to do, and do you know what, Gladstone actually believed him. Gladstone, unbeknownst to most of the public, had always been keen on the idea of time travel, and knowing that a reputable person like yourself did not make things up, he became a believer.'

'He, with his new Home Secretary, came up with the scheme, just as you did, to leave messages to be delivered at a point in the future. The only difference was, he did it through his government channels, direct to our government of the day. The first message was opened in 2015, and every six months a new one arrived. So, your tale was communicated about five years ago and have been waiting ever since. The area surrounding this oddity has been kept off limits all these years, as the phenomenon continues to happen, as you know.'

'We have had a couple of random Maori come through this time warp, and we sent them straight back with letters to inform the government of the day, that their messages were getting through to us. It worked. We did explain to the Maori before they left, that they might end up in another period, but usually, people seemed to be only about ten years out of sync. Though a few were only a year or two out. We haven't figured that out yet, so I believe it's not completely foolproof, maybe it's just luck. Bob Kydd was only away eighteen months. Even today our scientists have no idea how this is anomaly is happening, but it is, and so it's very important that it's kept secret. We don't want the general population travelling back and forth in time, you can imagine the problems that would create.'

She turned her eyes toward Blanche, 'So Blanche, we are fully aware of your past and your record. Don't worry, if you were to go back to your time of 1895, you would be free as a bird, as Gladstone gave you a pardon. So let me reiterate,' her voice softened with gentleness, 'from now on, there is nothing for you to concern yourself about, so you can rest easy, and know you are free to do as you wish.'

She stopped and took a sip of her water then continued. 'Now, there was a serious accident at Paddington Tube Station in November of 1895. Sir Anthony Purcell, the bloke that had sent the assassins after you all, slipped and fell onto the track in front of a moving train. It was an unfortunate accident. Then believe it or not, his home caught fire a couple of days later. They had been installing new gas pipes, and once Purcell had died, the work had come to a standstill. But it seems that they mustn't have disconnected the gas properly, as there was an explosion and the house was completely destroyed, everything he owned, along with all of his files, went up in a massive blaze.'

'Purcell was the culprit of course, but the Home Secretary Viscount Geraldine, was as much to blame. He was forced to resign from the government and went back to his country home in Wales. He died the same year in 1895. He had been out walking in the hills, slipped, then fell one hundred and fifty metres, that's around five hundred feet. He wasn't found for days. This seems all very suspicious knowing what we do today. We can only assume that their government may have been involved in cleaning up its dirty laundry, so to speak.'

'Well, that's our story in a nutshell. Now you

no doubt, will add a fair bit more information to the file, about your lives as we go on. So,' she looked at the clock on the wall, 'let's take a break for lunch and do the questions later.'

After lunch the third degree began, it took them a week altogether to work through each of us, to gather intelligence about the lives we had lived. They were skilled at sucking at the inside story, and in the end, they got what they wanted. However, it left us all exhausted, and I felt very annoyed by being interrogated like that. After-all, all I had ever wanted was to see my folks.

'I didn't come back just to talk to you lot,' I snapped. 'I need to see my parents—my son's grandparents, for heaven's sake I haven't seen them for 30 years. They didn't listen until our story fitted with theirs.

Eventually, Sarah made the decision, 'I think the next thing for us, Sam, is to collect your parents and bring them up here.'

'That's all I ever wanted,' my eyes flashed as I made her aware of my feelings. But she ignored my temper.

'We sent a friend of theirs, a government MP, down to see them and he met with Robert Kydd around the same time. We will put on an aircraft to bring them up, so they will all be here Monday morning. Furthermore,' she announced as she looked at my son Sam, Abe, and Blanche, 'we will start an introductory course for our century. Classes will begin tomorrow, so by the time you leave here, you will fit in to our present day, as if you were a native.'

I was overjoyed. Monday. I would see my folks again after all these years and my mate Brill. Then I started to feel anxious at the prospect and so did Sam. He confided in me:

'I'm apprehensive, Father, about meeting these new grandparents. What will I say to them, how will they react?'

'Well Sam,' I urged, 'just be yourself. Mum will love you, that is for sure, as you are quite a bit like I was at your age, you will be okay, don't distress yourself. I can tell you though, I'm sure looking forward to seeing them, and my little sister as well.' Heck, by now she'll be nearing twenty-three. I still found it unbelievable that only ten years had passed here, and yet it was thirty for me. Mum and Dad would be in their late sixties, so I would only be a year or two behind them. I grinned to myself, I hope I have aged well in their eyes.

There was a knock on the door, and Mary McInnes placed the book she was reading onto the table and called out to her husband, David, 'I'll get it, Davy.' She opened the door and looked up at her member of parliament and cabinet minister for science and technology.

'Jim,' she relaxed with a smile. 'It's not an election year is it, we hardly see you these days.'

Jim Cameron and Mary had both been teachers at the same school, in their younger days. She looked past his shoulder, and saw a driver waiting outside in the new ministerial electric Mercedes. 'Is this official?' she asked with a grin. She shook her head, 'I don't know, using your poncey car for your personal gratification. Come on in. Bring the driver in for a cuppa.'

'I'm sorry Mary this is official. Is David and your daughter home?'

'Yes,' she said as concern crossed her face. 'Is everything okay? This seems a bit ominous coming from you, Jim?'

She called out, 'David, Jim is here. Is Mary in her room?'

'No, Mum. I'm with Dad,' she said, coming through into the kitchen.

'Mary this is my friend Jim. Jim our daughter Mary. Would you mind putting the kettle on love?'

'Now what is this all about?' she ventured, as they went into the lounge each with a mug in their hands.

Jim looked at them. 'This is top secret, now I mean that, this is serious Mary. It's classified on a need to know basis only. I cannot stress that enough. On Monday morning, at nine o'clock, there will be a car to pick you up and take you all to Dunedin Airport. From there a RNZAF passenger plane will take the three of you to Ohakea Air Force Base. Also, Robert and Tui Kydd will accompany you.' He watched as the words sunk in.

'Look here, what's this all about?' David queried, a little put out that they had to drop everything.

'It's all about your son Sam,' he answered. 'He's back.'

Mary dropped her mug and burst into tears. David grabbed her and held her tight, and their daughter joined in a group hug. Jim patiently waited and drank his tea, as it took them a wee while to adjust to this revelation.

'How?' David insisted, as he came out of the maul, but still in shock.

'I don't know all the details, David. All I know is that he came back through the mist a week ago and has been debriefed and checked over. Now, there is another revelation brace yourselves, he has his son with him.'

'What, who? Our grandson you say?' Mary asked confused.

'His youngest son, Sam,' Jim replied gently, recognising the impact his words had on them.

'My God, he will only be a wee lad then,' Mary whispered, with joy raising in her heart.

'Well no, not exactly.' Jim said in a hushed tone, he squirmed in his seat, not wishing to upset them even more. 'It is not like that at all, Mary. I'm sorry, but even though Sam has only been gone ten years, thirty years has gone by in his time. So, your son is in his sixties, and his son's about twenty-six.'

Oh, my poor boy,' groaned Mary, as she bent over and sobbed.

'Look I have given you this information in good faith, so that you have the weekend to come to terms with it all. So, Mary, David,' he said, rising to his feet, 'a car will be here Monday morning, to collect the three of you. Bring enough clothes for a week.' Their daughter escorted him to the door.

'Take care of your parents, Mary,' he whispered. 'It has been quite a shock for them, but I know once they see Sam, all the lost years will vanish.' He turned and walked back to his limo.

They gathered together in the lounge doing their best to absorb the unbelievable story they had heard, when the phone rang loudly. 'I'll get it,' Mary said as she picked up the phone, 'Hello?''Mary, it's Bob here. Have you had a visit from anyone from a government department yet?' he asked.

'Yes Bob, he's just left. I'll put you on speaker.'

'G'day, Mary, David, what do you think of the

fantastic news? I tell you I'm over the moon to realise that he made it back. I'm so excited, and I can't wait to see him. He's actually home! We need to celebrate when we are all together,' his enthusiasm was infectious, and they all smiled. 'Look I know you must be thinking of all the years you missed in his life. But even if he was ninety, just to meet up with him once more... well, I can't express how happy hearing this, has made me. I never thought that I would see my mate again. Quite frankly, I don't understand how the years are so different in this time slip. Anyway, Tui and I will see you on Monday. It appears the aircraft will pick us up in Invercargill and collect you lot on the way through to Ohakea.'

'But Bob, how can we treat him like a son, don't you realise he is our age for heaven's sake?' David appealed.

'Like a son of course, Dave. Forget what he looks like. Look into his eyes, he will still be Sam, no matter what his age is. I gather your grandson looks just like Sam was at the same age. I feel so happy for you all. I'll see you Monday. We will have to ask Mum to take care of the kids for a week. Catch you all Monday.' He hung up.

'Mum and Dad, you know he's right,' Mary pleaded. 'He will still be your son and my big brother, no matter what. And I bet he can't wait to see us all.' She jumped up and threw over her shoulder as she walked into the kitchen, 'Another cuppa is in order I'd say.' Her parents sat with their arms around each other on the couch and cried, it was all a bit much to take in.

From early morning I had sat and looked south for the telltale spot of an aircraft. I was excited and apprehensive at the same time, as was my son Sam. If they left at nine a.m, with about two-and-a-half hours flying time, they should land around eleven thirty. As the morning slipped by, I was getting more anxious by the hour. All my thoughts accumulated and came to the conclusion that maybe I should have let sleeping dogs lie and stayed back in the past with all my family. Then the rational part of my brain kicked in and thought, be buggered, you needed to see your mum, dad, and sister before it was too late.

Then my son announced nervously, 'Dad I can see a dot in the sky.'

Sam, after being here only a week, spent much of his time alert to the aircraft flying around the base. Within five minutes a new Lear jet with New Zealand roundels screamed overhead, with wheels down, it turned in from the east, and dropped onto the landing strip. My heart was in my mouth, as we waited for them to alight, then climb into the van with the darkened windows. By the time the van drove up the drive of the house my hands shook, I was terrified.

'We will meet them in the conference room, Sam, out of the way of prying eyes.' Sarah informed us.

Sam and I waited, we could hear their footsteps as they came down the hall, then the doors opened, and in walked Mum and Dad with my sister. All of my anxiety fell away as I looked at my mum. 'Sammy,' she cried as she practically ran across the room, then broke down as she hugged my waist tightly. Dad was right behind her and then my wee sister, both added to the loving embrace. The three of us stood in the middle of the room and held each other and wept. My son held back, but my mother pulled out of the huddle, grabbed him by the arm, and pulled him into the group hug, we stayed that way for over five minutes, and showered each other with tears of joy. Age has no limits. We were a family once again. All you could hear was Mum saying 'Sammy, Sammy,' to both of us. Eventually, we broke apart, our eyes were red with crying. Then Bob came in with Tui. We grabbed each other, and the years just slipped away. We patted each other on the back with watery eyes, eventually we all pulled away and looked at each other.

'You have aged well, mate,' Bob told me with a smirk on his face.

'And, so have you.' I grinned.

'Tui,' I said. 'My God, you look like your—who is it—second great-grandmother. The resemblance is uncanny. This whole thing is incredible,' I divulged. I turned to my sister and said, 'I can't believe you are nearly twenty-three and at medical school. How long have you got to go?'

'A couple more years, I'll be twenty-five when I graduate,' she said proudly. 'Mum still held my hand with a firm grip and would not let go, and when she did, she replaced it with my son's hand. The day slipped by quickly, it had been a heartwarming day for all of us, but we felt exhausted by dinner time.

'You will have to come home with us, Sam,' Mum insisted. 'Come and live with us until you get your life in order, you too, Sam,' she said as she turned and smiled at her grandson.

'That is good of you Grandmama,' Sam replied.

Mum laughed.

'Such impeccable manners, Sammy, and with a lovely accent to boot,' she giggled. 'You know we have years of catching up to do,' she said with enthusiasm.

As we moved into the dining hall, I took my sister's elbow, 'You know your niece Margaret Fenton is a doctor, and also an Otago graduate, you two would have a lot in common.

'What!' Mary came to a full stop, turned and

looked up at me. 'That's unbelievable. Really Sam, is that true? Because there is a photo of Margaret Fenton in the halls of Otago, as she was one of our first woman doctors to graduate.' I nodded and grinned with pride, as my daughter had been honored in that way. 'Wow!' she added, 'To think she is my niece, now that is hard to get my head around.'

As Abe and Blanche sat down for dinner, I introduced everyone. It wasn't long before Abe and Bob began to talk about their experiences during the sacking of Auckland.

'Do you know that it's still not considered a Maori attack?' criticised Bob, annoyed that such a thing was swept under the carpet. 'They refer to it in the history books, as the devastating fire of Auckland,' he frowned and shook his head. I secretly smiled at seeing him hot under the collar again, it brought back fond memories of this happening all those years ago. Yep, that's my mate alright, bristling at anything he considered an injustice.

I told Bob about my life with Bella and how she lost her life. It shocked me, that it really upset him.

'Sam mate,' he cried, 'I did everything I could, for the life of me, to find her, I searched everywhere but I never came across a death certificate.'

'Look don't distress yourself, it's alright you

wouldn't have found one anyway, as no certificates were issued. I was out to it, and as there were no other kin around, all of the passengers from the stagecoach were buried quite quickly because of the heat. Only her christian name on a granite headstone, marks the spot I'm afraid. But my Bella would not have wanted anything else.'

'Well my main focus was on your life, of course,' Bob continued, 'I did well at first, then I hit a brick wall and nothing, but I want you to know I never gave up, mate. Even when the buggers warned me off, I just plodded on. And I made a point to give your parents updates each week. I missed you and Shane so much, to be separated like that, well it nearly did my head in. But I had Tui's support, and she's a part of Shane, so that helped a lot. Anyway, I'm so grateful that I have finally caught up with you, and to meet your son. And now I can find out what actually become of you, my friend.' Bob grinned from ear to ear, 'You know I'm on cloud nine because of this.'

A week later, Bob and Tui returned home. We stayed on for a few more days, but Mary had to return to university, so my whole family headed south to my parent's house in Dunedin. The government crowd had given us permission to continue to acclimatise Sam into our society on our own. But Abe and Blanche weren't so fortunate and had to stay on for two more months, before they came south. So, in that time, Bob organised a suitable place for them, not far from his cottage and right on the beach. Abe loved the beach along with the fishing, so he was happy. And Blanche was just delighted to be free. By the time their extra lessons on all the paraphernalia of the twenty-first century was finished, they were well equipped to settle into our way of life and had even learnt to drive.

Well my son had finally met his grandparents and his aunt, and I had made it back home. Was I happy? Only the future would decide. I gazed out from the shoreline of the Otago Harbour and watched a container ship slip by with the name Shrewsbury Port of Birmingham marked on its bow. My mind drifted back to my other family and wondered if I would ever see them again? Then Sam slid in beside me and nodded his head toward the ship. 'Looks as though it's heading home, Dad.'

'Yes, it does, son.' We looked at each other then turned and traipsed up the small hill to my parents' place, with our heads bent into the wind. Home. Are we really home? I thought.

EPILOGUE

Auckland 1899

On a cold autumn day as the rain came in from the south, we were huddled together in the passenger lounge on Queen's Wharf, waiting to board the SS Rimutaka. Many people were gathered outside, as the New Zealand rugby team were on a tour to Australia, on the same ship. I turned to my son. 'How do you feel?'

'Ecstatic, Dad, incredible to be going home. As much as I found the twenty-first century interesting, I felt out of place; I could never be at home there.'

My sister Mary stood beside me and clung to my arm. 'This is weird, Sam,' she whispered. 'It all feels so primitive to me, and I feel like a foreigner, this doesn't feel like the New Zealand I know.'

I patted her arm, 'Don't worry you'll get used to it, Mary. Look at it this way, you will be so much in demand, now you are a qualified doctor.' Turning to the rest of the group I said, 'I'm so pleased you all agreed to come.'

My parents stood close to me, 'Well Sam, coming with you wasn't really such a hard decision for us,' my dad admitted. 'Sam Jr has been so homesick, ever since he came back to our time. Besides, we have all talked about it for long enough. You didn't drag us with you you know, we made the decision to join you. I am surprised though, that Mary decided to come with us. We would've understood if she hadn't wanted to, and if that had been the case, we might not have come ourselves. So, with us all agreeing to make the trip, it was a no brain-er. Besides both of us had no really close family members left to keep us here.'

'What I think is so wonderful about it,' jumped in mum,'is we will all be together. I'm disappointed though that we cannot catch up with our granddaughter Margaret at the moment, as she is already in England. I was looking forward to meeting her.' Her enthusiasm waned a bit, then picked up when she added, 'I guess we will catch up with her and the rest of the family when we arrive next month. Imagine, we will have a wonderful English summer this year, and finally meet all our grandchildren and great-grandchildren.'

That day when I caught up with my mate Bob, he had been so surprised when I informed him that once Mary had qualified as a doctor, we were all going to attempt to return to the past, with the government's blessing. The nineteenth, or even the twentieth century, called both my son and myself home.

'Well at least mate, I found you, and to think we were able to actually meet up again, it's been an incredible experience,' Bob grinned. 'I had been so concerned about how you got along in the past and was so relieved when I found out you had done well. So now I can get on with my life knowing you are all okay.' He shook my hand, then gave me a hug.

Abe and Blanche had retired and were comfortably settled into their new life by the beach. They were very happy with the way things had turned out for them, so decided to stay on in the twenty-first century.

On an autumn day, in the beginning of May, the government arranged to pick up our family and deliver us up to the Tongariro National Park, where we spent the next several weeks waiting for the right weather conditions. When the mist arrived, much to the nervousness of my parents and Mary, we were transported through the time slip to Pukekawa, arriving at the cave in 1899 only four years after leaving, not the ten years we had expected. Funny that, as we had spent four years in the future as well, that meant we had aged as our old friends and family would have expected. I was 69 now, and hoped with a bit of luck, my Mum and Dad and myself would be around to see my family and grandchildren, and their soon-to-meet great-grandchildren, for a few more years.

We had hoped that we had dressed ourselves in the correct clothes of the era, so when we reach Tuakau we could see we were right on target. That same day, we waited at the railway station when the northbound train arrived in a cloud of smoke. Our government of the twenty-first century, had given me official papers in a satchel under lock and key, to hand over to the English government in the past. They had also apparently, sent reports through a few years ago, to my family, advising them that we were safe and well.

When we reached Auckland, I could see the four years we had been away had made a heck of a difference to everyone's way of life. The city had changed, it seemed much busier than before, even though many men were away fighting a war in South Africa, and cars were now seen on the streets along with horse and carts.

Our first stop in Auckland was the post office and cables were sent back and forth between New Zealand and the UK. The euphoria of the family in the UK was overwhelming when they heard that both of us were still in the land of the living and were bringing my parents home with us. I was surprised though when I found out that I was still the Earl of Shadymore, as my son Bernard was thrilled to pass the title back to me on the queen's say so.

Mary intended to visit from the USA with her children, whom I had not seen. And Bernard was as happy as a sandboy we were back. It was a shame that I never had a chance to catch up with my mates Shane and Tui, but maybe, in the end, it was for the best.

We watched the passengers walk aboard the ship then as a group, we followed. The captain was there to greet us.

'Welcome aboard, Lord Selkirk. A pleasure to have you and your family on board.' We were then escorted to our respective cabins. It seemed a long time had passed since I had last headed toward the UK on the Esk with Bella. Now my life had done a couple of complete circles, but I felt content to go home, and to have my parents and sister with me was a bonus. How long I have left on this world, only time will tell, but I know in my heart that this is what I was supposed to do, to live out my life with all my family in the UK.

The whistle blew as the ship slipped its moorings and slowly pulled away from the wharf. Hundreds of people waved at the New Zealand rugby team as we turned towards Rangitoto Island. The team would disembark at the port of Sydney before we headed up to the Suez Canal.

The rain had eased, and the sun poked its head out from behind a cloud. A perfectly formed rainbow hung over the harbour. 'That's an omen, Dad,' Sam remarked as he came over to stand next to me. 'A good one, at that.' We stayed and watched Rangitoto Island disappear as the ship cut through the waves. Black smoke from the funnel left a dusty trail behind us as we turned our backs to the sea and went inside to join our family. We would arrive home for an English summer, and Shadymore waited.

1911

At the church in Brittermore, family and friends gathered to say their final goodbyes to Sam.

Early in the year, Sam had a stroke but recuperated well, until a bout of influenza weakened him. He passed away quietly surrounded by his family. In his last spoken conversation with his family, he instructed that his ashes be buried with their mother, Bella, in Rhodesia.

At beginning of the spring in the southern hemisphere, Bernard and Sam Jr travelled out to Rhodesia to fulfil their father's request.

On the hill overlooking Fort Mangwe, at the start of the rainy season, two sunbirds appeared every year to sit on a granite headstone which read:

Bella and Sam together again.

OTHER BOOKS & CONTACTS

www.owencloughbooks.com

Whispers Series

Whispers of the Past
Shadows of the Mind
Clearing of the Mist

Upcoming Books

Liquid Gold
*Set in New Zealand
one hundred years in the future*

Bernie The Tram
A children's story

Get in Contact with Owen

owen.cloughbooks@gmail.com

NZ +64 276 496 687

Social Media

Facebook

/Book1WhispersofhePast
/Book2ShadowsofheMind
/clearingofthemist